River

of the

World

Book Two:
Selling Water by the River

Chaz Brenchley

ACE BOOKS, NEW YORK

THE BERKLEY PUBLISHING GROUP
Published by the Penguin Group
Penguin Group (USA) Inc.
375 Hudson Street, New York, New York 10014, USA
Penguin Group (Canada), 90 Eglinton Avenue East, Suite 700, Toronto, Ontario M4P 2Y3, Canada
(a division of Pearson Penguin Canada Inc.)
Penguin Books Ltd., 80 Strand, London WC2R 0RL, England
Penguin Group Ireland, 25 St. Stephen's Green, Dublin 2, Ireland (a division of Penguin Books Ltd.)
Penguin Group (Australia), 250 Camberwell Road, Camberwell, Victoria 3124, Australia
(a division of Pearson Australia Group Pty. Ltd.)
Penguin Books India Pvt. Ltd., 11 Community Centre, Panchsheel Park, New Delhi—110 017, India
Penguin Group (NZ), 67 Apollo Drive, Mairangi Bay, Auckland 1311, New Zealand
(a division of Pearson New Zealand Ltd.)
Penguin Books (South Africa) (Pty.) Ltd., 24 Sturdee Avenue, Rosebank, Johannesburg 2196,
South Africa

Penguin Books Ltd., Registered Offices: 80 Strand, London WC2R 0RL, England

This is an original publication of The Berkley Publishing Group.

This is a work of fiction. Names, characters, places, and incidents either are the product of the author's imagination or are used fictitiously, and any resemblance to actual persons, living or dead, business establishments, events, or locales is entirely coincidental. The publisher does not have any control over and does not assume any responsibility for author or third-party websites or their content.

First edition: April 2007

Library of Congress Cataloging-in-Publication Data

Brenchley, Chaz.
    River of the world / Chaz Brenchley.—1st ed.
       p. cm.
    ISBN 978-0-441-01478-1
    I. Title.

    PR6052.R38R58 2007
    823'.914—dc22

                                                                    2006037034

PRINTED IN THE UNITED STATES OF AMERICA

10 9 8 7 6 5 4 3 2 1

River of the World

Ace Books by Chaz Brenchley

THE BOOKS OF OUTREMER
THE DEVIL IN THE DUST
TOWER OF THE KING'S DAUGHTER
A DARK WAY TO GLORY
FEAST OF THE KING'S SHADOW
HAND OF THE KING'S EVIL
THE END OF ALL ROADS

BRIDGE OF DREAMS
RIVER OF THE WORLD

Part 1

Chapter One

IN a dark place, Jendre found herself thinking very much about darkness.

She could close her eyes—if she was allowed to, *if*—and that would be a kind of voluntary darkness, wilful ignorance.

No.

Outside, overhead it was night already, God's darkness; or it ought to be. More than moon and stars hung over the city now, though, and more than lamps and firelight spat back. There was a bridge, built by magicians on the dreams of children; that was a dark thing in itself, for all its sullen glowing.

To find the true dark these days—which meant all the long days of her short life; she'd never known any other days than these—you had to turn inward. Into houses, rooms, beds; into hearts and minds and motives.

Physical dark Jendre had found in a pinch-box, a black bier, the closed litter that had fetched her to her fate; the mind's darkness she had found in the man who had pronounced it. The Sultan, fat and mad, whose word had sent her here.

———

THIS, this was a dark place, despite its lights and fires. It was deep underground, as such places always were; she felt the weight of stone above her like a shadow on her mind. Real shadows shifted in every corner like her thoughts, tentative and fleeting and constantly renewed, every one a cold touch, a promise of what would come.

There was a table, there were chains; they were dark, made of dark things, old stained oak and iron. There was a brazier, its bars glowing almost as brightly as its coals. Bars and coals both couldn't hide their black dark hearts. Like the bridge, dark things did glow sometimes.

There was a box of knives and other implements, a heavy wooden box of them beside the table. They might have been bright and shining in the light, except that shadows lurked within the box.

There was a floor, she knew that, she was standing on it. Its flags struck chill through her slippers, and even the cold was an aspect of the dark. She didn't need to look down, to know how the floor would look.

There were walls, of course, without walls there couldn't be corners for the shadows to dance in. She had a wall at her back, only she wouldn't lean against it any more than she would look down. She kept her spine straight, her head up, her eyes open while the darkness ranged all around her like wolves around a sheepfold. All the walls were dark: dark stone, damp stone, sodden with misery.

The ceiling's shadows were complex and impenetrable. The men whose space this was kept it that way, she thought, holding all their lights low so that walls and pillars rose into a darkness thick enough to overhang all their doings here.

There was a door, a black door, and she might have thought that darkest of all, because she knew what lay beyond it, all the worlds of light.

She might have; she did not. There were men here with her, dark of eyes and dark of dress, dark all through to the core of them. Their white, deceptive hands—oh, she would not think of what those hands would do.

She would not need to think. She could watch it all.

She could watch it soon, soon.

THE door swung open, in they came: more men rapt in their cruel darkness, and among them her own beloved Salem. He was naked and beautiful by torchlight, but what of that? She had seen his skin before, and loved it utterly; today all she felt, all she could feel was a chilly relief that he was uncut, unmarked, not beaten or misused.

Relief and then belatedly surprise, because he should have fought and then they must have bruised him, that at least. He was bound, of course, but her Salem wouldn't have let them do that without fighting. He wasn't even fighting the ropes. His face was slack, and his gaze ran over her like water, catching nowhere. His feet stumbled on the uneven flags and he made no effort to save himself, letting all his weight fall on the men who held him, one at each elbow.

Jendre wondered if horror could undo a man's mind. But they brought him close by her—so close, she need only have stretched an arm to touch him; these men did not care, they would let her touch, claw, scream if she wanted to, and so she did nothing, nothing but stand, let that be enough—and she caught the rough scent of *khola*-smoke on his skin. Likely they had been burning the herb in his cell all day. That was a kindness, she thought, to numb his thoughts that way; and if they would do that, then likely there had been poppy put in his food to numb his body also. Cruelty glossed by kindness, that was always the way of it. She'd like to think it was a man-thing, but there were no men in the harem, where the same applied.

They brought Salem to the table, laid him down and shackled him. He stirred against the iron's grip, but that was all, no more than stirring. He was far gone beyond words, protest, understanding. Only she was allowed to understand; no smoke for her, no poppy.

Well, she would not want them. She was here for him, to stand witness. The Sultan thought this was a punishment. He was wrong. It would be terrible, but she would have made no other choice. This was defiance, rebellion, unsanctioned rage.

The chains that held his ankles hung like stirrups from a frame, holding his legs high and wide. That should have been a humiliation for him and a dreadful embarrassment for her where she stood beyond the table's foot, but it was neither. Fury burned away shame; it was all she had to give him, and would have to be enough.

A leather gauntlet sheathed an arm; a hooked blade was taken from the box and thrust into the brazier.

She would not think about the future now. Neither the short and savage future with all its pains and shadows, nor the long consequences of this night's work. Only the moment mattered: to watch, to breathe, to endure.

The blade was drawn from the fire, turned in its light, forced deep into the coals again. Not yet.

Watch, breathe, endure. All three of those were hard, and each was hardest: to keep her eyes open when she had lids to close them, she had a neck to turn her head away; to draw breath when the air was rank with men at their worst, at their foulest, when her body rebelled and her mind would have fled her if it could, if she would only allow it; to stand and endure what was unthinkable, monstrous, vicious beyond words.

The knife came out again with its own glow now, a dark thing, fit to cut and sear and seal all at once. The cruelty and the kindness, both together.

The world was dizzy about her, but she would not faint, she would not scream, she would not turn away. She was adamantine, she was herself: she would stand and bear witness, and remember.

Chapter Two

IT should have been the darkest watch of the night, except that here under the Shine there could be no darkness, and there was no one to watch. Strange but true, that being in the light could keep them secret.

Baris the dogtooth had rowed them all across the river of the world; now they came to Maras-shore, a soft and quiet landfall. Those same tides and currents that had brought shingle south to make the strand of Sund, here to the north they had brought sand and made a shimmering beach within the river's angle. There was some great truth half-hidden there, surely, something about the gods and their whims, that they offered the seductions of pleasure to the Marasi, while to the Sundain even their river brought only what was hard and useful.

So much time in such a little boat, suspended over so much water: Issel was in no state to hunt out grand and secret truths. Besides, no one took any pleasure from this beach now, where it lay directly underneath the bridge's arch, the very core of the Shine. It had a single use, tonight, for Issel and his singular army; it was the easiest way to sneak into Maras. It was also a stupid way, a deadly way, even for them. Especially for them, perhaps.

Baris, dogtooth, already too much tainted by the Shine: this long and close exposure might do anything, dull his mind further, twist his body still more out of human. Dogtooth skin was like hide, thick and bristly—more like pig than dog, to be clear—and Issel could see it shiver, see how the bristles stood all on end, see a greasy sweat that was nothing to do with Baris' labours. Even the work he did, rowing them all the way across this great river, pulling against tide and wind and current, even that could be a debt to the Shine tonight. Being in the light of it could magnify his strength, even as it poisoned his mind. Issel didn't know. He was only sure that Baris should not be here, where Issel had brought him, where he had to be.

Nor should any of them. Gilder had the water-magic, albeit barely; Rhoan had it too, a little more. Neither of them was accustomed to the Shine. What it might do to them or to their abilities, Issel again didn't know, and couldn't guess. Again it was a risk too great, and again they had to take it.

And then, of course, there was himself. His own gift of magic was stronger, and corrupted already, like acid in his water. All he could do was harm; he hurt his friends as often as those he hated. Oftener. He had hurt Rhoan terribly. And here he was back in the Shine, soaking up its influence again. He couldn't imagine what would happen if he used his powers here, now. Like Baris, he was shivery and sweating coldly; in Issel it was like a charge, he felt overfull and dangerous. That might be the river and the bridge, both working together; if he used them together, who knew? Perhaps they needn't go into Maras after all, perhaps he could break the bridge from here, from below . . .

But he gazed up at it and his eyes swam, his mind swam, his belly churned. Even from below it was malign, intransigent, untouchable. His thoughts couldn't get a grip on its slick, unnameable colours. You couldn't turn a spell against itself, any more than you could a weapon. That was fundamental. His own water-magic was half of the Shine already; if he used it here, it might break him entirely; he was sure it would not break the bridge.

"Issel? Don't stare up at it like that, you can't harm it by glowering. And it's not good, even to look at: I'm sure those colours get into your brain and do damage . . ."

It was too late for him, the damage was done long since. Still, she was right. He turned his head and won a smile from Rhoan. A thin smile, to be sure, but a smile none the less.

"And you stay here in the boat," she went on, "till Baris has hauled it right up out of the water. You don't want to go paddling in the river."

Again she was right, he did not. He thought his skin must be shimmering already, with that same strange gleam that the water had where the Shine fell upon it like a bar of putrid moonlight. He had dabbled his hand in it before, when they had barely left the strand; even then it had seized him, filled him, he had overflown with the seething surge of it. Now, after so long afloat, so long bathed in the Shine and all but engulfed in the river, only these few narrow boards between him and it—well, it was surely best not to touch the water.

Baris had no such anxieties. He had shipped the oars and stepped straight out of the boat as soon as it touched to shore. He stood calf-deep in the river now, laid two great hands on the stem and simply hauled. Even with the other three still aboard, even ploughing as it was keel-deep through damp sand, the boat rode up the beach, high and higher still, far beyond the reach of tonight's water.

They could step dry-footed, then, from Sundain boat to Marasi land. Not safe, surely the opposite of safe, many opposites, reckless and exposed and under threat; but still a little safer than wading ashore through that water in this light, still something to be thankful for. *Thank you, Baris,* and he'd never thought to say it.

He didn't say it, even now. He could hear noises—shuffling, grunts— eastward along the beach. He'd always seen well in the Shine; the water in his eyes, he thought, even that was tainted, touched by magic and perversion both together. There was something there, long and high and squared off, some work of man among the softer works of wind and water.

A guardhouse? Well, but what to guard? Nothing at night, surely. Even Marasi discipline would crumble under such an order. They could patrol the beach by day without need of a building; for a look-out post, somewhere higher on the river cliff would give a further view.

Besides, this wasn't a building. Not in the sense of walls and roof. What he was seeing, that angular shape was a framework, no more: a building without a skin, just bars, risers and crosspieces.

And movement inside the bars, great shambling figures, restlessly coughing and snarling their distress . . .

It was a cage, he saw, locked of course, and open to the Shine.

———

THAT was a cold moment, in a long cold night. He hadn't realised that the Marasi, even the Marasi could be so cruel, to pen any creature out in the

Shine. Issel wouldn't have treated a dog that way, for all his hearty terror of all dogs.

It wasn't deliberate on his part, not a choice; his feet had chosen for him; they were taking him that way, towards the cage. He could see a path beyond it, rising up through dunes. Above and behind were the lower levels of the city, where lamps and torches burned needlessly, pointlessly against the Shine. Perhaps he was going that way, towards the path?

Perhaps it looked that way, at least. When he glanced behind, he saw his companions following. No questions, no challenge. How did he get to be leader among these people?

Because he could, the only possible answer. The four of them were only together because of him, who he was and what he could do. Without him, they would fly apart like birds scattered by a flung stone.

What he was leading them to, whether they ought to follow—ah, that was something else. But they'd come this far; they had to stay together now, even though he led them blindly into darkness.

Darkness would be good, just now. The Shine exposed them twice, once to its own malevolence and then again to any eyes that watched. There should have been none, but suddenly there were, shining themselves in shoddy reflection of the bridge's light. He could hear Rhoan and Gilder muttering anxiously between themselves. Baris only snuffled, but Baris' eyes were as good as his, or better. He was sure that Baris knew what they were coming to.

As he did. As he had all along, if he'd been honest with himself. A cage of creatures, was it? And what sort of creature was it, that was found out in the Shine?

He had one of them at his back and a cageful, dozens, just ahead. He had the seeds of one, perhaps, the first signs of change in his own bones and in his mind already.

Figures who might have been Baris' twin came shuffling to the bars to stare at him. *In Sund, we drive them away when we find them; in Maras maybe they pen them up, no worse than that, and who's to say which is kinder . . . ?*

He knew, though. Oh, he knew. He didn't really need that well-beaten path to tell him that these dogtooth prisoners were locked in here only at night, nor the hammered chains on their wrists to say that they were slaves who had work otherwise by day.

The Shine made them what they are; so the Marasi keep them in the Shine; every night they do this, to make them stronger and more stupid, more obedient, better slaves . . .

Even so, even now, it was a chilling shock to see one thing more, the slimmer figures that were rising, coming to the bars, naked in this eldritch light: *those are men in their chains there, men like me, barely touched yet by the poison; and what, have they been put here deliberately . . . ?*

Yes, of course they had. Why not? Slaves, prisoners, rebellious soldiers—it hardly mattered, what they were before. The Marasi had found a way to exploit them, slowly, slowly. Strange, it was his own city that was meant to be thrifty. *Nothing is ever wasted in Sund,* and yet no one there had ever thought of this. They had as much Shine-light their side of the river, their end of the bridge, and they let it all run to waste every night; they hid from it and cursed those who could not, chased them away and never thought of putting them to use.

Sometimes, Issel was purely proud to be Sundain.

Just as he hadn't consciously decided to come this way, nor had he consciously decided to stop here, a few bare paces short of the bars. He should have had the sense to hurry past, but his body seemed to be making its own choices. Pity and horror: both were there in his head, and in Gilder's gasp behind him, Rhoan's soft moan at his side, the grip of her hand and, "Gods, what are those men doing here, why keep them in with beasts?"

She knew. Like him, she was only trying to pretend that she did not. Which was an instruction to him, to them, not to explain. Gilder understood that, seemingly, and Baris was too dull to give her an answer anyway.

And yet she was answered, unkindly from beyond the bars; a voice croaked back at her, "Why with beasts? To make beasts of us. They were like us once; soon now, we will be like them. What better labour to make roads, dig ditches, carry burdens in the docks?"

"Issel," she said with difficulty, as though her voice hurt her, "can you . . . ?"

That was all she said, all she needed to say. Yes, of course he could. Bare metal bars: he had a flask of perfected water at his belt, and would not need it. After so long afloat on so much water, he thought he had soaked up all the power in it, he could feel the river running cold in his bones; he could do this with a spit.

"No," Gilder said. "We dare not."

I dare, Issel thought; and, *I thought I was leader here.*

Gilder went on fiercely, urgently: "You can free them, yes; but where will they run? There is the river, one small boat we've left them; otherwise, all paths from here are watched from the city. And they are naked, chained—they have no chance of escape.

"And then, one sight of the bars and the Marasi will know it was the water-magic broke them. So they'll be looking for us, too soon; our only hope here is secrecy. These people, their only hope is us"—what they'd come to do, break the bridge and so dispel the Shine, but he wouldn't say it aloud where anyone might hear who could still betray them.

"You're saying we have to leave them here." That was Rhoan, cutting to the heart.

"He's right, Rhoan." Though it was hard just to say it, harder to do.

"Oh, he is right. Of course he's right. That's how this works, didn't you realise? We always do what's right, and it always means leaving other people to suffer. Usually our friends. I suppose I should, we should all be grateful these are, these are strangers . . ."

"Marasi" she might have said, to be another opposite to "friends." To make it seem a better thing, the wiser move, unkindness to their enemies. He thought he'd heard that hesitation in her voice, where she was poised on the brink of doing it. In the end she was too honest, and too bitter; she wouldn't give herself that leeway. Nor, of course, anyone she travelled with.

Nothing Issel could do, then, except make promises. "We'll come back. Not tonight, but I swear it, we will come back."

"Too late." The voice came from somewhere in the cage's depths. All the figures he could see, all those who stood and lined the bars said nothing. Issel had met that, the endless silent patience of the damned. "Too late for me. I know what this accursed witchlight has done to me. I can feel it in my bones, in my head . . ."

And sure, the voice had a slur to it and Issel could imagine the face it came from, the thrusting jaw, too long in the tooth; and all those silent faces were like a pale chant in echo, *too late, too late,* like an instrument played thinly by the wind.

The wind—that was a reminder, this cool breath that came every morning off the Insea, just before dawn. Even so, it took Baris to shift them.

Sturdy and bow-legged, he rocked past, heading up the path with barely a glance at his imprisoned kind, a few rough words hard-squeezed by his difficult tongue: "Sun will come soon. Why wait?"

Why indeed? All this sympathy, delicacy, fellow-feeling: Baris lacked it all, and the others couldn't afford it. So now they followed the one who was thinking straight, the one who found it hardest to think at all and so confined himself to straight lines and simple answers.

Up the path, and the path led up the bank, and so did Baris: a dune of sand and wild grasses, it should have been backed by a long reach of dunes. But this was Maras, city of hills, growing from the river to the height in little space with none at all to spare. It was how the Marasi saw the world, Issel thought, nothing free or forgiving, no leeway.

Rhoan might have made a good Marasi, he thought, the way she dealt now with the world.

So might he.

Perhaps that was how they hoped to conquer Sund at last, by making the Sundain think as they did, so that it truly was one city, Maras-Sund . . .

This dune-bank was topped by a road with another climb behind it, a tamed hillside where wooden steps were laid out between shrubs. Those shrubs had gone untended for years, but the steps still looked solid, embedded in weed-gripped gravel.

The road ran east and west, along the river. The beach was only incidental, a snatched moment in the river's course, a chance of rock and current. Easterly lay Maras-port, the docks of a great imperial city. Westerly, Issel didn't know; perhaps the road just ran and ran, perhaps it circled all the Marasi empire, except for Sund.

He took a glance back across the river, but could see nothing. Sund wasn't Maras, to rise so high above the bridge and burn its oil flagrantly. If there were any lights showing in his poor broken-hearted city, they couldn't penetrate the Shine even now, at day's edge.

No matter. He knew where it was; he knew why he was here. He knew he might never see Sund again, even from this side of the river.

He turned away, and followed Baris up.

Chapter Three

HE old palace might be half-full of women—bitter and sharp or bitter and silent, tactless or tearful, subtle or stupid, already working spiderlike to acquire power and position or else slumped into a helpless melancholy, all the wide range of harem women was here—but that meant that it was also half-empty. There was room enough, and to spare. Jendre had looked at spare rooms, corridors of rooms; then she had turned her gaze and her ambitions outward, found an empty pavilion overlooking the lake, and moved her entire entourage in there.

Jendre's own position was uncertain, unusual, undescribed. She was a disgraced wife, a runaway fetched back, which made her reprehensible, beneath notice; and yet she had been returned to the harem without punishment, which meant that she must have the new Sultan's favour. She had been wife and not concubine, their late lord's last-chosen and his favourite in his final days, and all of that should give her place and authority; and yet she had no children, was barely more than a child herself, young and foolish and utterly without influence . . .

Jendre didn't care. Let them make their anxious estimations of her worth, all these silly women. She had work to do.

It helped, perhaps, that there was no hierarchy of eunuchs here. In the

Sultan's palace, they constrained all life within the harem; they governed the roads of commerce and taxed all the traffic. If Ferres and his cohorts had been here, she would have been dependent on their goodwill, which was both expensive and unreliable.

As things were, the palace had been all but empty for so long, there were few servants who belonged. Every woman exiled by the late Sultan's death had brought her own, and those were engaged in their own struggles for supremacy. It might be months before any leadership emerged among them. It might be years.

Meanwhile, Jendre could take advantage. She had kept her own servants out of the squabbles of their compeers, holding them constantly at her side, binding them ever closer to herself. She had annexed her pavilion simply by right of seizure, declaring, "This will do. Teo, Mirjana, let them know in the palace, in the kitchens, at the gate; hereafter, we live here."

She had furnished and fitted the empty rooms in much the same manner: "We want beds, rugs, tables. Raid empty rooms, stores, wherever you can find those things we need. Plates and jugs, brooms and buckets. Firewood. You know how a house runs, better than I do."

"We do," Mirjana had agreed tartly, "and we know how much work it is, to fit out such a house. Are we to fetch all these things ourselves, the two of us?"

"If you're not competent to manage other slaves to do it," Jendre had snapped back, "then yes, you are. Habitable by nightfall, please. Lamps, we'll want lamps . . ."

HABITABLE it was by nightfall, though comfort took another day. By the time the slow litter arrived, on the day following that, the bare pavilion had become a living, working house. It was ready; her people said they were ready; only Jendre herself was utterly unready, and she could always pretend.

She was pretending now, indeed: standing on the pavilion steps with the lake as a view before her but her eyes entirely on the path, the litter, its bearers and escort. She stood quite still, quite calm, a widow waiting to receive one more to her household. His place was prepared, his future awaited him, there was nothing untoward or particular about it.

And that was a lie, this was all a lie, she was a liar where she stood. Her only immediate task was not to be discovered in that lie. Not to break down where any unfriendly eye might see her.

Her stance was a lie, so quiet and erect; her clothes were a lie, neat and clean and whole where she wanted to be tearing them, soiling them, lamenting. She never had been allowed to lament. She used to rage instead; here, in this newly dangerous world, she couldn't afford so much indulgence.

And so she lied, and lied again. Her manner was a lie as she greeted the eunuchs who bore the litter, the eunuchs who accompanied it; her cool distance was a lie, as she greeted the eunuch who lay within it. Only her fingers were truthful, for only the briefest moment that she permitted them to touch the cold sweat on his brow. They trembled, and so she snatched them back.

And then stepped aside, to let the bearers carry him up the steps and along the pavilion's open gallery to the wide waiting doors of the room she had designated his.

LIGHT and bright that room was, with pretty views for when he could sit up to see them, or when she could tear her gaze away from him, if either of those chances came about.

Gazing at him now, the first chance she'd had since his alteration, she doubted that either of them would.

What had happened in that dark place, the brute pain and the screaming, she had done her best to bury in a darker place in her head. For Salem, it was written on his body as well as his mind. She wasn't sure which would be more cruel or more dangerous over time, but for now, it was his body that was failing.

For the second time—and too soon, far too soon—she stood and looked down at a body she had loved, and thought that she saw death in the bed there. And this time she couldn't order the world's best doctors; the eunuch-slaves of a harem cared for each other, if they cared at all. For sure nobody else did.

He had been golden-bright and beautiful, the image of a young man in his prime, in his pride, perfected. He used to sit high on his horse, high in the city, commanding men and attention in equal measure; now he lay on a horsehair mattress in the Palace of Tears and not a man in earshot, and he too weak to cry.

The lovely sheen was gone from his skin, which was sickly-grey and sticky now. Half his flesh seemed to have gone from beneath it, though surely muscles should not melt so quickly; he seemed all bones and awkward angles, where once he had been smooth, taut strength.

His skin was restless, where his bones were still. He shivered and twitched and lacked any will to move, or else he lacked the power. That was almost the most dreadful thing about him, how he lay slack and feeble when he had been so potent and determined. She thought that they had ruined him; even if his body survived, she thought he would die regardless, because his spirit was dead already.

The most entirely dreadful thing about him was his head, his face, how drawn it was, like a skull with a drumskin pulled across. She would almost not have known him, even here. In the street, she'd have passed him without a second glance: just another death's-head beggar, no one she could possibly have known.

It was fever and despair together that had destroyed his beauty, but the rough stubble didn't help, where they had shaved him head and chin and lip. The law demanded it; even so, they need not have done their work so crudely. With his skin so tight, the hairs they'd missed stood out like bristles on a pig, stark and savage between the raw patches and the scabby cuts. Teo could attend to that, after they'd washed the rank sweat away and bathed his wound; but he'd need better treatment than water and razor and love could offer him.

She knew a little, a very little about treating wounds in war, from listening to her father and then to his doctors as they treated the Sultan. She had no access even to those few medicines she could name; she knew whose crafty hands could find them somehow, though, and whose long wisdom might offer better choices.

"Teo," she said—when her voice was back, when she had command of it again—"Mirjana and I can give Salem the nursing that he needs." And that was another lie. "You run to Djago, and tell him what else I want," a list of herbs and potions, everything her fractured mind could remember. "And his advice too, if he has any, I would dearly love that . . ."

"At once, my lady," but before he went—unusually, unnervingly—he kissed her. It was a boy's kiss, just a brush of dry lips across her cheek; and oh, she did miss her men, both men, the first who was dead already, and the second who lay here dying beneath her eyes, beneath her hand.

————————

IT was an hour or more before Teo came back, and in that time she and Mirjana had done everything they could, whatever they could think to do.

They had stripped away the soiled rags that Salem had been dressed in, coarse linen crudely stitched. Mirjana had taken those to be burned on the same fire that was heating water, while Jendre picked what herbs she could find in the near gardens. Anything that might help: lavender and rosemary for the perfumed strength of them, surely potent against a creeping fever; comfrey and agrimony to make an infusion for his wound. Weak warriors they might be, good for cuts and bruises and little more, but they were all the little that she had. The good general fights the battles he can afford, with the men he can afford to lose. Her efforts might be poor, but at least she was rich in poverty; she could try and try, fail and fail again. The gardens were vast, and there must be people who could say, "Pluck here, use this, this is sovereign . . ."

Meantime, scents and steam filled the room, and he had reacted to neither. *Dead already*, she thought, despite the heat in him.

But they washed him anyway, delicately, scrupulously, she at one side and Mirjana the other. When they had made their careful way from head to feet—and not till then, absolutely not till his last least toe had been daintily dried with a clean linen napkin—their eyes met across the bed. It was Mirjana who nodded, because Jendre needed her to do that; it was Jendre who reached out a hand to ease the matted dressing from between her Salem's legs, because she very much needed to do that herself.

————————

SHE had seen it done, in all the cruelty of its moment. She had screamed then, when he did, one brief indulgence. This was different—specific, particular, a close examination of cruelty in the cold—and she would like to scream again. Or rage, or faint, or run away.

And she could do none of those things; she needed to seem strong, to lie; and so she bent over his supine body—and that stillness in him was something else of horror, something more, and she couldn't even bring herself to mention it for fear of hearing what was obviously true, that Mirjana agreed with her—and dabbed lightly with a warm wet cloth, to wash off the dried blood and other clotted matter, to expose the hacked and seared flesh and see exactly what they had made of her lover.

Well, she already knew that, exactly enough. What she needed to see was how well he was healing; and the answer was not well enough, not well at all. No fresh blood came oozing from the wound after she had cleaned it, but it oozed none the less: a dribble of foul pus, where she would far rather have seen blood. And there were fierce red streaks beneath his skin, reaching down his legs and up towards his belly. She knew that was an evil sign; there was poison in the wound, and it was running slowly out along the body's channels. That was why he burned and why he sweated, why his body's weight was falling off him, fuel to the fire.

He groaned, and her heart broke. When would her man Salem ever, ever have let her know that he was feeling pain? His eyes were open, but whatever world they saw, it was not this one; they moved strangely, to follow sudden starts of nothing.

She wasn't sure whether she preferred him dead to the world, or alive to somewhere other. For certain sure, both choices scared her deeply.

———

WHEN Teo came, he had been so long about his errand, she could have beaten him; but he came with a shadow, short and squat beside his own lean grace, and she could have kissed him. She could have kissed them both.

"Djago! Oh, bless you for coming. Look, look here, this is not good, and I—I don't know what to do . . ."

The dwarf peered over Salem's thigh and down into the cleft of his injury.

"Open his legs a little wider, my lady; my arms are stubs, and clumsy. Do not mind him; his spirit is riding in the wind. Yes, better; I can reach now. If you would hold his, ah, manhood up, so . . . Yes. Thank you."

A long, patient examination, and then a grunt.

"What is it, Master Djago? What's to do?"

"Lady, you know what it is. The cutting was ill-done, the knife not hot enough, and the wound has soured. It happens; they are careless men, and sometimes vindictive. By order, sometimes." *The Valide Sultan*, he meant, *she gave word for this.*

"And must he die, then? Can he not be saved?" After so much, love and grief and dreadful punishment, must he too be carried off by poison at the old woman's behest? He might have preferred that to living on, unmanned; this was not done to punish him, but her.

"Say that the other way around, rather: that he need not die, but he can still be lost. The knife was not hot enough, but it was hot; the work was marred, but it was at least attempted. This is an imperfect art, this killing by clumsiness. Give me my bag here, folly."

When he spoke to Teo, his voice was crisply affectionate, and the boy responded with a whipcrack attentiveness. He had a leather bag slung across his shoulder, she saw now, that she had missed before. He laid it on the bed and held open the neck; Djago thrust his arm in.

A bowl, a silver tube, a little jar came out. There was more in there, other implements; they rattled as he rummaged; he had been ready for worse. She might take hope from that, perhaps.

He sent Mirjana for more water, hot, unscented. When it came he set the jar into it, to warm. Then he took his tube and parted Salem's raw, un-healed flesh, as gently as he could with awkward fingers. When he found that open fistula where the pus came leaking out, he slid the tube inside it.

And set his mouth to the other end, and sucked hard.

Jendre gasped. Teo half-swallowed a noise of revulsion that earned him a slap from Mirjana; Djago bent over his little bowl and spat, a glistening gobbet of putrescence.

"Now bring wine," he said. "Quickly."

"I don't think Salem will swallow it," Jendre objected. Besides, men in fever should never be given wine; she had heard her father say that. Heroes had died from heroic drinking after battle when their blood was overheated.

"The wine is for me," Djago said indistinctly. "To take the taste away."

Once he had rinsed his mouth—no, more than that, swilled and spat with water, swilled and swallowed wine—he put the tube's end into the wa-ter and sucked, and slipped his thumb over the end of it while it was still in his mouth. Jendre had done that with hollow straws in childhood, had taught the same trick to Sidië. She'd told the little girl it was magic that stopped the water dribbling out of the open end; she'd said it was a magic that only children had. Children and little people, perhaps she should have said . . .

Djago pushed the unthumbed end of his tube deep into Salem's wound, took his thumb away and blew; and then sucked, and held the bowl beneath to catch the water as it came sputtering out, stained and flecked with scabs.

"This will not cure," he said. "The poison is in the flesh and the blood of him, not in the excretions; but it will help, perhaps. Your boy should do this, daily. And then this, which will perhaps help more."

He unpicked the seal of wax on his little jar, inserted his tube and sucked again; slipped it into Salem's body, blew. When a little of the ointment dribbled out, he smeared it across the burned flesh and the raw.

"What is that, Master Djago?"

"Honey, lady. From my own bees, so I know that it is good."

Honey. What was she—startled? Amused? Appalled? She wasn't sure. Snappish, certainly. "And what, will that bring sweetness to his hurt?"

"Aye, perhaps; and healing, that too, perhaps. Lady, every soldier carries a pot of honey in his pack. Idiot boys eat it; this one would," with a nod at Teo, who smiled and nodded happily back. "The wise do not, and their wounds do not poison so easily. I think it draws out badness. Some drown a bee in the pot, for added potency. Like cures like, and the bee's poison attracts the poison in the flesh, or else attacks it. Some say one, some say the other. I do not know."

Nor did he say if there was a bee in his pot. But like did cure like, that was axiomatic. She was half-ready to take him on trust, untried; but that was Salem in the bed, so, "My father is a soldier, and has never mentioned honey to me. Nor were you ever a soldier, fool."

"No, lady, but I have had dealings with their kind. Officers perhaps have other, better medicines; the men in the field, they must rely on honey. And hope, those two."

And so must she, clearly, at least for today. "If there are other, better medicines, Djago"—*sweet Djago, beloved Djago*—"might you have a way to fetch them to me?"

"Perhaps. It would not be easy, with the city so—unquiet." He would have to go beyond the wall, he meant; and there were troops all over, gossip said, discontent in the streets, mutterings against the new Sultan. Maras was famously restive in times of change, and the Sultan was mad, she had seen that for herself. He had castrated the pasha's son, that was a madness in itself. She was surprised that there was not more trouble, open rebellion . . .

"Will you do what you can for me?"

"If you ask it. There would be a price, to be paid later. Eunuchs learn to be careful of their promises and not to look too high; like soldiers, we turn to honey, and to hope. Sometimes I wish my ladies would be as wise."

Well, she had honey, but she had little hope. *And less wisdom*, Clerys would have added; but Clerys was a house behind, a hill and two high walls away from here. She had to make her own decisions. This one was easy.

"Anything you can, Djago. Please. I do ask it. And I will pay whatever price you ask." Neither one of them glanced towards Teo; they both knew what price they were speaking of.

"Whether or not it saves your young man for you?"

"Yes, of course. Whether or not. Did you think I would cry off because he died? You do not know me very well, Master Djago."

"I do not, but I look forward to learning more." The dwarf's bow started low, necessarily, and went foolishly lower, with many flourishes; she might have laughed, almost. "I should return to my own sweet lady now, she grows fretful in my absence. But there is this to say, lady, because you have been married, and I know that you are strong. You think it is a cruel thing, that has been done to him; he will think it monstrous, irrecoverable. If he survives this crisis, he will still want to die. You will want to keep him. That may be unkind; I do not know. But I survived. I have lived many years in my condition, and I find my life worthwhile.

"If you can persuade him to stay with you—well, let me be blunt, what he has lost is less than you fear. He was fully a man, before he was cut; and he was cut badly but at least it was done the kind way, only his stones removed. Let me be as blunt as my body: he cannot father children, but that is all his lack. You can still take him to your bed and find some pleasure there, if he is willing.

"Some of us were less considerately treated. I was cut the other way, all gone with one stroke of a razor. The old man would not have us meddling with his women. We were his toys; it revolted him to think of us as men. When I piss, I do it through a pipe." He showed her where he wore it in his turban, the mirror of that silver tube he left beside the honey.

She thought he had still been talking about Teo, only that she did not know quite what he had been saying.

Chapter Four

SHELTER is as shelter does.

They had found a place that kept them from Marasi eyes in daylight; it more or less kept them from the rain; it might even keep them from the Shine at night if they dared linger here. Issel supposed that he had to call it shelter.

He'd slept in worse places, more exposed. Time was—and not so long ago—he'd have been grateful for this, he'd have fought to take it and fought again to keep it. He didn't need to fight for this; his only struggle now was to stay awake.

He didn't feel sheltered, and he was emphatically not going to sleep.

The rain helped, fizzing against his skin where he sat deliberately beneath a drip.

His companions helped a little. Less used to sleeping rough, Rhoan and Gilder shifted, talked, tried to doze and were alert again in moments. Their anxiety, their restlessness, their voices all served to snag at Issel's mind when he started to drift.

Only Baris was solidly, uncomplicatedly asleep. There was a comfort in that too; it was something to lean on, knowing that the strongest of them would be thoroughly rested before they had to move again.

Every little bit helped, but what helped most was his abiding sense of the river, where it went rolling by. The prickle of rain and puddle, this little lo-cal damp was nothing against that tremendous water. Its eternal wakeful-ness could feed his own; it flowed through his bones like pain and pleasure both. He felt almost joined to it, sworn to the river like an acolyte at temple given over to his gods. There would be a price, no doubt. Issel's life would no longer be quite his own; but price was inherent, nothing ever came for free.

THIS place they'd found stood above the river road and the slope that backed it, but still below the city proper. Here was another road, except that it led nowhere: a long broad esplanade lined with pavilions and pleasure houses, where the wealthy men of Maras would have come down to promenade and eat together. They would have talked business, Rhoan said, and arranged their children's marriages, and fostered their young sons to army families in hopes to see them rise. Those same sons, a little older, might have kept con-cubines down here, she said, politely outside the city walls, or else simply bought the attentions of prostitutes and slaves. It would have been a fair-ground, she said, a marketplace of bodies and drinks and drugs, exotic pleas-ures frowned on by their families or forbidden by their priests.

No longer. The bridge overhung it, the Shine must taint it nightly, when it should have been at its brightest and most alluring, torchlit pleasures and shadowy corners for secrets to be whispered in. The Marasi were no fools; they had abandoned their playground utterly, uprooted their fair and pre-sumably taken it elsewhere. Maras was famously a city of many gates and many views. They needn't look down on the river; all their empire lay spread out behind them, they could turn and look on that instead while they enjoyed the profits of it, flesh and fruits, coins and trade and information.

In Sund, all these fine fancy buildings would have been ripped apart and every nail recovered, every plank reused. But this was Maras, and they'd simply been left to rot where they stood. There was a grandeur in that, somehow, unless it was simply arrogance: *we were here; we have moved on.*

Happily, because this was Maras, even their wooden pleasure halls had been well made, of stout timber soundly jointed. Twenty years of weather and neglect, and they'd only now begun to rot. Hence this pavilion, where the rain might drip in but Issel and Rhoan were entirely used to that; he found it useful; where the caulked seams in the walls might have split but that was useful too; it gave him views of all the esplanade, and he could watch the rain.

He had done that half the day already, sat in its dripping and watched it fall. Nothing moved outside except the constant splash and run of water over cracked and filthy flagstones, where the weeds grew pale and twisted and robust. The Shine left nothing untouched.

Finally, he saw what he'd been watching for, something to justify the dull tension of these sleepless hours. He saw movement: first a flitting in the corner of his eye, a shadow scudding between one building and the next. His eyes were sharp, even without the Shine, but nothing was clear through the grey rain-heavy air. This much water could defeat even the water-magic, or else he simply didn't know how to use it.

Maybe if he was out in the rain, he could use all that water like a second skin, spread his senses through it so that anything the rain touched, he would feel. If the river stirred him at a distance, as it did, surely he could turn the rain to his advantage? Rhoan might have ideas how, but he wasn't going to ask her. For now he'd rely on what sight he had and what he could hear, though the rain dulled that as well, relentlessly drumming on the tiles overhead.

No rain could have muffled what came next, what he'd been afraid of, soldiers' boots and voices calling. They came cursing down the long parade, a squad of Marasi conscripts with heavy feet and heavy accents, like a mock of those sophisticated men this place was made for; they kicked their way in and out of every building along the way, and in a little minute they would be stamping up the steps of this pavilion.

And then Issel would have to kill them. With the others' help, he supposed, but they would need his lead to follow. And then there would be bodies everywhere and more soldiers come in search, and they would have to flee in daylight through the rain, with no idea where to run or how to hide again.

Unless . . .

"Rhoan." A soft call in the gloom.

"Yes?"

"Can you hide us? All four of us, in the corner there, if people come in looking?"

"With pure water, I can try. Not with this." Her hand gesturing at the spatter of rain on boards between them. "And it depends how hard they're looking, what they're looking for . . ."

"Not for us. Specifically. I think." Unless someone in that cage on the beach had tipped the soldiers off, *an invading army from Sund, all four of them in a little rowboat . . .*

"Come over here, then."

She'd been eager, amused, superior the first time, in Tel Ferin's study, when the master himself hadn't seen her. Now there was just a dreary acceptance in her voice, obedience to the inevitable. She was a traveller without hope, Issel thought, which made her the worst kind of companion.

And still he would use her when he could, as often as he needed to. He joined the others in their corner, furthest from the door. She tugged the two men in closer to Baris, nudged him awake and silenced him with a hand over his wide jaw, uncorked a flask.

There was so much wet on the floor and in the air, Issel could have used that without a second thought and preserved all they had of the purified water. But he didn't have Rhoan's skill in this, her delicacy of touch; she could be deceitful where he was merely savage, and it would be deceit that saved them now, if anything could.

She tipped a little water into her palm and it steamed, and no matter that some of it spilled over the edges of her hand, she had it now: her mind's light grip could dissipate it all and yet never lose a droplet, make it all hang like a curtain of mist between them and the doorway. Shadows would gather in the droplets, making the light dance off them and dissipate in its turn, hide her and all her companions behind that shifting barrier. Those who came in would see only the gloom of an empty corner in this empty room.

If. If she had worked it well, if those who came looked casually and expected nothing, if none of the hidden gave themselves away by other means: a gasp or a sneeze or a sudden movement, anything that might make the searchers peer and squint.

The waiting was the worst. They listened, they heard the stamps and growls come closer; Issel for one hoped fervently that the growls were only soldiers in their perpetual complaint, at rain and work and sergeants. Dogs' eyes might be fooled by Rhoan's little play with light and water, but he was sure she could not make it work upon their noses.

At last, at long last there were feet on the steps outside, and the door was kicked back in its frame. He didn't want to stare, for fear that they might sense his gaze and puzzle out its source, or just tramp over to this corner to poke about without ever really knowing why. Still, it was impossible not to look. He kept his head averted and stole glances on the sly.

Two figures in the doorway, darker shadows against the billows of the rain. One was a burly man, and one a youngster: the veteran and the recruit teamed together, sign of a good sergeant.

From where they stood, they might have seen this room was empty. If Issel had had a god, he would have been praying so. They came inside, though, a few steps. Not far enough to worry, exactly, but it would always be a worry to be in the same room as the Marasi and only a flimsy wall of magic to hide behind.

The young one shook his head, and his club of hair flailed around, spraying water. Rhoan flinched, Issel ducked, and either of those might have spilled the magic for a moment to betray them. But that spray had caught his senior full in the face, and the veteran was only interested in cursing and striking out, the recruit in covering his head, taking blows in his ribs, yelping apologies.

"Ach, no matter. I'm wet enough—and you too, no point trying to shake it off. Nor any point seeking shelter, when we've to go out in it again. On, now, there's nothing here."

Out they went, after that cursory inspection. Rhoan exhaled slowly and let her hands fall, her magic shiver into nothing. Issel crept across the floor to his original spying-point and watched the soldiers move away. They continued their steady search of every building, and he wondered what they might be looking for, if not for him and his.

Then there was a sudden scurry outside, bare feet on wet wood, and another figure came sidling swiftly in through the open door.

Sidling in and stopping, stopping dead.

———

ANOTHER moment, and that would have been all too true. There was water in the air, water on the floor, Issel was wet all over and sitting in a puddle. He didn't need to snap his fingers, nothing so effortful. His mind moved, his thoughts flowed over and through all that water; and just as Rhoan made her deceptive mists, so he could make a weapon of it, turn it lethal, turn the air itself against this newcomer, turn it to glass in his throat and tear—

Her throat.

That was what he saw first, in the shortest possible time between thinking and doing. She didn't know it, but he had her already, she was dead already; except that she was a woman, and the Marasi most certainly did not use women as soldiers. He held back that killing thought, even against the weight of all the river's water in his mind; and then he saw how her face was distorted, how broad her shoulders were, all the early signs of change. If she'd been smiling, he'd have recognised her teeth.

The Marasi did use dogtooth labour, they'd seen that on the beach; but those were men, and all in chains. This woman was free, or seemed so in her rags.

"Issel . . ."

That was Rhoan, and her voice said *don't*, too late; he had already decided. He loosed his control of the water and shivered, and moved out of the drip, away from the puddle. It made little difference, with all his clothes so wet and the air too, but Rhoan at least should appreciate the gesture.

It meant nothing to the newcomer, who could have felt nothing anyway except perhaps the tension, the danger between breath and breath. Issel's moving seemed to release her; she backed a step towards the door, until Baris' growl checked her.

Her eyes found him in the gloom. "Oh—one of us . . . But I don't know you. I haven't seen you here. And the rest of you aren't, and the Turds just left you here. I don't understand." Nor did she trust; her back was to the wall and a knife was in her hand, terror at war with determination in her voice.

Rhoan wanted to break that straining tension, perhaps; she said, "The Turds?"

"The Third, the third regiment. Janizars, the Border Guards, the Turds—but how can you not know that? Who are you? You don't even look like us . . ."

Except underneath, Issel thought, *where the bones are.* She was right, though; if she was a typical Marasi—in her blood, at least, before it was poisoned by the Shine—then their clothes were wrong, their skin was wrong, their hair and stature and everything about them.

No matter. He'd never imagined that they could pass for local, this side of the river. They weren't here to spy.

He said, "We're from Sund," confident at least that she wouldn't go running after the soldiers to betray them. For all their differences, he saw and felt a kinship. It was fed by poverty, by street food and street manners, a lifetime of beggary and hunger, getting by, surviving. She was barefoot and desperate; her clothes were ragged and filthy, but her knife was strong and clean and sharp. Issel recognised every aspect of that.

"Sund? What are you—no. Wait." At least nothing in her was dulled yet, or defeated. Her suspicion was as bright and sharp as her blade. "Why didn't the Turds take you? Wherever you're from?"

"They didn't see us."

"How not? My eyes are better, but they're not blind."

"We had a trick, to conceal us."

"A trick?" She blinked around, as though looking for blankets they could have hidden under, false walls to hide behind. Then, "Oh—you mean Sund-trickery, curses . . ."

"The water-magic, yes," Rhoan said, where Issel would have given her a hot denial. "Do they tell you it's a curse?"

"Of course. We know it is. The Sundain have poisoned all the river with their wickedness, to turn it against us . . ." But her voice faltered, as though she was listening to her own voice as she spoke, hearing how her words were slurred by the shape that her jaw had taken. Those who faced her didn't need to say a word.

"Why are you here?" she asked at last.

Issel told her, blunt and clear. "To destroy—that"—with a backward jerk of his head, nothing more needed—"and save our city."

She nodded, as if he had said something utterly mundane.

Gilder said, "So who are you, then? And why do you slip around behind the backs of your own soldiers?"

Issel could have told him that; he could have told her. All her life's history: it was written on his own body, in his own memories, more or less intact. It was only the city in which she'd lived her life that was strange to him.

He needed to learn that city. He kept quiet and let her talk.

"My name is Ailse. I was bond-born, to a man who trades in meat."

"I don't know what that means," Rhoan interrupted her, "bond-born?"

Issel did, although he'd never heard the phrase before. The words sang in her mouth, in his ears; they were the bitterness in her bones, lodged deep before ever the Shine shone down upon them.

"My family was bonded to his," Ailse said, "to be their servants in every generation. Choiceless, irredeemable."

"Slaves, you mean?"

"No, not that. The military, the nobles, they have slaves, they buy and sell their captives and their children too. That's not for us in the lower city, where we're all Marasi. Our masters don't own us—only our labour. We have to work for them; they have to keep us."

There seemed small difference to Issel. No matter.

"So your master was a butcher—?"

"No, a trader. He bought meat in, and sold it. To the army, mostly: fresh to the barracks, dried for the marches and the outposts. And for Sund."

Issel had seen it, in wagons and warehouses. Some he'd stolen, some he'd simply pissed on.

"And you, what did he do with you?" Gilder asked it as though she were meat of another sort, as though he knew how she should have been traded.

"My master decided that I should be married. To another bondsman, of course, one of his carters. I—decided otherwise, and ran."

"To this?" Issel asked, for all the world as though he hadn't done the same, seeking out a life in the bridge's shadow and a bed in the Shine.

"Where else? A bondsmaid can't pass the gates without her master's licence, mustn't be found on any road, daren't trespass on the farms or the plantations. All the land around Maras is watched as carefully as the city. This is where we run to, bonds and slaves and prisoners, because we can, because the whole foreshore has been abandoned. We hide in the shadows, we live on mussels and weed and whatever we can scavenge. And we grow strong, but not on what we eat," *because of the Shine*, she meant, *it makes monsters of us all*, "and so the Turds hunt us for their work-gangs on the docks. They keep us separately, but there is plenty of work for women, packing and sorting in the warehouses. We dodge them while we can, until we grow too stupid"—and her eyes found Baris in his corner, *until we grow like that, they would have him in a day*—"and we dream of what's impossible, an escape we can't achieve, a boat to take us free from here to the Insea."

She spoke of it as a priest might speak of heaven. Issel knew nothing of life on the Insea, and guessed that neither did Ailse, but he said, "We left a boat on the beach below the bridge. You could take that, you and whoever of your friends." *We won't be needing it again.*

Only for a moment, her face was lit with hope; then she shrugged, shook her head. "The Turds will have found that."

Likely they would, but, "It must be worth looking. Go see, Ailse, if you can go safely. If it's there, take it, use it, find your freedom. If it's not, come back. We could use your help."

He didn't offer her another kind of freedom, the kind you fight for, rather than the kind you run to seek. He wasn't so much of a hypocrite. If he found a way to destroy the bridge and give Sund its chance of freedom, that would have small impact in Maras unless it made life harsher for the poor and the powerless. Ailse and her kind: what chance did they have? He couldn't even advise her to row across the river. Baris had been a slave in Sund, and even that was rare. A dogtooth was more commonly driven out of the city and its hinterlands, hated as much as despised. What they might find beyond the hill-farms, Issel didn't know, but death seemed most likely.

Better to go further, Ailse. He only wished that she might send a message back, a map, a sign of hope; he supposed that he would be following her, sooner or later. Once the poison had done its work on him. He and Baris could go together, if the older one could wait so long. Or Issel could go sooner, not wait to see revulsion in the faces of his friends. Or pity, or fear. He thought those might be worse.

———

"SHOULD you have let her go?" That was Gilder; Issel wondered if he was fixing the blame, in case there was trouble to come.

"She won't betray us," he said. "Even if she's caught; she couldn't buy her freedom, so why should she sell ours? She should be safe enough, down to the beach and back."

"That's the point," Rhoan said wearily. "If she finds the boat, she won't be coming back. And we need her."

"We need someone, perhaps. There must be others."

"If we can find them. The patrols can't, and they know the land."

"We found her."

"She found us."

"Even so." They had magic, and they had Baris too; one dogtooth might sniff out another. Now that they knew what to sniff for. "We'll find them. Or we could go back down to the beach and ask help from those in the cage."

"And give ourselves away." That was Gilder, as determined as Rhoan that he had done the wrong thing.

"We have done that already," Issel said, "if they've found the boat." It should have been pushed back into the river, probably. Then there would have been nothing to tempt Ailse. But if they'd had nothing to offer, would she have helped them anyway? All they could do was make her a gift and hope it wasn't there for her to take: a stolen hope, a black promise, hollow at its core . . .

ISSEL sat and watched the rain, and cast his other senses further through the water. Sheets of it baffled his eyes, but he tried to feel past that, as a fisherman feels activity around his line: not just the bite on the hook but a wider impression of the water that engulfs it, what currents have taken it, what interest it attracts. So much water in the air and on the ground, so wet he was, he should be able to close his eyes and picture all the waterfront around him, the soldiers marching and the prisoners in their cage, the dogtooths and the runaways in their hiding-holes . . .

He reached into the dark behind his lids, tried to stretch through it, and found it not so dark after all. There were forms and structures that he could sense without seeing, that seemed to mirror the world of sight: as though water flowed over the buildings, over the ground, and he could flow with it, feeling out all the shapes and angles. And here, yes, at some distance now and moving further away, here were softer and changeable forms, indistinct among the buildings but he thought, no, he was sure that they were people, that squad of soldiers still searching, no danger now . . .

And then a hand gripped his arm, where he'd almost forgotten that he had an arm, a body, here where he'd left it; and he almost shrieked at the shock of that touch, and then again at the fierce burn of it, where it squeezed his wet shirt against wet skin and that steady needle-sting was suddenly red-hot needles; and he tried to see in the dark there, by the water-touch, before he remembered that he had eyes and could still use them.

So he did that, he opened his eyes and saw Rhoan on her knees beside him, confused and anxious and cradling her palm where she'd gripped him.

"Issel? What were you doing? You looked strange, so far away, and I thought the air was fizzing all around you, though I suppose it was the water; and it hurt when I touched you; it's never done that before, just when you were wet . . ."

He'd never had a river's weight of water run through his mind before. He thought that made a difference. And she had perhaps not touched him when he was actually working with water, except that one time when he'd been trying to purify it, not understanding how his own nature had been tainted. That time he'd been in agony, and she'd taken his pain deliberately to herself, and neither one of them wanted to speak about it.

He shrugged. "I was trying to sense where the soldiers were, through the rain."

"Oh." She looked a little blank, as though such a thing would never have occurred to her, although she was the subtle one. "Could you?"

"I'm not sure. I thought so, but maybe I was fooling myself." She'd been much closer, and wet all over, and if the soldiers really had been that flicker behind his eyes, she should have been flaring like a torch in darkness, even before she touched him. It wasn't the first time Rhoan had been this close, and he hadn't seen her.

"Well. Never mind, then. Don't trust it when you need it. I wanted to say I'm sorry, Issel. Of course you had to tell Ailse about the boat. Gilder wouldn't have, I know that; maybe I wouldn't have, I don't know about that. But you, you're not like us. You wouldn't have known there was a choice."

If she meant they were devious, political, manipulative, perhaps she was right; Issel had never really understood other people within-doors, in the frames and patterns of their lives. Put them in the street or the market, where he could be beggar boy or cozener, a thief either way; there he was devious and political and manipulative, all three, and better than any. And Ailse was a street-soul like himself. He'd known just what he was doing. Perhaps the boat was there and she was gone, grateful but useless to them. If not, if the boat was gone—well, she'd still have the gratitude. It was a gamble, he supposed, but street boys did gamble. With their lives, sometimes; more often with dice. He'd carried his own for years, rolling double-or-quits with storekeepers and more complicated games with anyone who'd play him, until no one would anymore. Not with his dice.

If this was a gamble, he thought the odds were good. Even if the dice weren't his. He might not understand people, but he knew a lot about fate, and about being hungry at the city's edge. A boat abandoned on a beach, unwatched, unclaimed; that must be a part of someone else's story by now, and he didn't think it would be Ailse's.

He smiled at Rhoan, didn't try to touch her. His fingers were still wet, and he had no reassurance in his gift. "She'll come back," he said. "Don't think I did better than you; it's not a kindness to tell her about a boat that won't be there."

"Can you, can you see where she is now?"

One person sliding through the rain, taking every chance she could to keep under cover, in the shadows, when this was a skill he'd barely invented yet, let alone mastered? "Perhaps," he said, "but I'd rather not try." *I'd rather talk to you*, except that they hardly had anything to talk about these days. "Can we just wait and see what happens? There'll be a boat, or there won't be. She'll come back, or she won't. If she doesn't, we'll find a substitute, or we won't. If we don't, maybe we'll just walk up to the gates of the city and tear them down. We'll do something. Sund has crossed the river now."

Rhoan nodded slowly, not taking her eyes off him. "Something's happened to you," she said. "Even since yesterday, I mean. Since we crossed the river. What is it?"

Nothing would have been dishonest; so would *I don't know*. He could lie to anyone at need, but he didn't want to lie to her. He didn't understand what it meant, to him or to them or to their enterprise, but he gave her what he had, knowing that she would understand it less than he did.

"I think I crossed the river."

———————

TIME passed. Rain fell. Silence puddled around them, all the hard and soft sounds of water only serving to underscore the fact that no one spoke.

No one until Gilder, who could contain his brittle energy no longer: "She's gone."

"No," Issel said. He had abandoned his watch from the corner and was sitting now with his back to the wall, his eyes closed.

He could feel Baris' heavy somnolence, Gilder's nervousness, Rhoan's dubious gaze. He felt his name in her mind, in her mouth before she said it: "Issel."

"Yes?"

"We should move. If they caught her, if they hurt her, she could betray us just to make them stop . . ."

"No. She's coming, and she's on her own."

In a more childish mood, in a less tense moment, he might have counted her in: *ten, nine, eight* . . . He did count in his head, for his own satisfaction, and only had to scramble a couple of numbers as she came a little more briskly, a little more confidently than he'd anticipated.

The water-shadow of her in his mind sidled along the pavilion's wall and up the steps; it filled the doorway, *three, two, one* and he opened his eyes.

"Ailse. Are you hungry?"

It wasn't really a question. Of course she was hungry. Hunger and fear together defined her days; he knew.

"Issel, we don't have much—"

"—And not enough to share. I know, Gilder. Even so, we'll share it."

There was dried meat, dried fruit, bread that had dried of its own accord even in this wet air. They didn't offer to share their water; the flaskfuls they carried were not for drinking. Rainwater here should be fresh enough, so long as it wasn't running off the bridge.

"The boat was gone, then?" That was Rhoan asking, waiting till Ailse's mouth was empty, even if her belly wasn't full.

Ailse nodded. "I don't think the Turds had it, though. The sand was churned up, but there were prints below the high-water line. Deep-sunken, only two pairs of feet and no keel-trace; they didn't drag the boat. They carried it."

"Two men couldn't lift that boat," Gilder objected.

"Two normal men, like you? No, that's what I mean." Her gaze found Baris, silent in his corner. "And their feet were bare. All the soldiers wear boots, always."

And a dogtooth went barefoot, always, because no boots would fit.

"You mean that your—your friends took it?" Rhoan asked.

"My kind." No friends of hers, if they took a boat she might have taken herself; and yet she was prepared to take that step that had terrified Issel for years now, to identify herself with them. "Yes. I think so."

"Good." That came out unexpectedly vehement; Rhoan looked surprised at herself, and qualified it quickly. "Better them than the soldiers, I mean."

Better that someone got away from here, that was what she meant, even if it couldn't be Ailse. Or herself.

Ailse shrugged, falling just that little step short of charity. Issel said, "Ailse, we need to go the other way, into the city. If you"—*your kind*—"can find a way out through the walls"—when all the gates must be watched and the traffic checked, coming and going—"can you point us to a way back in?"

She was a quiet person, the opposite of Gilder's twitchiness; great shock or fear simply stilled her. She was quite still now, under the moment of this decision, although she must have known that it was coming. Then, slowly, reluctantly, she nodded.

"I can do better than point. I can guide you, in and up. As far as you need to go."

"Oh," Rhoan said, "you don't need to—"

"Need? No. I don't need this, but you do. You could lose yourselves a lifetime, without my help. And what will that cost me?"

"Your life, perhaps," Gilder said, trying to be dark.

"Aye, but that's not so much."

"Your freedom?" Rhoan ventured.

"Oh, and what of that do I have now? Lurking on the foreshore, dodging Turds and fighting for scraps? I came here for a getaway, a boat. We all do. How many of us find one? I could count them on this hand, all those I've known." She held up just the one hand, deliberately the one that was clearly short a finger. "And my best chance just came and went today. I met people who had brought me a boat, but I met them too late. What point waiting now? I'll take you into the city, yes, and anywhere you want to go. What you do there, that's for you to choose. All my choices go awry."

Part 2

Chapter One

EVERY house has its rhythms and its moods, as a day does, a body does, a life.

It can be hectic, it can be tranquil; it can seethe by day and rest at night, or the other way around, or neither. It has a pulse that can be counted, whether it beats a dozen times an hour or a dozen times a day, or less than that. A house can panic, a house can smile, a house can wait. Generally, houses tend to be good at waiting.

A house can have preoccupations that set it apart from its neighbours. Such a house tends to be moodier than most, less steady in its rhythms, less predictable.

JENDRE'S house, now: Jendre's little pavilion had taken on all her own anxieties, necessarily, as her people had. Its lights burned late, and were lit early; in one room one soft lamp burned all night, where one of her people lay and was watched over constantly, by herself and others. The house slept as little as she did, and as fitfully.

Nor was it any more restful by day, except in that one room where every movement was quiet and slow, every voice was a whisper, as though in hollow mockery of the man on the bed.

Elsewhere the house had all of Jendre's nervousness, her peremptory demands, her sudden despairs. Doors were flung open, banged shut; people came and went, softly or suddenly, focused or distracted, sent or summoned or chased away. The house took its every mood from her; even its shutters could seem furious, its open doorways most unwelcoming.

Or else it could be sly, it could be sullen; it could be all cast into gloom, a shadow in broad sunlight, a shadow across the mind. It could lour, it could loom as though it squatted on a storm's horizon.

Occasionally it could be sunny, it could be singing to itself, if he had stirred or smiled unexpectedly, if he had made a good breakfast or sat up on his own account.

It was her house and her mirror, her message to a wider world, to anyone with wit enough to read it.

JENDRE had her own stool by his bed, which no one used those times she wasn't there. This was her place, her space. She knew that when he looked this way, he could only ever find herself, or her absence. He couldn't turn his head without thinking of her, one way or the other.

Sometimes he smiled, when he saw her come. It was a thin thing, that smile, but all of him was thin now, thin and weak. He had no strength and no certainty, he who used to be so swift and sharp and sure.

He couldn't bear to be alone, and so she kept one lamp alight to mitigate the darkness; he couldn't bear to be exposed, and so she screened his bed against the revealing sun. It meant that he lay in shadow all the time, half-light for this half-world he endured. *Half a man*, he might have said if he'd had the words for it, *it seems appropriate* . . .

He'd lost his words, though, along with so much else that had been his. He hardly spoke at all; sign and gesture were sufficient to express those few things he felt moved to say. A twitch of his fingers, a turn of his head; perhaps a smile for Jendre, but that was always an effort. His voice grew hoarse with disuse, hard in his throat and bitter in his mouth; it was better not to force him to it. Better to let him lie, to be content with gestures, smiles, any sign he chose to grace her with.

If that were contentment, it was limited to his sickroom, to that strained reduction of the world: walls and floor and ceiling, shuttered windows, screens and shadows. Outside its door she was miserable, vicious, tearful, raging, any or all of those. Occasionally elated, but that was as high and fragile as an instrument stringed with glass; it would shatter at a careless touch, and then there was always blood.

She and Mirjana snapped and grated at each other undeservedly, unendurably; they couldn't share the same room. Teo watched them both, sunk into his own silence. At last he left the pavilion without being sent, was back almost before he had been missed; it was no surprise, whom he had brought with him.

The only surprise was that Djago had brought his mistress Tirrhana, in the little cart he pulled himself.

"Djago, I'm sure this is kindly meant, but my lord Salem does not care for visitors, and I—I do not have the time to entertain your lady as she should be entertained . . ."

"Lady, he is not your lord Salem now, he is your slave Salem, and my lady does not visit slaves." The words were brutal, though the voice was not. "It is you we have come to visit. Your fine view of the lake here is entertainment enough for my lady, and I am certain that you can spare some few short minutes from your busy day to speak with me."

She gazed down at the dwarf, and as usual felt her height to be no advantage. So she glared at Teo instead, though he overtopped her now; her eyes promised him a beating that her hands would never deliver. He bowed like a devoted boy, the boy he used to be, and went to fetch the tea and delicacies that she had not ordered.

Sighing, she sank onto a bench that overlooked the lake there. "Will you seduce all my household from me, or is the one enough for you?"

"Ah, be easy, lady; one folly is enough to measure any man."

That was an opening, and for vengeance sake, she couldn't resist it: "Oh, and are you a man, then, Djago? By any measure?"

He shrugged broad shoulders, his equanimity quite undisturbed. "You must ask your boy. It's your own man I have come to talk to you about."

Of course it was, but she was still smarting. "My slave, you mean? My eunuch slave?"

"Even so. He will still be your man, whatever is done to him. Teo tells me that the infection is quite dead in him?"

"My thanks to you, it is, I think; but he is quite dead too. That is no living man you have saved for me in your wisdom, Master Djago. The Salem that I loved, that he loved to be, that man is lost to me."

"Indeed. And to himself, and to the world. Which is what I have come to say to you, that he must learn now to be Salem the eunuch, and you must learn to let him do that."

"I? I would not prevent him, whatever he wanted to be. If he would only rise from his bed, if he would want to live, in whatever way he must—"

"But you do prevent him, mistress. He needs to learn it from you first. So long as you cosset him, so long as you bring him fruits and favours with your own hands, so long as you nurse and comfort him and tolerate his idleness, that long will he be idle."

"He is not idle! He has been cruelly treated and terribly unwell, he needs time . . ."

"No, lady. Cruel treatment is behind him now, and so is his sickness. The last thing he needs is time to lie in bed and dwell on it all. When you geld a man, the kindest thing is to set him to work next day, while he is still hurting, before he's had any chance to heal. Give him other pains and other troubles, or this little thing will grow and grow inside his head and scar him deeper than the hot knife ever did. Your Salem has been ill handled from the first, and it will all be more difficult for him, and for you; but if you want him to thrive here, he must thrive as a slave, and only you can make that happen."

"I don't think I know how."

"You know as much as you need. You have been angry with your other slaves, all the time; when will you be angry with him, who deserves it more?"

Her heart said *never*, but that was useless and might not even be true. She could pretend, at least. As she did now, with a light laugh and an easy manner: "When will I be angry with him? Oh, when you are gone, Master Djago. I would not discomfort my guests, by berating a servant in front of them. Will you sit and talk with me awhile?"

"As long as you like, lady."

His mistress Tirrhana didn't eat before others, any more than she spoke. Jendre guessed that Djago must feed her with his fingers, in the privacy of their own pavilion. Here she sat small and stiff and ancient in her little cart, and gazed over the water and seemed to want nothing, even the little courtesies they offered from their bench. Teo served Jendre and Djago impartially, and when he had refilled teacups and fetched more almond cakes and used a scented napkin to wipe their sticky fingers, he sat on the ground between them, at his mistress's feet but equally close to the dwarf's swinging legs. Jendre thought the boy was getting kicked lightly where she couldn't see it, a boot nudging into his ribs; if she was right, he didn't seem to mind it.

For herself, she took hold of his ear and twisted it, tugged at the lobe of it, wondered aloud if it might look well pierced with pearl and gold. He didn't seem to mind that either.

When they weren't teasing Teo, they talked of the world out there, beyond the wall. Jendre began that as a ploy, but Djago knew far more about the city's doings than any harem eunuch had a right to; soon she forgot that she was being strategic, lost sight of her stratagem altogether. It wasn't hard. He was a trained fool; it was his work to tell good stories, or to make good stories out of the news he had to tell.

". . . How many, lady? No one is counting. The troops count only their own dead, and that only because pay and rations are calculated on a head-count. Rioters and rebels, curfew-breakers, troublemakers—who would care, to count? Individual soldiers may keep a tally, how many they killed today, this week, this month; but I doubt if most can count so high. Notches on a spear-haft, perhaps. No one adds them up."

"It's terrible," Jendre said, seeing her city in her mind's eye, dressed all in blood.

The little man shrugged at her side. "Change makes people nervous, and where there are too many of them together, so much nervousness makes them stupid. In the street, in barracks, both the same. Maras is overlarge, and—"

There was a snort from below. "Lady, he thinks everything is overlarge, being so small himself. Ow!"

That time, Jendre was sure that Teo had been kicked. Well, he deserved it. She cuffed him quiet for the sake of even-handedness, then set his cap straight for him. "Master Djago, I do apologise for my boy's ill discipline. You were saying?"

"Before my folly cut me off?" There was that disputed ownership, plain to see. "I spoke of Maras, that it is the beating heart that must sustain an empire, and so too big and busy for its own comfort. The people in the lower town are pressed as close as water-droplets in a pool; the soldiers too. Any change is a flung stone that causes ripples through all the city. A great change brings great disturbance. There will always be deaths, when a sultan dies; and more to follow, until the ripples die away.

"This time is worse, because the old man—your husband, I should say, the Magnificent, though my own duty was given to his father—he sat the throne so long, our lazy people thought he always had and always would. Now he is stolen from them, and they are not ready, and very afraid. And suspicious of his death, and overfed on rumour.

"It will all settle soon. The new Sultan may seem weak, but his mother is not. She will control her son, as she has always meant to. He will pay more dole, and as soon as the janizars see it, they will control first themselves and then the streets. The rioters will run home, the rebels will recant, and all will be—well, not as it was, but quieter than it is. The next trouble will build more slowly. There are young men out there who are angry at what has been done to their friend Salem. Do not tell him that, either of you; their anger can do him no good. Nor them. The impetuous ones, those are likely dead already, or marked for death; the others, the quiet ones, are more dangerous to the Sultan. Not to you or yours, lady." As though she needed that reassurance, as though she were afraid for herself or for her servants. "No ruckus will reach in here."

Salem doesn't matter anymore, he was saying. *What was done to him, that could still matter, but not the man himself. He is eunuch, which is less than being dead.*

"What of his father?" she asked aloud. "What is the pasha doing?"

"Ah, now, that is strange. The pasha is the most quiet man in the city. He sits at home and speaks to no one. I think the Valide Sultan will have her son send him to the wars. Live or die, she will want him out of the city. He should be raging, and he is not. That is very, very dangerous. You should not tell your Salem that, either. Do you hear me, folly? Shave his head, wash him, feed him—or better, chivvy him out of bed and have him shave and wash and feed himself—and talk to him of little things, eunuch things, nothing beyond the wall."

Teo counted his instructions off, one finger at a time. "Little things, eunuch things, nothing beyond the wall; oh, Djago, that'll be easy. I'll tell him all about you. Ow!"

Chapter Two

LL his life torn between the call of water and the fear of it, between the pain and the wonder, between the gifts and the costs, Issel had always struggled to keep himself as dry as he could, as far away as he dared to be.

To be sure, that was never very far, never very dry for very long. There had always been too much else to be afraid of, and too little else that gave him any sense of wonder. He always did come scurrying back to water.

Even so, he thought he had never been so close as this, nor ever quite so wet.

HE had crossed the river of the world, he and his friends in their tiny cockleshell boat struggling over all the water that there was. He had sat all day in a puddle, under a drip, in the wettest imaginable house in the rain, while his skin wrinkled and soaked, while the water fizzed and sparked as it dribbled off him.

Then when the sun had set at last, when the Shine took its place—below the clouds, so seeming brighter than the grey day, making stronger shadows—and the soldiers retreated, Ailse had led them out of that damp refuge and almost immediately into this. From sunlight to Shine-light to his own eldritch glow against the uttermost dark; from puddle-and-drip through a simple, dangerous rain and into—well, a torrent. A force of water such as he had never felt, never dreamed to stand in. Sund was a low, flat city that soaked up all the rain that came, and gave it back through wells and springs and fountains. This Maras was a city of hills with streets of stone, and profligate with its water as it was profligate with everything; he was learning all about run-off.

They hadn't been the only ones on the move in that shifting, oily light. The Shine made shadows of its own, but Issel could see more, real figures with a real purpose. With his new skill, his water-sense, he could reach out through the rain and find where it fell on others, out of his sight but not his ken.

None of them came near, none called a greeting or news or a challenge. All along the esplanade, people hid from the city's soldiers, scavenged a living, sought to get away; they had all the same fears, the same needs and the same hopes, and yet they avoided each other.

No—and *so* they avoided each other. There was nothing like this in Sund, but Issel understood it none the less. They weren't a community; this wasn't Daries, it wasn't even the strand where the last fishermen and their families all huddled close, watched each other's gardens, watched each other's backs. Here they were all rivals for the same hiding place, the same food, the same hope of a boat. They might not betray each other, quite— how could they, without betraying themselves?—but there was no safety in numbers on the waterfront. Numbers attract attention, and divide spoils too thinly for any to thrive. Try to fit too many within the narrow compass of a deck, and the whole boat could be lost.

Here, the poorest would do best alone or in small bands, not united. Unity would lead them to being caged out in the Shine; the only community here was a community of slaves.

Ailse led them upriver, away from the bridge. At the end of the esplanade stood a monumental building, too high and wide to be a private pavilion; some palace of common pleasure, then, a place for the rich and indulgent to indulge together.

There was a path of sorts, a narrow darkness between the building and the rising hill: a slaves' way, surely, access to the service quarters, overhung now by wild growth. More a tunnel than a path, perhaps, it led to a yard of beaten earth and cobbles.

The height of the building at their backs cut them off from bridgelight.

Ailse hurried straight on across the yard; Issel skipped on a step or two, not to lose her in the darkness.

Just as he did so, she stopped precipitately. He wasn't ready for that, couldn't do it, had one foot over the edge already before he understood.

And felt a sting in the air beneath his sole, and now he could smell it, feel the sting of it in his nostrils also, and a rising scorn at himself for not having felt it or smelled it out before.

He could hear it too, and could no doubt have heard it earlier if he'd been paying attention to anything outside his own skin. Even after a night's journey across the river of the world, even after a day of rain, even after pushing through that tunnel of shrubs run wild where every leaf and twig was wet and stinging at him—even after all of that water and the draining exhaustion of it, he surely should have been alert to this.

There must once have been a fence, but that was long since fallen or torn down. Without it they could slide—and Issel very nearly had slid, and it was only Ailse's sudden hand on the neck of his shirt that held him back from sliding—straight down from the dark of the yard into the deeper dark of a rocky gully beyond.

It opened like a sword-slash in the land, sudden and severe, slicing from the city to the river. It was sheer black down there, where even the Shine couldn't insinuate itself, but the rushing he could hear as he stood above it was nothing, *nothing* next to the rush in his blood, in his bones.

There was water at the bottom of this gully, water in quantities that would have terrified him once. Not so near as the rain, nowhere near so dominant as the river—which was in his head still, massive and portentous, where he thought it always would be now—but strong enough to strike up at him, to shrug off the rain's irritant and cut through the river's deep drag. A lot of water, and all of it in a terrible hurry. That simply didn't happen in Sund.

The others joined them now, standing on the crumbling rim and peering down into darkness, into the noise and the hurtle of it.

"Which way do we go," asked Gilder, "up or down?"

Up meant climbing the slope towards the city and its forbidding walls, the way they had to go eventually, just not necessarily yet; down meant towards the river, where the gully's walls might be less forbidding, the stream broader but easier to cross.

"Down," Ailse said, but she clearly meant something else entirely, because she went on the word, plunging directly over the edge and into the gully's maw.

Rhoan shrieked. Gilder cursed, but perhaps only because he'd caught all the shrill bite of that cry, direct into his ear. Baris gazed down after Ailse, unmoved.

Her voice came up to them, lightly contemptuous. "What, did you think there'd be a path? And lights, perhaps, to guide you? This is the secret way, the thieves' way in and out. Come down, or go home. If you can swim, or walk the bridge."

She knew which of those was worse. So did Issel. He crouched and laid a hand to the soft and sodden ground at the gorge's rim.

A grim light pooled like water around his fingers; like water, it found its swiftest way to fall. Over the edge and down, straight down, and glowing all the way: and no, it didn't find a path, but it did show them how it would be possible to grope and stagger down, lurching from one tangle of growth, one rock, one handhold to the next.

And it did show them Ailse, where she was already halfway down and staring back up this line of light, glowering and mockful, both at once.

"Secret, I said!" Her voice came at them, booming from the gulf, anything but. "Do you want the world to see?"

"The world is not looking," Issel called back, a little more softly. "And we need this, to find our way down without falling . . ."

Baris only shrugged at it and plunged as Ailse had, *as a dog would,* Issel thought and didn't say; Gilder was grateful but of course couldn't say so, stumbling and slipping his own way down, never quite in the light but always close; Rhoan couldn't make the attempt at all, just couldn't go over the edge until Issel took her hand and led her.

Damp in the earth beneath his feet: it lent him a strength he didn't own, which kept them both upright against the pull of the fall. She must have realised; after a short way, she gave up even trying to balance on her own account, and simply clung to him.

When he dared, he put his arm around her. Only because the slope was steeper yet, and he wasn't sure that she could keep her feet even with him to hold to. He was entirely certain that he could hold her forever if he had to. It felt to him as though he enfolded her in a wing of flame, so bright the water burned; he couldn't tell how it felt to her, though she did gasp just a little as he gripped her.

Trust me, his lips said, while he held his breath; he thought the air that came from him would have scorched all her hair to dust.

She said nothing, but her eyes were eloquent. He thought they said *never*, unless it was *always*. She was a girl; how could he know, how could he read her, he who had never learned to read?

Slow but steady all the way, that was how he wanted to do this, while the others skidded and sprawled. There was too much water in the ground, though. His slight weight and Rhoan's, just the two of them together were enough to start it slipping. Drawing strength from water to fight the tug of the slope, he didn't notice that the slope itself was falling until the ground had gone from under their feet, and they had nothing left to stand on.

So they fell, of course, the only choice they had; and slid with the soil and the tumbling pebbles, bruising elbows and pride together as they tried to slow themselves, not to go headlong into the furious roar of waters down below.

There was so much wet all around—spray in the air, rainwater trapped in hollows and clinging to the scrubby vegetation, mud all over—that he could have seized it in a moment and had it seize them too, stop all this calamitous falling, if only he'd had a moment to be still, to gather his wits, to command. But he was buffeted, jabbed, kicked—was that the slope that kicked him, or was it Rhoan?—and tumbled end over end, and there wasn't a moment available. All his strength, resilience, stubbornness, everything that made him Issel had been left behind; he'd fallen out of it like a snake slid free of its skin, there was nothing now except this endless rolling fall, and the brutal threat of water at its ending . . .

———

UNTIL he slammed into something very solid, and thought it was a tree; clung to it frantically, felt the warmth and smelled the stink of it and opened his eyes to find himself wrapped around Baris' leg.

Baris was standing on the bank above the flood—if you could call it a bank, where the slope of the gully barely shallowed before it met the frenzied hurtle of water. It was all dark down here; Issel was understanding it by touch, by smell, by other senses he didn't have a name for. None of them was refined enough to tell him what he needed most to know.

"Rhoan?"

He called her name into the darkness, barely expecting an answer; what was there to have stopped her going straight on into the hurly of the stream?

"Here." Her voice came back, breathless and surprised. "Gilder caught me—but only just . . ."

For once she didn't sound regretful, anxious, frightened: on the edge of laughter, rather, as though something in her had enjoyed that fearful plunge. The confident, bold girl she'd been, that Rhoan would surely have found something to enjoy in it. Perhaps that girl was not lost after all, only forgotten for a time.

"It's going to be hard," he said, "making our way up beside the stream, with no path," and the gully's slope trying constantly to shrug them off.

"Not hard," Ailse said. "Hopeless. We go in the water."

And she showed them, a shadow among shadows, jumping down into the torrent.

Issel wasn't the only one who cried out, though perhaps he did cry loudest.

Her laugh came back at them, only a little effortful. "It was not so deep before. Not so busy. Still, I can stand against it; so can you. Come, see . . ."

She had thighs like an ox and strength to match. More, she was Marasi; she had no sensitivity to water. She was dogtooth; she might have small sensitivity to anything, but she stood chest-deep in a flood of water and it was nothing to her. Oh, she had no idea . . .

Issel wouldn't have asked Gilder to do that, and he was the least skilled, the least trained, the least sensitive of the Sundain. Excluding Baris, of course, as Issel always did. He wouldn't have let Rhoan do it, if he had any hope of stopping her; and Rhoan had ways of avoiding the sting inherent in any touch of water.

In himself it was all bone-deep, banked up, fit to burn. He absolutely did not want to enter that stream; he thought it would consume him, from the inside out.

In a kind of hoarse bellow against the water's noise, he called, "Why do we need to get so wet? If we follow the path of it, on land—"

"—you will end up nowhere, at a cliff's face you cannot climb. I have come this way; I know. Follow me." She waded forward, while the torrent broke white about her body. That was startling, down here; Issel glanced up and saw a narrow cut of sky all bleached with Shine. That must be what the waters were reflecting.

They were all finding ways to force their voices through the torrent of sound; Rhoan's was a muted shriek, an octave higher than her usual dry tones. "I don't think we can do that, Ailse. We're not strong like you. It'll have us off our feet."

Issel blessed her privately, silently, for finding a way to refuse on his behalf; but Ailse said, "There is no other way into the city," and then Baris said, "We will help," as he plunged into the water to join her. At least, that was what he meant to say, or Issel thought so.

Rhoan turned her head to find Issel. He was seeing better now; he could read the helplessness in her.

He said, "I can help you too."

"Issel, no! How can you . . . ?"

"It's water," he said. "I'm good with water. And it doesn't have to hurt me; you keep saying that."

He closed his mouth on the lie, and took a breath, and jumped.

––––––––

FOR a moment, he was only astonished at himself.

Then he was engulfed, enraptured, awash, aflame; he thought he was a flame, a flame on water, with boy to burn.

Then he was utterly under the water, and couldn't scream when he wanted to. He thought he'd misunderstood how deep it was; he thought chest-high on the dogtooths meant drowning for him, an unexpectedly simple way to die in water. There were reasons why he'd never learned to swim.

It was only the force of it, though, that had sucked him off his feet. A great clawed hand closed on his neck and dragged him up to a frantic draw of air, deep into his lungs, as though breathing would be any help at all against the fury that had all his body in its possession now. He breathed mostly water in any case, the air was full of it, splash and spray; it was like breathing oil that burned as it went, so that he was scorched all through.

"You are not strong," Baris grunted in his ear. "How can you help?"

Ah now, there was a question. He could die, he supposed, and help them that way, not to be a nuisance anymore. But it wasn't a killing pain, not truly, that had seized him now; it was vicious and unrelenting, eternal, but never fatal. He should know.

He set his feet on the chill stone bed, leaning into Baris' strength to do so; water lapped at his shoulders but came no higher. He set his jaw as cold fires lanced up and down his body, through his bones. To Baris he gasped, "You should let go now."

The dogtooth's hand never moved from the nape of his neck. Fair enough. Issel reached out into this dreadful force of water: slowly, carefully, the most delicate lacy thought. A thought like a net that could hold nothing, that water mocked as it coursed through; and yet, and yet it could take something of that water's strength, draw out the force of it. And turn it around, use that force against itself, so that suddenly Issel could stand on his own feet and could step forward—out of the dogtooth's grip, but that was incidental—and walk against the current, though it roared and fumed around him every step.

He held his hands up, out of the water; he reached towards Rhoan on the bank, and said, "Come on, I'm here now. I'll hold you."

She said, "It's, it's too dark down there . . ."

That was easy changed. A soft glow coursed from him, forward and back; it ran through the water, but it wasn't the water that glowed, or the light would have torn and run away behind him. The glow came from his own wet self and shone through the water.

He said, "Can you see now, where to jump?"

No answer, only the splash of a body; but that wasn't Rhoan, it was Gilder.

Issel heard his yelp, and thought that was simply at the force of the stream. Gilder was a small man, not obviously strong; he needed Ailse's hand to hold him upright. If his skin was tingling, he'd probably barely notice.

Ailse had him, and that was good enough. Issel's concern was all with Rhoan.

Who stood on the water's edge above him, and cried, "Oh, hell," and leaped.

INTO his arms, as it happened. Whether that was her intent—or his—he wasn't sure. It happened, that was all. She leaped, he grabbed, she was there: wet and warm and gasping, gasping twice. Once at the water's sheer brutality, flesh and bone and hammer, hammer; once again at the rising sting of it, through clothes and skin and deep inside, flesh and bone and a whipcrack edge. Whether she felt his pain or simply her own, he couldn't say. She struggled, though, until she felt herself secure; and that was another shock to her, to realise how strong he was in here.

He smiled into her wide and doubtful eyes, and said—as privately as he could manage, more lips than voice—"It's not in the water, it's in me. You taught me that."

"So why's it hurting you so bad? You only ever pretended to learn it, anyway. You're a dreadful liar, I could read you every time . . ."

And then she pushed herself away from him and clung to Baris instead, worked herself around to the other side of the dogtooth, either to escape the lash of Issel's pain or just to be independent, free of his touch, she didn't say.

STANDING was one thing; walking was something else. Standing, he felt himself rooted, fixed, mind and matter and magic all three complicit; he chose to stand, and the magic wove itself through his body and the water and the rough pebbly bed that he stood on, to make it so. When he chose to move—well, he was like a tree rooted against a wall of water, a solidity; how could he move through that?

Thinking it was impossible. Doing it only demanded the impossible, and that was what magic was for. With his eyes closed against the distractions of cool light and furious water, he leaned into that elemental force, mind and body; he felt it, cradled it, possessed it; at last it seemed as though he allowed it to open, to yield, just ahead of him. And so there was a breath of space, and he could take a step into it; and then another as it ran ahead like silk that parts a moment before the blade that means to cut it; and so on, and on again.

He walked alone, as he always had. He had friends before and behind, or he hoped that they were friends, although he wasn't sure. He used to think that of Armina; but she had done what she had done, and he was here. He was here, and so were Rhoan and Gilder. So were the dogtooths, one fetched and one found. Tulk was dead, and always would be.

Another step. Another.

THE light moved with him, and so did that sense of rootedness, of being firm and fixed and absolute. Sometimes, where the gully twisted snakelike in its path, the water shattered against a stony wall and broke over his head, so that he was utterly inside the wave of it. It didn't seem to matter. The water, and the pain of it: he thought they were the same thing, echoes of each other. The water engulfed him and washed across his skin outside; the pain consumed him from the bone out and washed up against his skin inside.

Sometimes he lost all sense of his skin altogether, and his pain reached out to contain all the world. It was all of it his, from the rain in the sky to the river below; all of it was hurting.

And so another step, another.

SOON it was clear why they had to walk in the water. The gully grew narrower, and the walls more sheer; there was nowhere else to walk.

Issel felt drained and filled and drained again. What kept him going was the same that wore him away. All the world was water; all the world was pain, replenishment, ongoing.

They came to where the gully closed in on itself entirely, and was gone. Up at head-height in that slam of rock was the outfall, the source of all this water. Once, perhaps, it had been a natural cleft, a run for all the rain that soaked into the hills above and must go somewhere. The hands of men had made it something more, a round of darkness like a hollow promise, a mouth that bellowed water.

"I can't climb into that." Gilder didn't sound craven, only matter-of-fact. He spoke for Rhoan too, no question; perhaps he thought he spoke for Issel also.

"I can," Ailse said; and then, "I think I can." They ought to welcome honesty, but all they heard was doubt.

Baris grunted something. It might have been certainty, *I can climb this*, or it might not. Who could tell?

Issel said, "With my help, and the dogtooths', we can all climb this. See me . . ."

He walked through the downfall, and thought it parted just a hair's breadth above his head, so as not to batter him entirely to pulp. He was battered enough, in all conscience, but he survived. And came through to the other side, the wall of rock behind; set his back against it and fixed himself there, drew on all that water to make himself secure.

Here was his knee jutting forward, here were his hands held out: they made steps that a determined man, a determined girl could climb.

Rhoan's voice came at him, through the roar of water: "Issel, you can't hold our weight!"

"Yes, I can. The dogtooths too." Perhaps he should use their names, but he was too racked to be diplomatic. *It isn't in me, Rhoan, it's in the water,* except that he was too racked to be witty either.

"We still can't climb against that force." Gilder, being practical rather than concerned.

"Yes, you can." *If it's me you're climbing,* but he couldn't explain. "Come, see . . ."

He waited, and Rhoan surprised him, first through the downpour. Surprised him, delighted him: there was a spark in her that he hadn't seen in too long. Perhaps this overwhelming water did more than scorch her skin; perhaps it seared off waste emotions, all that dreary dead depressive weight of misery she'd carried.

"One foot on my knee," was all he said, "the other in the cradle of my hands, and—"

"Yes," she said, "I see. How much light can you give me?"

"As much as you need, out here. In there, you can make your own."

"This water's not been perfected, Issel . . ."

"It doesn't matter. You don't need that, not to make it shine. Try the walls, where they'll be wet."

Himself, he reached out through the water that was touching him; all up that pillar of flood, a slow light climbed against the flow. He thought he could probably send it further, into the tunnel that he couldn't see; wherever water ran down through darkness, he could push that light upstream. Better not, though. Far better to leave Rhoan something to do besides holding on.

Sometimes he seemed to think more clearly, more purely, when he was seized like this. Perhaps clean water scorched away the muddiness of Shine thinking? Perhaps even the dogtooths would be brighter, wet as they were . . .

She set a foot on his knee and her hands on his shoulders; there was no give in him, no hint of strain as all her weight came up. Her other foot was in his hands now, skin on skin; he could feel the buzz of what the water did to her, and then what his own touch did. He could feel how she drew from his endless strength, how that flowed from the water and through him and into her.

He could feel the flood's impact on her, head and chest; and how she defied it, how she reached into that worked mouth of rock and felt for handholds, found them, held on hard.

Then she stepped up, and was gone. He wasn't sure what would go with her, except what she had herself. Perhaps that would be enough.

He waited, anxious, breathless—though he hadn't seemed to breathe for a while now, and it hadn't seemed to harm. Rhoan didn't come spewing out again, a body broken; after a minute, he thought he could see a faint glow in the spouting water, mingling with his own.

Then Gilder came through the downfall, more bluster than strength, and Issel had another to help.

———————

THE dogtooths didn't need him. Once they'd seen their weaker companions scrambling up and in and not thrown out again, they made their own way into that gushing mouth, grabbing the lip of it and hauling themselves up, all muscle and no grace, no need of magic or finesse.

Ailse went first and Baris after, and that left him. He peeled himself away from the rock wall, stood in the monumental torrent, lifted his face to its source. Tel Ferin had taught him how to shape water into solid things, a sheet or a brick or a tile—but that had been still water, purified or otherwise apt to his hand. This was wild, tumultuous, not even Sundain; could he stiffen this outflow, make a stair of it, walk dryshod up into the cavern-mouth?

Probably not. He felt overfull of power, immense with potential, but not so vast as that. Besides, there wasn't the need. Baris loomed in the opening, crouched to one side of the stream and reached down a long, long arm.

Issel used just a little of his water-strength; he leaped like a fish from the water to grip that arm, coarse hair and hide beneath his palm, a whole history to come. Baris hauled him up without noticeable effort.

Lifted him and held him, secure in the flood, until Issel's feet found steps carved into the rock just where the water was most shallow, where the floor rose up to become the wall. Perhaps they had not been underwater at all when slaves hewed out this monstrous waterway. Perhaps not even when Ailse came this way, fleeing the city.

He took a little more from the water, enough to make a light, to help Rhoan's thin glow, so that he could see clearly where she and Gilder stood, holding to Ailse's strength in the turbulent stream; enough to let him shrug off Baris' arm, climb these steps and keep on going.

Sometime he would be able to stop; sometime he would have to. One would come before the other. Only the order was uncertain.

The others seemed to have stopped already. Daunted by the darkness up ahead, which Rhoan's faint light had only emphasised; or else waiting for him, waiting to be led; or else waiting for him more simply, him alone, for his own sake. He hoped for that but took the lead anyway, if only because it let him trudge past the others and so give Rhoan a smile as he passed.

There was certainly a lot of darkness down here. On his own, he might have been daunted. In truth, perhaps he was daunted. He simply wasn't going to let it show. He was Issel the cozener; how hard could this be, to set his slim shoulders square to the flood and wade forward, scattering light as he went, sowing confidence?

The grip of water was a toothache in every bone, keening like a wire. The force of it was something more, an unending hammer-blow. The darkness was worse yet, a great swallowing; they passed like a morsel down the throat of the land, and the water would have spewed them out, but the dark enfolded them. Their little lights were nothing, the scratch of a knife blade on a deep, deep lake, where the water would yield before it and close in behind it and show not a trace of its touch.

This was the dark's country, its true possession. They had come sneaking in like thieves, but there was nothing to steal except darkness, and they had no use for that nor any way to carry it off. Instead they did their best to break it, with their petty glimmers. The dark was unheeding, too grand to be contemptuous, not stooping to notice; it swallowed them whole, lights and voices and all.

ROCK and water. The rock had split and so the water had found its way, or else the water had done the work itself, splitting the rock as a root will, given time enough. Either way, men's hands had enhanced what the world had made before them. Not everywhere: there were places where the slaves had found no work to do, where the slope of the rock and the hurry of the water both vanished, where the walls pulled aside to leave open pools that seemed quiet and restful. His legs still felt the tug of hidden currents, secret streams beneath streams, the waters as layered as the rocks that held them here. Slow or sudden, his skin burned just the same; he thought his bones might be glowing by now, if there were any way to see so deep. Perhaps they would glow right through his flesh, like the fiery skeleton of Daries that exhausted Sundain parents threatened their children with.

There were branches, tunnels, natural fissures left and right, and all of them gouting water. He might easily have lost his way, if he had had one. With no map in his head and no sense of the city above, he was lost in any case; he kept to the main channel, and Ailse didn't call out to correct him. Besides, the men who built and maintained these deep ways must have had the same anxieties; there were marks cut into the walls at every junction, every point of doubt. Issel could not read, but he could understand an arrow where it pointed.

FURTHER up, further in: perhaps he would have to go on like this forever, drawing strength from the water to use against the water, and doing it alone when his companions failed him. He could believe in myths, in legendary dooms, in gods and hells and eternity down here, when there had never been time or space for it above. He kept his eyes fixed forward, watching light in water, watching for arrows on the walls, watching his way; every now and then he would call out just for the reassurance of a voice coming back to him, to say that he wasn't alone yet. It was always Rhoan he called to, though he never used her name; it was always Rhoan who replied.

Magic sustained him, but magic was exhausting in itself. As soon as he let it slip, he would be finished. He thought his companions were near enough finished already. Even the dogtooths were breathing in snoring rasps behind him. *They pant like dogs*, he thought, but there was no malice in it, and only a shadow of his former fear. A foreshadow, perhaps it was; he could still be afraid of what was to come, without being actually afraid of them.

The walls were brick-lined here, and there were colours in the glazes on the bricks, even here where no one would ever choose to come. He thought that was typical of the Marasi; it was said in Sund that they wrapped their shit in silk.

The steps beneath his feet were shallow now; the flood was broader, only calf-deep, and the ceiling was rising higher than his light reached.

He had the sense of walking into dread, into something greater than the heart of his enemy. He could feel it, like a great deep note sounding in his bones. He might have waited for his companions, but he couldn't break the focus that he had, step after step after step.

And so to the top of that last rise, and he stood in water on the edge of something vast and terrible, and he didn't understand it. His little light showed him nothing, only how close the darkness was. So he reached out and poured everything he had into the water at his feet, and on beyond that into the water he couldn't see, all the water that there was before him. He demanded light, to show him what this was.

He knew it would have to reach a distance, he could sense that even in the dark. He could smell it in the stillness, hear it in the echoing silence, in the wind's whisper where it ruffled cold against his skin, breathe it almost in how damp and heavy the air was . . .

He still didn't know how far it had to go, that light he made, until he saw it. Nor did he know what he was drawing on to make it.

He made a lightning, and it ripped the night apart.

He had found a lake, and all that water poured its strength through him; and he screamed, and lost sight and strength and everything before he even saw that lightning strike the further shore.

Chapter Three

O longer the prince abed, Salem still did not play the eunuch very well. His body might be on the mend, but his head and heart were not. Jendre would sooner have had him raging and threatening to run; she would almost sooner have had him back in bed and feverish. Instead she had him silent, sullen, heedless and morose. Sunk into himself, he gave scant notice to her or to anyone; he was a lean and pale shadow in her day, the embodiment of loss.

He could have practised at least a resentful obedience, but he did not. In particular, he would not kneel to anyone. He was an upright shadow, a ghost who stalked or stood in corners, no matter who came. She pleaded with him, and had nothing but a curt refusal: "I am my father's son, whatever else I have become. I knelt to the Sultan your husband, our loss; he was the Man of Men. I would not kneel to his brother, who had"—*this*, a gesture for which there were clearly no words sufficient—"done to me; I will certainly not kneel to anyone less. My lady." *Even to you*, that meant, *even for your sake.*

She spoke about it to Teo, who was meant to be teaching him his manners: "My lady, he will not. I wish you would give me a stick, to beat him with."

"Teo, don't even joke—"

"I am not joking. If he will not show respect to our seniors or their ladies, it will mean trouble. If I can't show him sense, maybe I can beat him into it. As you beat me, when I was new."

"Oh, I didn't, much," though she had a little, sometimes, if only to save him from the sterner discipline of his elders. In truth, there was something in Salem now that reminded her of Teo then—*boys*, she thought it was in essence, *stubborn, stupid boys*—but, "You were a child, and he is a man grown. And older than you, Teo, stronger. Try not to anger him."

A shrug came back at that. "He will not anger, lady. He has no, no passion left, I think. All he does is sulk and say no."

Perhaps he did need beating, just to make him see reason, just to keep him safe. But she couldn't do it, and for sure neither could Teo. "Let him be, sweet, if he will not listen. I will find some other way."

She did have another way, at least to make him listen. She could go to him in the dark, when they both found it easier: when neither one of them could see the other's face, when she was not dressed as his mistress nor he as her slave, when he was rolled safe in his blanket and the dark was like another blanket between them. They could talk, then, almost as they used to. Not so close, not touching, no more letting skin and sweat and muscle-talk speak for them, but still they could scent each other's bodies and listen to their breathing and try to rediscover the people that they were before, the bright and secret lovers. And fall short, of course, but not too far; and pretend, of course, but not too much.

In some ways, they were better people now. Not so proud, not so foolish, in no danger of overreaching. In daylight they saw the world as it was, at last, too late: bleak and bitter as it was, they saw it clearly.

Which was why she preferred to come to him in darkness, to avoid that threatening clarity. His voice had always been soft and husky, blurred at the edges; her memories of him were much the same, bar one harsh daylight scene, all swords and screams and the sharp intensity of fear. The rest were swathed in smoke or silk or shadow, and better so. Like this: sitting on his pallet in the alcove that was his now, fit space for a eunuch slave; smelling the musky odours that were irrevocably his, that had always underlain whatever immediate perfume or oil or sweat might have slicked his skin and hair; hearing the intimacies that neither of them uttered, the tenderness they only dared unleash where no one at all and least of all themselves could ever see it.

Once she had lain down beside him here, stretched out with only that blanket between them, whispered until she dozed. And roused, as close as she could come now to waking in his arms; and that had been dreadful, a cruelty inflicted on them both, that slow arousal through smell and touch and yearning. They had not done that again. Now she sat awkwardly on the edge of his pallet, hugging her knees and in no danger of dozing.

Still, at night they could be together and hurt only in a slow and sorrowful way, a bearable melancholy. By day it was harder, in the hard light of the sun, when she must look at him and see him watching her, and they could almost fight over who had lost the most.

By day, she took a lot of walks: alone or with Mirjana, or with Teo. Never both, because one must stay with Salem; never, ever with Salem. She didn't want him, couldn't bear him, wouldn't trust him.

She liked best to go alone, a privilege regained: a matter of illicit custom in her father's house, impossible in the Sultan's. Here, nobody cared. Or nobody who mattered, at least, because here there was nobody who mattered. She would greet other ladies on the paths, with their little knots of women or eunuchs in attendance, and hear their hissing disapproval and not worry in the slightest, pay them not the slightest heed. There was nothing they could do to her now, no harm in the world. She had all her harm already. She lived with it and in sight of it, her gelded man in the pavilion by the lake and her dreamlost sister in the pavilion up the hill, and she could help neither of them. That was her punishment, to be helpless in the face of their utter need; nothing else could touch her because that was absolute, it engulfed her, it was her sorrow and her shame.

Some days—as today—she would set out alone and find herself in company. Not of her seeking, but none the less not unwelcome. There was only ever the one companion who would thrust himself upon her uninvited.

"Master Djago."

"My lady Jendre."

"Your mistress is asleep, I take it?" He seldom left her side else.

"Asleep, or dreaming; it comes hard to tell."

Jendre didn't want to talk about that. It struck too near one of her own griefs. She said, "Well, then—shall we walk a little way?"

In his company, that usually did mean a little way. He would struggle gamely to stay with her, however far she went; but he was older than he pretended and extravagantly short of limb, and she knew too well that walking hurt him. Either he had the bone disease, or else his hips were simply malformed. Sometimes he would grunt at every step.

Even so, he wasn't to distract her from the purpose of these walks. She led around the lake and down, towards the wall where it overlooked the city.

"Lady, I think you will have explored every corner of these grounds, before you are satisfied."

"I hope I will," she said. "How could I be satisfied with anything less? If I must live here all my life"—which the law said she must—"then let me at least know the ground I live on."

He grunted at that, and she thought it had nothing to do with any vagrant pain in his joints. She thought he believed her not at all, and quite right too.

Left to herself, she would have plunged off the path and gone wandering over grass and into thickets, under trees and down rocky defiles. With Djago in tow, that wasn't possible. He couldn't keep up over rough ground, but more than that, he would wonder and ask questions and not be put off by her evasions. He saw too clearly; probably he would not need to ask the questions, even. Though he would still do it, if only to add her answers to his collection of lies that she had told him.

"So glad the rain has stopped at last," she said. "Really, I was beginning to think those storms would never pass."

"This is Maras, and you were right; they never will. These walls give us some degree of shelter, it's true—but if you could reach a little way beyond them, you would feel as I do, that the storm is building once again."

That wasn't fair. She was trying to be so neutral, so insignificant, and he was cheating; he wasn't talking about the rain at all. And she lacked his privileged access to the world beyond the wall, which made it doubly unfair because she barely knew what he meant, only what Teo had let slip about tension and unrest on the streets. If there was a conspiracy here, it was a most unequal one; she pretended not to know that he took her boy out in the city, and he pretended not to know that she knew, and so they could never speak directly of what he found out there. If she lost his confidence, then Teo's might go with it, and her world was already too starkly reduced. She didn't have so many friends that she could afford to lose one. Not even one. Two at once would be a calamity.

She'd play his game, but she had no counters; well, none except Teo, and him she thought she had spent already. That left her a beggar, rather than a player. She said, "Will you warn me, sir, before it breaks? I would wish to see my people safe."

Djago said, "What I know, lady, you will know. It may not be enough."

"No." That was unexpectedly generous of him; she supposed he had what he wanted already, so he could afford his generosity.

The path brought them to a shallow stream. There was a bridge to cross it by, but a second path ran down beside the stream, and Jendre turned to follow that without a thought at all. It was little used, beset with weeds and overhung with shrubs, a way she'd never been before, a way she had not seen; these were the ways that she was searching for.

Djago knew. He stumped along behind her, where he could not walk beside; he asked none of his awkward, teasing questions; he didn't complain even when they met a place where a tree's roots had broken up the bank entirely and the water had carried it away.

Alone, she would have got muddy and wet in some bird-brained scramble over those unreliable roots. Not being alone, she ought in decency to have let this be a check to the day's adventure; she should have turned back for Djago's sake, if not her gown's.

Instead she let him do the gallant thing, squirrelling into the shrubbery till he found a way around that tree and so back to the path again. He did his best to clear a route for her; she still had leaves in her hair and scratches on her skin before they were through. And, alas, mud on the gown. Mirjana would scold.

No matter. It was worth a little scolding, to know that the stream never reached the wall. Instead it dived suddenly and unexpectedly into a culvert, long before the wall was even visible through the trees, far too soon to be ducking underneath it.

An arch of stone built into a green bank, a brick-lined tunnel that gurgled with a constant swallowing sound as the stream flowed through iron bars and on into the dark.

The arch was not her height, though the dwarf would have no need to duck his head. If she stood in the stream, the peak of it might be at her breast. She'd need to bend double, or else to crawl: uncomfortable either way, almost impossibly awkward to carry anything heavy with her, and who could say how far the tunnel went, or how steeply down, or how much more constricted it might become . . . ?

Besides, there were those iron bars—or no, now she looked more closely it was a gate, a gate of bars like a cage or a prison cell, with its lock and hinges set into the stonework and likely rusted solid beneath their mantle of moss and weed.

She said, "Where do you suppose that leads, Master Djago?"

"To perdition, lady—which is why fortunates like you and me are safely locked away from it."

"Indeed, we should be grateful to be so well protected." She could match him back and forth, but she wanted better than irony and prevarication. "No doubt there are sewers beneath our feet that desperate men could use to break in and wreak havoc, seize our wealth and our persons, if it weren't for cold iron and good guard. But where do you think the water goes?"

"Out of our reach." And then, relenting at her scowl, he went on, "My lady Jendre, do you know so little of how your city works?"

For a moment, she considered pushing him into the stream. Then she gave him a reluctant smile, and, "Oh, Djago, I used to think I knew every little alley, every gutter, every door and window and roof-garden. Especially the roofs. But I was a child, and always looking up into the light. I never stopped to question what went on below the surface." Not in any sense. No doubt half her wild friends had spent their nights in cellars, caves, tunnels, even culverts, for lack of any better roof; they had not taken her to see, nor had she ever asked. Theirs was a friendship of the air, wind-blown and rootless, as pleasant and as trivial and as passing as a shower of rain.

She knew more now, looked deeper and asked questions of the dark. "Say I know nothing, Djago, and tell me what you can."

"This rock"—and he stamped on it, where he was standing on a little outcrop of raw stone—"is a honeycomb. There were always caves; likely that's how the city was made, a community settled in the caves and built a harbour. Houses came later, then walls, and more people, and so on. But the caves remained, though no one lived in them; and there was always water, and the channels that the water used to run down from the hilltops to the river. Some of those were above ground, streams and riverlings; some were not.

"Some say it was the great Sultan, Abeyet the first of his line, who made the watercourses. They might as well say it was God who did it; you Marasi are always confusing the two. One sure thing, it was not one man who did the work, nor was the work done in one lifetime. Perhaps Abeyet the Great saw what was needed and so began it; perhaps it happened later. Who can tell?" For such a small man, he had a very expressive shrug.

"Someone saw the need, if the city was to grow and be secure. So the work was done, slowly and painfully, over generations. Caves became cisterns and reservoirs; the hidden channels that the water took, those were dug out into sewers. Men died in the doing of it. Men and boys: boys can wriggle where a grown man cannot. Others followed, to lay tiles and carve stone and make beautiful what had been only useful; that is Marasi, to decorate the functional," and he spun and bobbed, an ugly little man in fool's motley.

"All over the city," he said, "there are ways and ways, from above to go below. From these palaces, more ways than anywhere; they use and need more water than the common folk, for all their garden pleasures." Jendre supposed that he meant to include her and all the women among those pleasures. Those greedy pleasures, that used up so much water. She could hardly deny it, who had spent days sometimes in the bathhouse, days on end.

She remembered another harem, another garden. The day the news came of the Sultan's accident, the news that changed her future and her city's, all at once: that day she had been frightened by a boy in the trees, heaving himself out of mud and nowhere. He had been clearing out just such a sewer. That might connect eventually to this, there might be only one intricate network, for anyone brave enough—or scared enough, or desperate enough—to use it. Anyone who was free to save themselves, who did not need to worry about others . . .

"And are these ways, these drains all so carefully closed off with iron, to keep us safe?" she asked.

"Lady, they are," he said, and bowed, and she didn't believe him for a moment. What was certain, he had his own ways in and out of this place. Perhaps he could bribe or bully or inveigle his way past the guards and through the gates, but she was sure he would keep a private route that was not dependent on other men's culpability. What better, then, than an unused drain, a sewer with its gate-bars rusted to nothing, a low and narrow tunnel that was quite high and wide enough for a dwarf to pass through?

A dwarf or a boy, or the two together—she might try to draw the

answer out of Teo, given that Djago was not forthcoming. Draw it out or
drag it out, demand it.

For now she said, "Well then, I can sit here as unworried as I need to be.
Do you go back to your mistress, Djago; I know you are anxious when you
are long away."

"Lady, I cannot leave you . . ."

"Why not, when I am as safe as you say? Go on, shoo," and she made
gestures with her fingers, as she might to a teasing kitten, just to annoy him.

"Well then, let me say that I would not."

"I know you wouldn't, and thank you for that—but truly, Djago, leave
me be. We both have troubles in our lives, in our houses; you are anxious to
get back to yours, and I am anxious to avoid mine. Get you gone, and let
me hide awhile. I will sit here"—and she did, on the stream's stony bank,
kicking her shoes off and dabbling her feet in cold, clear water—"and stare
into a darkness I cannot reach, and no one but you will know quite where I
am. If that makes them anxious in their turn"—Teo and Mirjana, it might,
perhaps; not Salem, who was so sunk in his own miseries he had no time to
spare for other people's—"then they can simply learn to live with being
anxious. It is not my task to keep my slaves content."

That was a lie outright, of course, it was absolutely her task. If she could
only find a way to content Salem, she would be satisfied; but she thought it
was impossible—you couldn't sew a man's stones back into his pouch, and
nothing else would serve—and so she ran away from the relentless truth of
that and dreamed of running further, with him and all her people.

Because that was impossible too, it didn't hurt so badly to find this,
what she'd been searching for, and to find it blocked with iron bars, un-
shiftable. She could sit here and stare into that summoning dark and not despair, because even if there had been no bars, she could still not have gone
that way. Sidië could not, so neither could she. There was no point going
without her. Jendre's own freedom meant nothing, and Salem wanted nothing that was out there, any more than he wanted anything that was in here.

———

ODD the things she noticed, when she was trying so determinedly not to
think. The stream sounded altogether noisier inside the culvert, as though
the water flowed more swiftly—and yes, it did, she could see now, where it
fell over a lip and was lost in a mist of spray.

The tunnel wasn't so dark as she had thought; she could see into it quite clearly. Perhaps the water reflected some of the day's light inward? No, that would throw it up onto the roof, and what she was seeing was a light rising from below, beyond where the water fell. Perhaps there were rocks down there that glowed slightly, or else something in the water, a weed or a growth of slime? There were fireflies and glow-worms, she'd played with both and kept jars of them to fascinate Sidië; there might be luminescent plants. Or perhaps it was a slave at work in the sewers with a rushlight or a lamp, there must be some way of access . . .

That light was definitely growing brighter. She was sure, then, that it had a human source; and she was right, because a figure came slowly into sight, beyond the fall.

———————

AND hit her head on that low and sudden ceiling, because she'd been watching her feet in the water; and cursed, which was how Jendre knew that she was a girl.

That wasn't right at all, for a slave at work in the sewers. The Marasi didn't send their girls to do that kind of work. And she was wet to the skin, likely wet to the bone of her, but even so Jendre couldn't puzzle out her clothes at all. Clothes declare a person's place in the world; she thought she'd never seen dress so nondescript, so unrevealing.

And more than that, worse than that, the girl wasn't carrying a light. Rather, light glowed within her cupped hands like water, and dripped between her fingers like water, and dribbled down into the stream and was borne away. And then the girl lifted her eyes to see the grille and the daylight beyond, saw how she would need to crawl to reach it; and opened her fingers and let all her light spill out at once, and Jendre couldn't pretend that it was anything but sorcery.

Still, she didn't run. She didn't move at all; only sat where she was and waited till the girl came crawling awkwardly up to the bars, and looked out, and saw her.

Eye to eye, stillness to stillness, silence to silence: how long could that last?

Only as long as it took Jendre to gather her courage and make a move, stand up. And then not run away, but walk towards the girl.

It helped, a little, that the sorceress looked quite as scared as Jendre was, and quite as determined not to back away.

Jendre walked in the water, as the other girl had. Here where the stream dived into the culvert, the banks rose steeply and were even more overgrown. This was the only dignified way to meet, face-to-face. If that meant wet and chilled from the knees down, then so be it.

She couldn't quite decide if it was very stupid or very trusting, to wade into the same water as a sorceress. Probably both. No matter. The girl had come this far, and if Jendre was right in her private, terrifying guesses, it had been a bold and a perilous journey; she could go this little way to meet her. She had taken greater risks than this, when she'd had much more to lose.

Even so, she wasn't foolish. She stopped a long arm's reach before the iron grille. The girl was closer on the other side, but not close enough to snatch through the bars. If that made any difference, to a sorceress . . .

"Please," the girl said, "what is this place?"

Jendre thought it was more proper for the intruder to explain herself, but, "This is the garden of the old palace."

"What they call the Palace of Tears?"

"I have heard that, yes." Heard it, used it, feared it. When you were frightened, it was more important than ever to act bold. Her father had taught her that, and so had her life, often and often. She said, "Are you from Sund?"

A moment's hesitation, which Jendre found comforting, that even a sorceress could have doubts, and wonder what was wise to do. Then the girl said, "Yes, I am. Do I need to tell you, not to be afraid of me?"

"No." Telling wouldn't help, fear was just a fact; but the girl had reason enough to be afraid on her own account. The Marasi had never been gentle with magicians, except those they employed. If she was found, the girl's fate would be appalling. "What is a girl from Sund"—that was easier, to call her a girl: she was clearly much of an age with Jendre, even if she had all those mystical wicked gifts of her people—"doing in the sewers of the old palace?"

"Looking for a way out."

That was blunt, at least, and Jendre matched it. "I'm afraid these bars prevent you." Blunt, but untruthful; what she feared was the opposite.

"They do. They wouldn't stop Issel for a moment, but—"

But she obviously thought she'd said too much, and that was two confessions at once: one, that she was not so powerful a sorceress, if iron bars could block her; and two, that she had at least one companion who would not be blocked. If he were here, which he was not.

Something to be thankful for, something to fear. Jendre said: "Will you tell me your name?"

A moment's pause, a thought; then, "Rhoan. I'm called Rhoan. Who are you?"

"Jendre." It didn't occur to her to lie. "Truly, Rhoan—what is it that you want in Maras?" *Your life must be risk enough in Sund, with the soldiers always on the watch for magic; why would you spit in God's face, to come here?*

"Truly? My people's freedom, my city's joy."

"You will not find that here."

"Oh, but I thought I might."

One girl, a sorceress who couldn't make her way out of a sewer? Jendre smiled despite herself, and saw that smile reflected on the other side of the bars.

"You're forgetting," Rhoan said, "I've given myself away already; I'm not alone in here. There are, oh, a full handful of us. And you've told me more than you ought, as well."

"Have I?"

"Yes. You told me that I'd found what we've been looking for. Don't be frightened, we won't harm you, or your people. If these are your people, these Marasi. Perhaps it'll mean your freedom too."

"Do you take me for a slave here?" For a moment, she was genuinely indignant.

"Hiding in the bushes, easing your weary feet in the water . . . Crouching in the stream-bed, to whisper to an invading stranger . . . I didn't take you for a high-born lady of the town. Was I wrong?"

Well, no. Neither high-born nor a lady; but, "I was the Sultan's wife, and Maras-born. My father is a general," or was, under the old dispensation. Whether that had carried over to the new, who knew?

Rhoan's lips shaped a soundless whistle. "Ailse told us that the old man's women would be kept here—but I didn't think she meant girls. No wonder you're so unhappy."

"No, you don't understand. It's not for me . . ." Though it was of course the hopeless search for an escape that had brought her here, and perhaps Rhoan understood her better than she wanted to admit.

"You want to take someone with you. Or more than one. Why not? It'll be an open door."

Jendre shook her head. "Even if we could, there's nowhere to go . . ."

"Sweet, this is the other side of the cage; there's all the world out here. These are your bars, not mine. Go where you like. We'll help, if we can. If you help us."

"I don't know what you want."

"Just point us towards the dreamers, the magicians. The ones who make the bridge."

Jendre shivered. Was this hope returning to her life, this icy chill down the back of her neck, like a trickle of melt-water? She said, "I can do that, if you or one of you can break these bars. But it is not the magicians who dream, and it is not the dreamers who do wrong. You must not harm the children, you must promise me that or I will show you nothing but guards with swords who hate the Sundain and all their sorceries . . ."

WET and solitary and shaken, a whole new kind of scared, Jendre made her slow way back towards her house, wondering how in the world she was to break this news. She had discovered depths of treachery in herself that were hitherto unsuspected, despite a long, long history of betrayals. She had betrayed her sister first by wilful ignorance, deliberately never understanding until too late that it was Sidië who was to be the victim of the bridge. Surely that did have to be deliberate, in some wicked deepness of her soul; if not, then it had to be stupidity, she had to be as blindly self-obsessed as some of the girls she'd met on her father's rise, daughters of his fellow officers. She couldn't stomach that.

So no, say it was deliberate, her first great treason. Then she had betrayed her lord and husband, the Sultan, the Man of Men: in his own house, with one of his own court. And then again she had betrayed his ghost, by trying to flee this palace of mourning women, with that same young man again; and had failed, and had so betrayed Salem to his brutal punishment and this half-life since.

And now she wanted to betray her city entire to its enemies, betray the Sultanate itself, and for what? Her own private redemption, another escape, so that she and hers could all live in fear and hiding in some desperate far-flung corner of the empire. Or in Sund, perhaps, which she thought was probably worse. Two women, two eunuchs and a child sick of a dreaming fever, all of them runaways and hunted: what kind of a life could they make for themselves, anywhere in the known world?

And yet she would do this thing, she had said so. She would meet Rhoan and her sorcerous companions tonight, and show them the pavilion where the dreamers lay, watched over by their masters the magicians. She had warned Rhoan about the insidious smoke-spell that had stolen her wits and Salem's too when they broke in to rescue Sidië the last time, but Sundain-magic must be stronger, surely. What were smoke and dreams against the power, the pervasion, the sheer impact of water?

They were victory, for Maras over Sund—but that was a voice she wouldn't listen to. That had been the genius of her Man of Men, his mas-terstroke against a city unprepared; this was the reverse, Sund striking back all unlooked-for in their turn. One swift and simple blow to destroy the magicians, spill their smoke, wake the dreamers and see the bridge fail . . .

And so undo at a stroke her husband's greatest conquest, his legacy to the empire. She was shocked at herself every time she considered the impli-cations; but every time she excused herself, she convinced herself again. Nothing good had ever come of that cursed bridge, so let it go. What was Sund to her? What did she care for an empire whose laws had condemned her to this death-in-life, whose new Sultan had condemned her light-hearted beloved to a grim and cruel servitude, as her own castrated slave . . . ?

Her thoughts tumbled over each other as her feet did, stumbling awk-wardly under her heavy wet skirts. Every step took her closer to the pavil-ion, to her people, to the explanations that she must make. She dreaded that. She was resolute, but she was entirely doubtful; she despised herself, but she was entirely certain of her course.

No wonder if her feet faltered, no wonder if they strayed. She found her-self taking a path she'd never followed, that led her to overlook the main harem-house; and there was a flurry, an agitation that was utterly unusual.

Which was utterly unusual in itself, that anything new might have penetrated the endless gloomy twilight of this palace.

Its constant mood was shadowed and sorrowful and still, endlessly still. Suddenly, here was movement and more than movement, here was rush. All around the house eunuchs were dashing, stopping, turning to run the other way; women were clustered in knots, nervous or excited or downright fearful, Jendre couldn't tell from this distance.

She didn't want to go any closer. Whatever was happening, she didn't mean to be involved. She had her own fears, her own excitements, her own troubles to face. This could only be a distraction; besides, Teo would know all about it already. Or if not, she could send him off to Djago, who most certainly would know.

So she turned and headed straight for her own pavilion, no more straying now, and even so that wasn't fast enough. Teo found her halfway; like all the other eunuchs in the palace, it seemed, he was running hard.

Breathless and capless, his shaven head gleaming with sweat, he said, "Lady, there you are, I've been looking . . ."

"Yes, so I see. What is it?" Her first thought was Salem; but no, this was an agitation that had stirred the whole nest.

"The Sultan . . . the janizars . . ."

"Yes? What of them?" She fought down the impulse to shake him, to slap him, to screw sense out of him any way she could; he wiped his head with his sleeve and tried to speak more steadily.

"There is a rising, lady. There are swords in the streets, janizars everywhere, and people say the Sultan is dead."

If it was true, she thought that few would mourn him. Who knew him well enough to mourn? And rumour was unreliable but Teo's sources were not, so treat it as true. Her immediate concern was her own people, and then her own plans and others', how this news would affect this night . . .

"Come on back to the house, I want to keep you close—and tidy yourself up," she scolded. "You look like you've been shoving through half the shrubbery in the park."

"Lady, I have. Djago said where you were, but I couldn't find you there, so . . ."

So he'd gone charging around heedlessly all over—and he clearly resented her for making a liar of the dwarf. No matter. She tugged his dress back into some semblance of order, asked where his cap was, cuffed him lightly when he shrugged, then took his hand as they walked homeward. The news was important, but not urgent. Its only impact on them lay in its impact on the city, whether fear and confusion might make it easier or harder to flee. Would the gates be closed, or thrown wide open? Would the roads and the river be empty of traffic and so treacherous, or crowded with refugees and so a place to hide even as they ran . . . ?

BECAUSE she didn't hurry, and because Teo had stopped hurrying, therefore they were nearly overtaken by the day's doom. Nearly is not quite, but the thought could shake her afterwards, how close they came to sauntering back, to arriving too late, to finding the world irrevocably changed without them.

As it was, they were just coming up the steps to the pavilion door when the sound of rushing footsteps behind them became too insistent to ignore. With her feet securely on her own territory, Jendre turned to see—and was amazed, confounded, almost terrified.

She had been terrified before, by this same entourage and its focus: old and crabbed and deadly, the scorpion in the garden. Never in this garden, though—and that focus never looking as she did now, grim and urgent and afraid herself, buckling almost under the loss of what she'd held before, power and position and prestige.

Jendre might have knelt from sheer habit, or she might have curtseyed from simple decency, respect, if the old woman hadn't looked quite so desperate, if her circle of eunuchs hadn't been carrying illicit blades openly in unsteady, unconvincing fists.

Instead she stood her ground, before the door of her house; she said, "Madam," and no more, as a way to say *you are Valide Sultan no longer, not the Sultan's mother now.*

"Oh, out of my way, girl. I want that boy I gave you, the pasha's son . . ."

She hadn't lost her habit of command, then, only the authority that drove it. Jendre didn't move.

"Madam?"

It hadn't been the Valide Sultan in any sense. Her mad son had decreed Salem's fate, where she would simply have killed him. She would have killed them both, Salem and Jendre too. Jendre was inclined to yield nothing to her; certainly she would not yield Salem. There were those knives, but . . .

But Teo had a knife of his own, and was picking his nails conspicuously at her side. She didn't know whether to slap him or hug him, so of course did neither. She only stood in the doorway there, not moving. Men with knives had been at Salem before, and she had stood and watched and done nothing. Not this time. This time, her body was between him and them, and not stepping aside for anyone.

She heard movement at her back, and that was Mirjana, coming to stand at her other side, no knives obvious; and then there was movement again, and that was Salem. She knew him by his step and by his breathing, she knew him by his smell, she thought she would know him by the way he stirred the air. He stood behind her and said nothing, for now, but she wasn't sure she trusted him.

The old woman gestured. "Him. I want him."

She said, "My regrets, madam, but you may not have him. He is mine." *Mine to me, the gift of your own son—and how much do you regret it now, that court of condemnation where he made his rulings? You set that up, you thought that he would follow your wishes, then and later; and you were wrong, and see just how badly wrong you were . . .*

Indeed, she had killed her other son, the elder, Jendre's Man of Men, because she thought the younger would be more malleable to her will, and so better for herself and her line. Perhaps for the empire entire, perhaps she really had believed it; but she had been wrong and wrong again. Jendre had been widowed for nothing, Salem had been castrated for nothing, and nothing was the old woman's portion now: no empire, no sultan, no son.

No Salem, that for sure.

"You cannot deny me, girl. You dare not . . ."

"On the contrary, madam. I deny you; I defy you. You have no voice here. Go back to your own house and your own people."

"They cannot protect me. I need—"

Her hand said what her tongue lacked the patience for: a withered claw stabbing upward to point past Jendre's shoulder.

"You need what—a hostage?" Now she was beginning to understand. "The pasha's son, you said. Is it the pasha, then, leading this revolt?" As soon as she said the words, she knew it. Of course it was the pasha, taking revenge for what had been done to his son. An honourable execution after an undoubted, undeniable crime might have been a different matter, but this shame was insufferable. Salem found it so, all too obviously; of course the pasha would feel the same.

So the Sultan had died, and his mother the Valide Sultan had fled her home and come here, in search of a hostage against the fate that the pasha must surely intend for her too; and who stood between the old woman and her want?

Jendre did.

She said, "Luckily for me and mine, your needs need not concern us. Too many people have died already, to appease your vanity; you will not threaten us. Do you hear me, madam? You will *not!*"

She reached out a hand to snatch that so-conspicuous knife from Teo, and did not need to. He must have been waiting, for exactly that; the handle slapped firmly into her palm, and her fingers closed around it. He grinned, pleased with himself and with her.

The old woman stared, in a kind of horrified disbelief.

"Do you dare, do you *dare* to raise a weapon? Against me?"

The blade of the knife caught the light and seemed to transfix her. Well, better through the eyes than through the belly. Would Jendre really use it, against her?

Best not to doubt it for a moment. "Yes, of course," she said, as though surprised that there could be a question. "To defend what is mine, I would raise a weapon against the Sultan himself. You are not Sultan," *though you would like to be, though you have tried to be. If you had trusted my Man of Men and been content, even content to lose a little, how different would the world be now? For you, for me, for everyone?*

As it was—well, the old woman had lost everything and did not know it yet. Jendre knew. She at least was no stranger to loss; what little she had left, she meant to keep.

"You are insolent, girl."

"Yes." It meant nothing.

"People have died for less."

She was sure. She had seen, indeed, how quickly and easily people died around the old woman. Nevertheless, "Last year, last month, last week—yesterday, even, I am sure that was true. Today? You are not Valide Sultan, you are mother to no magnificence now. You are fleeing a man who wants to kill you, and the only way you thought to save your life was to steal one who has been harmed already. So: you are a coward and a thief, and no one is going to strangle me for saying so. If your servants kill me at all, it will be to come at my Salem, because they can't get by me any other way; but I don't think they'll try. Look at them: they face two girls and a boy with a single blade between us, and they are as frightened as you are." *Just not quite so desperate*, she thought, she hoped. There was true danger here, and sheer weight of numbers could overbear them all; but not, she thought, with only the old woman's will to drive it. Not anymore.

And then a long arm reached past her shoulder and a hand closed around her fingers, dry and lean, and she shivered at the touch of it, as she did at the touch of his voice so close to her ear, pitched so as to sound private and yet to carry just those few steps down to the old woman's ears also; and Salem said, "No, not two girls and a boy. One man is all they face. But he is a man with a blade in his hand"—and he was now, his fingers had unmanned her and taken her weapon as easily as she might have taken it from Teo—"and he chooses not to be your hostage, great madam. He finds that your life is not worth his own."

Jendre's heart surged. In that one sentence he laid waste to her greatest fear, and gifted her a hope to be treasured later. She let his free hand guide her, round behind his body; she even pulled her two slaves back to join her, so that one defended three. If it was a bluff, it would need that much supporting.

If he had recovered something of himself, Jendre thought the old woman had lost herself entirely. What was she, if not the Valide Sultan and mother of magnificence? It had only ever been her title that mattered, the position it described, her place within this world; Jendre certainly didn't know her name. She might have forgotten it herself.

She said, "Your life is mine, as it always was," and that was a thin lie, pitiful almost, if anyone could ever have pitied her. Jendre had seen it proved untrue, even while the old woman's son was alive: her second Sultan son, the fat mad one who had wiped his mouth with his handkerchief and defied his mother, spared Jendre and given Salem this cruel chance at life even while she had been ordering death for both.

The old woman looked around now at her servants, and was just wise enough not to order them forward, where they would all too clearly not go. What she might have done instead, that could only ever be speculation. She was interrupted, forestalled by a rush of feet, a sudden clamour of arms and men on the path and all around the pavilion.

Her servants stood gaping, as they and their mistress were surrounded by soldiers. So too did Jendre, but her bewildered slowness was not fatal: at least not to her.

There might have been an order given, for those agitated servants to throw their weapons down. There was so much babble, so many conflicting voices, Jendre didn't notice. She did see a few eunuchs drop their knives, in obedience perhaps, or in fear or wisdom. Those who live long within the harem acquire a sharp instinct for self-preservation.

Sharp: not sharp enough, for these today. Other minds were sharper, better focused, more intent. Or else some fool eunuch did the wrong thing, raised his blade instead of let it fall, and so was the trigger for all his companions' calamity. She couldn't tell, she didn't see; later, thinking about it, she suspected that the order for their calamity had been given already, before ever these men came running through the garden to deliver it.

At the time, she didn't think at all. She couldn't; she was too amazed to see men in the garden. Whole men, entire, uncut. Janizars, the utilitarian slave-soldiers of the empire—but these were the High Guard, the Sultan's own. They should have been giving their lives in his defence, and his mother's too. No great astonishment that they had not; the High Guard had risen in rebellion before; but still they should not be here. Men like these, they were the foundation of all governance, the state's guarantee. Sultans died, but the Sultanate abided—and even after his death, the Sultan's harem stood intact, unsullied, preserved like a body in vinegar. It was the law, it was certain. Without that certainty, nothing could be trusted to survive.

It was more than a few old eunuchs, she thought, that they were destroying here. Whether they knew it or not, whether their master meant it or otherwise.

Destruction started, though, with those eunuchs. Those who had capitulated, those who tried to resist, it made no difference. They died, with or without a blade in their hands. The High Guard was as pitiless, as thorough as a wave of tidal water. Its men had the long straight swords of the janizars, and knives were as useless as begging, as submitting, as trying to run.

Jendre saw it as a flurry, robes and steel and tumbling, almost a dance or a performance of acrobats, except that grace was only in the janizars. The eunuchs slumped and sprawled before them, noisy and awkward and incomplete.

And then there was a ring of bodies, a different quality of incompletion, flesh without life. Jendre thought that she should have been shocked; a nice girl would scream or feel faint or turn away, that much at least. But she was treacherous and treasonous, not nice at all. And it was hard to care for the deaths of strangers, even so many strangers, when the High Guard stood around that circle in bright costumes with bright blades glinting and streaked; when the old woman still stood at its heart, bent and weak where she used to be bent and strong, gaping where she used to glower; when the pasha came pushing through to face her, the most impossible among all these impossible men.

Even without moving, Salem faltered at the sight of his father. Jendre felt it in him and stepped forward on the moment, to stand on his left so as not to obstruct his knife-hand though he had no use for it now. Her slaves—her other slaves, technically—should probably kneel, or abase themselves altogether; but there were whole men in the garden and all the rules were broken, and they stayed on their feet and she made no sign to them to change that.

Not face-to-face, because she was so old and small and her spine was twisted while he stood tall despite his age, but eye to eye across that narrow space they confronted each other: soldier and queen, rebel and ruler, the new dispensation and the old.

They had so many issues between them that mattered so much, neither one of them could find a word to say. The woman had poisoned her own son, the man's sworn-brother, oldest friend and master; the man had strangled her other son, her necessary; she had meant to kill his oldest son, his heir, but had settled for his gelding. Between them, they had brought the empire to this edge of destruction. How could they speak to each other?

All the impetus now was with him. All he did, perhaps all he could do, was to make a little gesture, one that had once been hers. Perhaps he borrowed it from her, or stole it; perhaps he meant it as a sign to her, one last tiny, timely cruelty.

He reached up to touch, to tap his throat lightly with two fingers.

In her, it had been a signal to her eunuchs, except when it was advice to her son.

In him, it was an instruction to his soldiers.

A janizar stepped forward, and he had put his sword up already; he had something else between his fingers, something too fine to see, that linked his two hands together in a curious parallel. He might have been a mimer, acting chains.

The old woman shook her head, but she did it to the pasha. She would not turn to face the soldier. Even now she had her pride, unless it was stupidity or hopelessness or simple disbelief.

The janizar dropped a loop of bowstring over her disarray of iron hair, and drew it tight around her neck. So thin, so scrawny that chicken-neck was, with the wattles puckered up; Jendre could see the string only by the line it drew, fine and straight and sharp, so sharp she thought it ought to cut the skin like wire. But it was waxed and fit for this, and she could see no blood. Only the old woman's distress, her confusion, the way her hands wavered towards her throat and could not touch; the way her eyes bulged and her mouth worked, just a little; the way the janizar's hands moved, slowly, slowly tugging apart.

That must have been the order, to go slow. The pasha wanted the old woman to feel her death, perhaps to fear it, surely to suffer it.

She would have liked to stand, Jendre thought, until it was over; but she lost her legs first, and staggered, and would have fallen except that the string could hold her up. She hung, then, like a puppet with its head awry. And still was not dead, not even unconscious, writhing and sagging while her hands flapped uselessly and the soldier's arms strained to hold the awkward struggling weight of her but he was still not kind, not straining in the least to finish her.

The pasha stood and watched, and her death lay in his gift but he would not give it. Jendre would have ached for her, perhaps, if she had had any feelings to spare. Right now, this seemed almost incidental. She had feared and hated the old woman for a long time now, and her fate meant nothing. Even acted out before her, even so cruelly kept dangling, it was an empty and meaningless event. What mattered stood beside her and behind her, her precious people; it stretched ahead of her, an obscure future, doubt suddenly where all had been so clear before.

There were more men coming down the path with weapons, with determination. There were familiar faces among them: one of them was Hedin, the wazir's son, whom Salem knew and did not like. She supposed the same might be true of herself. She had cause to be grateful to him—for her life, perhaps, for both their lives, that hot mad day before she married, when they met a riot in the street—but gratitude was seldom a good seed for friendship.

Another among these new-come faces, that was her father.

She had never thought to see him again, but this day, this desperate day had changed everything. For a foolish moment, she thought he might have come to rescue the old woman, to be loyal to his lawful master. But the Sultan was dead, so he was masterless, a general without a lord to serve; of course he served his old friend and comrade, the pasha.

The janizars saluted and let him pass their circle-wall. The two men stood together and spoke in low voices, while the old woman still hung suspended within the endless moment of her death.

It was grotesque, it was awful, and it touched Jendre not at all. She was only waiting for this to be over and the next thing to begin, the decisions that would change her life and Salem's.

The old woman was waiting also, waiting to be dead. For her, for sure, it was an agonising wait; it was meant to be. For Jendre, it was only long.

At last, she hung motionless in the janizar's string, a broken toy, abandoned. For certainty's sake, then he did pull hard. He held her aloft, adangle for that extra minute, till there was no hope of life in her; then he let her drop, unwound his string, bowed to the pasha and stepped back.

The old man shrugged and turned away from her, perhaps.

From Jendre's point of view, he turned to his son, the next business of his day.

"Salem," he said, "you are with me."

Jendre snatched Salem's hand, where he stood beside her. He said nothing; it was she who spoke, who said, "Where must we go now?" Meaning *how can we leave, how will we be allowed to live, how will you remake the laws of life and body?*

The old man ignored her magnificently, magisterially; he only spoke to his ruined son, and said more or less the same again. "Salem, you will come with me."

And he did, her man, her love; he slipped his fingers free of hers and went to his father's summons. And when she tried to follow she was prevented, by the flat of a janizar's blade laid against her body like a rail, immovable, unrelenting. The shock of it left her silent, without a curse or a scream or a plead on her tongue. Cruelty was implacable, she knew that. And her father did nothing to help her, though that was no surprise; and so she stood in utter, brutal grief, in her people's hands, while the last of what she had loved was taken from her.

Chapter Four

THERE was, of course, more water in the river. It was the river of the world, and all the waters of the world passed along it. That was a given, it was understood.

But there could never, surely, ever have been more water contained within walls, roofed over like a god in a cathedral. Awe was too small, far too simple a word; any words must fall short. Issel had fallen silent, long since. There simply wasn't the language.

At first, there hadn't been the courage either. Standing, seeing, understanding where it was that he stood and what he saw, all that had been too much for him. A cavern as vast as this might contain a lake too vast to measure, more water than he could possibly imagine; his mind could not contain the cavern nor its lake nor what else it held, himself, the boy who stood there looking. The idea of it was terrible; the sight of it unmanned him.

He couldn't stand, he couldn't look. So he had done the other thing, he had curled up on a ledge at the lake's edge and closed his eyes, turned his back on this underworld of water and shivered his way into silence.

One of them had to go away, the water or himself. The water wasn't moving, except for a gentle lapping all too close to his skin; he went himself, or tried to. His skin was all wet already, and his blood was surging with the force of all that water he had waded through; there was nowhere to go but inward.

He had always been wary of depths and darkness. He'd choose surfaces every time, trying to live on the skin of things, on the roofs of his city, on the strand. There were people he had known, street-jugglers and other wise and careful souls—and Armina too, but he didn't want to think about her—who had advised him to look inside himself, to seek a quiet place where he could rest and never worry what his body did. He'd find peace there, they told him, and the balance of the mind.

But Issel had always preferred living in his skin, in the immediacies of dirt and hunger, pain and water and release. He didn't trust peace, he didn't believe in balance; and if that meant he couldn't learn to juggle, which apparently it did, no matter. He had other ways to work a living out of the sparse pickings of the street.

Ways that had brought him eventually here, to this great echoing hollow where the lake might go down and down and never end at all; and his skin was sodden and the water called to him, it crooned at him with a voice like whips, it stung him with promises of sweetness, sweet power, indomitability.

Deep into himself, then, was the only way to turn; and if he could find peace or balance, that would be another kind of gift and very welcome, but truly all he wanted was a dry thought in a dry season, a place to hide from all this water.

———

IT was his companions who let him down, who wouldn't let him go. He felt like a man who had turned his back on the oasis and walked to the desert's rim, had seen his way ahead but not yet taken it, who could still hear the babble of open waters at his back; a man who stood in the ravine where the river ran, who gazed upward to the dry plateau but had not yet begun to climb. Close to water but turned away, towards where the water couldn't reach. He wanted to take that path, he needed the distance that it promised—

———

—AND his friends denied it him, they turned him round and dragged him back.

Hands clutched at him, lifted him up, set him with his back to the rock wall and so inevitably his face to all that water.

Voices battered at him:

"Issel, are you sick?"

"Can you stand?"

"Open your eyes, Issel, look at me . . ."

That last was Rhoan, and imperative. He did open his eyes, and found that even without the lightning there was light enough to see by. His fault, apparently. None of the others was making a light; they didn't need to. He was glowing, and there seemed to be nothing he could do to stop it.

Is it in me, or is it in the water? It was the question that Rhoan had challenged him with, constantly—except that to her there never was a question, she knew where the power came from, where the magic lay. She'd spent days and weeks trying to batter the same certainty into Issel, with the helpful use of a ladle against his skull.

Here, at last, he was certain. He'd found an answer, just as she had. Only that they stood on opposite sides of an unbridgeable divide, for all that she was crouched directly in front of him and trying to block his view of the water.

His skin was glowing, yes, but that was inadvertent. And the rock he sat on, that was glowing too, shimmering with light; and the wall of rock he leaned against, and the air itself where it rolled off him and out across that liquid dark of water, it carried light some distance as it went.

His skin was sodden-wet, his clothes were wet, and the rock he sat on, the wall he leaned against, everything. Even the air he breathed, it was cool but as damp as a steam-bath; he thought if he could turn himself inside out, he'd find his lungs glowing too.

It was in the water, not in him. That was his absolute conviction, and perhaps it was as well he couldn't speak, because Rhoan would only hit him again if he said that.

He'd passed beyond pain in the tunnel, in that thunder of water; here in this temple, this cathedral-lake he passed beyond awe. He felt crushed by the weight of it, even as he was stretched to its invisible, impossible limits. No mortal body could contain or control or wield so much potential. Necessarily, then, the power wasn't in him; he'd only ever been a vessel, imperfectly made and badly used, distorted under the Shine and dangerous to trust.

He had a purpose, though, and that was good. He tried to stand, and felt

Rhoan's hands grip his arm to help him up; and then heard her gasp, gasp twice.

And looked, and saw how she shone with light, how it had run like fire from his skin to hers, and so all over her. The others were glowing too, all of them a little, where they stood on the rock that glowed because he sat on it; but they were dim candles against a blaze. And Rhoan was biting her lip, flinching inside her skin, nearly breaking contact, then not quite.

She said, "It hurts . . ."

"Yes," though he still didn't think that was the word. There was a lethal liquid sharpness and an icy heat, as if his blood were glass, molten and shattered both at once. The sensation filled him, suffused him, overflowed him, as if he lay on a bed of knives and breathed a bitter flame in and out—but he couldn't call any of it pain, not now.

Rhoan still did, and there was no reason for her to suffer. He took his arm away, before she was ready to let it go, and watched that light run off her.

Where they stood was a narrow platform raised just a little above the level of the water: a walkway half-built, half-cut into the living rock. This must have been a natural cavern first, and perhaps it had taken a thousand generations of steady dripping water to fill it, before it began to overflow through channels that it found or made itself. But then the Marasi must have found it and remade it. A walled city needed an unbounded source of water to be secure, to feel safe; no wonder Maras was so proud, so arrogant in its dealings with the world. This was water enough to give confidence to an empire, as it had.

"Ailse," he asked, "how many ways are there, in and out of this?" Their own, the one they had come up must be one of the lowest and last, perhaps the final drainaway; by the way the air moved, chilly on his wet skin, he suspected many more.

"Scores, hundreds. I have never heard a count. There are many cisterns, all channelled into each other, and then pools and wells and waterways. So many ways to the surface, into the city, there might be more than anyone can number."

"Too many to watch, then," Gilder said.

"Yes."

Easier to watch the exits, catch runaways down below. And pen them nightly in the Shine, put them to work by day, make a monstrous use of them.

Issel said, "We will need to go up, to the higher cisterns," because all the world knew that the bridge was dreamed on a hill above the river, in a palace garden. He didn't understand that at all, but he understood his own strength, the damage he could do. He reckoned that he could wake any dreamer, and so destroy the bridge. After that, his city must fight for its own freedom; but after that, he was sure, his city would.

What happened to himself or to those he loved, after that, he didn't want to consider.

Before that, though, they had to find their way.

Ailse said, "The upways are the other side of this water. We could walk around, I did that coming; but I found a boat on this bank, and we could paddle over."

Issel was torn between dread and dread: circumnavigating this impossible lake on foot, or else taking the cockleshell route across the middle, bare planks of wood to shelter him from all its hidden depths. Both choices were appalling. He said nothing; his friends, even Rhoan, all voted for the boat. He'd known they would.

———————

IT wasn't like the boat across the river, although Baris did the paddling, although it seemed to take as long, although they made the journey through the dark and the only light they had was eldritch and unnatural.

This time there was black overhead, and black beneath. They moved as it were in a bubble of light, a glow they carried with them.

The others were grateful for it. He thought it hateful, dangerous, infective. He would sooner have been defeated by the dark. There was nothing he could do; touch a flame to an oil-soaked rag and it will burn. Put him in here, and there would be light.

Even so, the dark was master. Unless he played with lightnings, it engulfed them utterly. Once the walkway had vanished into shadow at their backs, they were adrift on unchartable waters, with no glimpse of anything still or solid to steer by: no stars, no landmarks, only the wall of darkness all around and above them, the unchanging lake below. They might have been endlessly paddling the same stretch of water, for all they had to tell them otherwise.

Issel had always steered by his native sense of water. "North" and "south" were only labels, against the immutable truths of wet and dry: where the river was, where the marsh, the individual wells and cisterns and the dry roads between. Down here, he was hopelessly adrift. He could feel water even overhead, water in the rock above like a great storm cloud building. Every direction looked the same and felt the same, equally true and equally wrong.

His companions were as disoriented as he was. They might use other skills to find their way, but nothing worked in this vast darkness; any sense of the world was oil-slick and impossible to grasp. They needed light, and not even Rhoan could persuade him to use the lightnings again, to burn them a flare-path to the further shore. Even in his head, he flinched away from that.

In the end they paddled back to the edge of the lake, where they could keep the wall and the walkway in sight. Which meant that they took the long way round after all, and they might almost as well have walked it.

Baris did all the work, though, which meant that the others could rest. For the first time, Issel was beginning to wonder if it might after all be bearable to live as a dogtooth. It was all about loss, but he'd been losing all his life, and there was plenty that he could still stand to lose. Most of that came with the water-magic, and most of it was fear. Lose those, lose both of those . . .

Not now, not yet; but once he had done this thing that they had come to do, he thought he could lose the magic, if that meant losing the fear too.

———————

AILSE had called this lake a cistern; as well call Maras a village, or the Shine a bad time to be out.

Issel sat and gazed at the walls of the cavern, as they drifted by in the light that leaked from him. It was a dark grey rock, shot through with streaks of milky white; in places that milkiness seemed to have dissolved and oozed like sap from between the slabs of grey, and then scabbed and set when it met the air, so that there were streaks and bubbles of white, dripping clots where the veins were cut.

Those were the places where the hand of man most showed. The walkway was mostly built from stones and pounded rock-dust and cement; but where the wall had spurred and shivered, where it had been easier not to build but to cut a path at man-height through all the jagged ridgings, there the milk-sap had squeezed out to mark where hammers and chisels had broken through the living rock.

Issel watched those sections go by, interspersed with the smoothness of water-worn hardstone, and the open mouths of natural crevices and true tunnels and sewers where the walkway made a bridge across open water, and the places where the wall must have collapsed to break the path because it had all been built up again with worked stone blocks. Even those looked old now, as though it had all been cut and built and abandoned long ago.

That wasn't true, and the boat proved it, although the boat itself was old as boats go, ready to die and lie stranded on some stony beach in the darkness here, to rot in silence until its ribs thrust up like empty fingers, like the stripped bones of a carcase telling lies about a life it never had.

———————

HE wasn't the only one to be puzzled by the utter emptiness down here, the lack of lights, of either guards or workmen. Gilder raised it eventually, speaking softly against the weight of silence: "How can there be no one to watch over this?"

"They're Marasi," Rhoan said. "They don't care, they don't know what it means. It's just, just *water* to them . . ."

Even as she said it, her face was saying that she knew that made no sense; as well say *it's just diamonds* to a jewel-thief.

"Even so. Their path gets broken sometimes; we know it does, we can see where they've made repairs. If they don't guard, they must inspect. What else are the pathways for? At a time like this, with so much water coming through, they have to be concerned. And yet there is no one, no sign . . ."

Don't complain, Issel thought; then Rhoan said it, and made his heart sing.

"Don't complain," she said. "We may still meet them higher up. Meantime, let's make the best of no one watching. Besides, if you're so sure, Gilder, why are you whispering?"

This water seemed endlessly wide, endlessly deep. When change came, it came as a sound first, a rising murmur that echoed flatly between roof and water; then it was a current, working against the hull so that Baris had to bite his blade in deep, bite and thrust. Then at last they were close enough to see a black spewing mouth in the wall. Ailse said, "This is the place."

"What about the boat?" Gilder asked, when Baris had brought it to the walkway.

"There is a ring here, see. Tie it there." Ailse might have been looking for the ring; Issel had felt it, iron singing to him from the stone as water did in a dry room.

"What if we need it, higher up?"

"Then we must want for it. You can't carry it," *and we're not going to,* meaning Baris and herself. She was ready to make common cause with him, and be his mouthpiece at need; he might have been a slave in Sund, but not so in Maras.

After a moment, though, she went on: "There are other boats, higher up. Some might be useful. Until then, we can walk."

At least this time there was no need to wade; steps mounted alongside the flow. They made for easier going, although probably no drier. If Issel hadn't been wet already, the spray would have soaked him through and through before he reached the top.

He might have carried the boat himself, or towed it, all unaided. The way he felt, he might have turned the water and had the current carry them up-slope. He might have been screaming all the way, but that was nothing. He felt constantly on the verge of screaming, just as he felt on the verge of breaking into flame, unleashing the banked power of all this water and tearing the hill apart above their heads, destroying Maras from beneath.

At the top of the rise was a broad pool, fed by three separate channels.

"Which way?" Gilder asked.

"Here."

A canal in a tunnel, outrunning Issel's light. A little way in, they found an iron grille set into the water, a small boat bumping against the grille.

Gilder said, "Ailse, how far do we go along here?"

"Far. I don't know. I only had one candle left, so when I saw that it ran straight, I blew my light out and walked in the darkness."

It was hard to judge distance in the dark, that was all she meant to say. What Issel heard was fear and courage, both of them renewed with every step of that long, long walk.

What Gilder heard, presumably, was the first word and nothing more. He said, "Baris can paddle against this current," and stepped into the boat as though that was decided.

Baris said nothing; Issel and Rhoan both looked at Ailse, caught each other doing it and then had to speak themselves, stepping deliberately out of Sund and into Maras.

Rhoan said, "If Baris is willing?"

That was enough of a step, for one day; but Issel was already going further. He heard himself say, "We can help," meaning *I can*, meaning *I can use the water, against itself.*

It was the last thing he'd meant to say, the last thing he wanted to do. Rhoan heard, and understood him entirely, and shook her head; Gilder heard, and nodded. Why wouldn't Issel use the magic, here where there was so much water, where he would be so strong?

The dogtooths heard and didn't understand, thought he only meant to share the paddling. Baris grunted and settled down in the stern of the boat, gripped the paddle and showed no signs of sharing. Rhoan's eyebrow twitched, in Issel's direction. That was a whole conversation about freedom and how hard it could be to recognise, how easy it was to refuse; and about how a free man might still choose the work he was best fitted for. It wasn't at all about dogtooth slowness of mind. They were the slow ones here, and they knew it.

FIVE of them filled the boat, almost to the point where water could slop inside. Issel reached just a fraction of his mind, a hint of a thought into the canal. He should have done so on the lake but hadn't dared, daunted by the sheer scale of the place, dwarfed by majesty; who would light his lamp from a volcano's fury? Here it barely seemed to matter if he worked the water, just a little: to make a stiffened cradle of it underneath the boat, to have it support the hull and carry them forward more swiftly than all Baris' power might allow.

Rhoan knew. She saw how the surface thickened glasslike around them, how there was no splashing, how the boat rose a little in the water; she saw how they moved on irrespective of Baris' strokes with the paddle. Her head rose with a sudden enquiry; Issel met her eye to eye and watched the question die before she spoke it.

He offered her an answer anyway, an honest shrug, *it's nothing. Like the light.* Like the light, he barely felt it; if he closed his eyes, he couldn't have sworn that he was doing anything at all except being wet, feeling the tingle of that.

And if he'd meant to do nothing, if he'd fought temptation and lost— well, he was never too proud to give up a fight. A broken intent had to be better than a flooded boat, sudden immersion, over his head in this flow that would tumble them inexorably back towards the lake and its mountain's weight of water.

AT the channel's end they found another cascade. They stepped out of the boat and let it go, watched it borne away by the current and swiftly out of sight.

"Perhaps we should have sunk it," Gilder said. "Issel, you could have done that. Stop anyone coming up behind us."

Issel could have done it without thinking. He still could, he could find the boat by feel alone, by the sense of it in the flow. But it was a boat, made for water; it was almost a sacred thing to him, and he didn't want to harm it in the least. He'd send it on its way with a blessing, if he could.

"Stop who?" Rhoan demanded. "There's no one down here but us."

"You can't be sure of that."

"For sure there's no one following us. From the gorge, against that flood?" *We wouldn't have made it without help* was what she didn't say, but he heard it regardless. "And climbing up into the city, it's a madness anyway. Who would want to?"

"Soldiers," Gilder said, "watching its vulnerable belly. If I had recruits, I'd send them up that outflow; toughen them up, and be sure they knew what they were guarding. Or maybe we were seen, one of Ailse's friends who would give us up, at a weapon's threat; or it was a patrol that spotted us, or found tracks in the mud . . ."

"The rain would hide them. Gilder, you're worrying about nothing. Worry about what's ahead. That's where the danger lies, where the people are. Where the soldiers will be, and the runaways coming in this direction, and the workers who keep the sewers flowing . . ."

. . . And all the countless ways out into the streets, into the city, a tiny band of Sundain adrift in Maras; and Issel still thought that Rhoan was wrong. He thought the danger did lie behind them, but it wasn't any threat of discovery. In that lake, in that seething monstrous mass of water, there lay what they should all be most afraid of. And if it was like oil waiting for its spark, and if he was the spark that could ignite it, well, then they ought all to be afraid of him. One thing he could say for certain, just now he was utterly afraid of himself.

He didn't say that; he said, "There isn't anyone behind us," which was true, and made it sound like he agreed with Rhoan, which wasn't true but would please her none the less.

"How can you tell?"

It was the wrong question to the wrong person, and Gilder knew it a moment too late. His mouth twisted, unable to call the words back.

Issel smiled thinly, and said, "I would know."

He could feel the way they had come, like a rope in the dark behind them: a rope like fire, bright and fierce and alive. It tugged at him; he could feel the lake like a monstrous weight, hauling, calling. It drew him constantly, the fascination of what's terrible coupled with the simple drag of lodestone. He thought he'd left some part of his soul there, snared and aware. He could feel the drift and suck of the water as though he floated in it; he could encompass the damp in the air and hence the whole cavern, to the height of its roof and the immense stretch of its walls. No one could move in there without his knowing it.

"WE should stop soon."

"Stop? Here?"

"Somewhere down here, where we're safe."

"Better to keep going. Find a way out, even if we don't use it yet. Anyway, there hasn't been anywhere to stop, unless you want to sit on the path and dangle your feet in the water."

"There must be a corner somewhere, a blocked sewer, a dead end, something. A drain they never finished, a natural cave they couldn't find a use for."

"Maybe there is, but why waste time looking when we want a way up to the surface?"

"Gilder—I'm hungry, I'm tired, I want to sit down. How long have we been walking? We've been underground so long, it could be sunset or sunrise up there, we wouldn't know. We need to be sensible: rest, eat, get some sleep. Issel needs to get dry, that above all."

"We all need to get dry."

"Not the same way he does. We couldn't take him anywhere near the surface like this. He's *glowing* . . ."

Some part of his mind listened, and even understood, in a distant kind of way. He couldn't respond. How do you make words happen when you're not sure what's your body and what water? He might think he was opening his mouth, and tear a hole in the stream of water beside his feet, or way behind in the lake; it might be his own skin he tore, or Rhoan's where she clutched his arm. Having no boundaries of his own, he clung to hers: the solid sense of her at his side, contained and absolute. He knew exactly where she was; it was himself he couldn't find.

At last, she brought him somewhere dry. Water wasn't far away, but not here, except in his hair and his shirt and his skin. In hers too, hair and shirt and skin; he was very aware of that, as she took the pack from his back and then the shirt from his body. Another shirt came from the greasecloth pack, and that was dry until she used it like a towel on his hair.

As he dried, so his glow faded till there was barely any light at all. He felt like a traveller returned, exhausted and overwrought, and he couldn't see what he had come back to. All the walls were shadows; Rhoan was a shadow too, where she bent over him saying, "Here, take this, eat it. Good. Now sleep, here, just lie down . . ."

The water had been cold, but this dry rock was warm. No pallet, no blanket: that didn't matter; he was floating on darkness, falling into it, gone.

––––––––––

WHEN he woke there was light again, but someone else was making it.

Gilder sat over a thin gleam that washed him pale, that flung his black shadow above and behind. There were walls, there was a roof for that shadow to cling to, close and rough-hewn; this was a narrow little chamber, and a stream rushed by in the dark beyond.

"Where . . . ?"

Gilder shrugged. "Some kind of storeroom, maybe? Or a bolt-hole, if the water rose even higher out there; we're a long step up from the pathway."

"No. Where . . . ?" He hadn't got all his words back, seemingly. He knew what he wanted to ask, but he was struggling for a way to frame it.

"Where's Rhoan? She's after what we came for. I'd have gone, but she does this"—a waft of his hand at his little puddle of light—"better than I do. She'll find her way and come back while I'd still be inching out there."

That was true, but still not what he'd been asking. He shook his head in frustration.

"Not Rhoan? Really? Well, the other two have gone to find another way out. Ailse says there are plenty of dogtooth servants in the lower town—well, there would be, wouldn't there? Not as bad as Baris, mind, but she reckons she can disguise just how far he's gone. They're after supplies, news, whatever they can glean."

That wasn't it, either. Issel had slept, and he didn't feel tired now, only utterly drained: bird-boned, hollow, dry inside. *Where's it all gone?* might have put it into words, that feeling of emptiness and utter loss, of having a world taken away from him.

Whatever words he used, Gilder wouldn't understand him. And he knew the answer anyway. He had gone to sleep in a river and woken on the shore. The world hadn't gone away; it was waiting just beyond the doorway, all the reach and power of it out in the dark there, the subtleties and the brutality, the pain and the possession. He could hear it, smell it, feel its call in senses that he had no name for. The rush of water in its channel was like the promise of water in his bones; he ached for it, feared it, desired it. And he couldn't reach it from here, where he was dry.

It was only a short crawl away, a crawl and a tumble, out and down. But Gilder sat between him and the doorway, and he thought that was deliberate. He thought Rhoan had left instructions, *don't let him anywhere near the water.*

Gilder had water, in that little dip on the floor there, where he was making his little light; but even that was a stretch too far for Issel, the way he felt, all the marrow scraped out of his bones. Gilder could hold him off one-handed.

Besides, Rhoan might be right. Maybe he was better dry, for now. Just the thought of water made his skin shiver.

Gilder noticed that; he said, "Are you cold? Your shirt's dry. Here . . ."

Dry it was, and stiff and scratchy from the soaking, and dusty from where they had laid it out on the rock. He wasn't cold, but he pulled it on regardless; and so sat up, and leaned back against the rock, and said, "Where's Rhoan?"

"I told you that. Looking for the palace garden, where the magicians are."

AILSE and Baris came back, loud of foot and heavy-breathed; Issel could hear them in the tunnels, almost feel the weight of their coming, long before they heaved themselves in at the doorway. They came with bags and bundles: bags of food, bundles of clothing. Gilder applauded, as his thin, nimble fingers unpacked and picked them over.

"You have done well. How did you fetch all this, without Marasi money?"

"Copper is copper," Ailse grunted. "There have always been Sundain coins here, from the time when coins were struck in Sund; it was good currency then and is no different now, except worn a little thinner. Besides, I can beg, and Baris can threaten. Some of this we stole, some we cozened; some we bought."

Issel smiled, in recognition of the life he used to live. It was good to learn that it existed on this side of the river also. It made him feel not so strange for a moment, to sit here quiet and dry and barely even fizzy, not a hint of shine to his skin, not a hint of Shine in the air and the soft talk of thieves about their business. Begging was thievery, that was absolute; it was an art, and he had mastered it, and missed it suddenly as he missed nights on the roofs and running secrets from window to window, the easy stillness of an empty house and his own practised silence, the lightness of his feet and the emptiness of his thoughts as he flitted from room to room, taking a cheap necklace here and a warm blanket there, whatever he could carry, whatever he could sell.

Not his life now, and never would be again: he had changed and been changed, more than ever he had asked for. All change was loss, he realised that abruptly, a lesson learned. Some of it might be growth also, some might be welcome, but it was always loss.

THERE was food, but he wouldn't eat it; there were clothes, but he had no need to change.

"I'm fine as I am," he said, and, "I'll wait for Rhoan."

While the others ate, while Gilder and Ailse dressed themselves differently and Baris discovered—or they discovered for him—that none of their new clothes would fit his bulk, Issel edged quietly around the chamber, around Gilder's little central puddle of light, to the open doorway. He was genuinely slow, genuinely cautious, rediscovering his own body in its unexpected weakness; he was also trying not to have the others notice what he did.

Once there, he didn't want to go any further. He slumped against the rough stone lip of the doorway and gazed out and down into darkness.

Barely a glimmer of Gilder's light was leaking out, and even Issel's breath wouldn't glow of its own accord, even where the air he breathed was damp and full of messages of water, not when he was so dry himself.

He could see nothing, so he watched that and waited for it to change.

After a while he heard, "My old master had a dog once that did that. Lay down on the threshold whenever he went out, whimpered to itself, watched the road. Wouldn't move until he came back. Useless as a guard dog, thieves could have stepped right over it . . ."

Ailse, was it, or was it Gilder? He couldn't tell; he was drifting again. They were right, of course, entirely right. He might look like he was on watch, and he was, but not for anything he ought to guard against. Anyone might come by below: soldiers, runaways, an entire parade of priests and worshippers come to offer to their secret water-god. Issel didn't care.

He sprawled on the stone and listened to the water that he couldn't reach, and tried to reach out with his mind anyway, to do the water-trick without the water. And failed, and knew that he was failing; and so pretended to himself, drew pictures in his mind, Rhoan here and Rhoan there, and always in trouble, and he wasn't there to help. He couldn't imagine Rhoan secure and content and coming back. He was sure she wouldn't come. He stared into the dark and tried to will it anyway, but he never believed it.

So the light, when he saw it, wasn't Rhoan's. Even when it pulsed and faded and died in a splutter of spilt drops and was renewed—as, for example, a handful of water set to shine, while it trickled away through the fingers because it took a greater skill or deeper concentration to make it ball and shine together, when it wasn't blessed and wasn't Sundain but only wild Marasi water—even then, it wasn't Rhoan that worked it. Some untrained Marasi with Sundain blood, perhaps, or another rebel from across the river, or . . .

Even when he could see her hair, her figure, the way she walked, the way she was: even then, she couldn't be safe in her return. She must be bringing disaster with her, soldiers at her back, news of some calamity, something . . .

And then, when she was close, she looked up and she saw him, and she smiled.

And she reached her arms up to him, for help to clamber up; and of course all her water spilled and her light went with it, but that didn't matter, because her groping fingers found his in the dark.

Her hands were wet, so they shared a sudden sting from palm to palm, and he hoisted her easily up and in; but he thought he could have done it dry-handed, just from the strength of that smile. She had seen him, and it had made her smile. That was enough, that was plenty.

What more she had come back with, she was bursting to say; but Issel made her change wet clothes for dry, made her sit and eat before she told them. And if he took her dripping shirt himself, to lay it out flat where the warmth in the rock might dry it—well, she had a mouthful and her hands full and her head full of news besides; for once she wasn't watching what he did. Like a wick soaks up oil, he soaked up power from that wet shirt; he felt strong again, clear-headed, fit and able.

Indistinctly, she said, "I've found it all. Everything we wanted, more."

"Explain?" That was Gilder, of course. Issel would take Rhoan's word entirely and never see the need to ask for details.

She said, "I followed Ailse's advice and she was right, I did find a way up to the palace garden. I wasn't sure, it could have been any garden, there are so many spurs and drains up there; but I found a way out and there was someone by the stream there, a girl . . ."

"Did she see you?"

"Yes, of course. We talked."

"You *spoke* to her?"

"Well, what do you think I should have done?"

"Hidden. Made yourself disappear, you're good at that. We can't let anyone know we're here; there'll be guards now, watching for us, we'll have to fight our way out, and then how are we going to—?"

"No, listen. *Listen!* It's not like that. Of course I spoke to her, how else was I going to find what we're looking for? We'd always have to ask someone. And she was right there, a girl my age and looking miserable . . . We talked, and I was right, she is miserable, and she wants out of there. So I said we'd help."

"You said what? Rhoan . . . !"

"*Listen*, will you? She's trapped in the harem there, and she didn't say so but I think they've been really cruel to her, or to someone she loves. She needs to escape, anyway. With her friends, I think. That's why she was down there by the sewer-mouth, looking for a way out. Which we can give her. So I promised her we'd help, in fair exchange."

"Exchange for what?"

"She's going to show us where the magicians are." And then she added one thing more, but this was direct to Issel: "I promised her we wouldn't hurt the children."

———————

PERHAPS it wasn't such a long walk in the flesh, in their little bubble of light. Perhaps it was only in his head, where time was washed away altogether. He thought they spent forever following the water's path, walking wetly beside it and eventually wading where it was shallow and the tunnel grew cramped, the walls narrowing and the roof dropping down. Everything not stone was liquid: light and water and air were the same thing, allengulfing, and they consumed time.

Until Rhoan held up a hand to halt them; and then turned back, came past Gilder and spoke to Issel, said, "We're here."

He blinked at her, then felt the shock of her touch, her wet hand against his cheek.

"Issel, are you listening to me?"

Oh yes, he was listening. It was talking that was hard. They had spent forever on the way, and forever had brought them to a crude rock tunnel they could hardly stand up in, and this was not what he'd been looking for.

Rhoan said, "Listen, then. The drain is just around the corner up ahead, and she's going to be nervous. A group of us might frighten her; Baris almost certainly would frighten her; and—well, Issel, you're glowing again. So just wait, yes? Let me talk to her first."

She said wait, so Issel waited. It wasn't hard. He crouched and leaned his back against cool stone. Calf-deep in water and feeling the tug of it, he might have let his soul slip away again—but Rhoan had said to wait, and so he waited.

Gilder was restless, impatient, pacing to the limit of Issel's light, peering to see where Rhoan had gone and then turning back, pacing.

The dogtooths were more restful. Issel could be comfortable with them, almost. They squatted, and so did he. With the Shine sunk deep into blood and bone, passivity was the easy option. They waited, and so did he.

WHEN she came back, Rhoan was frowning and anxious.

Gilder asked, so that Issel didn't need to: "What's wrong?"

"She wasn't there."

"I told you it was stupid, to trust a Marasi girl. Lucky you didn't find guards waiting. They could still be watching for us in the garden. Or in here. We should go back . . ."

"No. I trust her. Maybe she's just lurking out of sight, before she makes up her mind to trust us. What does she know of magic?"

"She can see the bridge, anytime she looks down on the river. And her magicians are right there in the garden, sustaining it. If she told you true."

"They're not her magicians—she hates them, fears them. I don't think they're Marasi. And they've got her sister, I told you that. Issel, come with me."

He gazed down at his arms, where his wet skin still pulsed and glowed; he didn't need to speak.

"Oh, come on. I said, she's not there; how are you going to spook her if she can't see you?"

If Rhoan was right, she'd be crouched in the undergrowth somewhere, peeping through leaves, and a figure that shone in the drain might scare her very much indeed. He went along, though, because Rhoan asked him to. There was another short stretch of tunnel, then a spur to the side; Rhoan took that way, signing him to keep quiet, to keep low. When she dropped onto hands and knees and crawled over a fall, so did he.

The stream ran in a channel of brickwork, easy crawling, and it brought them to the iron grille she'd warned of. Beyond was the garden: too dense and overgrown to show him anything, by moonlight or starlight or his own odd light. There could be a dozen girls out there, and his eyes would never find them.

He had senses other than his eyes, and he was hands and knees in water, soaked all over; it wasn't raining, but the stream ran like a road of molten fire in his mind, and the night air was damp. The garden opened itself in the darkness like a map.

"There's someone over there," he said, nodding through the grille.

"Is there? I can't see . . ."

"No. Nor I." Nor the hidden girl, presumably; she was keeping too far back to spy. "She is there, though. Trust me."

"Come on, then," she said. "Just you and me. If she's this nervous, we'd best not go in numbers."

"I'm still glowing."

"I know, but there's nothing we can do about that. I did warn her when we spoke before. I said you were reasonably human underneath."

That was meant as a joke, he knew; he struggled not to show how deep it bit. Truth could be so telling. Reasonably human he was, and so was Ailse, though not Baris; Baris had lost the art of reason. So would Ailse, and so would he.

Rhoan said, "Do the deed, then, Issel. Shift this grate."

The bars were thicker than his fingers, thicker than his thumb. Issel smiled at her and took a grip, two grips, one hand on the lock and the other on the topmost hinge. His hands were wet, and that was all he needed.

He felt the solidity of iron, under the surface decay of rust and lichen growing; he reached to make that wet iron soft, to make it bend and stretch. Gripping turned to ripping, and he tore the gate from its mountings, lock and hinge; it was sagging already before his hand reached to the lower hinge and twisted that into taffy, plucked it apart.

Even Rhoan gasped a little, as the whole span of grille-work fell splashily into the stream ahead of them. She'd seen him work before, but never so abruptly. Perhaps she understood a little more of what had been happening to him down in the sewers.

He led, out of the drain and into the palace garden. Physically he made a poor shield, too short and too thin, whiplash muscles and no bulk. Right now, though, his mind was whiplash too. With all this water in his head, he thought he could block a weapon between stroke and strike; he could catch an arrow in mid-flight.

There might be no guards in striking-range, no archers set to shoot. Even so, he meant to hold his place in front of Rhoan. Metal stood out to his water-sense like fire in the night. The figure crouching in the undergrowth—waiting, hiding, both—had a knife: one short streak of steel that blazed at him. Even a harem girl might carry a blade when she sneaked out at night to betray her nation to its enemies. He didn't blame her, he didn't fear her; he would still not allow her close to Rhoan until he was sure of her.

Sooner than climb the bank and tackle the undergrowth, they made their way along the stream-bed until they came to a bridge and a path. It wasn't far from here to the figure he could sense, huddled under a bush. Hanging back where she could watch the path, he supposed, as well as the stream.

If the girl was afraid—of them, or of discovery—it would be kinder to send Rhoan on alone. But Issel was not dealing in kindness tonight. Let her be afraid for a little while, what time it took to find her and reassure her. She would survive her fear, as he did his.

He stepped up out of the water, into what had been the moon-shadow of the bridge. His unearthly radiance went with him, brighter than the moon, casting shadows of its own. Ten paces on the path, twenty; and then he stepped to the side, to where a bush had grown so old and wild that its inside was all hollow behind its walls of green, where someone small or flexible could crouch and watch whoever came and never be seen themselves . . .

Never seen, but heard now if they gasped suddenly, knowing themselves discovered. And if they put their hand on their knife-hilt for comfort, for security, they might hear a voice crack down at them from this impossible figure, this djinn, this boy-creature that shone in the night: "Leave your knife there where you are, and come out without it. I will know."

———————

"ISSEL, stop it. You're scaring her stupid; how's the poor thing meant to move, with you looming over her like that? Go away, go back to the path . . ."

Rhoan pushed at him, then snatched her hands away, at the fierce buzz of water-shock between them. When she looked down, her palms were glowing. She tutted in self-disgust and tried to wipe them dry on her shirt, but that was wet already; all she did was leave streaks of light in the fabric.

So she scowled at Issel as though that too were his fault, and gestured him further off; and then she crouched by the bush and spoke to it softly, and might have looked utterly ridiculous to anyone who couldn't sense the other figure hidden behind its weeping branches.

So much for his protective instincts, so much for his vows to stand between her and harm. But Issel could be wise; he had learned that promises could be broken at need and still kept fresh in secret; he had an absolute grip over both of them, the figure inside the bush and the one without. The ground was wet, the air was wet, the leaves were wet between them; he held them both in separate bubbles in his mind, and they had no idea of it but neither one could touch the other without his immediate consent.

There must be a way that he could use the water to listen in, to catch their whispers and carry them to him. He was too tight, too focused to play with the idea now; he only watched both of them in his mind, his water-sense. When the one inside the bush went to all fours and began to crawl through the dense mat of branches, he reached and tugged with one casual finger of desire. The knife skittered out of the unseen figure's belt and through the mulch of rotting leaves, out of reach, out of sight and gone.

A yelp, a sudden hesitation; Rhoan rounded on him in a snappish whisper. "Issel, stop it! Leave him alone, he's quite safe . . ."

No, he wasn't. Not if he was close to Rhoan and within Issel's reach and not the girl they had both been expecting.

"He? Who is it?"

It was a boy, coming out now, shaven-headed and defiant and afraid. He scrambled to his feet and said, "I am Teo, my lady Jendre's slave," as though that was a proud thing to be; and he couldn't quite look at Issel directly, but that was all he let show of his fear.

"Where's your mistress?" Gilder's voice, coming from behind. Teo startled, and might have run then after all if Rhoan hadn't gripped his wrist to hold him.

She looked utterly exasperated, glared indiscriminately at them all—at Baris and Ailse too, where they were trudging up behind Gilder—and said, "Oh, did you all have to come and frighten him at once? Was Issel not enough, making a torch of himself to blind the night?" as though Issel had any choice about his glowing. "Never mind for now where his lady is; she has sent him instead, which is kind in her and brave in him," with a little shake of his arm and a smile that won her just a twitch in return. "She sent him to find us, but he sensibly waited here, where he could watch the stream for us and the path for anyone other. And look, he's brought towels and dry clothes; so first thing, Issel, rub that shine out of your hair and change your dress. The rest of us can dry too, but you matter most. Teo says there are unfriendly eyes abroad."

Rough towels, and Rhoan taking one to rub harshly at his hair and skin;

unfamiliar clothes, soft and light and silky, like wearing a warm breeze, and Teo had to show him where to tie and fasten, how to wear them.

"Is my lord a great mage?" he asked in a whisper, finding just a touch of light clinging to his fingertips, just for a moment, where Issel's skin had still been damp.

"What, me? No—"

Rhoan's laugh cut through his denial. "Him? Teo, he has been a thief and a beggar and a street boy; we brought him to school, but he kept trying to run away. He can do things we can't, but that's the only reason we bother with him. Otherwise, he's just a nuisance."

TEO had brought more than towels and dry clothes. A second rummage in the shrubbery produced a bottle of water sharp with citron juice, and soft oily breads flavoured with cumin and coriander, filled with onion and parsley. If the boy took long enough down there to find his knife again and sneak it back into his belt, Issel ignored it.

They sat on the bridge's stone parapet and ate, and passed the bottle to and fro, and Teo told them what had happened to his mistress and this whole discarded harem.

"The Sultan is dead," he said, his first news, his greatest.

"We know that," Gilder grunted, around a mouthful. "That's why we're here, why you are, why everything's different. The old man died, by poison or whyever, and—"

"No, the new Sultan. His brother. There is an uprising. The Sultan is dead and the old woman too, his mother, I saw her die. So did my lady. The pasha came and killed her, and took his son away. But he left guards on all the doors to the harem, and the ladies are inside; so my lady could not come tonight, so she sent me."

It was a short story, briefly told. In Sund they would have made a night's narrative out of it. Once the news had crossed the river, no doubt they would. For now, though:

"Why would he set guards on the harem," Rhoan asked, "more than you had already?"

"We are very dangerous people," the boy said, smiling lightly.

"No, truly?"

"Yes, truly. There must be a new sultan. Not the pasha, he is not blood and no one would accept him. The janizars would want their own generals, there would be other lords who claimed the throne, all of them would fight. It must be one of the blood, the last Sultan's sons; all their mothers are here. One will be Valide Sultan in the morning, and so dangerous. The others will all hate her, and fear her, and be dangerous to her if they can. So there are guards tonight on every door, and the house is full of whispers."

"If there are so many guards," Gilder said, "how did you get out?"

Teo shrugged. "They are there to guard the ladies, not me. And they do not know the harem. Or its boys."

That swift, elusive smile again. He had forgotten his fear, or shrugged it off under more urgent excitements, the company of rebels and mages. Issel wasn't clear whether he had eluded the guards or cozened them or pleaded; it was all one, anyway. Every beggar is a thief.

"Well," Rhoan said, "I wish your lady Jendre well—but will you help us, Teo, tonight?"

"Of course. My lady says I must," and his eyes said that he wanted to, that he was eager to see miracles and magic, now that he was past the first shock of it.

ISSEL'S hair was still damp, a little, if his clothes and skin were dry; and the grass was damp beneath his bare feet, and there was rain in the sky and dew in the air. His water-sense reached forward and back and all around them. More than that, he felt that he still had the power of the rushing sewers at his command, the potency of the deep still pools in the heart of the hill below them; it was banked, quiescent now but still there, to hand, at will.

Right now he thought he could make things happen with dry hands, with just the moisture on his breath. He wasn't sure if that was a comfort.

Trees and shrubs, sometimes a bed of flowers; grassy banks and empty buildings, the sudden boxy thrust of a straight wall and a clean corner, but all the windows dark and the rooms silent, open to the night. Streams that made his blood thrill before he heard their run, ponds and pools and little lakes that he smelled before he saw them, that he felt deep in his bones before he smelled them.

Up and up; sometimes their way would turn around a hillside and they would have a glimpse of the palace below them, a great range of buildings where one block had many lights burning at its windows, to mark the harem where wakeful women sat. One of those was Teo's mistress, Rhoan's new friend Jendre. What would her life be now, after another sultan's death—or what would it be, what would any of their lives be tomorrow, after Issel had destroyed the magicians and their bridge with them? All her plans and betrayals were in doubt; whatever happened, she wouldn't be escaping tonight with her rescued sister. She needed rescuing herself, but not by Issel.

An end to the magicians, and swift away: that was his purpose for tonight. No more than that. No pulling the children from their dreams, leading them into the sewers in a pilgrimage of hope; no wild romantic venture into the harem, to find Teo's lady and smuggle her out to join them. They must fend for themselves, or have others fend for them, or meet their own disasters as they could.

Sometimes the path turned another way and gave them oversight of the city beyond the wall, all the long drop of it down to the river and the bridge. Even down in the docks, there were lights bright enough to pierce the Shine tonight. Issel thought that some of them were fires. Maras might not be taking too easily to its new dispensation; that was all to the good. Only let the bridge go too, and it would be like stirring up an ant-hill with a stick; all the population would be agitated and afraid, every soldier and every citizen anxious for themselves and for their city, hardly likely to notice a handful of strangers slipping away as they had come, through the undercity to the river and beyond . . .

Those were subjects that they hadn't really talked about: how the bridge would break, and how they would get away after.

Maybe the bridge would fade, slowly and quietly, like a fire that's lost its heat for lack of fuel; maybe all the soldiers in Sund would see it pale and try to run back over the river before it was quite gone, and be too slow and fall through its insubstantial floor and plummet to the river and be lost. Or maybe it would snap, like a cable under tension; maybe some magic residue would come cracking like a whip through each of the cities, bringing mayhem and catastrophe.

———————

UP and up, and at last they came to a pool below a rocky peak, with a little white pavilion that overlooked the water and then all the gardens they had climbed through, the palace roofs and the city roofs beyond, the river and the bridge crossing it like a ribbon that glowed with sickness and the Shine falling all around it like a ring around the moon, poison turned to light. From this high—and perhaps with a little help from a damp breeze blowing into the wetness of his eyes, a touch of water-sense—he could see beyond the Shine to find his own city, Sund, small and dark and barely a glimmer showing this late into the night. There would be torches burning in the barracks, and lamps perhaps in some of the mansions, where those Sundain whose wealth had survived the occupation dined with their Marasi masters. Otherwise, oil was expensive and in short supply, and lights were liable to attract attention; Sund lived a daylight life, and mostly conspired in the dark.

Somewhere over there, betrayed by Armina and driven out of his own family mansion, Tel Ferin had taken shelter with one of his friends: another adept hiding his talents, surviving by discretion or else paralysed by fear, depending to whom you listened. Issel wondered whether Tel Ferin still counted as a conspirator, whether he had tried to gather his school again, whether there was still a rebellion to hope for. When the bridge came down, then surely something, someone in Sund had to rise . . .

———————

"THERE," Teo said, though he hardly needed to. "The pavilion with the children, the magicians, there it is . . ."

There it was, indeed. Any one of them would have known it, by the light that leaked from doors and shutters: alien and clouded, swirling with unnameable colours, a taint upon the air. If the bridge were a span of spider-silk, here surely was where it had been spun.

Issel would have known it with his eyes closed, blindfolded. Because there was nothing to see except blank walls, a roof, closed shutters and that ooze of light, he reached out with his water-sense, to find what more he could learn—and found nothing, a hollow, a space he couldn't penetrate. Inside a rock at the heart of a desert might be like that, so dry that there was no water, not even any memory of water to carry the hint of a whisper of a word—but he didn't believe it. He thought his mind had its own water now, the spirit of water; he thought he could ride the driest wind and seep like a century, a millennium of rain into the most ancient, most desiccated rock there was, and find its frailties, and shatter it if need be.

And this pavilion was a glance away—look, just there!—and he could not find it with his water-sense, only its absence like a hole in the world, a place where no light fell.

That ought to be impossible. If light leaked out, the breeze could go in, and there was water on the breeze. Besides, the pavilion was full of children, warm wet bodies that ought to shine at him like a torch in darkness . . .

"Issel?"

"Something strange," he said, when Rhoan prompted him again, this time with a nudge in the ribs. "I can't get inside, I can't feel my way . . ."

Gilder said, "No need to go inside. Just rip it down. That'll bring them out, like ants in a rainstorm."

He'd thought this would be easy; he was suddenly not sure. This was one more subject that they hadn't really talked about: just how he was to disrupt the magicians' spells, break the bridge and free his city.

It would mean violence, surely. He'd used other words, even to himself; but he had come to destroy their magic, which must mean to destroy the magicians or they would only build it up again. Almost certainly, that meant he had to kill them.

Well, he had killed before. With a knife, once, close-to, when he was asked; since then with water, and more often than he liked to think about.

Better not to think, then. Not about that. He might have followed Gilder's advice and ripped straight into the pavilion, hoping to fetch the magicians out in their wrath; first, though, he turned eyes and mind and water-sense to the pool he stood beside.

It was full and overfull, fed by rain and run-off from the rocky mount above; and yes, there was the overflow that kept it from turning all its grassy margin into swamp. It was an iron grid set into worked stone, familiar work; water dribbled constantly over its edge and ran on into darkness. Issel didn't need light or sight to follow how it went, along a buried culvert and over a fall into a deeper channel and so down to where he could almost draw a chart.

Where men had been before, to cut those drains, men could go again. "This is our way out," he said. "When I've done . . . what we came to do."

And he bent and gripped the weed-and-rust-encrusted bars of the grid and lifted it out, smooth and swift and easy, for all the world as though it hadn't been embedded fifty years ago in stone and concrete and left to the degrading elements since.

"Tight," Ailse said, with an anxious sidelong glance at Baris' broad shoulders.

"It'll be a squeeze," Rhoan agreed. But she said it to reassure, not to frighten further; and in case a tone of voice was just too subtle for them, she added, "Don't worry, we'll get you through. Issel can work it wider, if he needs to. If he's sure, we have to go this way . . . ?"

Issel shrugged. He wasn't sure of anything. "If we make a noise"—or a light show, sparks and flares of competing magic—"with all those soldiers Teo says are down in the palace, some of them will come to see. If the bridge is gone"—if it vanished or erupted, shattered or snapped—"then they'll come running to ask the magicians why. This way, we can be gone before they get here."

And he held up his hand, to show how it was glowing now after fleeting contact with the water of the pool. It was like touching fire to a half-burned log still hot. His blood seethed, his hand burned and his bones ached; he had all of this water at his command, and what lay behind it, below, where its overflow trickled down to meet and join with other streams, heavier flows, wider ponds and tiled pillared cisterns and so on further down to the great underground lake, one system like a circulation of the blood, all of it joined, all one, he had all of that if he should need it. He thought he might make quite a lot of light.

He said, "Wait here," and tried not to wonder whether any of them would, just because he said so.

HE walked ahead and didn't look back. His wet hand burned, his bare feet scorched the damp grass, his every step sparked lights about his feet; he was out in the world with all the impact of those reservoirs below him, and he was mighty, manifest, deadly. He thought he could rip this hill up by its roots if he had to. He could sense those roots, where the water reached to find them, down and down and further down. He thought he felt them tremble at his touch.

Small wonder if the earth bore messages, to say that he was coming; small wonder that the magicians came out to greet him.

A door opened in their pavilion, and that leaking light was suddenly a flood. There were silhouettes within it, shadows flung down towards him like a challenge, like an open road to war; it was still the light that seemed more dangerous. He had lived all his life under the Shine, slept too often in its bitter glare, and this was much like that. Where the light itself was poison, it was hard to fear the poisoners. It's the blade that cuts, not the hand that grips the haft.

What spilled across the grass was brighter than bridgelight, brighter than the Shine. And slicker, more oily, its distressful colours more intense. Here was the pure thing, the source from which the bridge must flow; it looked putrid. Pity the children who slept within that oozing glow, whose dreams were the fuel that must feed it.

Pity the children, but he had come here to destroy the bridge, the product of their dreaming; hate the bridge and its foundations, but he had been brought here to save the children. They were two goals, anything but twin; they pulled him in different directions, with contrary needs.

He could be happy, then, to see the magicians coming out. The dark seeds swathed in their luminescence, the grit at the heart of the pearl: if he killed them, then surely both his tasks would be achieved. The magic would die with its creators, the bridge would die with its magic, the children would be spell-free and released to their families' care again . . .

No need to reach far into himself, to find the killing strength of water. He had it all there at his fingertips, at his command. Weird to feel so strong, where he had no water to work with; but he did, of course, he had all the drains and sewers and cisterns of the city behind and below him and the river itself beyond that, all the water of the world. It was in his head now, and in his heart. He didn't need it in his hands.

He felt it like a flood that pushed him forward, like an ebb that tugged him back: both at one time, holding him poised but never balanced, always on the verge of toppling, one way or the other. More than that, though, he felt it as a simple force, his to use. And his targets stood before him, robed and mystical and hard to see, and he just reached out for them. He had always used water as his weapon before this, but now his water-sense was almost a weapon in itself. Once he had a grip it would take only a twitch of his mind to unravel them, to pick them apart by bone and muscle as though his will were a needle held in the hand of God. No need for an actual blade, or a blast of corrosive steam, or any of those crude and cruel tricks of his past. They could die and never know it, simply be dead on the threshold there, as they stood now on the threshold of death and didn't know it . . .

Except that his water-sense couldn't reach them, couldn't find them at all. It was strange, so strange: his eyes knew where the magicians were, but the water-sense was blind, when it was usually so much further-reaching. He pictured it sometimes not as thoughts but tendrils, gossamer-light, that quested in the dark like roots in earth. Fast, frighteningly fast yet still solid, a physical presence in the world. Not tonight. Tonight they lost all their solidity, all their coherence; they seemed to dissolve and lose themselves utterly in that shifting, shimmering light.

Never mind, then. Nothing delicate or subtle. He had the strength, and he used it: casting straight into the light, straight at the nearest smudgy magician-figure, definitely with a weapon now, a spear of thought, his mind shaping the force of all that water.

But it was still a thought, even dressed in a spear's hurl. All its focus, its integrity came from him, from his hatred and his fear and his fury; and he started to lose it as soon as it passed into the shifting light.

Not completely: he felt it pierce that cloudy barrier, felt it plunge deep before it began to fray. But nothing could be clear, where light swirled like smoke in currents of air. He closed his eyes to try to focus better, only then he felt dizzy and sick as though he were in a boat again, as though the earth beneath his feet were tossing and pitching him like flotsam on the river in a storm.

He could still reach back, to find the water. He could root himself in that and his connection to it; he could feel the immense reservoir of power that lay within it; he could feel himself like the lens of the eye, the point of the sword, the pivot. All that power could erupt through him if he chose. But he needed to direct it, and as soon as he turned forward like a pointing finger to say *strike here*, he was jabbing meaninglessly into a blankness, a bewilderment. It might have been empty space, it might have been solid rock. He lost that sense of being rooted; he lost all his certainties and flailed helplessly, like a man sinking in water, weak and afraid and almost overcome.

Almost. Never quite. The first time he had tried to infiltrate the light, it had shrugged him off scornfully, dismissively. This time—an invasion rather than an infiltration, forcing his way in where he had felt for it before—he had at least penetrated, even if the light engulfed his thoughts and sickened him and came close to overwhelming him.

If he could come this far, he could go further. These were magicians that he faced, although theirs was no magic that he knew or understood. They worked with light, or made it, or perhaps they poisoned it; to him, there was no difference. Where his magic met their light, it drained him, it drank his water and left him defenceless—but they weren't striking back as they ought to be. Perhaps this was all they had, the power to sap and confuse, the strengths of sleep and dreams.

He wasn't finished yet. He'd gone so far—into the light, into the giddy sickness of it, reeling, drowning—with just one stabbing thrust of his mind. He'd thought that would be enough, and he was wrong, but he still had more to draw on. He had a city's-worth, a hillsideful of water at his back, and he could use it all.

He thought he could.

He made himself a channel, a doorway, an open mouth. He reached back through the abiding link in his mind—unless it was in his soul, unless he didn't have one—to where all that water waited, and he clung to the great still weight of it to anchor him, and then he drew it forward.

Not all of it, not all at once, he'd need to be a mouth the size of a mountain to gush that. He was a tap, a sluice, a drain, no more: a tap for the power, for the magic. But he was Sundain, and if there was one thing he understood, it was water. He knew how a fat full urn and a narrow spout would make a tap spurt. He was narrow, and the hill was full. It felt like an impertinence, but he thought that vast potent reservoir should spurt through him, to make a weapon that the magicians' light could not deflect or absorb or defeat.

Whether there would still be an Issel after, who could say?

He'd lived so long closed off, it wasn't easy to open up. Nor to rely on something other than himself, a borrowed strength. When he worked water in his hands it was his own, he took possession of it. This was altogether different, a surrender, almost a defeat; and it was his mind he had to surrender.

He was rooted, restored, embedded; his bones ached with the surge and suck of water. He thought he was a sluice gate, closed and holding against the flood.

He threw back the gate, and let the water run.

———

DREW it on, indeed, poured it forth.

Here was the light, and here was his water-sense that had been drifting, abandoned, lost within it like a sailboat without wind or tiller. Now suddenly there was almost more wind than it could take, so much force behind it, the accumulated power of a hillful of water, and it still wasn't enough.

The light seemed to thicken ahead—deliberately, being worked against him—and it was like sailing a boat against a powerful flow, the wind striving to drive it forward and the current's suck dragging it back.

There was far more force in water than he could channel. He was the weak link, the fault, the failing: both flesh and blood, and hence weak, and untrained, unskilled in this. His sense of himself as water-carrier, as weapon, stretched a long way into the light, stiff and true and deadly as a sword blade, as a spear; but even with so much strength to back it, it had faltered now, it was stalled and still, a reach short of the magicians it was aimed at.

Issel couldn't see them clearly—with so much of his mind given over to the water, he couldn't see anything clearly—but he thought they had faltered too, as much at their limits as he was. They couldn't drive him back, any more than he could thrust further forward. It was a deadlock, futile and dangerous to him and his . . .

But he still thought he could draw more strength from the water. One last effort, then: he reached back in his mind and heaved at it, no passive channel now, not an open gateway but a pump. He wanted all that the water could give him, and never mind if it was more than he could take.

He heaved, and felt the dragging weight of it, even as he felt the responding surge of power.

Heaved again, and couldn't understand why it felt so heavy, at the same time as it gave him strength to haul.

Heaved again, and didn't feel what he was expecting, that clamorous rush of power, the force of it flowing through him and pushing deep into the light.

Instead, he felt a cruel bite at his feet and looked down, startled, to find himself standing ankle-deep in water.

Not a stream of water, not a flood, it wasn't flowing past him and on downslope. It was like a rope, rather, a coil that wound around his feet and was twisting higher as he watched, climbing his legs, oozing upward. When he looked behind him, he saw how it trailed over the grass and all the way back to the pond where he had left his friends.

No wonder it had dragged so hard; he'd thought he was simply drawing energy, but he'd pulled the water itself to him, ripping it out of its still bed and dragging it across the ground.

He wasn't sure how far or how deep that demand had gone, whether this was just water from the pond or whether he was sucking the run-off back up its channel, draining the cistern below and reaching further, perhaps the last echo of a whisper of a call running down as far as the heedless, infinite lake.

He wasn't sure of anything, except that he suddenly had water to work with, water in his hands, where he'd had only his water-sense and his intent before and they had not been enough.

That light might sap at his senses, it might dizzy and disorient his mind, but now he had a weapon that was physical, as well as being alive to his will. He could shape it, make it, shift it; it could be a rope, a blade, a poison, acid steam . . .

His hands were working, they were burning as they worked; he watched the magicians and didn't look down, but it felt as though his skin had melted half into what they held, so there was no distinction left, what was water and what was Issel. Or what was water, what was pain, what was Issel: pain was the margin between them. In the down-below world, water everywhere, he'd come through pain and found something vastly greater on the other side. Up here he was back inside his skin again and vulnerable to water; where it touched, it seared.

Still, he knew about pain. His hands didn't flinch, nor his mind. He drew the water up and shaped it as it came, made a harpoon of it. He had seen boats go out on the river of the world, half a dozen at once with four oars in each and a harpooner in the bows, to hunt the pods of beluga. That used to be the greatships' work, before the Marasi burned them. Now the little boats tried, every year at migration-time, as the pods came by; the rewards for even a single kill were too tempting to resist. Every year, some boats made it back to Sund, but only some. Issel and others would haunt the strand for days after, to salvage whatever came ashore from the ruin of those that didn't. More than once, he'd picked up a harpoon and sold it back to the fishermen. He knew harpoons, the weight and the balance of them in the hand, the trail of rope behind.

Now he made his own. The blade was long and double-edged with a wicked twist to it, such as a skilled ironsmith might have made in a hard hot day at the forge; Issel did the work with his fingers and his mind, a minute of pulling and shaping, and left it steel-hard and steel-sharp. It melded seamlessly into a short throwing-handle, which fined down in its turn into a string, a thread that came back to himself. It looked fragile but it was all water, all one; it was stronger than hawser. And that thread was still bound to the rope of water that came from the pond, and he was confident now that it did reach down through the overflow and into the reserves in the dark below. He could feel it, running back and back and further back, more water than a mage could dream of. He was no mage, only a wild and corrupt talent, half-trained and unprepared; he felt incompetent, inadequate, lethal.

He hurled that javelin without thought, almost without aim. He threw it with his water-strength, with all the force that he could channel. Then it had left his hand, but the rope it linked to was still entwined around his body; and it had all that mass of water behind, direct and unchannelled, to drive it on harder, faster. All he had to do was keep it true.

He had a street boy's eye and a straight arm too, developed through years of throwing stones at rats, at birds, at soldiers. That disturbing, drifting light engulfed it, though, and straightaway seemed to draw it off its course.

Issel nudged a little, like a fisherman with his finger on his line, except that Issel's nudge came from his mind, just a little twitch to bring the harpoon's point back into line.

Another drift, another twitch; and he was almost losing sight of the harpoon now, a slender streak of blued water in a haze of slick-coloured light, but he still thought it was aimed pure and true at the broad chest of the dark silhouette that was the nearest magician.

And his water-sense rode piggy-back on the point of the harpoon, and there, *there* was the great wet body of a man, so much water in it that even that heavy poisoned light couldn't mask it any longer; and then it was an eruption of wet, of dark wet matter and he drew back swiftly into his proper body and saw that shadowed figure fall, saw the agitation of his confrères; and then he heard the man scream, belatedly it seemed, as though the sound were coming from distance or had just needed time to travel through the light.

It was the light that faltered now, as the magicians were distracted, or their spell was weakened by a death, or both.

Issel had believed in that death from the moment the harpoon struck. He had felt the deep wet shock of it, the spill of life and fluids; he had been there at the heart, immersed in it. Now he saw the proof, how the light paled, how it contracted, drawing back almost to the doorway of the pavilion, almost to where the magicians stood, still on their threshold there. It had been reaching before, questing for him; now they could barely maintain it. He didn't think it would protect them long.

Except that here came other figures bustling out through the doorway, and no doubt more magicians could build their barrier of light back up again, fling it back towards him.

But he still had his harpoon right there, deep among them; and it didn't need always to be a harpoon, it was just a link of water, a tool that he could shape at will, easier with hands but he had the cord of it here between his fingers, and he could do this.

He reached his awareness all along its length and unshaped the blade of the harpoon so that it was just a heavy cord of water, nothing more. He made a snare of it and twitched it open, cast the noose around the nearest neck and pulled it taut—

—AND meant to kill, to strangle if he could, or else turn cord to wire and pull tighter, pull wire all the way through flesh and bone.

But that touch of water on skin, that first touch as it tightened gave him a clear sense of what he'd snared; and now it was his turn to falter, as he suddenly loosened the noose.

Just an image, a vision, a hint through smoke and strangeness: but what he saw was bulk and beads and mirrors in her hair and what he heard was bells, what he smelled was rust and spices, and the name in his head was—

THE name in his head was impossible. He left it there, where it could do no harm. No more harm. Too much had been done already.

He left the name alone, but still whipped his noose away from her neck; and thought to stiffen the end of it into a point, a blade again, and go stabbing for magicians.

He couldn't find them, though, he had no sense of where they were.

There was a dead body, he could find that, it was wet and bright and clear; there were figures bustling about it, but at least one of them was untouchable and he thought they all were, he wanted to give them all that same name, which was of course impossible. Somewhere among them or behind them must be the magicians, indetectable, unreachable. When he looked, the light was thickening like a shell about the doorway, and he could only vaguely make out shadows that moved within it. There was no way to tell who or what they were.

Frightened now, unless he was just defeated, he went to withdraw his rope of water, to pull right back and think again—and found that he couldn't do it. Something had gripped the other end. Not tightly, not like a hand or a cleat might grip a rope; more as though the end had come unravelled, and all the separate threads were tangled up in something. He thought that the water was fraying into the light, in the same way that he'd thought his skin had melted into the water, with no clear margin between them.

He'd been wrong before, his skin was still his own; this time he was right. *Nothing is easy, nothing comes without a price*—that was lesson one on the streets, where he'd never forgotten it. Here he was out of his proper place in the world, dealing with magics he didn't understand, doubly endangered, and he'd let it slip his mind.

He'd come here powerful, confident, ready to rip and destroy, carrying not a doubt in his head. He'd come as a fool, in other words, and he'd be lucky to go away wiser. He'd killed one magician—one out of three, he thought, and there might be more within—and had to work hard, wearyingly hard to achieve that much; and now here came the retribution, the price, that sickly light flowing back at him along his own snared rope of water.

It reached him and entangled him just as the water had, just where the water still coiled about him. He broke the rope in his mind, but only where the light hadn't reached yet, behind him, where the water stretched back towards its pond. It drained or ran away and the light had nothing to follow, nowhere further to go. It couldn't run on down into the sewer system and poison all the water in Maras; so Issel saved the city, perhaps, that he had come to doom.

He had no time to save himself.

The water burned like ice, his definition of pain, but the light was numbing, dizzying, bewildering. He tried to break free of the water's grip and so lose the light also, but physically he couldn't do it, it clung now as if it really had melded with his skin, he couldn't batter it off. And his mind was swimming, which was a terror in itself, to Issel the same as drowning; he couldn't shrug off the water, he couldn't drive it away, he had no way to resist the light it carried.

This was the Shine, the real thing, pure and direct: no longer its distant scatter, rumour of a whisper of a war far-flung. This was here, in his hands. There had been other people's deaths, some he'd caused and some he'd been responsible for; those were not the same thing, but the bodies had felt the same, broken and abused and ghostless. He'd never thought to hold anything worse in his arms, and here it was.

Sickly-sweet like rancid honey, insidious and vile, it crept into his blood and into his brain till he thought his whole body must be glowing again, beating with the pulse of that alien light as it oozed around his system, all out of time with his heart or his thoughts or his fear. When he was wet and surrounded by water, his own magic made its own light, and that was disturbing but justified, an expression of himself. This came from outside, invasive and terrifying. He wanted to shriek, but it lulled him, soothed him almost, drained him of energy. He wondered if he was still standing, rigid and amazed, shining with this new appalling light; he thought probably not, probably he was on his knees at least, if not on his face by now, still and deathly in the grass and glowing like a dead thing, half begun to rot . . .

NOT for the first time, it was Rhoan who rescued him, who caught hold of him and dragged him back to the pain and wonder and bitter disappointment of the world. Not for the first time, it was Rhoan who paid the price of that.

It was her hands that he felt first. His water-sense had rooted him before; he'd cut himself free of that, and so been lost within the drift of light. Now she seized hold of him, her hands on his shoulders, and suddenly he was rooted again, through her. She was something else to cling to, another kind of solid. So long as she held him, he was aware again, feeling his body, inhabiting it.

Hearing her voice scream his name, right there into his ear. Trying to find some way to answer her, but he had no voice himself and he couldn't respond in kind, his touch for hers, because his hands were entirely enveloped with the water and the light that beat within the water, the Shine made manifest.

Her fingers slid down his arms, and he could sense her hesitation; he wanted to scream at her, not to be so stupid, but of course he had no voice. He barely had any awareness, still giddy and sick in a lurching world where everything was currents and flow, and only she was fixed.

He thought she was going to grip his hands where the water had them and so share his peril, lose herself and both of them in this tidal suck of light. Instead, her touch was abruptly gone, although she was still close. He felt that coolness that he'd always associated with her: a breeze over deep water, moonlight on a still pool, silver in the rain; all his sense of her was like that, visions of what was strong and unreachable, intangible, a shiver on the skin, irreducibly female.

This time she wasn't touching him or talking to him. She was holding her hands out over what was left of the water, what the light had seized, what was possessed now by the Shine, as he was himself. She was trying to take that water back, to possess it in her turn; she was trying to purify it, as she'd learned to do in the upper room in Sund.

The last time she'd done this, that too had been to save Issel from his own pride and folly. That time she'd been hurt, grievously hurt. Armina had helped her burned hands, but it had taken time even to start soothing her mind.

What she was doing now was resoundingly brave, and resoundingly stupid, and Issel could do nothing to stop her.

He understood the argument as if it were all laid out between them, as if they were actually arguing, face-to-face: *if I can turn the water*, she would be saying, *then that makes it ours again, because blessed water is magic to us, not to them, it's no part of their working.*

The coolness he could feel was her working on the water, where it glowed with the Shine, where it lay on his skin. Where it soaked his skin, he thought, and permeated it, and slipped through into blood and bone of him, worse than a lifetime of sleeping below the bridge. Maybe her working would do the same, maybe she'd turn everything that was wet within him; purify him, or else possess him utterly . . .

It was too late for one of those, and the other had happened already, with no magic needed. It wasn't himself that was in danger here, on either count.

He felt the touch of her working like a lingering caress, like a breath on wet skin, no more vigorous than that. He felt the moment when the water turned, and wondered what she and the others had seen. Usually it was a shift of light, a darkness and a sudden flare, but this water was infested with light already. He'd hoped to feel the Shine retreating, and the pure burn of blessed water on his skin; he'd hoped to scream with the pain of it and so know that he was safe.

Except that it wasn't his magic, he wasn't doing the working, he was the one being rescued here. The battle was happening only on his skin, where the water lay; when it turned, it turned away from him. He felt hands—cool hands, yes—back on his arms again, and this time sliding down over his wrists, to where he still had a grip of some kind on what must be still some kind of rope, that weave of water.

Not just that rope, but that and all the water on his body, all the water in his clothes were straining another way now. Rhoan had turned it: more, worse, she was drawing it deliberately to herself. Of course the light went with the water, she drew that too, she made herself a willing target. First to save Issel, that was clear; and then to strike if she could, to use that perfected water as a lash, to drive the magicians back into their sick-lit house and slam the door on them. She wasn't a killer, and she lacked Issel's raw strength in any case, but with the water fit to use, she must have thought she could achieve that much.

She didn't know what she was doing.

Issel neither, but he had a whole long history of that. Rhoan was cautious, sensible, trained to be wary; she'd recently been badly hurt and worse, scared, by a heedless adventure with tainted water; here she was blundering forward to tackle something far beyond her strength or understanding.

The light had dragged itself out of his body, out of his head, like riverweed ripped free by the tide: tender and clinging and savagely strong, tearing wherever it touched. Shreds of his mind went with the Shine as it sucked itself free, and much of his strength also, all of his water-strength. Still, his body was his own again; the dizziness was gone, and he knew that he was standing on wet grass, even if his roots were broken. A push would knock him over, but no one was pushing at him now.

Someone was keening, close by. With a monumental effort of will, Issel opened his eyes.

There were the magicians, in their doorway, in their haze of light; here was Rhoan twisting and stumbling on the grass, writhing was the best word he could think of, seized by that same rope she'd tried to snatch, pulsing with all the misshapen colours of the Shine. He had made it, they had snared it, she had tried to claim it back. He was seeing now the magnitude of her failure, a mirror to his own. It clung to her like an octopus to a post, enveloping her, enwrapping her, threatening to smother her, seemingly, with its greatest thickness pressed against her face.

But she had at least achieved something with the water, which gave her a grip on it, some kind of claim to counter theirs. He was ready to snatch it back, only to see her free of it. If that meant that it seized him again—well, he'd just have to see what he could do with the changes she had wrought. He was more powerful with perfected water, as they all were. Perhaps he could resist them now, perhaps he could even strike back . . .

If he could take that water-rope from Rhoan, and not hurt her in the doing of it. He reached for it and hesitated, not seeing how; and then blessedly he didn't need to do anything, because she did it all herself. Like a fraying cable—or, indeed, like riverweed—the gleaming water-stuff had entangled her in countless fronds, reductions of itself. Now her arms pulled free of them in one mighty wrench, and it was Issel who screamed, picturing the ruin of her, flesh and bone.

But her arms looked whole and healthy still, and it was the water-rope that was harmed, losing something of its shine. Issel blinked, and realised that he hadn't properly understood what it was she'd done. She'd pulled her arms straight out, *through* the mass that confined her, as though it was only water and not rope at all. Which it was, of course, if you could see that and remember it and make the water remember it too. Water with lights in it, lights that could make you forget anything, everything, they could make you only drift; but Rhoan wasn't drifting now. Nor writhing. Purposeful, determined, she lifted her hands to the core of that cable, where it embraced her head.

Even before she touched it, Issel thought it was losing definition, losing its grip of her, slumping into water. Her hands didn't so much jerk it free of her face, more caught it as it fell away. For a moment she stared at it, coldly raging; he watched the light in it retreat, halfway back to the magicians, and again he thought she was going to do something stupid. Something much as the same as he had done himself . . .

You're not a killer, Rhoan, remember that—and she did remember, seemingly, just in time, before she tried to be one after all. At any rate, she flung that end, the bitter end of his water-rope down to the grass, a distance from either one of them; and she was already looking round for him as he reached for her, grabbed her hand and started running.

On the way, one small, small whisper of his mind reached back to touch that rope as tentatively as he knew how, just to undo the weaving that he'd made and have all the length of it relapse into water again, to soak away into the earth before those magicians could pick it up and learn something, make something of it, become even more dangerous than they'd proved to be already.

———————

IT was a short run back to the pondside, to their friends. Young Teo was the most nervous, the least used to magic, the most disappointed. He hung in the shadows of a shrubbery, where no piercing eye from the pavilion could make him out; he said, "I must, I must get back to my mistress. I must tell her . . ." And then, "What? What should I tell her?"

"Say that I'm sorry," Issel gasped. In fact, it was barely true; as he said the words he felt more elation than sorrow, simply because he had survived and so had Rhoan. Especially Rhoan, she had survived and come out stronger, more aggressive, some little more restored. And still not a killer, still Rhoan. He thought all of that was a gain. And the bridge might still be standing, but one magician at least had died, so they weren't immortal; and something else had happened that was bizarre, impossible and yet true, and that was something to be thought about and talked over privately, with Rhoan alone, which was something else to be looked forward to, however shattering the impossible thing might be . . .

"Say that we'll try again," and that was Rhoan being forceful as she used to be, all gain, and so no doubt it was true, no doubt they would; but not as they had tried tonight, a full-frontal assault, one magic pitted against the other. That was hopeless. And besides, they had killed tonight; next time they would not find so easy an access.

Tell her that we'll try, by all means—but don't say how, because he didn't know.

And then Rhoan sagged at his side, dropped to her knees and vomited, a thin and sour bile; and he crouched beside her and wished he had something to offer, a handkerchief at least to wipe her mouth; and she turned her head to smile at him in lieu, because she knew, and for a moment there he thought the Shine was in her eyes, all loss.

Chapter Five

HERE were lights high on the hill, which had to be somewhere near the dreamers' pavilion, which meant that they had to be something to do with the Sundain. Jendre was no believer in coincidence.

And she had sent Teo to guide them there, when she couldn't go herself, which meant that he would still be up there somewhere in all that light and mystery. She was no believer in his common sense.

And she was anxious for him, and envious of him, because he could be there and she could not; and either one of those, both of them together were going to earn him a cuff on the ear or worse if he didn't come soon. She wanted to see him, she wanted to know him safe, but more than that—far more—she wanted news. One version of her life, one future was playing itself out up on the hill there, while the other version was here, was this: a narrow suite of rooms, a confinement, a distant useless view of anything that mattered.

She used to think that she was good at waiting; she'd had a lifetime's training and was an apt pupil in the art. It wasn't only Teo involved in this, though, it was Sidië's future and her own and her city's too, which meant Salem's too, and everyone's. Everyone she cared about, everyone she despised.

It occurred to her that those two lists were—well, no, not identical. Disturbingly similar, perhaps. Both short, and sharing too many names.

She had her reasons; almost everyone she loved, almost everyone she'd ever liked had conspired in some way to put her here, in this room, this situation, now.

SHE'D never felt so brutally boxed in. All her life, home had been the women's quarters in a man's house, behind locked doors; the one time she'd begged a room alone, apart, there had still been a guard at the foot of the stairs. Even so, she'd always had a way out. As a little girl, that had been literal, over the roofs and away from her father's house, to seek out disreputable friends and earn herself a beating; she wasn't having enough fun if she didn't feel sore afterwards.

When she was too much grown to be let run free that way, when too much of her father's future depended on his use of her, she had at least had gardens she could run in, increasing views of the world, people she could listen to and argue with and learn from.

Recently, married and widowed and no longer bound to any living man, she had had wider grounds and further views and hopes of something better, a dream of life beyond these walls, outside the city even, some kind of curtailed freedom.

Now all of that was gone, snatched away in one night's work. She had no idea what might follow, new dreams or greater hopes; all she knew was that tonight, when so much was going on within the palace and beyond—when there was rebellion in the city and rebellion against it, fighting in the streets and strange lights on the hill—tonight when she did so ache to be involved or at the very least informed, she had been haled back from her private pavilion to the harem proper; she had been sent with her slaves to the mean little suite she'd had before, and she'd been forbidden to leave it.

Herself and all the women of the old palace, she wasn't being singled out here. They were penned up in their separate rooms, and there were guards on every corridor to ensure that they stayed that way.

She had tried being haughty, she had tried being persuasive, she had even—to her shame—tried to flirt. These men had been implacable. She must leave her little house and all her little comforts, especially the privacy that it afforded; she must be just one more among the dead Sultan's leav-ings. With Salem gone, there was nothing now to distinguish her from any of the others. She barely saw the need to keep her name, let alone her dignity.

It was still full men that watched them, even here in the close-quartered heart of the harem. Jendre wasn't sure why, except that it made an absolute statement, that the old order was gone and a new rule come. No doubt this was how the army behaved in a newly taken town on the borders of the empire, seizing its women and keeping them for the generals to distribute. She should have been appalled, enraged to find herself treated like a captive, like a prize; but this invasion had overtaken the whole harem and there was enough rage elsewhere in the house, she could hear the choking fury of it, along with the screams and the sobs and the sheer terror that had gripped so many of her sisters.

Perhaps she too should have been afraid, but she couldn't manage that either. Not for herself. She was afraid for her future plans, and very afraid for Teo; that was another reason to stay calm. She wasn't allowed out but her slaves were, necessarily. Food and drink and dirty pots must be fetched and carried. As soon as the guard was used to seeing people come and go, Teo was confident that he could slip past any guards; the house was vast and complex, with many hidden ways into the gardens.

He had taken a used chamber pot and was gone, and she was—well, not alone, there was still Mirjana—but left behind. Worse, this was the best she could expect, that she send her boy out to have adventures, while she stayed quiet in her rooms to wait for news.

She had waited; she was afraid she had not been quiet. After a while Mirjana had gone into the other room and left her, saying that she had no answers to the questions Jendre kept asking, and that if Jendre wanted to pace holes in the tiled floor, she was welcome to do so, but it really didn't need an audience, and that if Mirjana had to watch it very much longer, there would probably be slapping.

For a moment there, the slapping might have gone either way. But Mir-jana left, and Jendre paced; and humiliatingly soon thereafter she stopped pacing and just sat down. As Mirjana was doubtless doing through the archway there, and they really ought to be doing it together, only neither one of them was going to give way now.

So she watched the lights through the window, and worried, and listened for any sounds that might bring her news: the noise of booted feet, the clank of weapons and armour being run up the hill, perhaps; or voices calling, conveniently telling her as they told each other what was going on. There was nothing, though, or nothing she could be sure of. Perhaps a cry on the wind, disturbing and meaningless, that might have been a scream if she'd been closer.

Noisy or not, there must be soldiers on the hill. That was just another cause for worry, in case they caught Teo, coming or going. If they caught him and the Sundain together, that would spell a cruel end for him and likely for her too. If they found him on the hill alone, she could depend on him to weasel and charm, to justify himself with outrageous lies. Then no doubt the guards would send him back to her with welts and bruises, which Mirjana would treat with soothing lotions and a hard hand, which would be a touch of normality to end a monstrous, a monumental and unforgiving day . . .

———————

THERE were steps in the corridor, a word to the guards, a hand on the door and a figure in the frame.

Not Teo.

Not Teo but next-best, in a world where she could not have Salem, nor her sister.

A small, small figure in the frame, who walked with a hobble as though he limped on both legs at once, and with a swagger as though he did not care; who wore a gaudy hat with a peacock's feather in it, purely in order to doff it in a low and ridiculous bow.

"Oh, Djago—what will you bring me? News?"

"Nothing for your comfort, I fear, my lady," but he had brought it anyway. He was an honest man, if not a whole one; whatever his reason for coming here, he would pay the reckoning in any coin he had. And if there was one person in this palace with coin worth the having, that would be Djago the dwarf.

Whatever he had—and however uncomfortable it might make her—it was not word of Teo. That was clear in the way that he conspicuously didn't look around the room even once to confirm that she was alone; in the way that he absolutely did not ask after missing company; in the way that his eyes did move despite himself to the figure in the inner doorway, but his face said that he knew Mirjana before he found her.

He had come here looking for Teo, then, or at least expecting to find him. He was disappointed, anxious, not at all surprised.

"This is not a night to be comfortable." But there was no reason why they shouldn't make a pretence at it. Mirjana's proper duties did not include serving a eunuch slave as though he were a free man, but she did so gracefully, with every show of willing welcome: fetching extra cushions to raise him eye to eye with Jendre on the divan, bringing a jug of cool green tea and a plate of cakes, offering his choice of smoke if he should care to do that.

Blessedly, he didn't. "There are ways and ways," he said, "to beguile the night and its long watches. Smoke is one, and the companionship of generous ladies"—he included Mirjana, with a gesture that said *sit, drink, eat with us*, and she did, without a glance at her mistress—"is another, and it is always a mistake to mix them. Unless the ladies want to smoke . . . ?"

Jendre's mother did smoke, which was perhaps why Jendre never had. She shook her head; what she wanted was the news he had and was not telling.

"That is just as well, perhaps. There is too much smoke in the city tonight. And too much gossip, which is smoke too, because it hides the truth. Bad enough when it is honest: honest gossip, *khola*-smoke, sweet and silly; worse when it smells of wet and darkness and you can't tell where it's been. People are dying tonight, because the smoke misleads them."

Jendre was beginning to understand, she thought, why Djago was here. He had come seeking reassurance, and now he meant to stay until he found it, or at least until Teo came back and brought it with him. And the dwarf wasn't going to admit it, certainly wasn't going to ask where the boy had gone—they had their own odd ways of being, both together and apart—and would sooner spend all the good coin that he had, to justify his staying.

SO they sat and talked, and tried to waft the smoke aside to see through to the heart of the fire: how the pasha had the army at his back, and the wazir had the city well in hand; how any trouble that couldn't be bought off was being crushed, unless that was the other way around; how there had been a dark and unhappy scuttle from the New Palace to the sepulchre of the

Abeyids, not only a dead Sultan to be carried quickly and in shame to his last home but others too, some at least of his nephews. One must be kept for the crown, more kept in reserve; some she supposed were deemed too dangerous, too stubborn, too wilful to live. It was a hard thing, to ensure a tractable sultan.

Somewhere in this house, then, there were mothers who would learn in the morning that their sons were dead, that they were not and never would be Valide Sultan and the empire's hidden queen. Somewhere there would be one mother who would learn the opposite. It was a night to be glad, Jendre thought, not to have children.

"What would happen to me now," she asked quietly, "if His Magnificence had made me pregnant?"

Djago shot her a glance. Mirjana hissed under her breath. At least she could still surprise people, even on such a night.

"Did he?"

"No."

"Be glad. If he had, if it were known—well, a wise girl now would be praying for a daughter. Praying alone, in a dark cell somewhere with a guard on the door. A late daughter of a great father would be merchantable, worth keeping. A son, child of his last favourite—no. Neither the boy nor the mother would survive the birth."

Ah, they were all speaking plainly tonight. Why not, when the city burned and children died? There was nothing more that Maras had to hide, except the bodies.

Out of the barred window, the sky burned—but that view was away from the city, over the pleasure gardens and the park, sights even a widow was allowed. That wasn't flame-light, it was the strange shifting lights of the dreamers' pavilion, brighter and more intense and blazing like a beacon.

"Master Djago, what is happening up there?"

"Lady, I cannot say. Nor can any man in the palace. They have sent soldiers to discover, I know that much. Given where those lights are coming from, I don't believe that anyone knows more."

He was wrong, for once. She did; and Teo by now should know more than she. If Teo was uncaught, unhurt, alive . . .

That was victory or defeat, that play of lights, and she couldn't guess which.

She ought to tell Djago, but what could she say? That she had sent Teo out to cause this, and the boy had not come back? Not come back yet, that *yet* was important, but it wasn't enough . . .

She was on the verge, the very edge of confession when there was no need for it because the door opened abruptly, and the boy tumbled in.

He watched his heels anxiously, against the guard in the corridor; he looked around to find Jendre, with all the news from the hill bubbling up visibly inside him, ready to spill; he found Djago, and was utterly and immediately voiceless.

Entirely the discreet and dainty eunuch, he bowed to his mistress, he bowed to her guest. He'd have bowed to Mirjana too, Jendre thought, if he could've got away with it. Instead he took the jug from where she sat and carried it around to refill their cups, Djago's and Jendre's and Mirjana's too, for all the world as though he had no other duties here.

When Mirjana rose and went to the window, to close the shutters on the night, Jendre said, "Don't do that. I don't know what those lights are, but . . ."

"Lady," Mirjana said, "they've died."

"Oh. Have they?" So tangled up in the threads—no, the cables—of tension in the room, she hadn't noticed.

"I saw them dying," Teo said, softly and respectfully from the corner.

"Did you?"

He nodded. "And I saw them flare, at the beginning."

What were you doing there, boy? It was surely hers to ask, but of course she couldn't do that; which Djago surely knew, which was why he found an alternative.

"Tell us what you saw."

That was an invitation, and Teo took full advantage. He made a story of it, in the way that the street-tellers did, sitting neatly folded and erect on his rug and letting his voice slip into a half-chant that was first attractive and then seductive and ultimately bewitching, cozening, fit to steal time and coins both.

He told of seeing a figure in the night, a man who shone with a liquid light and wove a rope of water. He told of the magicians standing in their doorway and fighting the water with their own light, light like the bridge, smoky and halfway to looking solid, like molten coloured glass. Even at his distance, he said, hiding in the shrubbery, just the least touch of that light had left him feeling strange, losing his grip on the world and his own story.

It all sounded fantastical, invented, like a story on the street, like any one of Teo's elaborated fables. Especially that shining man: Jendre would have dismissed him out of hand, except that he came entire with the rest of it. And she had been inside that pavilion herself, she knew how the light was a drug into a kind of sick enchanted sleep.

And she had seen, they had all seen that light flare above the hill tonight; and of course she knew the story that he was so carefully not telling, how he had guided the Sundain water-mage and his companions up the hill to the pavilion.

So she did believe him, every word of it; and she wasn't at all surprised by the sudden eruption of another figure into the tale, a woman who went to save the mage when the light seemed to have snared him. And Teo told how they fled thereafter, to that pool below the belvedere where she had kept watch before; and how the Sundain—though he was careful not to name them, to let Djago infer it from their use of water-magic—one by one disappeared into a drain.

Teo had lingered, to watch the magicians. Their light still burned, broad and wide like a shelter around the pavilion. Then soldiers had come, and he'd slithered away before they started poking about for trouble. He'd been almost back to the harem, still looking over his shoulder, before he saw the light die down.

THE Sundain had failed, then. Jendre felt it as a burning disappointment, but really not a surprise. This was her life now, to meet hope unexpectedly, then to lose it too soon. Sorcerers from the belly of the earth, with a great and impossible promise: she ought never to have believed it.

The pasha's uprising, though, she had no choice but to believe in that. There was a guard outside her door, to guarantee her faith. Dare she hope for a little kindness, in the pasha or in her father who stood so close beside him? She had lost Salem, but there was still Sidië . . .

"If," she said hesitantly into the silence that followed Teo's story, "if the old order is so changed, if the pasha has charge now of who sits the throne, then there is not so great a need to give a hostage to the Sultan. Is there?"

If there had been silence before, it was a weak and pallid foretaste. This was something rich and dark and dangerous, silence like nightfall against the closing of a shutter.

Djago was the one among them brave enough to break it, wise enough to find a way. "I think," he said, "that the Sultan must be his own hostage, for a while now," which was just exactly what Jendre had meant, what she had hoped to hear. "But," Djago went on, "there will still be a need for the bridge."

And so for dreamers, children; and *why change these for others?* he was saying, *why ruin others' lives as well as yours?*

Because she is my sister! was the only possible response, and not enough. Jendre knew that; she had always known that. The words were on her tongue in any case. With her father risen and apparently still rising, he could surely use that influence to see one child, his own daughter, saved . . . ?

"The pasha also has a child with the dreamers," Djago went on, as though he read her thoughts in her face. No doubt he did; it couldn't be hard, when she was so distressed. "So do all the men about him. If he freed them all, the bridge would crumble."

And with the bridge, the state—that was manifest. No man could retreat from Sund and hope to keep the government of Maras.

This was it, then. She must be what she was, the Sultan's widow: fatherless, sisterless. Loverless. Alone, in every way that mattered.

Perhaps, she thought, the heart would prove to be like hide: the more you beat it, the tougher it became. Perhaps she wouldn't always feel so raw or bleed so freely. She didn't hope to heal, exactly, but scar tissue was strong stuff; and she'd lost so much, she thought there was little more that could be ripped away from her now. This last thing, being what she was, the Sultan's widow, no one could take that from her; and so she had this at least, this suite of rooms, these servants, something to hold on to . . .

———

DJAGO left at some point. Teo stayed—which surprised her rather, pleased her rather more—and eventually, towards dawn, Mirjana bullied her into bed.

She did sleep, which was another surprise, to be discovered on waking. It might have been pleasant, a languorous late rising, one of those times that are sheer slow physicality, all body and no mind at all. She thought she was entitled to that. It wasn't late yet, though, the grey light in the room there said so, as did the low sun and long shadows outside, as did the ache in her bones and the ache in her head; and she was being shaken into the unready morning all unready in herself.

She tried to slap those shaking hands away, and found her wrists caught and held like a naughty girl's. If she'd been anything better than half-awake, she'd have met that with a volley of abuse, her wrath transmuted into pure molten words. In this condition, though, her fury only choked her; which gave Mirjana the chance to say, "Jendre, stop this! You need to be up and dressing, and I need to have you thinking while you do it."

"Wha—? Why? Give me my hands back . . ."

"If you've stopped hitting out."

"Yes, yes." It was true, she had now. Mirjana let go, and Jendre sulkily pulled the bedcovers back up to her shoulders. "Why do I need to be dressed?" There were monumental matters afoot in the city, to be sure, but they hardly affected her. Whatever they did out there beyond the wall, whoever rose or fell or faltered, in here she was secure.

Or should be. Though the Valide Sultan had thought that, no doubt, until men had come and taught her differently, in the circle of a string.

Not till she was out from under the covers and getting dressed did Mirjana condescend to answer her question, why she needed to. And then it was an answer with no heart to it, a brick without straw. She said, "The women of the house—and yes, my sweet, that does mean you, and all your sisters: wives and concubines and slaves, all your great husband's choices for his womenfolk—are ordered to be ready, to be seen."

The frown that came to Jendre's face was magnificent, she could feel it, pure widow, woman of the Man of Men; she said, "Ordered? By whom? If there are any men in Maras who can order me in such a manner, I am not aware of it." She was meant to be divorced from such demands, wasn't she? Her man was dead, who could have sent such a message. That death gave her a place here and a position that could not be usurped or challenged. Widowhood was a most certain state; it had that much to be said for it.

"The order comes from the pasha, sweet."

"Oh." That would make it hard to resist. The pasha had come here himself, and seen death done, and left his men behind him; if there were any niceties surviving in this new world, he had small regard for them. Even so, "And by whom are we to be seen, in this so-gratifying order? Will he come here himself, to cast the grace of his gaze upon us?" *And why would he do that, why would he ever want to, it runs so hard against everything he has ever stood for or believed in or supported; he is a man of the old world, my husband's man, why should he want to trespass now . . . ?*

"That I do not know. It is not said. But, Jendre"—and Mirjana was utterly in earnest, catching her mistress's face between her palms to be sure of her, speaking close and eye to eye—"be careful, yes? Tread lightly here. We walk on glass."

"We walk on broken glass," she said, and was surprised by the bitterness in her voice, in herself. She had not thought to find herself so sour.

BUT she dressed, and ate, and waited; and at last there were eunuchs in the corridor calling her out, and she came, as did other women from their rooms; and they stood confused in their doorways, seeing eunuchs and men too, men with swords, and not understanding what had happened or what was due, until the pasha came with a small party and cried out, "Here is His Magnificence, the Sultan Mehmet VII!"

And then it was easy to know what to do, and Jendre did it: she dropped neatly onto her knees, and lowered her gaze, and thought that her husband had never needed anyone to announce his magnificence, it had been a burden that he carried in and of himself.

But then, he had been magnificent for fifty years; and here was a boy trying to step not only into his clothes but those of his brother too, who had been fat and mad; and small wonder if he needed some protection, some shoring up against those two reputations. Just a boy . . .

Just a boy who had been held in the *Kafes* himself all these years, since his circumcision: who should have known both his father and his uncle, who had grown up in their successive shadows, who might yet be as great as one or as mad as the other, but for now was only a pair of legs come to stand before her. They were good legs, she thought; he was at least a boy her own age, the best part of a man. The pasha hadn't chosen to keep a child alive and slay all the rest.

And then he was a pair of legs and a hand, fingers beneath her chin to lift her face to the light; and then necessarily he was a face too, an entirety even, with a smooth and chubby face that was like his late uncle's, little marked by life. Less marked by the sun, after years in the Cage: his skin was pale and slightly sticky-looking, like unbaked pastry.

Only his eyes were sharp. She thought they glittered, with a hawk's hunger.

His voice was like his skin, soft and rounded, as if it had hardly been used. He said, "This one too, she is lovely. I will have her too, uncle Pasha."

And the pasha, who was not his uncle but whom she had thought her friend, listened and nodded and made a note, and by the time she understood anything it was too late, they had gone and she was left with the men and their strong hands to take her.

Part 3

Chapter One

H E can't! He *cannot* do this! I, I was his father's *wife . . . !*"

That seemed not to matter anymore, in this new dispensation. His young Magnificence had emerged from the *Kafes* to find his harem all but empty, while the abandoned palace on the nearest hill was filled with women. That they had formerly belonged to his father meant nothing. Nor did the tradition that they should be left to mourn their late lord in solitary woe, in a palace as empty as a mausoleum.

He had come, he had looked, he had chosen. His picks—slaves more often than concubines, and Jendre the only wife—were the young, the slender, the girlish; he still had a boy's tastes, evidently.

And a boy's heedless vulgarity, to do this thing at all, when it outraged all decency; but at least he didn't have a boy's needless cruelty. She was allowed to take her people with her.

She almost felt cruel herself, to take Teo. But he said nothing, and Djago likewise, and what else could she do? The boy could have no position outside her household; Djago's adoption of him was hardly official, and carried no weight. She wouldn't have let that friendship develop so far, if she'd known they'd be leaving like this. She'd thought they were here forever, and she'd been wrong. Again.

They called this the Palace of Tears, but if Teo wept he did it privately, internally, with not a sign to show. Herself, she was nowhere near weeping; she was raging. And had just sense enough to understand that this was absolutely not the time for temper. When the outburst did come, as it must, at least it came in a whisper, and only to Mirjana.

Who looked at her, as calm as she always was, and said, "Are you not the one who complained because you did not want to spend the rest of your life being your husband's widow and locked in here to lament him?"

"Yes, of course I am. But that's different, that's not—"

"Jendre, it is exactly the same thing. This was a life you did not want or deserve. Now you have another. It may not be so different; one harem is much like the next. You know this."

She did—she had gone from one to another to another again; but she'd never thought to retrace her steps. "This is not a proper harem, such as a man builds around himself. To pick, what, a hundred women from his father's house . . ."

"Softly, softly! I did not say that one man was like another. This is a boy, a pretty puppet to sit on the throne and own the name of Sultan, and run to play in his gardens. His masters will not care what he does there; they have the empire beyond the wall. The boy-Sultan wants toys to play with, and he has chosen you. And all these others"—with a glance around—"because he sees no reason not to take as many as his fancy falls upon. There is no reason; who could give him one? Why would anyone be troubled? They keep you here, or they keep you there. No difference.

"So his garden will have pretty flowers in it, who will flatter His Magnificence and help him forget that he matters not at all in the world, that what keeps him on the throne and out of the sepulchre is exactly the width of a bowstring."

This was deadly talk, and Jendre should have shushed her direly; their own lives were no broader than that bowstring if anyone heard, if anyone passed on what they'd heard. But Mirjana was speaking in a low murmur close to her ear, and Jendre wanted to hear this. Perhaps she needed to. Mirjana always had an instinct for what she needed, which was often and often not at all what she wanted. This time, though, the churning fury in her gut craved a palliative, and Mirjana was offering exactly that, and she was grateful.

"What else comes, we cannot know. I am not saying you should be pleased to be chosen—rather, I think you should be extremely careful—but if you must complain, at least complain honestly. If he only takes you from one palace and leaves you in another, with not so many women as there were before, then perhaps you should not complain at all."

"Wait and see, you mean."

Mirjana smiled and nodded, as though to encourage a slow pupil who has finally, grindingly produced a proper answer. Jendre sighed, and squeezed the older woman's hand; and then she shuffled her feet and gazed about her and waited for the gate to open.

THEY were standing in the small bare court behind the palace gate, over-looked by walls and janizars: the boy-Sultan's pick of his father's women, with a scatter of servants—those who had them, those who had been anything more than slaves themselves—but nothing else, no bags, no property. Jendre had asked about her things, and been told only that she would not need them. Not need her clothes, her jewels, her private precious mementoes? That was fuel to her flaring anger, but only if she let it be.

There were too many women squeezed into too small a space, and most were crushed uncomfortably close. There was nevertheless a space that made itself around Jendre. It wasn't the sharp elbows of her friends that had caused that to happen, or not that alone. It was in herself, her status, the only wife selected. She thought it was pity, more than respect or envy, that kept the other women distant. If there were degrees of freedom, she had known more than they had, concubines and slaves; here in this courtyard, all at the whim of a boy, they were suddenly equal. The others were not new to this, to any of this, the abrupt uprooting and the fog of what was to come; she was the one who had fallen, fast and far.

When the gate swung open, she was no more ready for it than any of these anxious, clustering women, but she was perhaps the most grateful, simply to be moving on.

What waited them outside the gate was not the long parade that had brought them here, on foot behind their master's body. They were spared another walk under the eyes of a curious, salacious city with its own fears today, its own reasons to spy from windows and spread news in whispers: *the women, he's taking the women from the Palace of Tears, his father's women, he's taking them . . .*

Instead there were covered carts waiting in a line. Ox carts, and oh, she could have bridled then, she could have risen up in passion and refused. But none of that would have helped at all; she had been chosen, by His Magnificence himself, and one way or another she would be taken.

So she submitted, gracelessly, angry again; and made a point of helping Mirjana and Teo up onto the wagon bed, not to seem demeaned by this treatment. She wouldn't give anyone the satisfaction: not the Sultan who had ordered this, nor his eunuchs who had planned it, nor these men who came now to enforce it. If they noticed her at all—and they should, she could hardly help but stand out in her dress among these others, a butterfly in the roses—then they might see her anger, but they should not see her flinch.

––––––––––

MAKE a virtue of necessity: that was a lesson well learned, in the harems of Maras. There was nowhere to sit in the wagon, so she sat on the floor; there was no other company to sit among, so she sat with the slaves. There was no room to sit apart, so they were all crowded together, barely room enough to sit at all. Her hips were wedged tight against Mirjana's on the one hand and Teo's on the other, her feet were poking some other girl's bottom, and her own was being poked in its turn.

All of this fed her rage, but it was a tutored anger; she flung it all unseen and scornful in His Magnificence's face. No matter if he neither knew nor cared. She could still make a sacrifice of this debasement; she could endure it proudly, wilfully. She had already chosen to be angry rather than humiliated. Now she would choose to make herself easy company, to draw no distinction between herself and those she travelled with.

The girl in front of her, whose bottom she was poking with her slippers: she poked her back as well, with a gentle fingertip.

That won her a twitch of the shoulder-blade, no more.

She tried again, a little harder, a little more deliberate.

This time the girl turned round. She was darkly pretty, with startling green eyes: from some conquered northern city at a guess, sent as tribute or a gift to the Sultan, or else given as a bribe to some imperial official who had had the sense to use her in buying favour for himself, passing her on and up until at last she'd ended here, like all of them, one step further on than she could ever have imagined, one step in the dark.

"My name's Jendre."

That won her a stare, and no response else. The stare was enough: it said *I know that, of course I do*, and *what do you want of me?*

Even unvoiced, it was a good question. Perhaps she wanted friendship, perhaps only kindness. She said, "What's yours?"

She might as well have said, *please, talk to me, I'm desperate here.*

They were all desperate; it was only that for some of these women, most of them, that desperation was commonplace. They had lived with it for years, some for decades; they knew its taste and savour, they knew the weight of it and the sting of it, they knew how it was sometimes a sourness in the throat and sometimes a whip against the skin. Sometimes a hunger in the belly, always a burden to be carried, a fact to be lived with. They knew. Her own people, Mirjana and Teo, they knew. Jendre was still learning.

The girl said, "I am called Felice," and that might have been a name she had brought with her or it might have been given to her at any time in her captivity; there was no way to tell, no way to ask.

Jendre said, "These are Teo and Mirjana, my friends," and her luggage, all that she had been let bring; and at that she was luckier than Felice, and ought perhaps not to be drawing attention to it. Salt in a wound, it might be. Or it might be just a shrug, a nothing, the inevitability of rank. She was trying to deny that, to evade it; she carried it with her in her every gesture, her voice, every little detail of her life.

"Was it His Magnificence who selected you too?" Perhaps he had only deigned to grace the widows with his personal regard. Even the question gave her away, though, she realised too late; she was trying to be friendly and only sounded superior.

"Of course. We are what he wanted." His indulgence, his pretties. "He said I was lovely, when he looked at me."

He had said the same of Jendre. It was clearly his word for beauty, the one he used, the only one he needed.

Felice was doing what Jendre was trying to do, what the Sultan had done, drawing no distinction between them; they were all in the same wagon, all selected by the same eye, the same hand, the same word.

Jendre said, "Please, Felice," *give me a little kindness, a little grace, your favour,* "you will know the harem better than I do; I hardly came there, what little time I was married to His Magnificence." She had known the corridors, full of women, full of eyes; the Sultan's apartments, full of shadow and mystery and wonder. Just the once. Otherwise, she had kept—or been kept—in her own place, apart. "No more did Teo or Mirjana." That was absolutely not true. Mirjana would have found out quickly where to look for whatever was needful, and Teo had been everywhere like a rat in the cellars, like a boy. "Will you help us to find our way about?"

Felice blinked slowly, and said, "You will learn. Quickly, I think."

And then she turned her head away, and said something in a rapid undertone to another woman. Jendre couldn't make out the words.

Nor could she make out if she'd been snubbed or complimented, if Felice was sympathetic or indifferent or dismissive.

Well. No doubt she'd learn. Quickly, as Felice suggested, would seem to be a good idea.

———————

THE wagon jarred and rattled over cobbles, swayed and lurched, tipped unpredictably when wheel-rims met broken roadway. Wedged as they were, the women still rocked and slid, and shrieked, and clutched each other; Jendre felt someone's hand seize her arm, nails digging in. Before she could pull free or reach around to offer better support, before she could even decide which to do, she heard a sudden yelp and the hand was gone. *Teo.* She might have turned one way to apologise for him, or the other to remonstrate with him; again she was undecided, and the wagon lurched again, they all slid and grabbed again, and the moment was past. It was like shuffling stones in a bag; she had no idea whether the same woman was still behind her now. She was only sure of her own people because she was holding on to Mirjana, which she hadn't realised, and Teo was holding on to her.

The Sultan—no, better, the wazir, Hedin's father—should be made to travel this way, say once a year, to help him understand the city's state of repair. Not that he would have the budget to make improvements to the roads. A new sultan was always a drain on the treasury, and the boy Mehmet was the second in far too short a time. Installed by violence, too, that had to be expensive. There would be so many bribes to pay, to ensure the loyalty of generals and janizars; so many spies and informers to be hired or bought, to keep watch on how that loyalty worked out. He—or his guardians and protectors, the pasha and his cohorts—would be lucky to find loose coin enough to see them through the month. She foresaw wagon-loads of imperial treasures leaving the palace, to be melted down or sold.

And this, this wagon-load of imperial treasures heading to the palace, this train of wagons with their pretty perfumed cargoes? She supposed they were an easy way to keep the boy amused. If he were penned within the harem walls, then he was safe and controllable. And cheap.

If she had been more closely caged, if she had spent years locked in the *Kafes*, she thought she would never want to eat or sleep or sit within four walls again. She thought she would run from guards and barred gates and weapons drawn; she would demand swift horses and open plains, high mountains, oceans, wide views and far horizons. A boat, perhaps; a tent might be better. A cabin was too much like a cell, she'd have to sleep on deck and sit out in the rain. A tent would definitely be better, somewhere with walls she could cut through if the mood came on her, where she could have a different world to wake to every day.

Even as she was, less a prisoner than the Sultan had ever been, she thought she'd like a tent.

She had this canvas hood, a wooden floor, the movement that she dreamed of—but not for long. Down one hill and up another. She couldn't see, but she could feel their progress, she could map it in her mind, back and forth the winding ways that led wheeled traffic through the city.

Winding and watchable, protected. There was precious little noise out there; she fancied all of Maras keeping terribly still, crouched like a mouse between the cat's paws. There would be no markets today. People would stay within-doors, with their shutters closed and their doors barred even to their friends. How reliable was friendship, at a time like this? There would be soldiers on every corner, and distrust at every table. Perhaps it was a good day to be a woman, to make one short and guarded journey and be walled up again . . .

If she were Sultan, she thought she'd ride to war, sooner than live sheltered within walls. But then, this Sultan—she thought he'd not be allowed the choice. That would be a trouble for kingmakers, they would need to keep their king secure for their own heads' sakes. Only let him fall outside the city, beyond their control, and who knew how many rivals might arise? Few could actually sit the throne, but there were many who'd like to be kingmaker in their turn, to set one child or another there and stand behind him with an empire to beckon.

Any empire might fracture, under such conditions. She thought this one might fly apart. Too many generals, too many cities; too many armies, too many miles apart. She thought the pasha had taken an extraordinary risk already, to depose one sultan and install another. He wouldn't chance his luck further. He'd keep his young Sultan close, by any means he had to hand.

Herself included, evidently. She should be a garden ornament to a lonely, imperious boy, for as long as he should want her; and then what . . . ?

No, it was unbearable. It was not possible, to live such a life. She would not.

They arrived, and the boom of the gates and the slam of their bars behind the wagon were trumps of doom but too late, too slow; she had already decided not to let them pen her in. The Sultan could submit if he chose to, if he understood how he was to be kept in bounds. She would not.

Time passed, and they stayed where they were, where they sat, on the bed of the wagon. No one came. Hot sun bit down on the canvas; there was no shade, and the air grew thick and wet and rank, as her throat grew dry. None of them had thought to bring water. There were a few pieces of fruit, found in pockets and shared between friends; none for Jendre. Mirjana whispered an apology, but she shook it away with a glower. She might have thought of it herself, and hadn't; they were none of them used to saving food against the risk of going hungry. It might prove to be a lesson worth the learning.

At last, there was a tug at the ties of the canvas. The rope pulled free, the flap opened, there was a waft of clean breeze, cool on sweating skins, and a collective gasp, a communal snatching at it. Jendre joined that, she couldn't help it. However reluctantly, they were all sisters here, and they would choke each other for the air they breathed.

Someone let down the tail of the wagon and a voice called the women out.

It was so unlike the other times she had been brought here—and yet, it was so very similar. She sat in gloom, and was called out into sunlight. Previously she had been alone, stepping the first time from a palanquin in glory and the second from a pinch-box in shame; this time she was one in a crowd that hustled and hesitated, flinched back and started forward like a brood-flock of fowls, that needed one to start them, then went all together. If she had a mood, it was too complex to pin down with a word. She simply went when the others did, an awkward slither down from the wagon bed and onto cobbles.

Where a handful of palace eunuchs waited for them, and of course Feres was one, wasn't he always? He was the constant star that determined her course in this palace: always there to greet her—in glory or in shame, or in this more confusing state today—and direct her, to comfort or punishment or purpose.

Previously, she had been the new wife arriving or the runaway returned, and his having the voice that called her and the face that met her was an expression of her status, but also of his. This time, she was one in a hundred women debouching from wagons and clustering together. This again was an expression of status, new to her; perhaps, by his face—drawn and hungry-looking, tight-lipped and anxious—it was new to him too. A falling-off, out of his master's favour: a lesser place, herding servants where once he had instructed wives. Perhaps he was lucky to have this. Jendre had always thought he was the Valide Sultan's creature; she was dead, and he might well have expected the same. Two throats, and but a single bowstring.

He had survived that night, at whatever cost to dignity or office; and he did herd them, with great sweeping gestures that set his sleeves to flapping. It was another eunuch who led them through narrow ways to a courtyard behind the great harem. Here was a sprawl of out-buildings, the kitchens and the laundry; here too were memories for Jendre, bright and potent pictures, a day of death and sorrow.

She was not afflicted by ghosts, but she was very much by doubts and questions; she let her footsteps drag, so that other women hustled past her. Teo was holding her hand; when he tugged at her, *don't dawdle*, she tugged back. A meaningful glance, a twitch of her head, and he scuttled forward to keep pace with Mirjana.

Soon Jendre was last in the pack, the one Feres was flapping his sleeves at. She dawdled that little bit slower yet, and there he was at her side.

"Jendre. I am sorry to see you here."

That was blunt, at least. It was the first time he had ever called her by her name alone, which must mean something, but was hardly the sign of pleasure she had looked for. They had not been friends, and certainly not allies, nor co-conspirators either; opponents, rather, when they had engaged at all. Opponents across the chessboard, though, where mutual respect and the satisfaction of a challenge laid and met can breed a form of liking . . .

"Feres." If he would not use honorifics, nor would she. "If that's true, then I am sorry also. I had hoped to find"—well, what? She couldn't lie to him, he saw clean through her—"a welcome." That, at least, from one player to another.

"And I wish that I could give you one. But in these circumstances . . ."

"Oh, but what circumstances are those? Feres, you have lost your old master and your new. If you have to be lowly for a while, you can do that. You will rise again; and I see no reason for you not to welcome an old friend." She could say that, so long as she was saying it with irony. "I hope you still have that chess set that I gave you?" It was tradeable goods; he might have traded it himself. If so, no matter. They could make shift with perfume-bottles on a mosaic floor, though she was fairly certain that would not be necessary. Feres might have fallen, but not that far. He was too clever a man, too consummate a politician.

He said, "Jendre, my dear,"—and that was new too, a stretch too far; she didn't like this at all—"it is not my circumstances that are troubling me."

He looked shrivelled, bent in body and spirit too, as though he lived under a burden of fear, and she thought his circumstances troubled him a great deal. He was old, he had lived his life in the harem; it must outrage him, to see the boy-Sultan bring so many of his father's women back. Perhaps that was all he meant, that he saw how she had been demeaned and was resentful for her.

She had almost forgotten to be angry for herself, in all the shake and flurry of the journey. She might try being grateful, for having found someone else prepared to do so on her behalf.

She smiled at him, both to thank and to reassure, *don't be troubled on my account*—and then had to hurry forward, to where a sudden hallway opened to let all the women group together, to take away her chance of being private at the tail of a queue.

Narrow corridors branched from the hallway, with a dozen doors opening off each. Jendre stole a glimpse through the nearest open door: a bare cell with a pallet on the floor, a chest, a bowl and ewer, little more. Slave quarters, unadorned; and being fetched in here with so little, these women would have a hard time buying or bargaining for those little trinkets and cheap luxuries that should furnish their lives.

They were being told off, two to a cell. Jendre waited to be fetched away with her friends, no doubt when these other women were all settled, to be shown where she was to live now. Not the separate quarters she'd had before, that was certain; not the wives' quarters at the top of the house, because she was not a wife here; so where . . . ?

Doubt blossomed into realisation, sharp and stinging. She spun around, words rising like bile in her throat, burning and incoherent. "Feres, no! You dare not—!"

The ageing eunuch took a step back from her fury, spread his hands and said, "Jendre, I have said that I am sorry. It is not I who dares, it is not any of us here. The choice lay with His Magnificence. We are all his creatures now."

That boy, that pale chubby nothing? She seethed, and would have spat if not for Mirjana's sudden hold on her arm. She was a general's daughter and a sultan's widow; she would be no one's creature, and least of all—

Mirjana or no Mirjana, she might have spelled out then just what she thought of His young Magnificence, at great peril to herself and those she loved; but just in time she saw how Feres had his own grip on Teo's elbow, how he was drawing the boy away. How Teo looked suddenly terrified, and yet went in obedience to that light touch, that demanding gesture.

"No! You cannot have him, he is mine!"

"No longer, Jendre, I regret. None of these can be yours now. You have nothing, beyond what your master will allow. This boy will be taken into the household, as I was myself; you need not be concerned for him."

Save your concern for yourself was the implication, but she could not do that, not yet. "Teo . . ."

He said nothing, he only looked at her, and he had his face schooled to obedience now, as his body was, a stranger would read nothing from it—but she was no stranger, and to her he seemed desolate, bereft, unbearably alone.

And afraid, as though he knew good reasons why he should be. And it was her own fault entirely, her own selfishness that had brought him here. She could have left him behind with Djago, where he was happy.

Feres was leading him away already, she had only this one last moment; she called to him rapidly, "Teo, as soon as you can, find your little friend from the woods, the water-rat—he'll show you where to go . . ."

He'll show you a way out of here, she meant, *a sewer under the wall.* And what then? She had no voice in that now. Perhaps he'd find his way back to Djago and be happy again. She could hope.

He gave no sign of understanding her. The slump in his shoulders said he was defeated already, resigned and broken. *Nothing survives Maras*, she thought bitterly. Not even her giggling, resilient, ever-talking boy . . .

And then there was herself, now there was herself in this new understanding, and nothing to shield her anymore as waves of rage and misery rolled over her. She did what she could, all she could do: she seized Mirjana's hand in both of hers and hung on grimly, utterly determined that whatever else happened between now and the end of the world, no one was going to take this woman away from her.

<h1>Chapter Two</h1>

THERE was a dead man in the water.

It was no one's fault, just a thing that had happened, and no one else seemed to care, but to Issel it was a taint in the water and a taint on his soul.

The body was far out of sight now, but he felt it still, like a touch of Shine running all through the system, upstream and down. It made sense to see it as one more of the Shine's perversions, because the dead man had been a dogtooth too.

He'd been far gone, further than Baris, almost demented; and he'd blundered into them on their way back to the precarious safety of their bolt-hole.

Shaken as they were, perhaps none of them was taking care enough. For sure Issel wasn't paying attention to anything, anyone beyond Rhoan. He'd wanted to carry her back, and she wouldn't let him. Then he wanted to walk with her, side by side, himself between her and the water, but there wasn't room on the path. Nor any point, to be fair—as she pointed out to him, with a thin savagery that wasn't fair at all—because their first cramped slither down through the overflow drain had left them all equally wet and equally vulnerable.

So he'd been walking behind her, as close as he dared with her so weak and scared and snappish, which wasn't really very close at all. The man had come barrelling out of a side tunnel, where the dogtooths should have smelled him and Issel should surely have felt him out with the water-sense, even Gilder ought to have heard him coming, but they were all of them distracted one way or another, and so none of them did.

And so he charged straight into Rhoan and wrapped his vast ham arms around her, roaring threats that none of them could understand. Gilder had a knife but he didn't dare go close enough to use it. Not with a massive hand clamped round Rhoan's throat and half-choking her already, strong enough to crush her neck entirely.

Baris and Ailse between them might have tackled the creature without blades, but the same absolute applied. Thankfully, they could see that, and held back—or Ailse could, and she held Baris.

Issel had a knife too, he had all the strength of the water all around him, and he didn't think of touching either one.

Issel spat.

The Sundain do not spit, but Issel was getting a taste for it.

Issel spat, and that little shining ball of spittle shattered the man's skull.

For a moment his grip on Rhoan visibly tightened, and Issel thought he'd killed her. She flexed, though, and fought fiercely against the weight of him. Perhaps she knew already, that deadweight was all she was fighting now. The chokehold on her throat slipped first; wheezing, gasping, she straightened up with a great straining effort and flung him off. He fell loosely, backwards, into the canal.

From then till now, Issel had been haunted by regrets. Dogtooth skulls are thicker, stronger, massively reinforced; for a while he hadn't understood why the man's face was so distorted in those moments before he fell, or how it seemed to slump into shapelessness where he floated in the water. Like a tent with its poles broken, Issel thought now, the fabric all unsupported and folded in on itself. The skull beneath had simply disintegrated.

It was an ugly and a pointless death, and he was not consoled by any thought that his friends could offer—"Issel, he's peaceful now, he would have thanked you for it"—nor even by the constant knowledge of Rhoan alive where otherwise it would have been she who died. She first, and then the dogtooth anyway, because he couldn't have lived a moment past her death. He couldn't have been allowed to.

"I suppose he came up the same way we did, through the outfall," Gilder said. "Once he realised what was happening to him down by the river, once he understood that there were no boats. I'm surprised there aren't more like him, living in the cisterns here, going out into the city for food and coming back for shelter."

"Perhaps there are more," Ailse said. "The city says it is unlucky to come below, but some of us are not lucky anyway. There are many miles of sewers; you have seen only the main trunk and a few byways. There could be dozens, hundreds living down here, and we would never meet them." They wouldn't have met this one either, if he hadn't flung himself upon them. Drawn by the light they made, perhaps, or driven finally mad by it, after weeks and months of darkness. "He was past scavenging for food outside, though. He must have been living on whatever comes down in the water, what he could smell in the dark."

And so he was desperate, out of his mind perhaps with hunger as well as their light as well as the Shine; and now he was just something else in the water, going down. The current had taken him out of the fall of Issel's light, rolling him over as he went so that it looked almost as if he were swimming. Nothing could take him beyond the reach of water-sense, though, now that Issel knew he was there. Even sitting dry on warm stone at the back of their bolt-hole, as far from the water as he could come, he could taste him, almost, a lingering taint like oil on the water. And it was just one more death when there had been so many, and yet this one mattered; it drove Issel deep into himself and far from his companions.

People came and went like shadows against the light of the water, and they talked and asked him questions and tried to make him eat, while a dead man floated further and further away from them like a stray mote of dust in a sunbeam, and that still and silent body held all the attention that Issel had. It wasn't a ghost, only an emptiness, a lack, a space that he could follow in his mind and fill with guilt and sorrow and regret.

———————

PEOPLE came and went. They spoke to each other, sometimes they spoke to him. He found that he could listen, in the same way that a rock listens to the rain, entirely on the surface of its skin. It wasn't at all the way Issel listened to the rain, deeply and flinchingly attentive to every drop; it wasn't at all the way he usually listened to Rhoan, but it mostly wasn't Rhoan who did the talking.

She was almost as quiet as he was. Her throat was sore, he knew that from the hoarse and broken voice she used when she did speak. Her neck was stiff and her body badly bruised, he knew that from the way she held herself. It was her spirit, though, that had been pulled down into that well of solitude and silence. He knew that because they shared it, though each of them was alone in there.

At least they were alone together, but that was small comfort to him. She shifted away from his hand when he reached to touch her; she only shook her head when he tried to speak. Which only drove him out again, reaching for the body in the water.

She had been hurt and scared, but both of those were true before. This time she must have felt the man's death, that intimate moment when his spirit left him; she had been struggling hopelessly against the brute strength of a dogtooth, then suddenly she was only struggling against the slump of his empty flesh.

And more than that, of course, it had been Issel who had killed him. Quickly, casually, as a man might kill a dog. She would see it that way, she must, there was nothing more to be seen: only that swift spit and the man's destruction, his deadweight on her back. She probably thought that Issel expected her to be grateful.

She'd have to be confusing him with Gilder, if she did. He couldn't bear that, so he slipped away. Outside there was an infinity of water that could carry him off if he would let it. If not, he could still ride it, up and down, to feel out every corner of this subterranean city. *An empire is its roads*, Tel Ferin had said that to them once, when he was trying to make them think beyond their own bodies. This was a sheer example, a skeleton stripped bare; there was nothing to it except the sewers and pipes and cisterns, all the ways it had to carry water.

Anywhere it carried water, it could carry Issel's water-sense. Even sitting dry in this dry hole, he found moisture enough in the air now—from their breaths, from their bodies, or just his own sensitivity climbing again to another level, another layer of skin burned off—to carry the weightless whisper of his thoughts. But he had no imperial cravings, and no wanderlust; he had to be reminded—even now, even after the dogtooth had caught Rhoan by the throat, all of them by surprise—to search for people.

Constantly, all he did was reach for the body and ride with it, slowly down into the dark.

PEOPLE came, and he knew it, whether he was looking for them or not. These people—so many, so loud, dark shadows against the shining waters— he could not have missed.

He said, "They are searching the sewers."

"It's taken them long enough," Gilder said, snorting.

"I expect they were scared." That was Rhoan, rousing herself, remembering that she needed to be scared again herself. Reminded, of course, by Issel. That was all he did to her, to bring her where she needed to be hurt, or afraid, or both. "Where are they, Issel?"

How to tell them? This undercity, this empire of ways, it was a web in three dimensions, and the people were there, and there, and over there . . .

He could point, not usefully; or he could shrug, and say, "Everywhere," which was neither useful nor true, and he did that.

"Can we still get out?" Gilder's voice was sharper suddenly. "Into the city?"

"Yes." There were so many ways in and out, so many little streams of water, hot bright wires in his head; wherever the soldiers came, Issel could lead his people somewhere else.

But, "We don't need to leave," Rhoan said. Scared, unhappy, withdrawn, she was still herself. "When they come, I can hide us."

"Are you sure? We'll be trapped in here . . ."

"I'm sure."

And of course she was sure of the other thing also, that if they were discovered, Issel could save them. She had seen it, felt it, watched it fall.

It was far away now, still floating, still drifting.

PEOPLE came, and they were in the channel, on the path with their torches and lamps. The path was narrow, and the bolt-hole would be hard to miss, even without the rungs in the rock below to point the way.

But Rhoan was sitting with her fingertips dabbling in water—Rhoan who had claimed to be hopeless with it unblessed, yet hadn't given this a second thought—and whatever it was that the men below were seeing, it wasn't a hole in the wall and a handy ladder leading up.

They might have gone straight by, but they had dogs with them. That was a good thought by those who had sent them down here; a bad thought, a dangerous thought for those they had sent. It is not wise to hunt the Sundain with dogs.

When one of those they were hunting was Issel, it might have been a fatal thought, though not for those who'd thought it.

He heard the dogs bark and whimper, just below. He'd felt them come, of course: water-sense is neither sight nor smell nor hearing nor touch, and yet he'd known that these were men and those were dogs, in all their wet fur and their rankness.

They were wet, and the air was wet, and the path was wet beneath them. And they were dogs, that above all, and Issel had grown up throwing stones at any—rare—stray dog on the street. The dogs could have died then and there, and their handlers, and the other soldiers too, the half-dozen men in single file who had penetrated this far. But Issel had killed too recently, and harmed more than himself in the doing of it, as he always did; he didn't want to kill again. Not so soon, not with Rhoan sitting close and watching him askance.

He didn't even kill the dogs. He could forestall them with just a tingle beneath their paws, just a breath of acid in the air, enough to make them hesitate, to crouch and whine and sneeze, to tug against their leashes and want to jump into the water.

"What's this, then? What's their bait?"

"Dunno. But they were on a scent, and now they're off it."

"Good and proper, I'd say."

A dragging sound, a yelp.

"Oh, look. If the dogs stop here, then so does the trail. You know that."

"Oh, and what? Climb the walls, did they, run along the ceiling? Or do they fly, these witches, is that it?"

"Maybe they do. How would I know? But they're Sundain, if we've been following the right trail—"

"—the wrong trail," an unhappy mutter from someone who clearly thought that following Sundain witches was a path to suicide, that at best—

"—and the only thing we know about Sundain witchery is that it's water-magic, right?"

"Yeah, right. So?"

"So what's this here, where the dogs want to go swimming?"

"What, you think they walked on the water?"

"Might have done. I dunno. What I do know, there's a lot of boats down here. Maybe they just got into a boat."

"It'd be something to tell the sergeant," that same muttering voice again.

"Something, right. Not enough. We go on."

"What about the dogs?"

"Kick 'em."

SO the dogs were kicked on, yelping and whining and scuffling enough that they didn't notice where the scent truly went, or else the men didn't notice when they did.

Rhoan took her fingers from the water, though she kept the pot beside her.

Issel followed the soldiers, on and down, though he never moved a handspan from her side.

WATER-SENSE is not hearing, but he could use it to carry their voices back to him:

"Wait. What's that?"

"What?"

"In the water there, up against the grille."

"That's a boat. That's what you said they . . . Ow!"

"*Between* us and the boat. In the *water*."

"Dunno. Garbage."

"How much garbage have you seen down here? That big? Shine your lamp over . . ."

"That's a body."

"Right. Turn it over."

"I'm not reaching into that. Not if those witches have been playing around in it, killing people. How do we know what he died of?"

"That's what I want to find out."

"Or maybe he's one of them, maybe they've been killing each other."

"That too. Use your spear. You're the one insisted on dragging it down here, banging all our shins bloody in that crawl—"

"I don't like swords. You have to get too close."

"Right. Witching-distance. So use that bloody spear, and turn him over."

"Gods!"

"How many gods do you want?"

"You get as many as you like, down here. If you have to look at that and not chuck up. What happened to him?"

"Sundain witchery. What else? But look, look what he is. What he was."

"I can see what he is. What was he?"

"Oh, look. Even the sergeant hasn't got shoulders like that."

"No, but I dunno what you mean."

"Haven't you ever been down the docks? Or on the river shifts?"

"What, with the Turds? Not me. Strictly High City Watch, with my eye on the High Guard."

"Aren't you too old to have ambitions?"

"One thing for sure, the High Guard'll be having their eye on you. But look—all right, we see it, this thing came up from the beaches. Must've done. We still don't know if they killed it—"

"—Yes, we do. What else could do that?"

"—All right, what I mean, we don't know if they just found it here or if it was with them. One of them, even. That was the word, that they had at least one beast among them."

"What, and they'd kill their own, would they?"

"Why not? Witches, they might do anything. And they were running, sure, and that would slow them down. I had charge of a string once, unloading a cargo for the palace under special guard, and they're so awkward—stubborn as mules, thick as fog. I'd sooner drive bullocks any day. You don't start off trying to reason with a bullock, you just go for the whip first thing. Instead of last."

"What kind of cargo is it, that calls the High Watch down to the docks?"

"Never mind his cursed cargo! And it doesn't matter whether this was with the Sundain or not. That's not our problem. All we got to do is report it."

"Shouldn't we take the body back?"

"What for?"

"So they can see, what's been done."

"We can tell them, they won't want to see it, and do you really want to be carting that, all the way upstream?"

"We could put it in the boat and tow it back."

"Maybe the dogs'd do the pulling."

"Maybe they would too. All right, it was a good idea—but I'm still not fishing in this water for that thing. Anyone wants it, they can come and fetch it. We'll just tell them where to look. That grille's got it fast, it isn't going anywhere."

"Tell you what, though, there's got to be a better way out of here. I didn't like that squirm coming down; it'll be worse going back, with the water in our faces. And it's raining again, up top. There'll be more to come down."

"Well, but how else do we get out?"

"Keep the breeze in our faces and follow the dogs."

"Fair enough. Just mark the corners, so we can find our way back if we have to. I've never lost a man yet; I don't want to lose a whole damn squad in this dark."

———————

PEOPLE went, from this channel and from others; like sparks in the darkness, in the dark of Issel's thoughts, they went out.

People came.

———————

PEOPLE came and he found them, like sparks flowering in the darkness: awkward things, stuttering and slow beside the awful burning majesty of water.

He watched them, followed them, felt them leave. His own people he watched over, wherever they went. He couldn't follow them out into the city, but within the waterways he was an ever-present whisper, a trace of thought, an eye that never closed.

People came, and most they avoided. Some they hid from. One, just the one, they went to fetch.

———————

ISSEL had found him wandering, adrift. He'd thought of the body in the water, just as lost, just as helpless. But the body was a peaceful thing, though it tormented him; this sobbing, shrieking boy was the opposite of peaceful.

And there were still soldiers in the underways; if he made so much noise that Issel barely needed the water-sense to find him, then sooner or later he would be found by others and given better reasons for his sobbing.

And anyone down here who was not a soldier might prove to be a friend. Issel sent Gilder to find out. "Once you get that close, past the cistern with the pillars, you'll find him by yourself. He's very loud."

Ailse went too, because Gilder was not good at giving comfort and Rhoan should really not leave the bolt-hole, in case they needed hiding. That chafed her, but was hard to argue with. The boy would have to be quieted before he could be brought here; Gilder's suggestion was a blade to the throat, which was why Ailse had to go along.

So then there was nothing to do but sit and wait, in the silence that had fallen on the bolt-hole. Baris was silent by habit and growing more so, less easy to understand when he did speak. Issel followed the other two with one thin thread of his mind; another, heavier, stayed behind, unhappily with Rhoan; the rest watched the body where it lay sodden in the water.

———

HE was aware when Gilder and Ailse reached the cistern of the pillars. The waters in his head made a strange distorted map, but he knew just exactly where they were.

Water-sense is not sight, but he could have drawn an image if he'd never seen the space: how there were slender pillars rising from the water like young trees in a plantation, too many to count comfortably; how the pillars and the walls and the ceiling were all tiled in rich deep colours, greens and blues, the colours of deep water; how the water itself was darker than any of these, seeming inky and almost black and yet as clear as any when they dipped a handful; how there was nothing natural left anywhere, it was all a rich man's plaything, a cavern turned into a pretty toy.

A useful toy, to hold a rich man's water. Or water for many men, rather, many households; channels led from here in all directions, like spokes from the hub of a wheel. The boy was still howling when Gilder and Ailse came there; still howling as they hurried on towards him. Issel could see his voice almost as a living thing, hurling itself at walls and roofs and water, desperate for release.

Gilder had small talent, but even he could raise a light. If the boy was howling in the dark—and what else could raise such a cry of despair, such

utter abandonment?—then the first thing he'd see would be two grim figures coming towards him, in an alien glow.

Issel felt it, when the boy fell silent. Relief or terror, no matter. Either
way, it would pass. Gilder had found him, Ailse would keep him quiet, and
between them they would bring him back.

Here in the bolt-hole, this other silence that had fallen between himself
and Rhoan: that too would pass. One way or another.

The body was caught, trapped, held while the water flowed around it.
Sinking, despite the current's best efforts to hold it up. Silence was a heavy
state of being.

———

ISSEL knew the boy, when he came. They all did. It was Rhoan who remembered his name.

"Teo!"

He still wasn't talking. He only crouched against the wall, huddling in
on himself, taking even less space than the squeeze of all their bodies would
allow.

His clothes were sodden, his face tear-stained and filthy when he glared
around at them, half-sullen and half-scared. Rhoan said, "You might at least
have let him wash," and that was so like what had been said to Issel and
about Issel, his first day at the school in Sund, he thought he heard their old
master's voice overlying hers.

There was nothing of Tel Ferin in what she did, though: dipping the tail
of her shirt in the water she kept ready for her hiding-spells, wiping Teo's
face gently as if he were a child.

He let her do it, too, as if he were a child; and when she let him be, his face
worked as if he was on the verge of crying again.

If so, he swallowed it down. And looked at Rhoan and found a voice of
sorts, said, "Thank you," in a thin whisper, even tried a hint of a smile as a
well-trained boy no doubt should do.

It wasn't convincing, but no matter for that. It was Rhoan's to notice,
and she smiled back brightly, like applause.

"Are you hungry?"

He shook his head abruptly.

"Sure? . . . All right, then, but do just say. We have food here." Not
much, and not good: it might have surprised a boy used to a palace diet.

Still, he shook his head again, and Rhoan went on, "Can you tell us what happened? What are you doing down here?"

Wailing would have been one answer, the unkindest truth. *Looking for you* might have been another, and Issel thought that Rhoan was expecting it; but where the boy had been found was so far from where they'd seen him last, Issel guessed that there was a surprise coming for Rhoan and all.

"My mistress told me to. She sent me to the water-rat, and I knew what she meant, but . . ."

But his voice died away unhelpfully. Rhoan shook her head at him.

"I'm afraid I don't know what she meant. Who is the water-rat, and why did your lady Jendre send you to him?"

"She has been—taken," Teo said awkwardly. "To the new palace. For the new Sultan's . . . pleasure. Us too, Mirjana and me, but I was not let stay with her. They would have made a palace servant of me, and I don't—I don't want that." He seemed briefly startled by his own vehemence, not accustomed to finding his wants paramount, even to himself. "My lady said to find the water-rat, who is one of the boys who keep the drains clear in the Sultan's gardens. She meant that he could show me a way down to here, that I could run away. But I lost my light, and I couldn't find my way . . ."

And that had been brutal, terrifying; no wonder he had been wailing. Issel couldn't achieve darkness in among all this water, but he could still imagine it.

"Oh, Teo," Rhoan said. "What were you looking for? Where were you trying to get to?" They knew what happened to runaway slaves in this city, Ailse had shown them; those who weren't caught on the way ended up on the beach, in the Shine. In the cage, eventually. It was impossible to imagine, this fine-boned boy turned dogtooth labourer, vast and hulking and useful to the state.

Privately, Issel thought the Marasi would have felt the same. Teo would more likely have been taken back to the palace and punished cruelly, an example to his fellow slaves.

"I wanted to go back to where I was before. I have . . . a friend there."

He said that as though it were a great treasure. Perhaps it was.

"Well, we can show you the way. But, Teo—can your friend hide you? For a lifetime?" There would be nowhere else for him to go, no other life to live. Not for him, not in Maras.

"The palace is very big," he said, "and no one cares anymore, about the women there. Or their servants."

That might mean yes, but . . .

"No."

That was Gilder, unexpectedly setting limits, or making demands. Issel didn't understand; no more did Rhoan, he thought, or any of them.

"There is little danger," Teo said hesitantly. "The palace is full of servants, eunuchs like me; nobody asks us questions. And my friend will protect me."

"Nobody asks you questions," Gilder said. "That's the point. You can come and go, in and out of the Sultan's palace, in and out of here; you can be a spy for us. We'd be stupid"—to the others—"to take him back to that other place. We've been there, and failed; it might have killed us all. A spy on the Sultan, though, an eye in his palace, a guide . . ."

"To do what?" Rhoan asked warily.

"To strike, of course. To kill him. What else?"

"They seem to be happy enough, killing their own sultans. The empire endures, and it doesn't touch the bridge. What would be the point?"

"The *point* is that we would have done it, for Sund. It would be a blow struck, a beacon lit. When the news reached our people—"

"Oh, and how would that happen?"

"We would tell them. There must be a way to cross the river."

"Ailse's people have been looking for one a long time now, and not found it."

"They are dogtooth," with all that that implied.

And so will we be soon, Issel and I—she might have said that; he waited to hear it, but she was merciful, or frightened of the truth. She said, "Even so. And if the news did reach Sund, what then? If all the city rose as one, which it would not, it could still not defeat the Marasi regiments. We have no soldiers, Gilder."

"We have water-mages, Rhoan. We have the water you can make, you and Issel together, more powerful than we have known before. If we killed the Sultan and found a way back, the mages could lead the people, and the regiments would run . . ."

It was even possible that he was right. Chaos at home and fear abroad: the slave-soldiers of Maras might not stand.

Or there might be slaughter, massacre, a return to the brutal policies of the invasion.

Either way it didn't matter, it couldn't: not while the bridge still stood. Issel understood that as an absolute; he thought Rhoan did too; he was bewildered that Gilder did not.

He said, "Gilder is right."

Rhoan stared at him; so, probably, did Gilder, but it was Rhoan's gaze he was holding.

He said, "There has to be a way to cross the river."

Without that, there could be no way to bring down the bridge.

She said, "Well, Teo can't find it in the Sultan's palace. And I don't think he wants to be a spy for us, do you, sweet?"

He said, "No, but—I would like to help my lady."

"I thought you were running away?"

"Because she sent me, and because I knew no way to help her. I didn't think that I would find you again."

"We found you," from Gilder, a none-too-gentle reminder of the state they'd found him in and so how much he owed them.

"Yes. Thank you. I will go back, if you ask me to. If you will help my lady."

"How can we help her, Teo?"

"Take her out of there. Soon."

"And, what, bring her here?" Rhoan gestured around them, at the sparse quarters and the bare rock walls, *no place to bring a lady*.

"Better here than where she is, what she is now. I will help you do what you want"—he would be their spy—"if you will help my lady. My friend will still be at the old palace, after." That much, at least, was certain.

"Teo," Rhoan said, "you give away too much, too quickly."

Of course, his shrug said. *I am a slave*.

"What we will do," she said, "we will show you the way back to the palace where you came from. I'm sure Issel can find that for you. And then we will show you the way from there to where you want to be, the Palace of Tears." A glance at Issel, who nodded back; he could do that too. "And when we're sure you know that way, and the way here from both of them, when you're not afraid to be alone down here, then you can choose where you go and what you do. You can serve your lady, you can help us, you can run to your friend: any of those, or all of them. Down here, it's your decision. You're not a slave to us."

LATER—and it was a while later; they did as Rhoan said and it took time, it took a long time to lead a nervous boy through complex ways and teach him where to turn, which tunnels to follow and how far—when they were alone again, Issel took Rhoan by the wrist and tugged her lightly out of the bolt-hole and away from their companions.

Gilder watched them go but asked no questions, did not try to follow.

Rhoan asked no questions either, though Issel was sure she didn't understand.

He led her downstream, to where eventually there was a grille across the water, before it spilled into a wider pool.

Here was a boat, bumped up hard against the iron. Nothing else to see now.

Now at last she spoke, as he slipped off his shirt.

"Issel, what . . . ?"

He shook his head, and stepped off the path into the canal.

WATER closed over his head.

It had happened before, but never quite like this. It was like wilfully stepping into a burning building; it demanded that degree of courage, or of folly. It was like flames against his skin, flames within his skin, flames running up and down his bones. Inside and out. Flames in his skull; his thoughts were flame.

His mouth opened, but there was no air to scream with; there was no air to breathe. It didn't seem to matter.

He opened his eyes, and there was all his own light to see by; down here, he burned with a living, liquid glare. All his skin paid the price of it, in a pain so intense that it was barely pain at all.

He saw what he was looking for, and claimed it.

It was bigger than he, more massive and massively swollen, massively sunk. Even so, he tried to handle it honourably, giving the dogtooth a respect the man had probably never known in life.

He held the body in his arms and walked to the canal's edge, where he could see Rhoan's distorted, distressful figure staring down into the water.

He lifted the body high, above his head; and felt her take a grip on it, and between the two of them they rolled it out onto the path.

Then he found the rim of the canal wall with his fingers and hauled himself up to follow.

Water streamed from him, and it felt like a world ripping itself away.

Rhoan was staring at him, mouth agape, and it felt like a world on the edge of ripping itself away.

He groped swiftly, desperately for anything to say, and all he could find was, "Help me lay him out, somewhere in the dry. Some hole like that other that we found, where he can rest in his own tomb. He deserves that." And there was nothing more that they could do for him.

Chapter Three

**E**VEN now, she hadn't really understood it.

Not until now, at least: not until this exact moment, where she stood with other women in a bright fall of sun, and His Magnificence the Sultan strolled to and fro before them with half a dozen eunuchs in attendance.

His Magnificence was fresh from the bathhouse, wrapped in a simple silk robe and slippers, his skin still flushed, his hair still damp and perfumed. It was as though he could never sweat or soak enough, as though the years in the *Kafes* were a taint that could not be scrubbed or worked or oiled out of his skin, though he meant to go on trying till they were. He had rejected his father's suite of rooms in the main harem block in favour of an airy pavilion in the gardens; he lived between there and the bathhouse, dallying back and forth with his eternal entourage.

If he had been fully dressed once in this last week, Jendre had not seen it; and she had seen him daily, several times a day. That was his order, that his women, the fair flowers of his garden should be arrayed before him in this constant progress, coming and going. They were kept close at hand, in other pavilions, far from their own mean cells; when he moved from bed to bath or back to bed again, they were stood in clusters and congregations beside the path that he would walk, like flowers in their beds.

Like a youth picking flowers, he would choose: this one, this one, this. His picks would go out onto the lake with him, in the great imperial pleasure barge, silk-curtained and discreet; or they would attend him in the bathhouse, hour upon hour; or they would follow him to his pavilion, to music and dancing and so eventually to his bed, two and three together.

Jendre didn't know if it was his choice to keep within such narrow limits, or if he was being compelled. The men always with him were palace eunuchs, not soldiers; if he went another way, if he went to the gate and demanded to go out, she didn't think they would stop him. Of course, the gate was in other hands and might simply not open. Perhaps he was wise not to try it; no door is ever locked until you do.

Or he was still a boy, caged a long time and easily frightened. Perhaps he locked himself away because the pasha had demanded it; perhaps he did because he wanted to. The wide world of empire might seem too much to him. He could be wiser than she guessed, taking one step at a time, learning the gardens beyond the *Kafes* before he thought to tackle the world beyond the gardens.

Learning the ways of women too. If he didn't seem to be learning much else, if he'd shown small curiosity beyond this little triangle of boat and bath and bed—well, he was a boy, and easily ensnared. And it had only been a week; and at the start of the week he must have thought himself set to die, right up until they declared him Sultan. He was surely allowed a little time to recover. Even to hide for a while, to bury himself in these new luxuries, his new possessions. After the deprivations of a *Kafes* cell and never a fertile woman allowed inside, he must be dazzled by space and sunlight, drawn by the shadier intimacies of bathhouse, bed and beauty.

———————

SHE could make him all the excuses that he needed, but she still hated these constant parades, where she must be displayed with all the others, chivvied around by eunuchs whom she used to command. Told to come out, to kneel when he passed; told to simper for him if he paused to look—she would not do that, though they told her and told her; she was his father's widow yet, and not his petty plaything—and told to go back indoors after, to shield her skin, to keep herself pale and attractive.

Mirjana stayed close by her side, to keep her from folly, she said. She was a shield and defender, and endlessly welcome, but even she couldn't shield Jendre from her own stupidity.

All these days, living so differently, watching and being watched, and still she hadn't really understood how the world, her world had changed.

Until today, until now: until the young Sultan paused in his magnificent progress, just in front of her, playing his long silk handkerchief between his fingers. This was a trick he had picked up from his father, as though it were an age-old tradition. In the Man of Men it had been an expression of casual style, of arrogant ownership, of absolute entitlement; in his son it appeared more as a nervous gesture, a rude assertion of a right he still didn't quite believe in.

He paused, he played the silk between his fingers; he said, "What are you called, girl?"

"My name is Jendre," she replied, "Magnificence," which had so nearly come out as *boy*.

"Jendre. Why do you dress so differently from your sisters?"

"I was your father's wife, Magnificence," *and these, these were his concubines and slaves*, and even she could not have said whether she was explaining why she had sent Mirjana to scour the upper levels of the harem for suitable dresses, or simply denying her sisterhood.

"Oh dear, were you? His wife? That old man . . ." And he giggled, and pressed his handkerchief to his lips just as his uncle used to do. His sad, mad, strangled uncle . . . It was easier to feel sorry for the dead. Especially now, with Salem taken from her, all her life taken from her, when it was so easy to feel sorry for herself. But to see that same gesture remade in this boy, when it was associated in her mind with a dark place and dark promises: that was like a shock of water, chilling, breath-taking.

And then he laid the handkerchief over her shoulder, in just his father's manner, and now she really couldn't breathe, she couldn't believe this. He was saying, "You are not married now. You are mine now, and no one's wife at all. We will find you some more suitable clothing. Later," and that called for another giggle that was not like his uncle's at all but all his own, breathy and boy-like and sending a shiver through her. It wasn't fear, no, there was nothing to be afraid of here; it was rage, pure and clear, the unadulterated thing pouring into her like water, needing to spill over . . .

Mirjana understood her, better and more swiftly than she understood herself. A hand closed tightly about her arm, to hold her down there on her knees, to stop her standing where she could tower over this wet-lipped child in his sordid greed and tell him just exactly how and why he really should not be laughing right now.

First the hand and its wiry strength, then the voice cutting through her blind fury, addressing itself to the Sultan of Maras as though to a nursling: "Magnificence, what pleased an old man in his decline is hardly fit for the empire's new hero. Would you have the people say that you dressed yourself in your father's clothes? It would demean you in their eyes, and in their hearts."

"There are those who would say that it demeans me more to be chided by a slave." By luck or good judgement, she had lighted on just the right way to speak to him. Perhaps it was familiar, his daily treatment from the old women of the *Kafes*; perhaps it made him think back to his life before that, when he had been truly a child, and surrounded by women who spoke to him so, and perhaps had been happy. From the corner of her eye Jendre saw his hand reach down, to lift Mirjana's face into the light.

"She is not my father's now," he said. "That man is dead. See, I wear his ring; everything that was his is mine, to do with as I like." *Within these walls*, but he wasn't going to mention that. "I suppose I could order her divorced from his corpse, if you think it wrong for me to bed a widow. I could see it done in temple, truly in the people's eyes, where they would not need to spy," and briefly Jendre thought that he meant it. He giggled again, and she saw what he was seeing: her lord's coffin paraded through the streets and ripped open on the altar steps, there where she had married him in his pomp, in his prime; his rotting hand held up to repudiate her, in public as the law demanded, as all the Sultan's doings must be done.

The pasha had rebelled against his lawful master, for the insult done to Salem. Fathers should defend their children, she thought; but where was her father now? There would be no uprisings to save her honour, or revenge her body's abuse. She had always been expendable; if she helped to keep this boy quiet, no doubt he would think her once again well spent.

She didn't feel particularly inclined to oblige him—*fathers should defend their children*, and he never had—but there was an awful inevitability to her life these days, to the whole progress of it from wife to widow to runaway and so on down to here, where she was what, a concubine, a slave . . . ?

If she hadn't truly understood that before, she knew it now, by the weight of that handkerchief that hung across her shoulder, by the weight of his words as he discussed her with Mirjana. Who used to be her slave and was now his, she supposed; and her equal, entirely her equal as he bit off his giggles and said, "No, we will not divorce her; death has done that for us. 'Widow' is a word, no more; she is my woman now, and she delights me. She will learn to delight me. You, too." And those fingers that had cupped her chin were stroking Mirjana's face now, catching lightly at her lips, pushing into her hair where it was bound up as she liked it.

And then he was turning away and speaking to his eunuchs: "I will have them both. Yes. They will be good together. Bring them now."

————————

THE last time she had been brought to a sultan's bed, there had been such ceremony to it: not just her entry to the room, chased in by his mother with his ortolan piping hot under its jewelled lid and he in such a stately hurry to engulf it, so stately slow to engulf her afterwards. Before that there had been a thorough, immaculate bathing and detailed instructions to follow, a punctilious preparation.

But that had been in Feres' hands, and for the Man of Men. Those days were lost. This was an immediate world, predicated on a boy's urgent appetites. He strode on to his pavilion and didn't trouble to look back. His eunuchs hauled Jendre and Mirjana to their feet and pushed them along in his wake, all soft hands and hissing. Jendre wanted to slap those hands away, she wanted to stalk alone in her anger and shame; instead she was flurried, surrounded, swept along like a toy boat in a running gutter, out of all control. She needed to speak to Mirjana, urgently, but the eunuchs were between them now. Deliberately or otherwise, they were given no space to come together.

Bad enough that she couldn't defend herself; now it seemed she couldn't defend her people either. Teo was lost to her, barely glimpsed all week and always hurrying away; the best she could do was trust him to Feres' care, and she didn't trust Feres at all. And Mirjana had suddenly become a toy for the Sultan's playtime. As Jendre had herself, but it was Mirjana she could have wept for.

Her own would be the violation that shocked the city, and the Sultan was a fool if he thought the city would not hear. The wall had been porous even in her husband's day. Now his eunuchs had far less to do, fewer women to watch and a less rigorous master; for sure they would gossip more, steal more, have more contact with the world outside. She gave it one day before the news was all through Maras, that His new Magnificence had trespassed where his father had been lord.

It wasn't the kind of news to bring the city out onto the streets, or to raise the janizars in rebellion. She wasn't that important. In herself, she didn't count at all. But it would make Mehmet less secure than he imagined, and leave the pasha wondering if perhaps he strangled the wrong sons.

It changed nothing, it would save no one, but if the seeds he planted tonight sprouted into vines that might yet grow to—yes, to strangle him, Jendre could foresee some satisfaction in that.

It was good to have something to look forward to.

———————

LAST time there had been pumice-stones and powders, delicate and scrupulous attention, a gorgeous robe and a liberal bedecking. This time . . .

Were slaves all treated like this, being made ready for their masters? She didn't know, and was ashamed to ask. She'd never considered before how much she'd been protected, all her life, especially by those who served her. It had been a kindness in them, surely, to shield a child from too much understanding; but she was not a child now, and had not been for a while. She felt unprepared, exposed—and was almost ready to blame Mirjana for it, *you should have let me learn*, as if the other woman could have known that they would come to this, both slaves together.

Despising herself for that and more, she stood stiffly silent while she and Mirjana were stripped and scrubbed, cold water in a tiled outhouse. A rubdown with a rough towel as though they were horses or dogs; a spatter of perfume, cheap and coarse; loose and open robes to wear, diaphanous wafts of coloured silk and ribbon that concealed nothing, that somehow left her feeling more naked, even more exposed and vulnerable than before.

"His Magnificence likes his women to be simply clad," a eunuch told her sharply, the one time she demurred, when he knotted a sash around her waist so slackly that the sheer silk beneath was sliding apart even before he took his hands away.

His Magnificence is a leering, snatching child, she thought, and managed to swallow the thought down before it became fatal, words spoken aloud. The cheapest harlot in the street would never choose to dress so revealingly. He was a boy, after all, she would not have looked for the sophistication of his father; but he was the Sultan, after all, and she would never have looked for the debasement of a dockside brothel.

They were hurried thus from the outhouse and across the flagstoned court behind the pavilion, and so indoors again. A narrow corridor, the smells of smoke and coffee, the sounds of music; and then a doorway, a curtain twitched aside, and they were gestured in.

Here was a luxury plundered from a dozen other rooms, thick carpets heaped three or four deep and hangings too long for the walls they hung upon. A score of lamps cast conflicting shadows, so that light rippled like water through the room. An ornate brazier burned incense in one corner, next to a marble table—a marble table-top, at least, supported by a great bronze elephant—that held bottles and flasks and a goblet; in another, a boy played a flute while a woman danced. She and the music both were slow and languid, smokily erotic. Her skin glowed golden in the fugitive light.

All of this and everything else in the room was peripheral to the one thing, the focus, the heart. In the centre of the floor, magnificently astride the carpets and gleaming with its own burning glow, casting its own vast shadows was a bed. A bed the size of a barge, and surely the same weight too; half a dozen full-grown men could lie on such a bed and never touch each other. If they chose to. Jendre wouldn't willingly go near it. To her it was worse than ugly, it looked poisonous: gilded and shimmering, adorned with sinuous shapes on every pillar, climbing vines and serpents. Atop the pillars was a gathered tent of fabric, and that too was heavy with gold thread and pendulous with swags and fringes, all of them showing hints of this and that, creatures and plants unreadable through the folds and shadows. She had seen rich beds before—yes, and slept in them, and more than slept, exulted—but this was monstrous, monumental, an abuse of furniture. At a guess, it had been a gift from some foreign potentate, unless it was the spoils of conquest; either way it would have come here in tribute and been left in some neglected corner of the palace, unwanted, unregarded.

Until this pale boy came out of his bleak cell and found it, or was led to it by some encyclopedic eunuch—"I want a bed," he might have said, and heard, "We have just the one, Your Magnificence," in response—and had it carried here in pieces, and built to fill the room.

Massive as it was, repulsive and compelling, it was not the bed that drew the eye, nor held it. It was for their master that the boy played, the woman danced; and he—*master of us all*, Jendre thought, *master of the world*—lay sprawled across the covers in a nest of pillows, like some young demigod in the soft comforts of his pomp. His own robe was no more secure than Jendre's scanty silks; he lay half-naked and revealed while he watched the dancer, while one hand played between his legs.

———

AND then he looked up and saw them, and said, "Does either of you two know how to please a man with her mouth?"

———

IN the awful silence that followed, that the music seemed only to punctuate and not at all to puncture, Jendre's prime realisation was not that they were in the hands of a monster. That had been obvious all week; however kindly sympathy tried to paint him, the truth of him had always been laid bare below. You can gild a skull, but it will still be bone and teeth and cold hard hollows only cushioned by their shadows.

No, what struck Jendre with the force of sunlight through a falling shutter was that her beloved Mirjana—her reliable Mirjana, who had so often stood between her and trouble, facing whichever way she needed to, to defy the trouble or her mistress, depending—was not going to step forward, not going to say anything, not going to save her this time.

Indeed, that Mirjana had said nothing and done nothing that she was not ordered to, since that courageous moment where she had tried to turn the Sultan's eye aside and drawn it to herself instead. Since then she had been conspicuously silent, stiffly enduring as Jendre was but giving her no signs of comfort, no sharing moment, no touch of hand or eye.

Jendre glanced at her now and saw her standing with her fists clenched, her head down, trembling visibly; and understood something suddenly about her friend that had eluded her all these years in the harem, where it could never have shown itself before.

And understood at the same time what that meant, what that laid on her, how it was her turn now to play shield and defender.

How it was down to her to lift her head and meet him eye to eye, to say, "I do, Magnificence."

"Of course," he said. "My father's wife. How not?"

And he smiled, and beckoned with a finger, and she went; she went clinging to the only good thought that she had, all there was left now to cling to, *if it's me, at least it isn't Mirjana* . . .

———

AT some point the music had changed, all unheeded, at least by Jendre. She didn't think the Sultan had taken his eyes off the dance; at least, surely not to look at her. Now that she could lift her head to look at him, now that he'd—blessedly!—pushed her away from the soft, sticky skin of his belly and the smells of sweat and musk that overlaid it, all those tastes that meant a man to her and were so cruelly deceptive here, she saw how he lay propped up on his pillows just as he had before, how his gaze was still turned towards that corner.

Her own eyes followed, they couldn't not; and yes, the music had changed. It was the woman's playing that she heard now, the same flute but a different voice to it, like two tongues that spoke the same language. The boy was dancing, dreamingly slow; as he moved, light gleamed on his shoulder, on his flank. He seemed dusted with gold, in this lamplight.

So had the woman when she danced, before she sat back in the shadows; and so did the floor, the carpet where the boy's bare feet traced a tempered pattern.

It amused this Sultan to take a great man's widow to his bed and degrade her there. No doubt it amused him also to have his slaves' skins powdered with something immeasurably more valuable than they were. It must still be cheap in the pasha's eyes, if he could buy a sultan's complaisance with a few warm bodies and a cold bag of dust.

She could still feel sorry for the boy Mehmet, with his hard history, but she chose not to. Sympathy is a gift, and not an obligation.

Besides, she had the taste of him in her mouth and could not spit, not drink until he let her.

His reaching hand found a bunch of grapes somewhere in the shadows. He dangled them above his head—his other hand was in her hair, the fingers all entangled—and bit them one by one from the stem. Once he knew that she was watching, he did it lingeringly, pulling at them with teeth and tongue and then bursting them against his palate, with his mouth open so that she could see. It was all wanton, lascivious, crude: boy-play, she supposed, but she had been used to more grace and gentility even in her boys.

The last grape on the bunch, he took that between his fingers and bit into it, bit half of it away and then offered the rest of it to her, holding it just a hand's-span above her mouth.

When she lifted her head to take it, his hand in her hair gripped tightly to stop her reaching it. His giggle was a mockery, but his little jerking gesture with the grape was a command. She tried again, and he prevented her again.

The fourth or fifth time, he let her take it from his fingers, though she needed to use tongue and teeth together, and then he left his fingers a moment too long in her mouth.

He fed her like a dog, teasingly, unkindly; and she ate from his fingers like an obedient dog, teased but not protesting, not at all tempted to bite.

The grape, the half-grape was wonderful—velvet-skinned against her tongue and running with juicy sweetness to counteract what was sour in her throat, musky in a better way, darkly flavoured—and not enough.

It gave her an excuse to spit too, pips politely into the palm of her hand, and that too was wonderful, and not enough.

Then there was a snap of his fingers, and, "Serve me wine, girl," and even as she rose onto her knees on the bed to go and do that thing, she saw Mirjana instinctively rising to her feet to do the same; and even as Jendre was thinking *no, not you, keep as you are*, that movement had caught the Sultan's eye and turned his head.

And he said almost what Jendre was thinking, almost but not quite, not enough; he said, "No, not you. This one," his hand in her hair again and giving her head a shake, which she might have thought almost affectionate if she hadn't learned already at two men's hands how affection turns to play, even rough play. This was purely contemptuous. "My father's grieving widow can fetch me wine. She should at least be familiar with it; it is his cellars I am drinking. You can come here. What do they call you, girl?"

Jendre slipped off the bed and went to the elephant-table, sniffed at what was open until she was certain—*thank you, Salem*, for those nights he had come to her with a bottle in his pocket, doubly sinful, to seduce his Sultan's wife with tenderness and alcohol besides—and filled a goblet near to the brim. Mehmet was a boy, with a boy's appetites and an untrained boy's body that could not hope to match them; if she could get him drunk, swiftly and deeply drunk, then—

————————

THEN it would already be too late. It was too late now.

It was too late because Mirjana had been slow to move and slower still to answer, had not spoken yet. The Sultan had been content, and might have proved tolerant; now he was impatient.

"What, no tongue? Is that why you cannot use your mouth to please a man? Show me."

"I, I have a tongue, Magnificence . . ."

He knew she did; he'd heard her speak before, when she was trying to turn his eye away from Jendre.

"No name, then? Would that be it?"

"My name is Mirjana."

"Well, I don't intend to bellow it across the palace. Come *here*, I said."

Summoned like that, she came: puppet-stiff, as awkward as she was used to being graceful, as though with every step she was fighting her own stronger desire to run away. With this sudden new insight of hers, Jendre thought that actually that was probably true.

She couldn't stand and watch and do nothing; she stepped back to the bedside and said, "Magnificence, your drink . . ."

He grunted and held his hand out, without turning his head from Mirjana's creeping progress. He had his father's intensity of focus, she thought, one thing at a time—*the ortolan and then the woman, all night the woman, and duties in the morning.*

She pressed the goblet into his fingers, then—trembling slightly, feeling that tremble against the warm solidity of his own flesh and bone and hating herself for it, knowing that he would feel it too, knowing that he would enjoy it—she cupped her own hands around his and said, "Magnificence, please . . ."

"Mmm?" At least she had drawn his attention away from Mirjana. "Well?"

"Let me serve you tonight. Me alone," and she wished she could sound more lascivious, more wheedling, a girl with ambitions to rise. But he wasn't stupid and he was frowning already, not ready to be deceived, so she settled for straightforward, honest betrayal. *Forgive me, Mirjana . . .* "She's not suitable, Magnificence. She's never pleased a man, even when she was in my father's harem, where there were barely a dozen women when I was young. I don't know why he allowed it, but she avoided him—"

"You mean she's a virgin?"

"Yes, Magnificence. Exactly that. And she knows nothing, she would seem coarse and clumsy to you"—*flatter him, yes, make him feel sophisticated and experienced*—"you would have no pleasure from her. At least let the eunuchs teach her something"—*let me have a chance to gentle her*—"before you take her to your bed. You have so many, many women better trained, better able; or tonight, my lord, my master, you have me . . ."

And now she was being lascivious, crawling onto the bed and never mind how the flimsy silks fell away, that was half the point, to contrast her immediate eagerness with Mirjana's dread.

"Of course I have you, I have everything I want."

It was another of those moments of instant understanding; oh, she was sharp tonight, she was at her best. It was an utter truth that he gave her there, terrible to realise. He genuinely had no hopes, no desires beyond this. Food and drink and luxurious comfort, a garden full of pleasures, women and boys and absolute indulgence. Why should he look to the world beyond the wall, why should he want to govern it, or anything? In here, he didn't even have to govern himself.

Nor was he going to let himself be governed by a girl's suggestion; she knew that in the same moment, saw it with this unaccustomed clarity even before he said it.

"Tonight I want her," he said, as his eyes went back to Mirjana. She stifled a moan, but only barely; he had heard it too, his face showed it. A little twitch, half a frown and half a smile. "I want both of you," he said. "For now, her. You later."

"Magnificence . . ."

"What? Weren't you a virgin, when you married my great father?"

"Yes, of course, but—"

"But what?"

It was a lie, a calumny on both of them, but, "I do not think he much enjoyed the night, Magnificence."

It was a calumny and a waste of time; he said, "He was an old man, my father. Sometimes I think he was born old."

If age equates to wisdom, I think he was born older than you. "He had lived a long time, and he did know—"

"Know what? How to take what he wanted from a woman? Well, and so do I know that. Whether or not she knows how to give it."

He took a swallow of wine, but Jendre had overfilled the goblet in her hopes, or else he was clumsy in his drinking, propped on one elbow and not watching what he did; it spilled around the corners of his mouth, onto the skin of his chest and the silks of his bedding.

He scowled and thrust the goblet at her, saying, "Take this and hold it for me. And light me a *khola*-pipe. I can train a girl better than any eunuch." And his hand reached out across the bed to where a leather switch was lying half-concealed in a fold.

Jendre's fingers were trembling again, but not from nervousness now. She set the wine down neatly to hand and turned obediently to look for pipe and *khola*-jar, and couldn't spot them in all the shadows of the room until the boy—all his gold-dust streaked with running sweat but still swaying dozily on his feet, rapt in the music but never heedless of his audience, not when that audience was master of his world—pointed with his chin, to a shelf above the brazier. Sure enough, there were the makings of a smoke. By the way his eyes were rolling in his head while his body went on dancing, Jendre judged that the boy might have smoked a pipe or two himself, before his master came.

She dipped a handful of dried herb from the jar and filled the pipe's bowl, overfilled it indeed, much as she had the goblet. Mehmet might have been allowed his fill of smoke in the *Kafes*, it would have been a kindness in his father to give his captives that much freedom; his son might be long used to its effects. But he might not, it might be as new to him as alcohol. If he could be brought swiftly to a dizziness and the dense sleep that would follow, then she could still save Mirjana something of the night . . .

She was still thinking clearly enough, at any rate. She noticed that in herself and approved it, as she packed the *khola* tight with her thumbs, as she noticed that the tremble was still there inside her and fighting to get out.

Fighting to hold it in—*he shall not beat her, he shall not*—but a glance behind showed that the Sultan had left the switch where it was and was only exploring Mirjana with hands and eyes, not roughly, something to be grateful for although she didn't look grateful, she looked wild, terrified, appalled—Jendre looked for a spill to light the pipe, and couldn't find that either. The boy was no help this time, drifting with his eyes closed. She felt unreasonably abandoned; how could he guide her to the makings and not to a light? So many lamps in the room, any one of them would furnish a flame, but she needed a way to carry that to the ready pipe. Her temper was equally ready and perhaps this stupid boy might be the spark to ignite it, perhaps she would flare at him instead of His Magnificence though it was the Sultan who had earned it, deserved it, set her into this shaking fury . . .

She choked suddenly, on a waft of smoke from the brazier; and glared down at that in lieu of the dancing-boy in lieu of the Sultan, and—

———

OH. That would be why the boy had not guided her to a light, then; because he thought he had. Tears of frankincense were scattered among the glowing charcoal in the brazier, where they burned and smoked. The brazier sat on a tripod, and between its feet was a basket heaped with more of the little golden nuggets.

There was a rod lying in the brazier with its ivory handle toward her hand, its tip buried in the heart of the charcoal. It looked like a branding-iron in miniature; really, she supposed it was a delicate kind of poker, meant mostly to stir the charcoal into fresh life when the time came to recharge it with incense.

But it would light the pipe too, it must be keeping hot enough in there. No wonder the pipe was kept close to the brazier, and the *khola* too; no wonder the boy thought he had done enough. Indeed he had, and she had simply not been bright enough to see it.

While she'd been complimenting herself on thinking so sharply, thinking through her rage. Flattering herself, more like. Blundering about, blind and incensed, addled by this incense-smoke so that she couldn't see what was just under her nose . . .

She gripped the poker and drew it out; saw one of the pea-sized tears of frankincense clinging stickily, smokily to its tip; and frowned, and went to wipe it off against the iron rim of the brazier—

———

—AND was interrupted, brutally forestalled when Mirjana screamed.

Jendre spun around to see her friend thrown across the bed now and the Sultan on top of her, pinning her down.

And that was—God! this was a wicked world, a cruel world, but that was what they were here for, all in all, and there was nothing she should do to stop it, so she should just stand back and let it happen, stand by to comfort Mirjana in any way she could when it was over.

Any other woman, and she would have done exactly that. But this was Mirjana, who was so much stronger than her and so much wiser in everything but this, and so horrified by this, and Jendre loved her too much to be still; and—oh, fool!—she was *struggling*, clawing at him, trying to get away. And Mehmet was cursing, slapping at her, reaching out and fumbling across the covers for his switch; and Jendre honestly didn't know, couldn't have said afterwards whether her first impulsive move was to calm Mirjana or to protect her: to say "No, don't do that!" to him, or to her.

But it takes time to move, even if that time is measured only in moments; and in the time it took Jendre to cross from the brazier to the bed, Mehmet had found his switch and struck Mirjana savagely across the face with it.

And it was Jendre who screamed then, and not her friend; Jendre whose fury finally cut loose; Jendre who swung her arm with the glowing poker in it, just as the Sultan had swung his switch, and Jendre who struck him as he had struck Mirjana, ruinously on the cheek.

Jendre who had to stand and watch as that gobbet, that tear of frankincense fell free, to glow and smoke and burn its way into the Sultan's eye while he was screaming now.

Chapter Four

E said, "We need to go back to Sund."

He was astonished that they still listened to him at all. They needed him, of course, they could do little enough without him—though Rhoan was stronger than she used to be, to his deep anxiety—but he'd become so strange even to himself, he'd gone so far in his power and inside his head, he must seem simply mad with it. Not dogtooth-slow or bestial—not yet—but frantic, cackling-mad, like the man who sat in the gutters and drooled and poured water on his head.

Him, Issel could understand. To a man of Sund, to a mage of Sund, even to a scratchy street-mage with a sickness in his bones, madness and water should sit close together. Water could drive anyone mad when it crept into you.

When you crept into it. Sometimes Issel thought he saw the world from underwater; sometimes, he thought that he was mad. He was sure the others thought so. And yet, when he spoke, they did still listen.

And argue, and at least that was normal, that was right.

"Issel, no. Why? We can't come and go, across the river. We were lucky the first time: not to be caught, finding Ailse, finding our way in here . . ."

"Where we can do nothing but lurk." That was Rhoan, arguing with Gilder, and that was right too, though it didn't mean that she agreed with Issel. "What do you want to do, attack their soldiers here the way you did

in Sund? It's pointless, Gilder. You can't drive them out of Sund by nibbling at them in Maras. Worse, it's suicide. I can't hide us forever. They'll
bring dogs again, or they'll spot one of us coming or going and just follow us back, or they'll come while Issel's asleep and so we'll have no
warning, or—"

"No," Gilder said, "that's not what I want. It's not what we came for."

"We can't *do* what we came for. We tried, we failed. If Issel can't get
into that pavilion, none of us can, so . . ."

"Not that, no. But one big strike, enough to shake the city, enough to let
Sund see that if we all stand together, we can stand against Maras and all
her armies . . . Oh, I've told you already, you know what I want."

"To kill the Sultan. Yes. And we've told you, that's pointless too.
They've killed two of their own, and Sund is still Sund"—captive, divided,
defeated, oppressed.

"But if it is Sund that kills the next one, if it is known to be Sund—"

"Then they are united as never before, and their armies march over their
bridge and destroy every last vestige of our city and our hopes. They would
kill all our people, burn the buildings to the ground and sow the fields with
salt. We can't move, we daren't move, unless we can bring down the bridge.
You know this, we've talked it over already, over and over . . ."

Issel was on the verge of changing his mind: they didn't listen to him after all, they only used his words as a trigger, to rerun the same arguments
again and again. And reach the same place, which was nowhere.

Unexpectedly, it was Ailse who brought them back. Doglike, she had
hung on to what he'd said to start this; as the argument died, she said,
"Why's Issel wanting to go back to Sund?"

That turned them all round to him again. He took a breath and felt the
spark of water in it, the dampness of people in warm air; he said, "We have
to find Armina, and fetch her back here."

Baris said nothing, but he'd hardly spoken for days now. Ailse shrugged;
she didn't know who he meant, or why he wanted her, or why it would matter who she was, when the simple getting of her was so difficult. The other
two stared at him, for all the world as though they really did think him mad.
Then they both started to say so, their voices clambering higher and higher
as they fought to speak over each other.

Issel was quiet by nature, and would never have thought that two people could raise such a clamour on their own. He sat it out until one or the other remembered that they were meant to be hiding here, until they had shushed each other, until they had come back to him with the one bare, bone-bitter question, "Why?"

"Because we need her," he said, "if we're going to break the bridge."

"What *for*?"

"Rhoan, you were there with me"—*you pulled me out, or I did you, I forget*—"didn't you feel something familiar about the magic in that place?"

"It all stank of the bridge," she said slowly, knowing that there must be more, "the colours and the lights . . ."

"What else, though? Apart from the bridge?" He wanted to make her see it, if only to confirm what he'd seen himself. She had the clue now, but he did still want to hear it from her.

She stared at him, shook her head, confessed it. "Armina's magic. Her—truthsaying, fortune-telling, whatever it is. Picking holes in the future, and catching what spills out. When that rust of hers gets in your head, it's like that, all sick and swirling patterns . . ." And she shifted her gaze down to her hands, her palms, where Armina had used that same magic to heal the damage Issel had done there, not very long at all before that woman went off to the Marasi and betrayed them all.

"Yes," he said, "and the magicians have women in that pavilion who tend the sleeping children, who all wear their hair as Armina does"—as nobody in Sund did, nor he thought in Maras either, except for these—"with bells and mirrors in . . ."

Gilder's shrug was almost a snarl in itself, and his voice was harsher. "So?"

"So she is of their kind, however she came to Sund."

"I understand that. I am not stupid." *Nor likely to become so*, his voice implied viciously, *no dogtooth I*. "I meant, so what would you do with her, if you could find her, if you could fetch her here?"

"I would . . ." Well, what would he do? It was no bad question, even despite the malice that drove it. If "malice" was the right word. If it was, then it was aimed at him; Gilder's feelings for Armina went far beyond malice, into the deepest pits of hatred. "I would have her"—no—"I would *ask* her for help to defeat their magic. She must know what it is; she uses it herself." Or at least some shadow of it, something from the same foreign source, where he could not speak the language nor hardly see in the light that his eyes could barely use, the colours he could not name.

"And you would trust her? First with our safety, and then to tell you truly, how to defeat her own people's magic?"

"Issel," from Rhoan, "Tulk died, because of what she did."

"And Lenn," from Gilder.

"Yes, and others, I know." Too many to count, some whose names he'd never had the chance to learn. "I *know*," and he was shouting at himself as much as them. "But I have known Armina longer than you"—all his life— "and she has not always been kind, but everything she has done, it has all been for a purpose." She had ordered all his life, or so it seemed from here, looking back; he thought she had seen the same pattern from the other end, looking forward. "I think she always meant for me to be here, now." And if Tulk, Lenn, others had to die to achieve that, then so be it. Whether she wove the pattern or only saw its weaving, there was a ruthlessness there that he had long since learned to live with.

"What for?"

"I don't know. Perhaps she wants to see us break the bridge. Perhaps she wants to help." She was slave, in Sund; perhaps she saw her own freedom in it, somehow. Or perhaps she had been one of them, here, and they had sold her, and she wanted her revenge. He could make up stories all the day, and they would be no more true than the fancies told on Sundain streets every day and every hour of the day. It was his city's strength; perhaps it was the strength of every captive, to tell tales of being free.

"Then why are we here and she in Sund, if she needs to be here with us, if she saw it all so clearly that she could kill our friends to make it happen?"

"I don't *know*." He hated these guessing games, that took him further and further from what little he was sure of. It was all uncertain ground, but this was bog, and men could drown in it. "Perhaps this is how she comes here, because we send for her?"

"Issel," Rhoan said doubtfully, "if she wanted to come, if she needed it, if she saw that—why wouldn't she just have met us on the strand, that night we left Sund?"

"Because we would have killed her," he said simply. "Gilder would have done it, you would have done it. I might have done it first." Tulk had died that day, and Lenn, and all the others.

"I would kill her still," Gilder grunted.

"Not if we needed her." He'd said it himself, earlier: he was not stupid. "If she could show that she was useful—"

"—and if we could trust her," the eternal question—

"—and if we could fetch her here," Rhoan interrupted, or finished off, perhaps. "Did you have any ideas about that, Issel? Because I don't."

"No." There was the bridge, which was guarded and impossible; or there was the river, where they had no boat and small hope of achieving one. "We could try the docks, there are boats there . . ."

"All of which are guarded," Ailse said, "behind locked gates."

Of course; there were dogtooths all along the waterfront, looking for escape. Every manageable boat, every stealable boat would be protected, unless it was a trap leading to the cage and chains, to the work-gangs on the docks. "We could break the locks, and overcome the guards."

"Perhaps. And take the boat, perhaps, and go to Sund. And find this woman Armina, and then what? How would you bring her back here, with the docks alert and double guards? As soon as they saw you in the water, they would fire your boat and all of you, you'd never reach the dockside."

They had heard that the Marasi could do that. Not magic: some tar that clung and burned like oil, which they could fling from a machine. Not everything said in Sund was true, but who could tell? Ailse clearly believed it. She might have seen it.

He said, "We don't have to land at the dockside. We could come to the beach at night, in the Shine, as we did before," when the bridge's light was better than darkness to hide them, because it promised that no one would be looking.

"You could; but you have attacked the palace and killed a magician since you did that before. And fled down here, and your enemy knows that. They may think you have gone away"—at least the patrols were fewer now, more a lingering threat than a daily danger, so long as the Sundain hid here and did nothing—"but the outflow will be watched, and the beach too." *Shine or no Shine*, she was saying.

"Then there will be more deaths. There must be. We need her." He might have been driven back by the magicians, but he was confident of the soldiery. He had death in his fingers, so long as they were wet; he almost had death in his eyes. Which were always wet, so always had that promise.

"Well. If you must go for her, I will come."

"Issel, it's impossible." That was Rhoan, quiet and absolute. "You think you can slaughter your way onto a boat, cross the river without being pursued, come to land unseen in Sund, find Armina, come back the same way, kill more soldiers to get back in here and still not be pursued, go back up to the palace and kill however many guards they've set around that pavilion now, so that she can help you break through their magic so that you can kill the magicians too? Do you really?"

No, not really, though he was still confident about the killing. "I think we have to try," he said.

"Even if we need her," Gilder growled, "do you really imagine we can trust her?"

"No," Issel said. All his life's history said the same: that she would keep him and feed him and send him where she thought he most needed to be, and always for reasons that were obscure and obscurely her own, that could in no way ever buy his trust.

"Well, then—"

"But I think we have to try."

———

IN the exhaustion of a hopeless argument, unwinnable on either side— Rhoan and Gilder having no alternatives to offer, because Issel was demonstrably right, but so were they—Issel let his mind drift.

Not casually, not sulkily. This was duty now, a watchful care: his mind drifted like mist over water, like breath on a mirror, the lightest of touches, feeling its way upstream and down. Feeling for form, for warmth, for sounds, or for the odd echoes of those things that were his water-sense.

Feeling, and finding; and saying, "Someone's coming down."

"Soldiers?" Gilder asked, while Rhoan sighed and stretched out a hand, to where water stood always ready.

"No. I don't think so. There are two of them." Patrols were five or six men; workers and watermen always came with guards. Occasionally there would be a random pair of soldiers, coming down and going up by unexpected routes for unreadable reasons, but he could tell a soldier first touch, by the hot glare of his steel.

Rhoan murmured, "How do you know?" but it wasn't a question asking for an answer. Even at this distance, this tentative a contact, he knew.

"Where?"

That was Gilder again, and it did need answering. "Up at the cistern of pillars." One waiting by the waters, while the other ranged up one tunnel and another, as though trying to discover which way forward. For any meaning of forward, where there were choices that led to choices and the purpose was unknown.

"Can you tell us who it is?"

"Wait."

———————

WATER-SENSE is not smelling, and did not bring him scents; but he reached over water, over distance, and that restless, anxious, hesitant figure was lamp oil and bath oil and boy-sweat all entangled, and he knew.

"It's Teo," he said. "And his friend, I suppose. Someone should go to fetch them, or he'll get lost again."

"We showed him the way from one palace to the other. Issel, you marked it for him, didn't you?"

"Yes, but not the way down here, in case a guard followed the marks. I think that's what he's looking for, I think he wants us. Rhoan, will you go . . . ?"

———————

SHE went, she came back; she had Teo with her and his friend too, squat and stumping.

Teo was clutching his little lamp like a talisman against a greater dark, the world and its unkindness. His eyes clung to them hungrily, needfully: telling Issel that he was right, but not why.

It was Gilder who pinned him down, blunt and brutal. "Teo, stop jerking about like a fish on a line and tell us. What's happened, and what do you want?"

"My mistress . . . She hurt the Sultan, and she is seized, condemned . . ."

<h1>Chapter Five</h1>

IRJANA was dead, then.

Jendre had heard this, in an aside intended to sound casual, dismissive, meaningless. It was not punitive, she was meant to understand: only that slaves who had heard their Sultan screaming could not possibly expect to live. The dancing boy and the woman, they were dead too, for the same cause.

She did not ask how. They might refuse to tell her, these guards who had so lazily let her overhear; they might tell her true; they might lie to her. She could not know, so why torment herself? The thing was enough, the fact of it.

They had lied to her already, she knew that. This whole letting-the-news-slip, as though she were not meant to know, that was a lie in itself; so was the reason given. Of course it was punitive. Mirjana had died because that would hurt Jendre, and for no reason else. The Sultan was a boy, and he wanted a boy's vengeance, lashing out all over. She was half-surprised he had not come himself to tell her, to gloat over details that might or might not be true. He had lost his eye, though; he might still be in too much pain. His mother, the Valide Sultan, had him in her care and would be fussing, she might not let him out of bed.

It could be a mother's vengeance and not a boy's, to kill the slaves and be sure the culprit heard it. Left to himself, Mehmet might just have ripped and torn at her, with blades and irons and who knew what. This was colder, harsher, more considered; on second thought, Jendre was more inclined to lay it at the mother's feet. Particularly the way the guards broke it to her, so incidentally, the very opposite of gloating. There was nothing of the boy in that.

They gave themselves away, though, when they asked her directly where Teo might be found. If they couldn't find him, she was unclear how she might help, who hadn't seen him for days; and so she said. They were rough in response and determined that she knew.

Perhaps she did, but she said nothing, only shrieked a lot until they went away. Their hands had hurt her, but the shrieking not at all; she had no pride left. Only stubbornness, and that was better hidden.

They could have no reason for wanting Teo, except to punish her further, which was what gave the lie to all they'd said before. They were fools; they had spoiled that and given her this, some fragment of hope to hold to. If Teo couldn't be found, he must have slipped out of the palace. Perhaps he'd found a way back to Djago, who would surely look after him. Security, even happiness for one of her friends: that was a hook to hang a comfort on.

Otherwise, there was nothing. Mirjana was dead, and of course Jendre was dead too, only that it had not happened yet.

She could have wished for that same swift dispatch. She had been picked to be a slave, no different; it seemed unfair to distinguish now, between one slave and another . . .

Well, no. Not really. She had been the one who set her mark on the Sultan. Of course there was a price to pay for that. She was sorry that Mirjana had had to pay on her account, but dead already was better than being tortured still; and whether it was vengeance or justice or necessary politics, the greater cost would have to fall on Jendre.

And then—politics, yes—there was her father. He would need to be appeased. She couldn't imagine how the pasha had kept him quiet when Mehmet picked her to be one among his slave-girls; unless they had hoped to hide that, to leave him thinking that she was still with the other widows in the Palace of Tears. She did not think it could have been kept secret long.

Now, of course, there could be no secrets. Her father might have raised a protest, before; he might have raised an army, raised a rebellion at the news that his daughter was being bedded by this puppet-Sultan. Unless he'd been bought off by some promise of influence, a seat at the pasha's side. He might have thought that worth a little honour lost.

Or, if his influence was strong enough already, he might have used it to buy her freedom back. But that his daughter had assaulted the Sultan, for whatever cause; that she had wounded him, scarred him deeply, that took her beyond any protection, beyond negotiation. There would be no rescue from her father. He would condemn her himself if he were asked to sit in judgement.

Of course he would. She would probably have done the same.

Just, not Mirjana. Not the innocents. Oh, she did hope that Teo had got properly away and was safe, but she didn't really believe it. There was no safety: not for her and hers, in this city, now.

––––––––

SHE sat in the dark and waited to die.

She seemed to have been doing this a long time, though there was no way to measure that. No glimpse of sun or starlight, nor did they bring her meals. Why waste food on the condemned? Or light, or water, information? Sometimes they talked outside her cell, but only to torment her. Just that once they had come in, heavy-handed, to ask questions about Teo.

Did pain make the time pass quicker? She wasn't sure. It had at least made the end more certain. If there were any chance of her surviving this, the guards would have been more careful, of her and of themselves. A soldier among the high learned to be circumspect. Lost influence could be regained, and power shifted fast; that woman he brutalised last week—under orders, or just because she was here, in a cell and destitute of friends— might be giving the orders again tomorrow, and against his head.

That they had made so free with her body, that they had left her bruised and bleeding and appalled, that was an absolute guarantee. She was condemned already, as she had to be. It only waited to learn the manner of her death, and how slow her progress towards it.

She did wish that they would hurry up. She couldn't measure time, but there seemed to be an intolerable burden of it. No comfort there, all these wasted breaths, this eternal hunger. She did have a hunger to be dead already, but astonishingly—at least, it astonished her—she had a base and earthly hunger too, a ravenous craving to eat. She thought it was indecorous, to be swallowing empty against an appetite on what might be her last day alive. She ought to be more noble, or else more craven: fear what was to come, or rise above it. Turn to prayer, perhaps, or think of her beloveds.

Instead, she thought a lot about food. Without it, even her bowels made an unreliable day-clock. Her stomach gurgled and hurt her, her dry throat longed for sweet waters, but her mouth really ached to chew. She wanted breads and meats, pastries and the tang of spice, soft fruits and nuts to bite on.

Wanted and would not ask, so perhaps she had some pride left after all; or else it was just wisdom—too late!—not to ask for what she knew would be refused. They didn't even bring her water. She had a bucket; perhaps she was meant to drink from that.

Meantime, she could wait. Sit, and wait. At the end of this long darkness was another, longer, easier to bear. Eventually they would come, to bring her to it.

———————

EVENTUALLY, they did. The guards were veiled here below their helmets, which was a curious inversion of the world she knew, where women went veiled among men. It used to be that there were no men here in the women's world, only eunuchs; previously, it had been Feres and his fellows who walked her this way, down stairs to a hall, a door, a lamplit chamber with vaults and pillars to carry the weight of the harem above. Today it was soldiers all the way. Mehmet must be nervous among his women; or else the pasha was nervous for him, or just strengthening his grip a little, making his possession clear.

She had known this before: the dais with its cluster of the highborn and superior gathered around the throne, the reed mat on the floor before it. The surprise to her was to find the throne occupied. She'd thought the boy would delegate his justice, but not so.

She had thought he'd want to hide his face, from his court and especially from her who had caused it, but not so.

There sat Mehmet, waiting; and even these thick shadows couldn't be kind to his face, not now. That gobbet of burning incense had seared the eye from its socket and scorched the orbit of bone around; the poker had branded a seam across his cheek. In decency, in pride, he might have veiled all of that, if veiling was the mood.

In cold spite, she thought, he had not. Let her see the face that judged her; anonymity was for shadow-folk, guards and lesser men. And for his mother, the Valide Sultan, who stood stoutly beside his throne, in the place of influence. She was veiled, and Jendre couldn't recognise her; they might have met in this palace or in that, the one harem or the other. They might not. It couldn't matter now.

Those who surrounded her were barefaced, except for the shift and fall of shadow; blessedly, Jendre couldn't recognise them either. Not her father, not the pasha, no man she knew. This was a play-court, then, a toy to keep the boy amused. As she had been, as was all his world of women above. The real world, as ever, lay outside the wall.

Except that suddenly there was one face she did know: at the back and standing away from the dais was Hedin, the wazir's son. He had been a colleague to Salem, a rival perhaps, certainly not a friend; but he might be serving Salem's father now, as well as his own. He stood here as their eyes, she guessed, to see how the Sultan conducted himself, what he ordered done. Whether it was his order, or his mother's. All of that, and how the men behaved around him, more. A witness, a spy, a watchfulness.

Whether Hedin himself would carry word to Salem, how she conducted herself at this last trial, she couldn't guess. He might do it: from respect, or from vindictiveness, or anything between. If not, what he told would still get back to Salem, one way or another.

Well, if he wanted to disparage her, he'd have to lie about it. She knelt because that was her place before her Sultan, but she did so as upright and graceful as she could manage after days of no commons, when she was dizzy with hunger and sick with anticipation. She had been here before, and not disgraced herself; she would not do so now.

The Sultan—Mehmet One-Eye, she supposed they would call him, if he didn't earn himself some better name—glared down at her. Briefly, wildly, she thought that he wore his new face well. Pain and fever had drawn his flesh more tightly to his bones, so that he looked far less the child in his young man's body; that ruined eye gave him a strength, a solidity he could never have achieved by merit.

If it gave him also a malice that had not been his before, she shouldn't be surprised at that.

She thought this was a good harem to be leaving. Once she was gone, that malice might well linger and fester, and turn foul. How long before he let his marring and his captivity consume him, before his life was all grievance and resentment, to be taken out on those he could?

For now there was still pain, she could see that, and fury, and distress; and she could be glad of all of those, because they were at least clean, the heat of flame as against the heat of fever.

He said, "You have lifted weapons against the body of your sovereign lord, to our great harm and outrage."

He spoke the line as though he'd been coached to it, as surely he had; she thought his coach was standing by his chair.

She said, "Magnificence—"

"No! You will not speak, you will not be heard," and that was still what he'd been taught to say, the great difference between this trial and the last, as though lessons had been learned in the meantime, although no one, it seemed, had survived from then to this. No one except her, and she was dead already.

Her voice had sounded dead to her, just that one word, and she could only croak it; as well, perhaps, that he was trained not to listen.

He said, "You have been condemned. This is your doom: that as our fathers did with wicked women, you shall be sewn into a sack and cast into the river."

The river was sown with bones, they said, from earlier harems. One famous sultan, famously mad, had drowned his entire house this way. Perhaps she could be grateful, that it was not to be worse.

And then he leaned forward, and this was all his own and nothing of his mother's teaching, because he wanted to tell her that it would be worse: "I have told them to prepare a sack of leather," he hissed. "Oiled leather, with wax in all the seams. The water will be slow, slow to take you, and you will be struggling and screaming all the way . . ."

She wouldn't, no. He was a boy, an imperial son, he had no idea how other people lived or felt or suffered; he had never had to learn.

She wouldn't scream. She would go quietly, and be glad to go.

Perhaps she'd float, if her sack was full of air. Perhaps she'd bob away downriver to the ocean, and leave all the court and all the city laughing at him: Mehmet One-Eye, the Sultan who couldn't even see how to drown a helpless girl in a sack.

THEY took her away, and would have liked to drag her, she thought, these soldiers of his, to please him; except that she walked cooperatively, obediently between them, and never gave them the chance.

Then it was back to her dry thoughts in the dark and the iron door bolted behind her. This would have been worse: simply to be locked up in here and left to desiccate, like an insect in a bowl. Strange that he hadn't thought of that, he who'd been locked up himself for so long, who must surely understand the dragging horror of so much time.

She detected his mother's hand again. The damage done was so visible, so public, Jendre's death must needs be public too. He might have preferred to have her close, immured, where he could come and whisper hatreds at her while she starved, while she dried; it was a wiser choice, and so she thought it was his mother's, to send her openly and wetly from the world.

And Mehmet was so new on his throne and so uncertain in his hold of it—so unlike his father—that his Sultanate would need to be asserted through the city, any way it could. Any way it was allowed. What better than to put an errant harem girl to death in the old way, the sultan's way? That would suit the pasha and keep her father quiet too; and it would be an object lesson for the people. Give her to the river, and let the city watch . . .

That would be why the condemnation before the court there, that swift charade: to make her death official, the Sultan's decree, heard and witnessed. It would be why she'd been returned to this dry waiting, to let the word spread wider, so that the city should know to gather and look. There would be ceremony about it, a great portentousness; she might be the only one who couldn't see it happen.

She and Mirjana, who was dead, for whom all this was happening. Jendre sat in her darkness and lost touch with time, and was glad to be too dry to cry.

THE dark might have been frightening, it might have been meant that way; in fact she found it restful. Now that she knew, she had nothing to fear in here. And little to regret. She had tried to remake the world—to save the Sultan her husband, to save her sister, to save the man she loved, to save her friend—and had failed at every turn, but at least she had tried.

Had she ever tried to save herself? She thought not, at heart, though others had tried to save her. They'd failed too. That was the world, the way of it: too big to turn aside, too cold to survive. Implacable.

It sounded like a description of the river. That was accidental; she liked it anyway. It felt strange to be smiling in her death-cell, but at least no one could see. It was good to be private, these last moments of her life.

Private with her ghosts: her husband the Man of Men was there, and so was Mirjana. And Sidië and Salem too, both of them in a forced seclusion and so dead to the world, differently dead. As she was, dead to them, although she hadn't quite died yet either. She wondered if she haunted them at all. Salem, she hoped, perhaps. Sidië she thought was beyond reach of any ghosts, living or otherwise.

Soon, so would she be. Unless the dead could be haunted, but she doubted that. She would drown and die and be gone from here, not linger; whom would she need to haunt, except Sidië who was lost in dreams, who would not see her?

———————

WHEN they came, she wanted to think that she was ready. She wanted them to think it, very greatly. She tried very hard: on her feet while the bolt was still rattling, before the door slammed open, not turning her head aside although the glare of their lamp burned her poor dry eyes, stepping forward before they could summon her out.

Two of them, big smelly men, but then she was smelly herself. They were rough with her because they wanted to be, not because they needed to. Their hands seized her arms, seized and twisted as they forced her along; she didn't cry out because she was determined not to, because she bit her tongue savagely hard to ensure it.

A little blood was warm and welcome in her mouth, in her throat. It tasted better than the dust and drought of these last days; and soon, of course, she would have water.

Not yet.

For now she was taken to a small room where a sack was waiting for her, and a woman too.

The sack lay on a table, stiffly collapsed in on itself, pale new hide glistening in shafts of sunlight. It was good to see the sun, although it burned her eyes.

The woman said, "Hold her," which the men already were. Neatly and swiftly, she began to undo the laces of Jendre's dress.

Jendre struggled, uselessly; croaked, "I can do that."

The woman ignored her. With all the fastenings undone, she nodded to the men, who shifted their grip just enough and long enough to strip Jendre naked. It meant nothing, except that she would have preferred to strip herself. She waited quietly for the opportunity to step into the sack—and instead found herself being as roughly and rapidly dressed again, in a simple sleeveless white wool robe.

It was scratchy, but she had itched all week; it was clean, though she was not. She could be grateful, even through a dizzy bewilderment. Why were they dressing her, to drown her in a sack? The sack was surely dress enough . . .

THE answer, of course, was that they were dressing her for the streets, and she would get to see her own execution after all.

All but the end of it, at least.

They made her carry the sack.

Out of the room and out of the building, then out of the harem itself: herself and the soldiers—she was thinking of them as hers now, her own soldiers, the tall one with the black moustache and the one who shaved, perhaps because the scars around his lips disfigured any beard, and she wondered what on earth he'd done to be cut so; had he chewed on a knife?—and the woman too, which was a surprise.

Weak from days of hunger, dizzy with sunlight after so long in the dark, she stumbled as she crossed the threshold, as she passed under the arch of the opened gate; only the soldiers' grip on her arms held her upright. She wanted to thank them gracefully, to be sure they understood it was not fear that had halted her when she saw what was waiting in the street. She couldn't do it, her lips were cracked leather and her throat was baked sand. A little blood was not enough to loosen words, where they were caught so dry.

All she could do was show them. Her bare feet trampled weakness on hot paving-stones; her mind flared like a candle-wick, dispelling dizzy shadows. She couldn't shrug her body off altogether—not yet—but she could bend it to her will. For a little while, until that will failed too. She could feel its failure coming, building like a storm. She was too dry, too hollow; her mind was as clear as a glass bell, and as fragile. It would break, it must break; she could be proud, she should be astonished that it had not broken yet.

The soldiers had to let her elbows go, if only for a moment; there was a step up into the wagon, and that was only wide enough for one.

So she stepped up alone, it could almost have seemed voluntary; and by the time they had clambered up to join her she had already walked forward to where a pole thrust up from the wagon bed. She had put the sack down at her feet, indeed, and was surveying the way the pole ended in a cross-bar at waist height.

Apparently she could talk after all, when it really did matter, when it was a little more than saving face before a pair of soldiers. She said, "If you want me to hold this, I will do that. You do not need to tie my hands."

They didn't say a word. One of them—the moustached one—took her wrists and drew them behind her back; the scarred one had a leather thong ready.

And so she was bound to the pole in the back of an ox cart, and so she was displayed in the public streets, all through her city of Maras.

———

SHE had been paraded before, but discreetly, behind the drawn curtains of a palanquin. She had been paraded openly before, on a litter, but then she had been veiled and the Sultan's bride-to-be, with soldiers and gallants— *oh, Salem*—to attend her. She had been run in shame through these same streets before, but in a black bier, a pinch-box, where no one could see her face or anything about her.

Now she was dressed, but she might as well be naked; she was exposed brutally, and people were called forth to see her. In front rode a janizar astride a great horse, with kettledrums slung on either side of the beast; he pounded them alternately to the slow rhythm of his progress. Behind, a clerk on a mule recited her sins in a flat, dull repetition that was none the less penetratingly loud:

"Come out, come see! This is the woman who dared harm to His Magnificence. She goes to the river, come see! Her name is nothing, dust in the stream. His name will be wonderful. Come see!"

And they did come, to stare and spit and gossip. She could be glad to be so high, so separated from them; none of their spitting reached her, though their voices did, calling down curses on her head.

It was not love of their Sultan that made them spit and curse, she was sure of that. Nor hatred of her; they didn't know who she was. None of them, surely, would recognise in her the adorned and glittering bride-to-be of the Man of Men, those few short months ago. Chances were, they barely remembered him, let alone his last of many wives. They were afraid, she thought, after two dead sultans and now a boy on the throne, a vulnerable boy who could be hurt even by his women. Their city had been rocked, the empire was not built on such firm foundations as they thought, they needed to blame someone and she was one who could be blamed without cost. That was all.

So they spat and cursed, and she endured it. When they threw an occasional stone, she ducked aside if she saw it coming, as far as her bonds would let her. Those she didn't see, they were mostly badly aimed and flew by, or else they fell short and skittered across the wagon bed. One or two did strike her, but her flesh was dried like saltfish; nothing hurt.

That was remarkable, but true. Nothing did hurt, anymore. Nothing in her body, from the too-tight bindings on her wrists to the rowel of hunger in her belly to the cutting sting of a flung stone; she felt them all, but not as hurts. And nothing in her mind, from all the cruelties of her recent life to the losses of her friends to the anticipation of her nearing death; those things that had made her huddle and scream and rage before this, now they were shadows, like curtains to be torn down in search of the light beyond.

Her mind had broken, then, as she'd feared that it would. If even Mirjana's death could not hurt her anymore, then she was no longer Jendre. She wondered who she was instead: some creature untouchable, ethereal, transient. Otherworldly. That was good, that was a blessing. Perhaps it was given to all the condemned, to be unbuttoned from their lives before they lost them . . .

Perhaps this is the first touch of delirium: too much sun after too long in the dark, on an empty belly, nothing more . . .

That was a sane thought, rational and unwelcome. And persuasive. No matter. She could shrug it off as she did her body, slip free of it as she did her mind and still soar on these new-found wings, far above her body and its suffering, far above her mind in its anguish. She almost felt that she could look down on herself, in her slow procession. She could let go this wagon and ride with the soldier instead, with his relentless pounding drums; or with the herald behind, although the drums were better than that raven's voice.

Or she could swoop ahead, rise higher, overlook all her city and the river too: count the vessels in the docks; see the fuss about the royal quay; wonder at the crowds where they had gathered on every point of vantage, lining roads and rooftops, spilling through gardens and being squeezed out onto beaches from where they would see nothing but could at least still say that they were there . . .

It might be foresight; perhaps it was insight. There was said to be truth in dreams, and it might also be true of delirium-dreams. This couldn't be the clear sight it seemed to be, but she did still think that what she saw was real. Little by little, she was sure of it. The people had come out to see her die: not only in the hundreds who stared and spat and threw stones and ran to follow the wagon down, but in thousands. Highborn and low, janizars and merchants, urchins and sailors and saddlemakers, clerks and whores; they were packing every outlook on the river, even into the shadow of the bridge.

She supposed she was famous now. More so than her marriage-days, when they had come out to see her wed. From today she would be a hiss and a spit, a hawk in the throat whenever people met to talk about the calamitous history of Maras. An assassin in the harem, so near to murdering her master: the city's strength was the strength of the Sultan, and this was a crack in the armour, a breach in the walls. Maras hated her, and rightly; it needed to see her die.

Happily, she was in a mood to oblige. She half-thought she'd died already, or else she thought she'd half-died; her body was away from her, below, an anchor perhaps but only that, no more, and cables could be cut . . .

———

SHE drifted, floated, in and out of her own senses. Sometimes she thought she borrowed others', birds' perhaps; she saw with strangers' eyes and heard unexpected voices from far away or long ago. Ghosts, too: Mirjana walked beside the wagon. Sometimes Jendre thought she was Mirjana, walking, and this was somebody else entirely up here tied to the pole.

She felt nothing, though she did know that there were still pains to be felt: in her bound arms, in her trembling legs, even absurdly in her belly, hunger-cramps again. They lingered, waiting for her attention, but her head was full of light and had no space for her; she was squeezed out, and so she had to float.

SHE floated down to the river, in the wagon's lee. On the royal dock she was untied from the post and rudely handled down, to the distant jeers of the crowds; janizars held them back, though they were pressing close. Sometimes she thought she pressed with them; or eluded the soldiers and pressed against herself, but could find no way inside.

Janizars took her, and she watched more than stumbled inside that heavy awkwardness of flesh she'd always called her own, that had been taken from her in every way she could think of now. They took her, it, all the way to the end of the quay, past the imperial vessels with their awnings and rich embellishments to where a common sailbarge was moored.

That woman walked beside her, the one who had stripped and helped to dress her. Now she was carrying Jendre's sack, and just as well; someone had to, or it would have been left behind. She wouldn't have wanted that.

What she did want, all she wanted was a swift end now. Cut the cable, sail away and let the anchor lie . . .

WHICH was, of course, why she was made to wait. A distant figure to those who had come to see her end, just a scratch against the glare of sunlight where it reflected off the shifting river, she came closer to herself again as the tide turned, as her shadow crossed the boards beneath her feet. Not soon, but eventually she was back inside that flesh and bone, that body. Too dry to sweat, she shuddered in the heat, and clenched her fists and glared dry-eyed at that shadow and fought to keep herself upright against the dizziness and the shaking and the dark that threatened in the corners of her sight. The drifting, the separation had been better, so much better than this. She couldn't recapture that, it wouldn't come at will; right now she could barely remember it, like a dream that fades in the first minutes of waking. Now she had her body and nothing else, and that was barely under her control, and all the world was watching.

She would not faint, she would not fall. She had faced their hatred; she spurned their scorn, and would not earn it.

The sun was a weight like an iron bar across her shoulders, but she could stand against it. Thirst was a demon crouched in her mouth, its barbed and scaly tail flexing in her throat, but that was an old foe with nothing new to say, no further harm.

It would be cruel, if her body failed her now. The world was cruel, she knew that, but there were degrees of cruelty and it would be sheer malevolence to add humiliation to what she'd suffered else, what more stood ready. She bit the insides of her cheeks ragged, to give herself those fine sharp pains to focus on, to hold the darkness back.

At last the Sultan came, with his promise of an utter end. He might have waited longer yet, but that the crowds would not. This was about his authority, which meant his safety, how securely he sat the throne; he could not afford to have his writ overrun by a mob, even if they enacted his revenge for him.

So he came, sooner perhaps than he or his mother would have preferred; he came in his own procession, bright and loud with trumpets, whose bold brassy voices blew Jendre almost entirely out of herself again, unless it was simply that she rode high on the wind of relief, that the waiting was over now.

Nearly over. Mehmet and his entourage progressed slowly out along the quay, and stood in formal congregation while the herald called over her crimes, her condemnation and his judgement, as though nobody there knew all of it already, and Jendre had to keep standing where she was.

Then the imperial party boarded the imperial craft, slowly, ceremonially, and Jendre had to keep standing where she was.

The whole little fleet of luxury put out onto the river, one by one, to the accompaniment of music; the boy-Sultan had more flautists to beguile this slow time away, while Jendre had to keep standing where she was.

By now, though, Jendre was flying again, rising high and soaring in circles, leaving her body to fend for itself this last little time. Perhaps she trusted it; perhaps at last she had decided not to care. Let it slump, let it fall if it needed to. She had her end in view; it couldn't hurt her now.

FLOATING as she was, she saw her body muscled onto that fishing barge. Perhaps they thought she was resisting, because she didn't step where she was ordered to; they hadn't realised that she was barely there. At any rate, the soldiers half-dragged, half-threw her down to the deck. And then jumped down beside, while the woman made shift with an awkward, arms-full scramble. The crew cast off fore and aft, and pushed away with long oars.

They didn't raise the sail, not for this. She was surprised almost that they bothered with a boat at all. No doubt the Sultan would go for a pleas-ant jaunt downriver, not to let his whole day be spoiled with this unpleas-antness; for herself, they could as easily have thrown her off the quay's end. A girl could drown in a hand's depth of water, and here the river ran deep.

But no, not that. Not for her. This had to be a show, all the city had to see; she must be taken out into full view of its tiers, up and back.

Her barge didn't follow the imperial fleet, once they were out in open water. It turned against the current and rowed upstream: into the shadow of the bridge, she saw, with a hollow eggshell understanding. She must not only be drowned, she must be degraded, poisoned in death and her bones deformed, disgraced by where they lay.

––––––––––

HER body was an anchor, drawing her after, drawing her down.

They put her body in the sack, and she didn't struggle, she was barely in there with it; but then the woman produced needle, twine and wax, and now Jendre understood what she was for.

While she threaded her needle, a crewman came with weights, ugly bulks of ballast lead. A soldier took them—one at a time, he could not man-age more—and dropped them into the sack with Jendre.

Her body was an anchor, but these were heavier; they caught at her soul and hauled her in, just before the woman closed the sack above her head and tacked it with quick stitches.

Back in the dark, then, back inside herself, Jendre settled to the slow motion of the barge. And wished to fly, and couldn't do it now, cut off from sky: sealed in slowly—everything about today was slow, everything bad, which meant almost everything—with twine and then wax, all she could do was wait. She felt unkindly sane, where she had been hugging madness to herself like a stolen treasure, like a gift.

She hugged her knees instead, and wondered vaguely if she could use the sharp edges on the lead weights to slash her way out of the sack once it was cast under; but she needed both hands just to lift one, and the stinking greasy hide was fresh raw leather, thick and tough. She would drown long before she could cut her way free.

There was no freedom anywhere in this world, not for her.

She couldn't drift any more than she could fly; the men had weighted her down, the woman had sewn her back inside herself, with all her pains and sorrows. Well, she was here, but not for long. She felt it, when the woman left off sewing; felt it, when she left off rubbing wax into that last long seam.

She felt it—how not?—when the men lifted the sack between them, and swung it back and forth against the weight of her and the lead between her feet, and cast her out.

She felt the slapping impact, and then the slow fall down; she felt how the sack bulged out and stiffened like a bladder as it sank, but how it went on sinking. The weights made sure of that. There would be no floating away for her, no bobbing sack on the surface to make a mockery of the Sultan's justice.

Down, down. It had been dark already in this sack, even with the utter sun outside; now in the water it was dark as dark, all black, and she was—at last!—afraid.

She could feel a wetness about her feet, where a slight leak was forcing its way in. The water was deathly cold, as was the leather where she pressed against it, though it tried to squirm away from her. Theirs was a slow and awkward sinking, rocking back and forth in currents; her skin was clammy now, the air she had was wet, and the little relief of that against her lips and throat was lost in her gasping, because there seemed to be little goodness in it and less with every breath, and she thought perhaps she would choke before she drowned . . .

———————

PERHAPS she was drifting again after all, even if she'd found no way to fly. Fly in air, drift in water; that made sense. Of a sort, if you were mad, or madly tending. Eggshell-fragile, and close to death.

She did feel very close to Death now, and yearned for his coming. She thought perhaps that this was him, this light that encompassed all her sack, all her little darkling world. The only dark left was in herself, in the corners of her eyes, like sleep closing in. She had seen that before, and fought it off, but fighting was too hard now.

The light was a glow, soaking in like water. Perhaps it was the water; there was a lot of water now, and she could see it all around her legs, and it was glowing. But then there was a blade, she could see that, because it glowed; it shone, burned almost with its light, as it slashed in through the leather.

And then there was a boy, on the other side of that cut, and he glowed too. Could Death be a boy? She could think of no reason why not, except that she hadn't expected anyone. Perhaps he was an angel. Or a devil, more like, come to drag her down and down.

He wasn't smiling; he looked overwrought, as though he were very ill, or very much in pain. Unless he was very much in wonder, overawed. He ought to be, for this was wonderful. He cast the sack aside and pulled her out of it, and his hand felt solid, flesh and bone, although it burned to touch him.

And now she had no air at all, although she wasn't gasping. There felt no need: as though she'd passed beyond breath. Which should mean beyond life, she should be dead, she must be dead; but she simply didn't feel it.

She felt mad, that for sure. Twice mad, as he tugged her after him in a slow, stepping motion. The water beneath her feet seemed more dense than the water that he pulled her through, so they almost walked on top of it, although it was still water and she could see through it by his light, all the way to the river's bottom where indeed there were bones sown in little heaps, where they must have spilled out of sacks long rotted away.

Part 4

Chapter One

WILL go to Sund for you, Issel, if that will help, although I don't know your friend or how to find her."

They were back in their bolt-hole again, squeezed in with yet two more warm bodies now, though one of those was slender and one was very small.

They had light in plenty, because Issel was still glowing, because he wouldn't let them get him dry; and that meant they could all of them turn to stare at the one who had spoken, who was Jendre.

She spoke to him although he hadn't said a word, not to her and not to anyone, since he brought her to the beach where his friends were waiting. He was aware—vaguely, distantly—of how his silence oppressed them; just as he was aware of how they really didn't understand what had just happened, how he could go down into the river and emerge again a long hour later with a girl in tow, a living girl who had not a trace of the water-magic or any other.

They had wanted explanations, how and why. He had given them nothing. He knew their disappointment, their confusion, Gilder's distrust; but he had been in the river this day, and everything else was less than trivial, meaningless. He had nothing to say. There weren't the words, for anything that mattered.

The others had talked and talked, once they were back in here. It was eventually Rhoan—who didn't agree with him—who told Jendre what he wanted, Armina fetched from Sund.

And Jendre—who was sitting with water in one hand and bread in the other, alternately sipping and chewing with an endless, impossible appetite while all their words seemed to wash over and around and away from her—lifted her head and said that she would go.

That stole all their words from them, for a little minute. Then there was a flood, intended to overbear her: everyone saying at once how she was ridiculous to offer, the thing couldn't be done, it wasn't sensible or safe even for those who were Sundain, even if they could get across the river, which they couldn't; why on earth did she imagine they would allow her to throw her life away so casually, on a fool's mission, when Issel had only just given it back to her . . . ?

And she said, "If fetching your friend across the river will break the magicians' power in that pavilion and give my sister back to me, I will do it."

"We can't promise that," Rhoan said quickly, regretting perhaps that she had mentioned Armina at all. "Neither half of that. We don't know that she can help us, even; and if she can, we don't know that she will; and if she will, we don't know that we can rescue your sister."

"Only to break the magicians, break the bridge: that would be enough. Even if I didn't get Sidië back after. Knowing that she was safe and cared for, that would be enough. And if you try, if you fail, if you only *try*—that would still be worth it, to me. No one else is trying."

Gilder said, "This discussion is pointless. We have no way to cross the river. Unless Issel thinks he can walk it?"

That was a bitter joke. The bitter truth was that Issel could, or thought he could, but that Rhoan wouldn't let him. He knew that before she said so.

"That's not funny, Gilder. Have you seen him since he did that, that *dive* to rescue Jendre? Look at him now. He can't even *talk*. If he tried to cross the river that way—well, I don't know what would come up the other side, if anything did, but it wouldn't be Issel, and I'm not sure it would even be human anymore."

Issel wasn't utterly human in any case; he had dogtooth in his bones and they'd be showing it soon enough; he wasn't sure it mattered, what happened to him between now and then. It did seem to matter to Rhoan, though. Besides, he had no words to argue with. She was right, that the river had taken speech away from him, even if she was totally wrong about what it meant. He might not be human, but he thought he was becoming more and more himself.

This was what Issel meant: this boy who sat alone, who stripped water from his shirt with a finger and played it with the shadows of his mind, barely a thought turning it to tiny crystal spheres that snapped and danced on his palm, to mirror how they snapped and danced in his corrupted blood, all pain, all wonder; this boy who had nothing to say, but who could feel the swell of the river in his bones, the rising tide in his head, all the great masses of water at his back only waiting for his hand to turn them to his desire; this boy whose jaw was clenched around a word he dared not utter, who thought he could feel that jaw shift and thicken from day to day, as he waited for his thoughts to shift and thicken and slow down.

He was an achievement, he thought, an astonishment in the making. Strong beyond measure, dangerous beyond measure, and yet unable to do the one thing that he wanted, what they all wanted, what had brought them here; soon to be strong and stupid, like any dogtooth, magnified to a terrible degree. Then he would be dangerous in other ways, a tool to others' hands.

For now, at least he could still choose, even if he couldn't argue for his choices. He would not choose to walk the river, but that was for his own reasons, not for Rhoan's. He might still do it later, if it turned out that there was no other choice.

Jendre said, "He doesn't need to do that. There are other ways across the river. Human ways."

"There are no boats, for the likes of us—oh." For once Gilder stopped to think, to wonder if perhaps he might be wrong. "Are you saying that you could command a boat?"

"No. Once, perhaps, I could have asked. I have been on the river. Now, though—well, in my own name I'm dead, and the city has seen me drowned." She paused then, and they waited, letting the weight of that sink into her, watching it happen. After a moment she roused, shook her head, went on: "An unknown girl with no name to give, without an escort—or worse, with a shabby escort sporting Sundain accents—no, I couldn't command a boat. The best I could command would be the sudden curiosity of the guards."

"And if we could steal a boat, we wouldn't need you—but there are too many guards, and the boats are carefully watched. We know that, we've looked. So—"

"So," Jendre said nervously, determinedly, speaking over him, "there is still the bridge."

"We can't use the bridge!"

"No. You can't. That's what I'm saying."

"What," Rhoan said, gently butting in, "that you can?"

"I am Marasi."

"You are dead. Officially. And I don't suppose they let unnamed girls wander to and fro across the bridge, any more than they would runaway wives."

"No, but that's the point—when I wanted to run away, it was one of the plans we looked at. No one would search for us south of the river. And there are Marasi families living in Sund, and they do come and go. Across the bridge, sometimes. A closed carriage, drawn by servants because beasts won't do it, with an armed man for escort: we could have bluffed the guards. But it would need a Marasi accent, to be persuasive."

"The escort would need the accent, and we don't have that," Gilder objected. "If we did, we could order a boat."

"Yes. There's something else, though. We had another plan, in case we couldn't take Salem, or he wouldn't come. Mirjana came up with this." And there she glanced at Teo, and stalled.

He held her hand, and said, "I know she is dead."

She nodded, and visibly stiffened herself, and almost managed a smile as she said, "So am I. Officially. She should have known, she couldn't leave me behind. But there was always the chance that Salem might have to stay; so she found this other way."

Jendre seemed to have stalled again, as though she had to say something she didn't want to, as though the saying of it would commit her to something she didn't want to do. Issel recognised that, because he remembered it in himself. On the streets, a spoken word was like a paper full of promises. He just couldn't think that it could matter anymore, whatever it was. She had been in the river, with him; why would she care what else she did, from here on?

It was Gilder—of course!—who poked her. "What other way?"

"A pinch-box." It was almost a whisper. Issel heard her clearly—her mouth was wet, which made the words wet as she shaped them; how could he help but hear?—but didn't understand; nor did the others, except seemingly Ailse.

"What is that?" Rhoan asked.

"A black bier. Oh—you don't have them? They are, um, boxes. Carried like a litter, but locked. A way to fetch runaway women back for punishment. I have—ridden in one, once. They are terrible, but I could do it again. For a reason."

"No, wait. Locked, you say?"

"Yes."

"Well, then," Gilder was adamant, "it needn't matter who was inside. Any of us could go. If we felt it was worth it."

"You could—but I would not risk that. An escort would carry the key, and the guards at the bridge might demand that it be opened. Or they might ask questions of the woman inside, through the grille. At which point—"

"Yes, yes, it would need to be a woman. With a Marasi accent. But you bring us back to the same problem again, that we do not have a suitable escort."

"We have Teo. For a woman in disgrace, a eunuch is the perfect escort; all the better, because Teo is only a boy. I ran away from my husband because he lives an impoverished life in Sund; I stole a boat in Sund, where that is easy; I sailed it across the river and made my way back to my family, because I am stupid. They held me till my husband sent a pinch-box to fetch me, and a boy to hold the key and trot beside . . ."

"No."

That was unexpected, the bark of a voice they'd barely heard till now, had almost forgotten about. It came from the dwarf, Teo's friend Djago, who was sitting in his own space to leave Teo room to be with Jendre; and once he had all their attention—or as much of Issel's as he could attract, when the river still echoed and thundered in Issel's skull—he went on:

"This is not for Teo. It is for me. A dwarf is more contemptible even than a boy." The look they shared then, these two eunuchs, was entirely private, and even Issel could see that and understand it. "I can ride atop the black bier, and kick my heels, and amuse the guards entirely. Teo will not go." That was an absolute, apparently. If Teo didn't argue it, then no one could. Djago's mistress was dead, they had gathered that, though he wouldn't say how; free, he remade his world by fiat. "Who is to carry the bier? And how are we to find your friend?"

"Baris," Rhoan said, and it might have been an answer or it might have been a summons, *pay attention*. "Baris, can you find your master Tel Ferin? Do you know which house in Sund he fled to when his own was raided?"

Baris grunted. It was barely a word, but certainly an answer. Rhoan nodded, and thanked him, and turned back to Jendre. "Baris will carry one end of this—box—of yours, and he will take you to a man who will know where to find Armina. But you need another carrier, and—well, I suppose, with Baris . . ."

". . . it should be another of us." Ailse completed the thought for her, where she faltered. "I am willing."

"No." That was Djago again, being absolute again. "The story would not hold. No Marasi man would send a woman servant to do that, however—changed—she was. It must be another of your kind, that is right, but it cannot be you."

There was a silence, uncomfortable, unhappy, but the whole conversation had been unhappy; and then Gilder said, "Down on the beach. That cage, full of dogtooths," which was the word that everybody had very carefully not used, until now. "One of them, surely, would be willing. For his freedom."

————————

PROBABLY they needn't all have gone, but somehow they all did. Perhaps no one wanted to be left behind, huddling in the dark, with nothing to do but wait; perhaps some of them wanted to say good-bye to those they might never see again. Issel could remember having those same feelings himself. It was only that feelings didn't seem to matter anymore.

He led and they followed, down what were familiar ways now, tunnels and canals and pools of open water. He didn't pause even at the great lake, even when they passed the boat; he walked on, and nobody called him back.

For a while, in the river, he had thought that he reached from the Insea to the ocean. Then—and only then—had he been afraid.

Now and only now, by the last pool before the channel that would lead them to the open air, did he wait to let his water-sense slip ahead of him, just a little way, down with the rush of water, just to find what waited.

It was dark out there; that didn't matter. Water-sense cared nothing for the light. There were bodies strewn on the bank below the promenade, but he knew that. Those had been guards, set to watch the gully; he had killed them early in the day, and insisted on the time it needed to lift their bodies from the water. The force of it here would have carried them quickly to the river. To Teo, that had been a reason to leave them, to hurry to his mistress's rescue; he had argued that fiercely, oblivious to the people gathered above to watch the pomp of Jendre's execution. To Issel, it had been entirely a reason to stop, to pull them out.

The bodies were still there, but now there were living people too. Issel could sense them on the banks and in the water, wading up towards the outfall. He had expected that. A change of guard, the discovery, the alarm: of course there would be soldiers here again. Many of them, hesitant, unsure of what had killed their comrades and reluctant to seek it out in the dark of the sewers.

They would come, though. Slowly, inevitably, they would come. Soldiers do.

That wouldn't matter, except that they were in his way, and not even Rhoan could hope to slip past them unobserved. If he killed them now, though—as he could, from here, sight unseen—it would be hard to hold the bodies where they were. Nor was there time to haul so many out of the gully, nor would the steep banks hold them all.

Instead, Issel stopped the water flowing.

Just here, where this last gathered pool of water ran over its rim and down into the last worked tunnel, where it could smell light and air—even though it was the Shine it smelled, and the tainted air below the bridge—Issel caught it and stilled it, lifted it and turned it back on itself like a tongue, to make a wall that blocked all the water behind.

The tunnel ahead of them gargled as though its throat were sore. Standing under that rearing tongue, in the Issel-blaze of it, their shadows were flung far after the retreating water.

"Is it—safe?" Ailse asked, with a stammer in her breath.

No, it was not safe at all, though it would hold. Issel had no voice to tell her so; instead he simply led them in the water's wake, barely wet-footed. Where they came to side-passages and tributaries that still spewed water, he blocked those too; and so eventually they reached the outfall, and there before them stood a small army, gathered bewildered in the gully where it had suddenly run dry.

NO, not dry. The stony floor of it was almost bare of water, the torrent reduced to pools and a muddy trickle. That would still be wet enough, here in the narrow twisting confines of the gully, between water-slick rock walls; but then there would be a great crush of bodies to clamber over, and there would still be a great head of water behind them, enough to carry all those bodies down to the river when he eventually released it. Which was what he most wanted to avoid.

The soldiers closest to the outfall had seen him already, but he wasn't worried. None of them carried bows; those were weapons of the battlefield, not for tunnels in the dark. Besides, he must look awesome, a brightly shining figure outlined against the black of the tunnel-mouth; those who could see were pressing back, against the weight of all the men behind them pressing forward.

Issel ignored the soldiers and followed the soak of water with his watersense: down into the subsoil and the rock beneath the stream-bed, where still more waters ran unseen; back along the gully to where it opened out, where there was a slope to the banks, where there was soil and scrappy growth. Where the previous guards had found just ground enough to stand on; where their bodies had been left.

This new band of soldiers snaked through the gully and all the way back to there. Issel found the last of them down on the stream-bed with his cohorts, bewildered by the water's vanish but feeling bold, no doubt, feeling safe. If the water returned, his bolder barrack-mates would meet it first, and he'd have time to scramble up to safety . . .

The banks that loured above him in the night were soil and rock, loosely compounded; Issel remembered that from the frantic slide down their first day in Maras, when Ailse had brought them here. Besides, he could sense it. Wet soil, wet rock. There was rain in the air, though that was hardly necessary; the water's fury made so much splash and spume in this narrow chase, there was so little sun that ever found it, it must be constantly wet.

Wet enough for Issel. He gripped it in his mind, all that thin soil, all the pebbles and the splintery rock beneath; he gripped it, tore it, wrenched it down.

Those soldiers at the rear couldn't have known what killed them. They'd barely have had time to feel the rumble and the shake of it, before uncounted tons of rubble came crashing down upon them.

Further up the gully, they would still have had small warning, less understanding. They would hear something, to be sure, echoing up that tight squeeze of rock; they would have time to turn around, time to feel afraid. They couldn't have light enough to see what was coming, only the looming darkness of it, a noise blacker than the shadows that they stood among, a high wall bearing down, filling the narrow gully like liquid rock, like fog turned solid, swallowing, engulfing . . .

Issel dragged that avalanche of wet rock and soil upslope into the gully like a storm, a roiling cloud of filth, and never gave a thought to the weight of it; and as it came, as it filled the stream-bed and mounted the walls, he pulled those walls down on top of it, shearing rock from rock to lay a new road-bed atop the dying and the dead.

He heard the silence at his back, the shock of it, louder than any voices. Without looking, without listening, he knew that Teo was terrified, Jendre appalled, Rhoan wearily disgusted with them all. She'd blame herself, he knew, for allowing this.

Gilder was content, seeing Marasi soldiers die. He'd likely have the image of Lenn in his mind, her death not outweighed by any number of Marasi dead. Djago was neutral, hard to read; water-sense was not telepathy, though it told Issel more than his regular senses ever had.

Some of the men died quietly, some died screaming. Some few died more slowly than he'd meant. They all died.

And when they'd done that, when he was sure, he went on working, beneath the settling slabs of stone that were the new floor of the gully. He churned up rock and mud and water, deep deep down, working by that mental touch that was neither sight nor sound nor feeling; he broke the old bed into shards and splinters and sharp gravel, and rolled it all over and over like teeth to chew and crush and rip apart.

The others didn't understand, he thought, why he made them wait. He didn't explain, there weren't the words; but by the time he was done, there weren't the bodies either, anywhere under that mass of fallen rock. Only a coarse cement to set these stones in, to fix the stream's new bed. It would have taken a patient man a long, long time to pick apart flesh and soil, gravel and bone; soon enough, it simply wouldn't be possible. The river would abide, as clean as it was, as clean as any water could be that flowed within the Shine. Issel would abide, his soul no more tainted than it had to be. The men were gone, their bodies nothing now. Even their steel—blades and mail, buckles, helms—had been eaten into unidentifiable twists and splinters.

The gully's floor was higher now. With no pour of water over the tunnel's lip, it was an easy task to slide down; only the dwarf needed assistance, and there were willing hands to give that.

Issel walked slowly forward, light spilling from his damp clothes to guide the others over the broken ground. It should have been soft and shifting underfoot, but he had crushed it down hard, to let the stream run clean and clear when he finally released it. He could feel the pressure building, back inside the sewers; that open pool they'd walked by, that whole chamber was water-full now, and the tunnel behind it was filling. Soon the level in the lake would start to rise. Infinitesimally.

It didn't matter. He could hold even that weight, as long as he chose to. Truly he was a water-mage now; the river had baptised him.

Actually, he thought the river had drunk him, drowned him and spat his altered spirit back into his body, so that he was not Issel the boy he had been, though he was still a boy; he would never be Issel the dogtooth he should have been, though he would still be a dogtooth.

He was a water-mage, as perhaps he never should have been. It cost him in pain, in levels and degrees for which the names of pain were no longer enough; it had brought him friends and cost him friends, and would do the same again, he thought, before the end. It might have cost Rhoan her own future, exposing her as he had to the wizards' magic. It was all cost, but even that didn't matter.

It might yet free his city. He might have been in the river, but that hope survived; that did still matter.

That was why he could kill a squad of men and have the wet land digest their bones, and light the way over their souls, all down this gully that provided deep and secret access to the river. It felt to Issel like walking in the hollow of a bone, in the echo of a voice. It was a steep drop and grew steeper; before they reached bottom, the dwarf was riding Teo's shoulders and the boy was unsteady under the weight of him, laughing under his breath as he swayed and staggered and nearly lost his footing. Djago clung to his ears and issued terse, useless instructions. "Careful! Remember my dignity, and do not let me fall . . . !"

He didn't, quite, though he did plunge past Issel on the last and steepest incline, desperately running to keep upright, charging headlong into the Shine.

THE stream debouched into the river behind a little spit of land, that had masked them this morning from the crowds. Tonight they did the other thing, climbing over that spit in the full glare of bridgelight, coming down onto the open breadth of the beach.

Last time they were here, the night that Baris had rowed them across from Sund, the beach had been sensibly empty, the cage of dogtooth labourers left quite unguarded. Issel might have freed them then, and had not; he should be glad of it now, or guilty. Both.

This time, tonight, there was a difference. More than one: it was raining, and they were challenged before they were halfway to the cage. The Marasi had left a platoon of guards out, in the rain, in the Shine; heedless of their soldiery as they were of their civilians, in these days of strain.

A voice cried, "You, there! Stand!"

Issel reached through the rain, through the wet sand, and found half a dozen men at the high point of the beach. His friends could see them straight; so could he, no doubt, if he used his eyes, but the water-sense brought him closer.

Rhoan said, "Two of them have bows, Issel."

"Yes," he said, and kept on walking.

In sunlight, he might have been afraid of arrows. In the Shine, in the rain? Not he. He wasn't invulnerable, but he was very well protected, and his friends were too.

They shot their arrows when he ignored the cry to halt, when his friends did. One shaft came at him, one at—well, he wasn't sure. One of the others, behind him. It didn't matter.

Arrows are swift, but these came through rain; he was ahead and behind and all around them, he caught them in mid-thought and snapped them into pieces, and moved on.

The soldiers were unthinking, inattentive. The archers had already loosed more shafts; their earthbound brethren were running down the sands, towards Issel and his friends.

The sands were wet, and deep. Once Issel had broken these new arrows and then the bows that shot them, still in the archers' hands, he sent his water-sense plunging into that dense, heavy darkness. It was like thrusting his arm into the beach, fingers worming deeper and deeper—except that his arm was a slender and a limited thing, contained within his fragile and inhibiting skin. His water-sense seemed limitless today, reaching as far as he chose to reach. Walking here by the river, sunk into these sands that were soaked by the river, he almost felt that he was the river, which meant he was the world . . .

The steep slope drew the soldiers on, towards this helpless little group of strays where it marched so defiantly forward. It was only one by one that they looked down, to watch how their feet were striking so deep into sand that seemed softer than it should, how the slope was steeper than they had thought.

Looked down and could barely understand what they were seeing, in the shifting and treacherous light from the bridge; and still tried to heave themselves on, until the pit that had opened up before them closed again around their legs, their waists, and they felt the sucking sand begin to draw them down.

Then they screamed, and beat against it, and tried to heave themselves out, burly arms thrusting or scooping or flailing wildly.

The sand swallowed all their efforts, all their strength. The screaming was dreadful, so Issel stopped it; with all this rain in their faces, it took barely a thought to fill throats and lungs with water.

They drowned, then, in a sea of sand, and were drawn down deep; and again Issel spent a few minutes to abrade their bodies in that grinding wet darkness, until there was nothing that could be handily separated from the sand that held them.

"Issel, must—?"

"Yes," though it was Gilder who said so. "Yes, Rhoan, he must. How else can we get Jendre and the dwarf safely away, except by making sure there are no witnesses, no one to see or follow?"

"Even so, it's not, not *good* for him. Always to be killing. I wish it didn't have to be him all the time. It's too easy, he just—"

"It doesn't matter."

The voice startled them all, himself included. He was already groping wildly with his water-sense, trying to find whoever had spoken, before his mind caught up with his body and recognised the voice as his own.

Words had come back to him at last, if only that one empty phrase. He gazed around at the others, at a little circle of eyes glinting oddly in the Shine; and shrugged, and walked on.

THERE was no other guard, no watch kept on the cage itself. No need. Strong as they were, these dogtooths, iron bars and a stout lock were stronger. The floor was sand, indistinguishable from the beach around it, but here it was only a skin; Issel could feel the rock beneath, and how it gripped the risers of the cage. There would be no shaking those loose, however they raged within.

It was crowded, within. It was all men, huddled together in their chains because there was no room to be alone. There was no matching cage for women, out here in the Shine to make them dogtooth faster; perhaps strength mattered less in female slaves, or intelligence mattered more. Ailse had said they had other work, picking and packing in the warehouses.

Despite the running and shouting on the beach, despite the screams that had ripped the air just minutes earlier, the captives largely had their heads down, their shoulders hunched against the rain.

Heavy heads, broad shoulders, largely. Many sprouted hair all along the ridges of their spines. There were still cleaner, slimmer forms among them: more than before, Issel thought. It was mostly those, new prisoners not yet tainted in their blood, who were watching his approach. A few had even come to the bars, though more had backed away. Fear was a constant, Issel knew; you could be trapped in one fearful situation—a cage, say, under the bridge, naked in the Shine—and still be just as afraid of something new, something equally fearful, say a sorcerer who could open the beach and have it swallow soldiers . . .

A brave man, a bold man said, "Who are you?"

"Sundain," Issel said, when none of his friends seemed inclined to speak for him. He did have his voice again, when he needed it; he added, "I have not come for you."

"For who, then?" and the man clenched his fists around the loose length of his chain, to say *there is no one here who is undefended.*

"One of those"—with a gesture towards the slow and bulky dogtooths, who were starting now to stand, to turn, to come shambling towards the conversation.

"Not to harm," Gilder said sharply at his back. "We will give him freedom, if one of them will come."

"Come to do what?"

"And then," another voice inside the bars, "freedom to do what? How can he be free when he has no way to live?"

"We will find him a way," Gilder said. Issel thought about Sund, and how the poor of Daries would kill a dog without thinking and drive a dogtooth out of the city with hurled stones, and said nothing.

"He won't be alone," Rhoan put in. "He'll be with Baris here, we just . . . Oh, let's be plain. We need two dogtooths, to carry our friend here across the bridge. We have one. We hoped that we could find the other here. Please?"

"We are caged," the man said, "and chained . . ."

Issel stepped forward, towards the cage door; Gilder said, "No, wait, let's have their promise first."

"We can't promise for them," the man said. "Not for any one of them. But you can't have any one of them without opening the gate—and, look"—a jerk of his head to underscore it—"the gate is ours."

It was true, they couldn't come to the dogtooths without going through a cluster of these fresh prisoners first, where they had gathered all inside the gate.

Issel heard Rhoan starting to negotiate, "What's your name, and what do you want?"

It didn't matter, not to Issel, what the man's name was; he already knew what they wanted. Men and dogtooths together, they were in the cage, and they wanted out.

That much lay within his gift. He ignored Rhoan's soft voice and Djago's too, when his joined hers more roughly; he walked that little further, up to the bars of the cage and away from the gate, towards where those already deep-sunk in their change were pressing close together, confused and anxious. They might have been herded there by their smarter fellows, to demonstrate who was in charge here, who mattered within the cage.

Issel set his hands to cold wet iron.

"Issel, no . . . !"

That was a shout, Gilder; it didn't matter.

Issel pulled, and ripped those bars right out of the rock. Two, and then two more: a gap wide enough for any man to squeeze through, however distorted his body.

A gap narrow enough for a water-mage to stand in, against any rush.

"Baris," he said, "you come. You choose, who to go with you. If he will."

Chapter Two

THESE people, these Sundain bewildered Jendre.

Bewildered and terrified, in equal measure. And yet, she would work with them against her city and barely care what happened to it or to her, so long as what they did would free Sidië. That wasn't bewildering to her at all, she understood herself perfectly; but these people . . .

Gilder was a ferret, a predator, small and sharp and lethal. He didn't trust anyone, he didn't invite trust; he didn't believe in Issel's friend, he didn't want to send for her, he doubted Jendre's ability to fetch her anyway. And yet he had done everything he could to make this happen, as soon as he understood that it was possible.

Issel was silent, remote, barely human. He hadn't spoken a word to Jendre, barely any to his own companions. She thought he was possessed, demonic: the very image of the Sundain sorcerer that harem talk had frightened her with, all through her childhood. She'd grown up believing it was nonsense, and now here was a sorcerer in the flesh, a water-mage, and he was appalling. And bewildering, she didn't understand him at all, but she didn't mind that so much; she was allowed not to understand a water-mage. That he was kind too, that he had rescued her—and only because Teo had asked him to, not for any gain he knew of at the time—that only added to the bewilderment, and could be tucked away and not considered. Mostly, he was appalling.

But then there was Rhoan. She was a girl, Jendre's own age, she should be easiest to understand; and yet she had some kind of deep engagement with Issel. That was obvious, and bewildering enough in itself: how any girl could feel close to someone with such monstrous powers, however kind he might appear.

And that was the least of it, because Rhoan too was appalled by what Issel had done tonight on the beach, perhaps by the person he'd become, and yet that made no difference, seemingly. And none of them here had any idea what he would do now, left alone with Gilder, Ailse and all those prisoners in the cage; and yet Rhoan had done that, she had left him and come with Jendre and her suite.

"I can't fight," she'd said, "or not as Issel does," which wasn't fighting at all, of course, it was slaughter, and nothing to regret, "but I can hide you if there's trouble along the way."

Jendre didn't understand that, and would prefer not to learn what it meant. Altogether, she would have preferred fewer people with her, simply because a larger party was more likely to attract the kind of trouble that they might need to hide from.

But there were the two dogtooths, and Djago; they were essential. And then there was Rhoan, who had come because she chose to come, unless it was because she chose to leave Issel just then, and Jendre didn't understand it; and then there was Teo, whom Jendre understood entirely. He had come because he had to be left behind in the end.

"When you go to the bridge," he'd sniffed, all sullen boy, "then you can leave me, if you want to. Not till then. And I won't leave you," and it wasn't clear at all whether he meant Jendre or Djago or both.

Altogether, what was clear, they were too large a party to be sneaking through Marasi streets this way. She'd rather be up on the roofs, where it was quicker and safer for the skilled and the nimble; but the dogtooths would be a cumbersome liability up there, and Djago would be impossible.

Street-bound, then, they clung to the shadows and were nervous at junctions. Teo said there was a curfew, these difficult days; there would be patrols, there would be standing guards. They were lucky not to have met any yet. With Issel, they needn't have worried; she was glad not to be with Issel, but the worry was great. If they were caught, she didn't know what they could do. Two girls, two eunuchs, two dogtooths strong but slow: they were not a fighting party, and yet she supposed they would have to fight.

Better not to be caught, then. Pray not to be caught.

Teo was leading them, because he insisted, although she knew these short streets and narrow alleys at least as well as he did. He was wary enough, slow enough that Djago could keep up, stumping along in his shadow. That looked practised: a time to be glad, she supposed, of their nocturnal adventures together. Not that she'd ever resented them. Envied, yes. Now she was having one of her own, and she was far more anxious than exhilarated, glad to have guides ahead of her and simple strength behind, the dogtooth called Baris and the one who seemed to have forgotten his name. Baris' choice: she supposed she could trust it.

She was trusting her life to it, to that and other choices. Gilder didn't trust her; after what had happened in the river, she wasn't sure she trusted herself. She was finding it hard to remember, let alone to organise those memories into any coherence. All she knew for sure was that after Issel had brought her up out of the water, when he led her back into the day—though he did it under the shadow of the bridge, in the stream-mouth where there were no people to see, except his disturbed and disturbing friends—she'd come back into an altered world, and the prime alteration was in herself. She had no notion of how Issel had kept her alive down there, but with her first free gasp of air, she'd felt something slip and run away from her with the water that was cascading down her legs.

She might call it caution, she might call it self-control; she was still fumbling to understand it. It wasn't fear. She was still afraid of almost everything that encompassed her, from Mehmet to Issel and all that lay between. She was afraid of her own city now, and this creeping about within it, the chance of capture and the chance of escape. Escape meant the bridge, and she was afraid of that; beyond the bridge lay Sund, and she had always been afraid of that, glad to live this side of the river.

Fear simply couldn't stop her anymore, that was the thing. She had always been bold, in pursuit of what she wanted; now she felt reckless, heedless, unbridled. Released. Which was why she was doing all of this, going from fear to fear, still in pursuit of Sidië. She had thought before that she would do anything to achieve her sister's freedom; now, it was simply true.

TEO held his hand up to still them at a corner, then melted into the shadow of the wall. She tried to do the same, knowing that fouled as it was by river water, her white robe was still working against her. Far better the dark dress of a eunuch, shadow-grey; it might almost have been designed for slipping unseen from street to street. Perhaps it was. They led a twilight life, these half-men. Not Teo, who was too young and carefully trained and her own sweet boy, but generally they were secretive and self-possessed, creatures of the shadows themselves. No surprise, then, if their dress was meant to ease them in their pursuit of hidden things, power or pleasure or prestige . . .

After a moment, Teo sidled down towards her, bringing Djago with him as he came; the others gathered at her back.

"There are soldiers, a little group of them, standing in the middle of the way."

"A patrol?" Jendre asked. A patrol would move on, if they waited.

"No. There is a brazier, and a kettle steaming." A stationary watch, then, for the hours of curfew, dusk till dawn.

"Where do we need to go?" Rhoan asked.

"Ahead. We must cross this road, here or higher; wherever we cross, they will see us."

His voice faltered, though, on those last words; Rhoan smiled thinly. "Not necessarily. Take us higher, Teo, to give me a little distance to work with. Hurry, though, this rain is good, and I don't want to waste it."

She made no sense to Jendre, but the others seemed to understand, even Baris. Not the new dogtooth; Jendre thought he understood little of anything. She thought his promised freedom was an unkindness—he wouldn't be able to use it.

She thought her own was an illusion. Being dead was a good story, but it was likely to prove short-lived. If these men took her, if anyone recognised her, if Mehmet learned that she was still alive—what then? She wouldn't die so easily the second time, but she would most certainly die. In flames, probably, being as far from water as the city could achieve. And all these others with her, Sundain witches and Marasi traitors, a conspiracy of eunuchs . . .

Perhaps Issel would come to save her a second time, save them all; she couldn't guess the limits of his power. She wouldn't like to count on it, though. She didn't think that anyone should count on Issel. Rhoan included.

Teo took them uphill, to another alley that brought them back to that same road. The guards would certainly still be able to see them if they crossed here; but Rhoan beckoned them all near and said, "Listen, then. I can hide us, while we cross. I think I can. It'll be hard, with us all moving; anyone who falls behind or dashes ahead is only going to make it harder. Stay close to me, and stay together. Move slowly and don't hesitate, don't turn back. Don't talk. Try not to look at the soldiers. Remember, you can see them quite clearly; that doesn't mean they can see you, but they will if they look directly, if you give them any reason to. This is about misdirection as much as magic. Stay *close* . . ."

And she took a flask of water from her belt and poured herself a palm-ful, although it was still raining and she might have dipped it from any gut-ter, any puddle round about. She stowed the flask away again as though it were somehow precious, and then she dipped her fingers into her palm and flicked little drops of water at all her companions, although they were wet enough already.

When those drops fell on Jendre, just for a moment she thought they stung more than water ought to.

She didn't understand how this would help, how it could hope to hide them; but one thing was clear that had not been explained before. Rhoan really was a Sundain witch, if nothing comparable to Issel.

Once she'd flick-splashed them all, Rhoan dabbled her fingers in her palm, took on a look of abstract focus, and walked out of the alley into the road beyond.

Slowly.

The others all clustered behind her, drawing Jendre along in their midst. She found herself walking with the dogtooths, while Djago led them, and Teo hustled them along from behind.

Her sister had been sold to magic, and the bridge that Sidië and others dreamed hung in the sky behind her. She had seen too many soldiers killed, swallowed up by magic this very night; she had been saved herself by a magic that terrified her even in retrospect. She had walked within the river, and she shuddered when she thought of it.

That was all magic she could see, touch, detest. This was something ut-terly other; this was like religion, being asked to believe in something intan-gible and unlikely. It was an act of faith, to walk blindly out into full sight and trust Rhoan when she said that she could hide them. Jendre's legs ached to run. She did press too closely on the dwarf, but he made a good vanguard; he simply couldn't walk faster than he did, rolling painfully from hip to hip.

She did also look downhill at the soldiers, though Rhoan had cautioned them not to. Of course she looked, she couldn't help it.

There were half a dozen of them, and they were doing what men will do on a long watch in the rain, where there is a fire. They had gathered around it, much as they had gathered greasecloth capes around their shoulders; everything turns inward, to the core, to the heat. Their backs made a wall against the world.

But these were janizars, trained men, and the world was no place to turn your back on: not with a new Sultan insecure on his throne, a would-be assassin executed today and all the city restless under curfew. They kept a careful watch, even while they clustered around their brazier. Every second or two, one of them would lift his head and stare, uphill and down, the city and the river. Here in the lower city, there was light enough from the bridge; it was a drear kind of light, casting strange and shifting shadows, but he could see all that he needed, all that he was required to see.

He could, he must be able to see Jendre and her companions, walking slowly and steadily across the road.

She looked, and saw him lift his head and gaze about; she saw it turn in her direction; her footsteps faltered despite herself, despite all instruction.

If they'd been closer, she'd have said she caught his eye. In fact his face was shadowed beneath his helm, with the shine of the bridge behind him. Even so, just at that moment when their eyes might have met, his head did pause in its turning, he did seem to look fixedly in their direction.

And just at that moment Teo pushed her, quite forcefully, and she stumbled forward, and when she looked again he had turned away, turned back to the fire, and another man was lifting his head to scan the street.

Where they were still walking, and still somehow entirely overlooked. Rhoan was still touching her wet fingers to her wet palm, still flicking occasionally, though that little handful of water was long since spilled or used up; all she had to work with was the rain now. It seemed to be good enough. They walked slowly and steadily from one side of the street to the other, from the shelter of one alley to the shelter of the next. Unseen, uninterrupted, undelayed.

JENDRE wanted to know, oh so badly, what the other girl had done, and how she'd done it. Rhoan was Sundain, which meant a witch, and she was playing with water: that should be enough, but it wasn't. To name a thing is never to explain it, and curiosity burned in Jendre like a brazier in the rain, hissing and hot and deeply attractive.

She didn't ask Rhoan or Teo what just happened. She kept quiet, she kept alert; she let Teo take the lead again, and he brought them up from the lower town and higher yet, to the broad ways and big houses of her own family's recent elevation. High walls, less light, more darkness but fewer shadows, less contrast to conceal them. Here there were no standing guards—no one would try to enforce a curfew on the élite—but there were patrols to elude. Patrols that walked on by as they crouched in gateways or clustered behind a monumental plinth, and she was never sure whether Rhoan was working any magic to assist. The girl worked so quietly, and what she did was so opposite to Issel's dreadful gestures and yet was still so effective, it was hard to understand that they came from the same city, let alone the same school.

Teo brought them to a particular gate, and here it was Djago who stepped to the fore. Indeed, he waved the others back out of sight, around the corner. Teo left him reluctantly, Jendre thought—and she caught the boy's hand with determination, held him to herself. *Just for a little while, for this moment, now . . .*

They heard Djago hammer on the gate, they heard him call; after so long in delicate hiding, suddenly to be making noise and demanding attention seemed barbaric. So did the gate's opening, a great slamming of bolts and creaking of hinges, fit to rouse the city.

There was a murmur of voices, indistinct; she had to imagine it, but what she imagined was a clink of coins to go with. Perhaps not physical coins, actual gold. Perhaps the trade was in information or promises. Eunuchs deal; it's a definition. Their world is a marketplace.

Whatever the coin, the deal must have been done. There was a soft whistle that she recognised; Teo responded immediately, pulling free from her, "Come on," with a broad beckoning gesture for the dogtooths.

Obedient to that summons, they all followed: back to the gate where it stood wide now, empty of Djago, and swiftly in.

Here was the dwarf in lamplight, holding the lamp indeed; and here was another eunuch, in shadow, drawing the gate closed behind them but not bolting it.

Here was the back of the house: a cobbled yard, a stable of horses—she could hear them stamp and whinny at this unaccustomed disturbance—and a number of out-buildings, all outline and shadow.

Here were no words, no need to speak. Djago led, and the others followed. The eunuch of the house stayed at the gate, in the shadows.

Here was a long wooden coach-house, doors so high and wide they should probably be called gates. One was standing open, ready for them; there was perhaps a hint of movement behind it, a shuffle of feet, a stir of breath, the sure feeling of a presence, another body watching. Oh, they were being cautious, these men, hiding their faces in hopes of saving their skins. Unless it was their necks they hoped to save, if they understood just who they were helping here, and to what purpose. She wondered what Djago had chosen to tell them, and what he'd had to offer in return.

Inside were carriages and litters, all the transport of the house. In one corner, Djago's little pool of light found what they had come for: a pinch-box, a black bier, a squat little wooden crate with a grille pierced on each side—the holes cut, she knew, at random angles to let in a modicum of air and as little light as possible—and two poles by which to carry it.

The first time they'd found Djago, he'd pulled his withered mistress in a cart, up and down the steepness of a knoll. It was his practice, and perhaps his duty. For sure it was not his pleasure, whatever he might have claimed. It had taken Jendre a while to understand how much it cost him, in effort and—mostly—pain. Since then, it had amused her to see how he delegated physical work to Teo, and how the boy jumped to do it.

Not tonight. Tonight, Djago unlocked the front of the box and lowered it silently on its hinges, stretching up above his head to take the significant weight of it, to stop it falling with a clatter that might disturb the horses and so the house.

He brought it lightly to the floor, which must have strained all his body, all his joints in succession; and then he walked round the pinch-box, dagger in hand, and worked the blade into all the air-holes, twisting it like a drill to enlarge them as much as he dared and as quickly as he could. Again it was work he could have given to the boy and did not, although it meant his standing on tiptoe and working above his head.

Only when he could push a pudgy finger into each of the holes, only then was he satisfied; only then did he step to the side and bow low, with a flourish that was all respect and not a hint of mockery.

"My lady?"

"Thank you, Djago."

She stooped, turned around, and shuffled backwards into the box. Squatting on the floor, she saw him start to raise the front; at the last moment, Teo came darting forward with a cushion that he must have scavenged from one of the carriages.

"My lady?" The words were an unconscious echo of Djago's; the voice was not, breathy and unhappy, anxious for her but also for himself, she thought, being left among strangers, abandoned by both the people he loved. There was nothing to be done about it; she had to go, and Djago had to leave him behind. A dwarf might be sent to see a runaway woman home; she knew men who would find that amusing; she couldn't imagine a story where his catamite was sent to keep him company.

"Thank you, Teo." A cushion would ease the worst discomfort of the journey, which was the least she had to worry over; a word and a smile were the least that he needed now, and the most that she could offer. "Be good, be careful, and I'll see you soon."

"I hope so, my lady."

"Depend on it. We'll find this Armina, take a boat and come straight back. One night, maybe two. You be waiting, down by that stream."

"I will." His eyes moved from her to the dwarf, still seeking promises that neither could honestly give him; she'd made do with lies, which he knew. The dwarf contented himself with a grunt as he raised the front of the box. Teo moved to help, whether he would or not; they finished the work together, closing Jendre into darkness as they argued about the lock.

"Give it me, it's too high for you."

"You just hold this, so; I can manage."

"Only if I lift you up—Ouch!"

She could hear them perfectly well, through Djago's air-holes; she understood them equally well. This was pantomime, played out all for her benefit. She obliged them with a chuckle, duty done, a gesture for their sakes. They were all of them playing roles. Two at least were frightened—for themselves and for each other—past the point of being able to talk true. She didn't know what Djago felt, inside; she hoped that Teo did.

―――――――

INSIDE the box, in the dark of it, with her friends the thickness of a plank of wood and a world of light away, she felt for one little moment like a child playing hide-and-seek, crouching in a cupboard, one little word from discovery. It was a tremulous, breathless feeling, bounded in security: she was here because she chose to be, and one little word would release her, safe into the company of those who loved her.

Then the pinch-box lurched and lifted, and she felt the hollowness of space around and herself just dangling in it. She lost the last of her light when Djago gave up the lamp; she heard his voice and Teo's, Rhoan's, with a sting of resentment that they could all talk to each other but not to her; she heard the slam of the gate at her back.

Nothing had changed. She was still only the thickness of a plank away from the world, she was still here because she chose to be, one little word would still release her. It was still her friends who would hear that word: Djago and Baris, and the other dogtooth who could not give a name.

But discovery was no longer a step into safety. She was bounded by danger, and the planks of the pinch-box felt perilously thin. They had skulked in shadow half the night; now Djago and her bearers were out in full view, abroad after curfew, inviting challenge. She had only the box's shadows to hide in, and it felt too small, too frail. Issel's brutal strength was gone, and Rhoan's nimble enchantments too; all she had to rely on now was Djago's tongue. She was suddenly not at all sure that it would be enough.

―――――――

THE box swayed and jerked around her; she bounced and slid within it. After a few minutes, she realised she was still absurdly hugging Teo's cushion, while her bottom was banging about and acquiring splinters from the rough-cut planking of the floor.

Awkwardly, she worked the cushion underneath her—and in the process, she found what was long and stiff inside it. Long and cold and stiff, something of metal; long and cold and stiff and sharp, a blade.

Carefully, where there was a hole picked in the seam, she probed two fingers into the lamb's-wool padding and found the haft, drew it out slowly, discovered it with her fingers.

It was her own knife, or it had been: a pretty ivory-handled toy to dangle at a girl's waist when she wore a military costume in flattery of her father, but also—because he was her father, and she her father's daughter—a two-edged blade of the finest steel that she kept lethally sharp.

She'd given it to Teo because he was a boy, and unhappy. And now he'd given it back to her, because he'd seen that she had nothing but this skimpy robe, no defences against the world, and she was going into the greatest danger that she'd faced since—oh, since this morning, when she'd been tossed into the river in a sack and a knife really would have been useful.

It was a sweet gift, and he'd made it privately because it would have embarrassed him to do it face-to-face, and she would have argued, and Djago might have laughed at him. She didn't honestly think that a blade shorter than her hand would save her, in Sund or elsewhere; and it left him without a weapon just when he really could have used one, when he and Rhoan had to skulk back through the streets and down to the river again. Without it, he'd be relying on her gifts of concealment entirely; which was probably wise, but he wouldn't see it that way. He'd feel inadequate, dependent; which was why she'd have refused the knife, which he knew, which was why he'd slipped it to her unannounced . . .

———

WELL. She was glad to have it, though she didn't expect to need it; sorry he had to go without, though she thought he was better so.

She spared him one last hopeful thought, that he and Rhoan should make it safely back to the beach and so to the other Sundain, that they should all hide up securely in their bolt-hole until she came to find them again. One way or another, with whatever company she could. She wished that Teo and Rhoan could have found a swifter, safer way through the sewers, but it was a labyrinth down there. Teo had been lost before, and only found by Issel's magic; he wouldn't go down again without Issel.

She spared him anxiety, good wishes, hope. Then she let him slip from her mind, squeezed out by darkness, by jolting, by sore elbows and anxiety. She was anxious for herself and hers, these unlikely servants, a dwarf and two dogtooths: the four of them off to walk on her sister's dreams across an impossible bridge, to find a woman with bells in her hair and so hope to bring down the bridge, to wake her sister, and—Jendre realised now, surprised—to destroy this new brute Sultan. If the empire went with him, so be it; she couldn't care.

———————

THE first time they stopped, what little light came in these little holes was all yellow and hot, lamp and fire. Not at the bridge yet, then. There was an abrupt brief thunder against the front of the pinch-box, which startled her, until she heard Djago's voice from above. He had said he'd ride on the roof, but she'd thought he was joking. Obviously not. Of course not, now that she thought about it; he couldn't have kept up on foot, and where else would he sit?

That noise must have been his heels, drumming. A signal to her, *be alert*, an apparent mockery of her to the guards who must have stopped them.

His voice boomed overhead; he cried, "Greetings, noble protectors of our civil peace!"

The man who answered him must have been a conscript from some border province, taken in the levy as a boy. His voice still harboured accents of his home, as Teo's did.

He said, "What are you, little man? And whose? And where do you think you can go, in curfew? Why should I not have your throat at my knife's edge now?"

"I am a fool, of course"—which the soldier would have known, if he had been native; Djago still dressed the part, even though his foolery was long years, decades behind him. "I am my master's man, who lives in Sund across the river; and I am going to the bridge, with my cargo here"— another sudden drumming—"and our bearers, as you see."

"What cargo, then, little man, what is in the box?"

"My master's wife is in the box; his newest wife, his little one, his dear. She ran away, because he is old and crabbed and ugly. She is said to be lovely, but alas, she is certainly stupid. She ran to her father, who had sold her for a handsome price already and would not take her back. My master sent me, and his black bier"—another drum—"to fetch her home again. He is very angry, and I left him counting out his irons and heating up his knives. She may not be so pretty tomorrow. Would you like to see her now, be the last to look upon her beauty, something to boast about? She would only take a moment to unlock . . ."

"Nay, crafty," came back the hasty answer. "I know your kind. You would tease me into a breach of your laws, then hold it over my head all my life."

"If I could reach so high," Djago said amiably. "Don't worry so, I don't seek to trap you; but don't look either, if you don't feel the need. Just let us pass. My master wants her back by sun-up, or else I wouldn't chance my own loveliness on the bridge in its high shine, let alone hers; but hers is transitory and his temper is volcanic, so . . ."

"Enough, enough. Go on, then, and welcome; I would not do it, I. I have trod that bridge in daylight, and that was bad enough. When it glows like this, it shines into my bones, and I can feel its coldness. I would not touch foot to it."

"Nor I—which is why I ride. On, beasts, on . . ."

ON they went, on and down; and gradually there was a light that crept in through her spy holes, that was not caused by any good work of this world.

Less constant than the moon, it shifted like silk on water under moonlight, flaring and fading, changing its colour as often as its mood. Even these cloudy beams that probed her darkness, even these pale spots of light that skittered up and down the walls of her confinement as the pinch-box swayed were enough to mark it unnatural. She flinched away from them, as she would from a scum of oil on a drink of water; and couldn't avoid the touch of them, and felt nothing when they did touch, except that she was reminded of the sleepers' pavilion and the night she'd broken into it with Salem, the swirling colours of the light in there and the swirl of them in her head, sucking and dispossessing.

They hadn't reached the bridge yet, let alone begun the crossing, and already she was disturbed. Jendre wondered what it must be like to live in the bridge's vivid shadow—but the question was disingenuous, downright dishonest. She knew what that was like. She had seen what it was like, writ in bone and skin and muscle, writ in blank bewildered stares. These people who carried her now had been distorted and remade by it, a light that poisoned and corrupted flesh, stole thought and language from the mind.

They came to a halt again, and this time the dwarf was not so jokeful. This time he was silent, indeed, after a sharp voice called to them to stand. She wondered if he was feeling daunted. Men crossed the bridge every day, but only because they had to, because there were whips and worse to drive them on. All these with her now had chosen to be here, to do this thing; perhaps all of them were sorry now.

She wondered if it was better or worse for her, in her box. She thought she'd rather be able to see, but that could be delusion.

There were footsteps sounding a slow circle about the bier: a soldier in authority, working the silence. Walking it. She knew these men, she knew their tricks; she'd met them often and often on the streets.

Keep still, Djago, keep quiet, wait for him . . .

Djago knew them too, clearly. Of course he did; he had fifty years' start on her, and doubtless a far richer experience. She flattered herself, she knew, with her own baby adventures; romanticised them, painted them in brighter, bolder colours than they deserved, made herself out to have had a wilder and more dangerous street-life than was ever true. Once, that had been a consolation.

Now she was locked in a box at the bridge's foot, and fear was a rank bitter taste in her dry mouth, and even the memory of the river couldn't wash it away. She could hear the river, she thought; or feel it, perhaps, a low thunder in her bones. Her memories of this morning might be washing themselves away, but something remained, some more intimate connection. She had been hand in hand with a water-mage, deep below the surface, and that touch of wonder and terror would not leave her fully. Blind and deaf, she still would have known that she was close to the river.

Above the river's rumble-and-suck, she could hear distant cries, noises of battle and destruction. Too far away to be distinct, but close enough to carry: she thought that must mean fighting on the docks. Which was un-heard of, impossible to imagine. The docks were the empire's military and commercial life-line, still practical when the roads were mud and ice; janizars kept watch there day and night.

And she had left Issel on the beach close by, and from her short and dreadful knowledge of him, the impossible was what he did by nature.

She and Djago had taken this mission because the Sundain had no access to a boat. She wondered if that were still true, if the whole adventure was not suddenly redundant.

Too late to know, no way to learn; emphatically, too late to turn back. The soldier was speaking to Djago. As he too must be hearing those noises below and couldn't go to investigate, that might explain the tension in his voice, the edge of very real danger.

Or it might only be this post, standing at the bridge-mouth hour after hour, perhaps day after day. It might be that constant new levies were needed to stand replacement for those whose bones had thickened and whose thoughts had slowed at this duty. And that he knew it.

For now he had authority, and was still sharp; he said, "Why are you here?"

"To cross the bridge, sergeant." *Careful, Djago*—but he had said it simply, as a matter of fact, with no hint of any other meaning in his voice.

"At this time of night?"

"It is my master's order. It will be day by the time I reach his house, when he wants me there."

"Who do you have in the pinch-box?"

"His new wife. Run away, and so fetched back." No fooling here, no drumming heels, only straightforward answers to what questions came.

There were more questions—his master's name, his family, his rank, his houses here and in Sund. Djago was ready for them all. He gave the sergeant no reason to detain them, even on a night of riot; in the end, they were let pass.

Jendre was almost disappointed. Here on the brink, it would have been a relief to be turned back. But the river's bass thrum was in her blood, to remind her how she had stepped through death and every moment of this second life was already bought and paid for; and Sidië's image was in her head, to remind her that her sister's life was worth any risk, any price for its recovery.

————

SHE felt it, the moment her bearers set foot upon the bridge.

Until then it had been a distant image in her mind, never seen close-to; it was the sight that even her most foolhardy friends turned their heads away from, rather than creeping up to steal a better view. It was a legend all through the city, but that kind of legend that was hissed in whispers. The wizards and sleepers in their pavilion were a matter for common gossip, but the bridge itself lay across the city and the river like a brand, a scar of shame. She had felt it all her life, and she was not unique. She knew that, simply because no one liked to talk about it, here in a city that dealt in talk as in coin, lasciviously.

Now she was on the bridge: not quite treading it, but the next worst thing. Her box was small protection. The light here was a mist, just as it had always seemed to be, just as the light was in the pavilion; it oozed in through her air-holes and filled her little space, filled her mouth and nose and lungs, oily and clinging. She breathed it because she had to, and waited for the dreadful dizziness of the pavilion to overtake her.

It did not. Well, of course it did not; otherwise no soldier would ever pass from one bank to the other, they would all be lost in dreams across the span of it.

It didn't make her dizzy, it didn't steal her soul away into dreaming. Nothing else was good.

Not being able to see was terrible. She wanted to know where she was and what was coming; she wanted to know that they were with her, the smart and subtle and the strong. She did believe that the dogtooths were still carrying her, because she could feel their slow progress—but she could be wrong even there, she could be deceived. There were constant motions in the bridge's light; perhaps it had seized her up, perhaps she was being blown about like a leaf on the wind, or sucked down like a cork in a current. She couldn't tell. Even the largest of her spy holes showed her nothing. This was the kind of light that conceals, not illuminates.

She was moving, she was sure of that, but she was deeply disorientated. Something lurched inside her, from moment to moment; she had been sick once in a boat, on the river in a sudden summer storm, and she remembered it as feeling somewhat like this. That sense of losing any balance, any understanding with the world, even the simplest *I will stand, and you will be beneath me.* It was as though she—or her bearers, rather—plummeted with every step, as though there were nothing solid to take their weight: more like falling than floating, and yet—she was sure, she believed—they were not falling.

She wanted to scream, but she was sweating and sick, and it was hard to catch her breath; she needed what little greasy air she could find, just to keep breathing. It was a wonder to her to hear a voice, calling down thinly:

"My lady? Be still, be strong. We will come through . . ."

Djago. The effort was louder than the words themselves, far more persuasive; but he was with her still, and he could think of her, give her what she needed most, a moment's human contact.

If he could talk, so too could she. And without vomiting, she was firm about that; she would not consider vomiting in here. No.

She took another unsatisfying breath, ran her hands down over the sweat-slicked skin of her face as though that could help at all, swallowed once—but not against the vomit, no, there was none—and called back.

Her voice was a traitor, carrying a living image of her, stinking of her own sweat; she could smell it, taste it, hear it in every word.

"Master Djago! It's good to hear your voice," and not a word about how his betrayed him also; he would know. "How is it out there?"

Somehow, he managed to sound dry, though she could hear the way it strained him. "Be glad," he said, "that you are in here."

And then his heels drummed on the door again, a skittish little patter.

She could not do that, but she understood him to be saying that it was very, very bad out there. Very well. She would endure in here, uncomplaining; and when they reached the yonder bank she would sympathise with him, and she would never give him to understand how very, very bad it had been for her in here.

Meantime, "Master Djago? How are the bearers holding up, Baris and the, the other?"

"Yes. I hope," and he spent a great deal, to emphasise this hope, "that he will be able to tell us his name, if we have the quiet for it on the other side. They are—enduring. Their kind is good at endurance."

So could she be. She set her jaw, she stilled her hands, she sat on Teo's cushion. Little else. There was little else she could do, except to be as easy a burden as she might manage. She tried to sway against the box as it swayed, to keep the weight steady. And of course she was not sick, there was no question of her being sick. And if her thoughts tumbled as her balance tumbled—well, there was no need to prevent that, so long as she held her body upright against the sense of fall, so long as she kept her mind from tumbling mad, so long as she kept her roiling belly-stuff inside . . .

———

NO more talking now. Her mouth was sealed, necessarily.

———

THE more she shifted and rocked, the more the world twisted around her. Soon she had arms and legs splayed out into every corner she could reach, thrusting herself back and down, wedging her tight onto that cushion. The box could move as it must, but she didn't need to move inside it. No. She was rooted, absolute, adamantine. Nothing could shift her now.

_____

TIME tumbled, and was all displaced. She was a foul slick falling thing braced in a box, and she had been that way forever and always would be.

_____

AND yet, others did not fall, or fail. They clung on, they kept going. Eventually—gods of all faiths!—they came to solid ground again.

_____

SHE knew this, because that was the moment that they dropped her.

_____

IT was a bruising tumble, but she was braced for it already; she barked an elbow and bit her tongue, collected a number of bruises, no more than that.

And lay for a while where she had fallen, on her side, on one side of the box; and through the air-holes on the other side she heard laughter and mockery, taunting cries: "Up, get up, don't roll there with your cattle, come on, up—oh, begging your pardon, sir, I see you are up. I thought you were still kneeling. What's this, then, what are you bringing into Sund?"

"This is my master's business," Djago said, and she was astonished that he could force his tongue to it, "a stray wife returned—or will be, when I can get these on their feet again, and moving."

"Oh, we'll help. Won't we, lads?"

Laughter in strange accents, boots on flesh, and the heavy grunts of the dogtooths as they were kicked to their feet again.

And she was lifted, or her box was; for herself, she just sprawled on the floor of it, all ungainly and hugging her cushion again, while they carried her away.

Chapter Three

ISSEL had opened the cage because that was what he could do, what he was here for. He had stood in the opening and cowed them all because he could do that too, until Baris chose one. They talked in bone-bare grunts like drumstrokes that seemed to carry all the meaning they needed; eventually they went with Rhoan and Jendre, the eunuch and the dwarf.

That left Issel with Gilder, Ailse and a cageful of dogtooths: new and old, long-gone and barely showing. The freshest prisoners were rioters and rebel janizars, still human all through, new-caged and not yet tainted. They weren't as strong, of course, but they weren't as fearful either; they were the ones who led the rush, out through that gap in the bars, where Issel was no longer holding them back.

And then there were all these men, naked and still chained, all across the beach. Issel expected them to disappear like cockroaches in lamplight, swarm over the sands and up the banks and away. Instead they gathered in little knots and tangles, all looking back at him; and one of the bold ones, one of those who were still men came to him—cautiously, not close, but close enough—to ask, "Can you break these fetters?"

They knew he could, they'd seen him do it for the man that Baris chose. Issel said, "If I break them where you stand, I will break you too." To judge by his own voice, how it sounded in his ears, he didn't particularly care either way.

The man edged closer, sliding his feet through the sand. He talked too, suddenly and shrilly: "Only, as we are, we have no hope; as soon as the janizars see us in fetters, they will know us for prisoners and take us again. And where are we to go, what freedom can you give us? There is no escape from the city, all roads are watched . . ."

As soon as the man was within reach, Issel gripped the cuffs of his fetters and simply shattered the wet iron. He thought that was enough, as the chain fell away; but the man didn't move, so he said, "What more do you want of me?"

"A life. A way to live. I have no food, no dress, no road; what can I do? What can any of us do?"

Issel had never thought himself wealthy, in any of those. He had perhaps never been quite this naked to the world, except when he had gone deliberately bare to beg; and outside the walls of Maras, he guessed, would be no good place for beggars.

He said, "Wait," and gestured the man to one side; there was a line forming behind him, other men in their chains. He couldn't leave them here to the soldiers' vengeance in the morning, death for some and a return to the cage for the survivors.

He was aware as he worked that those he'd freed were gathering around Gilder and Ailse. Asking them the same question, he supposed, demanding some more promising freedom. It didn't lie within their gift, or Issel thought not.

Perhaps he was wrong. He wasn't sure whose idea it had been, but when he had broken the last chain from the last dogtooth's wrists—a craven, slavering creature, tossing his head like a wild thing, needing two of his cohorts to hold him still enough that Issel could work—he found that it had caught like a brush-fire in summer, sweeping them all.

They were standing united, as one, and gazing past the empty cage, up the path that they knew well, that they trod daily, that would lead them to the docks.

ISSEL didn't know whose idea it was, but he did know it was a truly bad one. This wasn't what they were here for; it wasn't what they'd agreed.

They were meant to go quietly back to the sewer outfall and wait for Rhoan and Teo; then they would all wait together for Jendre and the others to bring Armina across the river. This wasn't the time for rash adventures. They were only here to bring down the bridge, and they only had one hope to achieve that, which was Armina. Nothing else mattered.

But here was a rumbling, urgent crowd of men, filled with fear and anger and their own wild hope; and that hope had come from him, and Gilder was busy stoking up their anger. That made him twice responsible, and he couldn't simply turn his back.

So when they said, "We want the docks. There are warehouses there, there will be clothes and food; and there are boats there, we could take boats and flee," and it was clear that they couldn't take the docks without him, he didn't see how he had a choice.

————————

THIS was, of course, what Gilder wanted, what he had always wanted: to attack the Marasi as and when he could, with whatever means he had to hand. In Sund his means had been Tel Ferin's purified water and his own small band of rebels with their limited water-gifts, and his strategy had been ambush and retreat and agitate, trying to win more Sundain to his cause. If the effect of ambushes was to irritate the Marasi into brutal retaliations, well, that also served his purposes, banking up the city's hatred and helping to sway new recruits.

Here, his means had been Issel, and Issel had refused; but now his means were Issel and a mob, and if Issel abandoned the mob, then all these men would be recaptured or killed, and it would be Issel's own fault.

Issel didn't know much about people, but he knew Gilder's mind. He knew how the little man thought, and how he worked. He saw the trap, and its gaping mouth; but he was inside it already, and there was no way back.

Ailse was speaking to her people, trying to calm them as they dug stones from the sand—but that was only to hold them here, to make them wait and follow, not to run off down the path armed with stones against bows and swords and spears. Her heart was with them, she was with them, she supported Gilder absolutely in this sudden new strategy, to seize what they could take from Maras.

Seize it and hold it if they could, destroy it otherwise. To take the docks would be almost as great a blow as bringing down the bridge. It wouldn't save Sund so directly, but it would shake the empire to its foundations, wreck its commerce, turn its thoughts towards rebuilding and recovery. The pricked snail seals itself into its shell to heal. Only turn Maras' attention away from Sund, and the city might save itself.

That was Gilder's thinking, and he had the means now to follow it up. His means were a mob armed with stones, and they wanted to go up against an army; but because they would do that, Issel had to go with them. He had freed them; only he could save them now.

He hated the argument, and he hated its conclusion, and he had nothing to set against it. It was true.

IF he had to lead his own small army, it should be armed with better than stones. They had no blades to spare, and he couldn't spare the time to be clever. But the Marasi had picked his soldiers for him, and even the un-altered men were fit for heavy work; the dogtooths were strong in the way that oxen were, fit to heave and haul all day.

Issel went back to the cage.

With even an hour to play with, he could have fashioned weapons with an edge. But if these men fell to fighting trained soldiers hand to hand, a rude sword wasn't going to help them. Better to give them a long iron club and let them do what they could at a distance. Many of them would die in any case, but that was their choice. Unless it was Gilder's.

He took that cage apart, wrenching iron bars from rock and bending them, breaking them into sections half the length of a tall man. That was a great weight of solid iron, but these dogtooths could handle it; some took two, one for each hand. For those not so massively muscled, he broke off shorter lengths and stretched them, to give the same reach with less weight.

They wouldn't win the docks by force of arms, in any case. The weapons were for protection, not for assault. Issel would have to carry out the as-sault himself.

AND so this: not what he had come for, not at all, but he marched at the head of an army.

At least, he walked up the path from the ruined cage and a mob fol-lowed, hopeful and afraid. He thought they still had the sense to be afraid. He might have lost half his army before they reached the docks, and wouldn't have minded that; it was their choice to make. But Gilder was everywhere, murmuring, exhorting, whipping up their tempers with his words, whipping on the hesitant.

Some of the time Gilder was with him, for the same purpose.

Issel walked that path without looking back, bitterly aware of the murmur of voices behind him, their lives in his empty hands. The path climbed up from the beach, to meet the road that ran between cliff and river until it turned around the headland and showed them the full spread of the docks: a dozen quays lined with moored vessels; an open harbour beyond, protected by a stone breakwater, where more ships were anchored to wait their turn at the quay; a long line of warehouses and another road, where the cliff fell away to a more gentle slope, climbing to the city wall and a high, protected gate.

The docks had their own encompassing wall with just a single break in it, a single gate where that road ran up to the city.

At the gate and regularly along the wall, watch-platforms stood high, and every one of them was manned, even now. The Marasi were careful of their goods and their access to the river. There were barracks in among the warehouses that held the docks' own garrison; Jendre would have known that, probably, and thought to warn him.

More guards were clustered around the gate. Not many, though, at this time of night; the gate was barred, the warehouses locked, the ships and quays quiet, with only an occasional lantern showing. What Issel saw, he saw largely by Shine-light, where the bridge arched between river and sky. No soldier would welcome duty in that light; most would be safe—they hoped—in their barracks, sleeping or waiting nervously till morning. If they were nervous enough, Issel hoped, they might run, if they saw a clear way up to the city.

Not through the gate, then. Leave the gate for them, and that swift tempting road. He'd go in through the wall.

If the men of his army lacked the nerve to follow him—into the breach and an awkward scramble over rubble into defended territory, a classic way to die—so much the better. Let them stay out here and be safe. They could be small help to Issel in there.

The sky would be most help, full of low clouds, dense and wet. He had a riverful of water anyway to work with. He had the river in his head still, unless it was in his heart; he felt it, he knew the shift of tides before the moon did, he knew where the hidden currents ran and where the wrecks lay splintered among rocks, where the bodies mouldered and the big fish lurked—but wet air was better. It left his water-sense as unbounded as his strength, not limited to streams and drains and courses. Anything the rain touched was his for the finding, for as far as his sense could stretch—and he had not yet found the borders to that stretch.

The same rain would help to hide the dogtooths, his whole little army, for so long as they stayed back this far. He signed to Gilder, *keep them here*, and went on alone.

This road ran down to encircle the wall from its near end, where masonry plunged into the river to become the great breakwater that protected the harbour. Issel didn't need to follow it far. He was surprised, actually, to get as far as he did, almost to the foot of the wall, before a voice hailed him from above. It was hard, he supposed, to keep good watch in the Shine, let alone in the rain in the Shine. It was a shifty, deceptive kind of light that made shadows of its own, and the rain did the same thing while breaking up the outlines of what was really there, and all the time any guard would only be wanting to take shelter from both, hunch his shoulders and turn his back and find a roof, a wall, a dark dry space to hide in.

Issel had no trouble feeling sorry for these men who served his enemy, who were his enemy, who would scorn him and fear him and destroy him if they could. The sympathy was wasted, but it was real none the less.

"Stand, there! What are you, boy?"

I am your enemy. He didn't glow so much out in the open like this, wet only from the rain; if the guard had seen it at all, he must have thought it was an effect of the Shine. Now, though—now that Issel had lifted his head to look up, and it must be clear that he was most unnaturally lit—there was a cry that was nothing to do with a challenge, rather a panicked startlement.

That same rain-in-Shine worked to sharpen Issel's water-sense. It gave depth and meaning to everything his eyes could see and a great deal that they couldn't: so that he knew the guard had stooped behind his parapet for a crossbow kept there, loaded and cocked; he could sense the tension in the cord, the spring of the steel, the weight of the bolt. Sense it, and use it. Wet metal fused with metal; the guard might as well throw the bow down from his platform now, as the trigger could no longer loose the bolt.

As he learned, as he tried to shoot it, hasty and desperate, not really knowing what it was he shot at. Issel did sympathise, but it made no difference.

Close-to, he could see how the watch-platforms were built up like scaffolding, to stand higher than the wall. How long was it since he had believed that water had no authority over wood, since he had been taught that they repelled each other? One short summer, that was all; and now . . .

Now wood snapped and splintered when he reached for it, with the lightest touch of his mind. Now he wrenched all the supports out from under that scaffold, so that the whole platform teetered and fell, and the man with it, shrieking as he went.

If that brought all the garrison out to face him, so much the better; he could face them all himself, and save any of his rag-tag army from the need to die tonight. He'd need to bring the wall down swiftly, though, to let the soldiers come at him before Gilder or one of the smarter, more stupid men decided that he needed help.

He stretched his water-sense like fingers—no, flatter and finer than fingers: like a net, like a web, like a skein across that wall, on both wet sides of stone. He felt for the mortar in between the slabs, the cracks in the mortar, wherever dampness crept. The roots of moss. He found that infiltrating skin of damp and gripped it, claimed it, possessed it; and then used it, turned it against the stones it held. Like a lever, like a grapple, like a chain: he tilted and heaved, hauled and twisted and pushed, and stone by stone, course by course, that wall came down.

It took time, but not too long. Not long enough to suggest that he needed help, or that people would need to swarm the wall half-high. Not long enough—he hoped, he thought—for the dogtooths at his back to overcome their fear. They had been afraid of him before, and that was right; he hoped it might save their lives, if they were afraid of him still.

Time enough for the soldiers to mass on the far side of the wall; enough for them to organise themselves more or less into troops, with duties. He was aware of voices, commands; he could have silenced those wet voices, choked those liquid throats if he'd taken time away from the wall. Instead, he let more stones fall on that side, or hurtle, rather, towards where the men were gathering.

Some would crush and kill, he knew that. He heard the sounds of it, the dull slams, the screaming; he felt the double impacts, stone to flesh to ground. That wasn't so much what he wanted. What he did want was the growing restlessness, the muttering, the fear. That wall used to be a barrier against thieves, a sneer of Marasi invulnerability, *no one touches us, or ours.* Now suddenly it was their last defence, and failing, and there was a sorcerer on the other side.

He wanted them terrorised, he wanted them to run. He left the stones alone for a moment, only to reach further along the wall and strip off the next watch-platform, let another man scream his way down. Then he came back to breaking down the wall stone by stone, and tossing those stones about within the compound.

That was a regiment of janizars he faced, though; their lives were all discipline and ruthlessness, all for moments like this. Terror worked both ways, and their training held. They were still there, standing squad by squad, not falling back from the barrage of stones. Standing and dying, some of them, and he might as well have killed them all already . . .

Or they might kill him, of course. He wasn't invulnerable: a crossbow bolt he didn't sense, that would be enough. Any surprise attack, he supposed, if they could only catch him somewhere dry. Small chance of that in this city, in this rain, but he ought to be aware. This felt easy, and that was deception; killing was never easy in the long run. Never as easy as dying. That came naturally; killing you had to learn. He had learned, he'd been learning all his life, but his skills were superficial, masking, not ingrained . . .

For that and other reasons, he did want to make the janizars run. Enough of nibbling. He ripped a hole in the wall and ran up the rubble while it settled, so that when the rain washed the risen dust cloud out of the air, there he was already, standing in the breach and deliberately shining brighter than the bridge at his back.

And yes, there were archers and crossbowmen too, and they began to shoot as soon as they could see him. Unsurprised, he was not unprepared; and he found a new way to interrupt their bolts in flight. He could weave the rain into a kind of chain-mail that would deflect an arrowhead or shatter it. Every separate falling drop was caught and held for the moment it was needed, in a rigid matrix that existed only for that moment, then it was falling rain again. The water knew, the water learned; it was as though he'd cast a spell of ward all around himself. He'd never felt so benignly watched, so protected. Armina had watched him all her life, but she'd never made him feel protected, she'd never let him feel safe.

There were no spells, there was no watcher except himself, his own water-sense. He knew that. But still he could turn his mind from bolts, turn his eyes from the soldiers in their clustered troops—if they charged him, if they had the nerve, they had all that spewed rubble to scramble over, and then the minor mountain of the fallen wall to climb—and look beyond, to where the river lapped at ships tied up against the quays.

Wood hates water, wood and water have nothing to say to each other— very well, then. Let the water spit it out . . .

——————

IF anyone had been watching besides him, they would have seen the nearest vessel dip down strangely in the water. She was a three-masted barque, but that was all he knew, and that from seeing them on the river, distantly; ships of this size had never come to Sund in his lifetime. She dipped until her hull was invisible even from where he stood, high on the rubble of the wall; until she strained all her mooring-ropes close to the snapping-point; until her crew—awake and alert already, gathered nervously on deck for the most part, with the bolder few swarming up to the masthead to see what was happening at the wall—had finally understood that something strange was happening beneath their feet, beneath the hull.

It wasn't truly the ship that dipped, it was the water: the great river of the world, or this little fringe of it, this fussing at the edges, drawing down like a mouth that puckers before it spits.

It spat.

That vessel—as big as a house, bigger than any house Issel had ever hoped to call his own—was spat up out of the water like an olive-pit. She snapped her tethers like cobwebs as she went; she scattered her crew; she rose till her keel was roof-high to the warehouses.

It was the force of the river that had thrown her up; it was the strength of the rain that held her. It might look, it must look as though she flew, as though she sailed the air, although her sails were all furled for harbour. She was unmanned now, too, which was likely worse, he thought: a ship with her own will, who sailed the winds because she chose to do so.

Just for that little time, the soldiers must have thought so, while he amused himself by sailing her in the rain. What did she need of river water to hold her up, when there was all this rain? Her master unappreciated her, she was able for so much more; she could loft on a storm clear to the far dry north, a ship with no need for ports or water . . .

And then she fell.

Sank in air, wet air.

Smashed like a hurled toy into the staring, scattering ranks of janizars, breaking bones, breaking skulls, engulfing and crushing, killing those too slow or too entranced to flee; and splintered as she smashed against the stone, and those splinters flew like hurled knives to pierce the legs and backs of runners, to kill and maim again.

Those not caught by the splinters or the wild flailing ropes, the hurtling blocks, any of the wreckage, those lucky men just kept on running. They chased their luck all the way to the compound gate; all the garrison broke at once, and when they found the gate barred against them, Issel needed only to lift another ship from the water. They slew their own officers and those men standing guard, threw the gates open and ran for the city, a long desperate spew of men, a voiding of the docks.

———————

THERE were the wounded, yet to be dealt with; there would be stragglers and lurkers, sailors and civilian workers hiding here and there throughout the warehouses and other offices; but the army was gone, the battle was over. One man—no, one boy . . .

One water-mage.

One water-mage working by bridgelight, using terror more than force to be his weapon. Men had died, but not half so many as he had feared, not a tenth of those who might have died; and not one of his. They had the docks; they could take all the boats they wanted. He'd break the rest, and the big ships too. That would prevent the Marasi from chasing after their stolen craft to punish or recapture the runaways, and it would cripple their trade at the same time, loosen their grip on empire. He could break the quays as well, destroy the warehouses and everything they held, maybe even block the harbour with sunken ships and heaped rubble. If the river would let him, if that wasn't straying too close to heresy.

And then . . .

Then he was supposed to retreat quietly into the sewers again, and wait for Armina.

MOVEMENT at his back, a deal of movement, a sudden rush: Gilder, leading his dogtooths on. Issel felt that as a pressure, pushing him into the chaos of rubble and shattered wood, shattered bodies. He wanted to stay ahead: especially here, among the wounded, where he didn't trust either Gilder or the freed prisoners. He barely trusted himself. These were Marasi; more, they were janizars, the soldiers he had hated and feared all his life. He had killed them before; he had killed them today, here, many and many of them. If he killed more, what matter?

Some of these, it would be a kindness. Crushed or pierced, they couldn't live with such injuries; death was coming, slow and infective and agonising. He could bring it quickly—except that he couldn't, as it turned out. He stooped over one suffering man and then another, drawn by their screams or else their silence, their desperate movements or else their desperate stillness; he had death in his touch, almost in his glance, absolutely at his fingers' ends, and he couldn't use it.

Pitying and appalled, he made his slow way between them, this way and that, like a ship tacking into a headwind and getting almost nowhere. He wanted Rhoan and couldn't have her, she'd gone and he wasn't sure why; he wanted Armina also and couldn't have her either, they would both of them come too late. He wanted Rhoan because she would work to save these men, and make him do the same, and it would feel right. He wanted Armina for the opposite reason: because she was ruthless and would be content to let them die, perhaps to help them die, and she would make him do the same, and it would feel right.

On his own, with Gilder coming, he simply didn't know. Only that Gilder would do something where Issel couldn't, and whatever he did, it wouldn't feel right.

He wished he could recover the detachment that the river had given him, that remote and utter certainty that nothing mattered. It was gone, though, another measurement of loss: he still had the rolling strength of river water surging at the back of his mind, but his spirit was his own again, entire and inadequate.

He bent over one more man who was lying tremendously still, although the pulses of life surged within him, strong enough that Issel barely needed water-sense to pick up the suck and surge of blood in his body. Among so many dead and dying, the man blazed like a beacon in the night. Here was one, surely, who could be cured; at last an end to doubt and ducking choices, he could be clear about this—

———

HE reached to touch, and the man's eyes opened.

Fear and hatred twisted his face, and a wild, reckless determination. Issel saw it and understood it, and was still too slow.

This man isn't hurt at all—

but the blade was already in Issel's belly.

He was hiding among the bodies here, only hoping for a chance—

to do this, twist the knife in the gut of the water-mage if he could get it there.

Chapter Four

HEY set her down at last, after a long slow time, too long. In the swaying darkness, with the sick shock of the bridge and the immediate danger of exposure behind her, Jendre had drowsed a little and might have slept entirely. She could almost forget that she was adrift in an alien city, an enemy city. Worse, an enemy city subdued. To the Marasi she was a traitor, dead already and fetched back by sorcery, doubly condemned; she couldn't trust the loyalties of any Sundain who discovered her. She wasn't really confident that she could trust this Tel Ferin she'd been sent to find, and she was utterly certain that no one trusted the Armina she was pursuing.

She trusted Djago, though, and that was good. It was his voice that she clung to, like a thread in darkness, to stop herself drifting too far. He talked to Baris constantly, a soft murmur of reassurance and encouragement: "This is the way, is it, Baris? It's good that you remember; I wouldn't like to be caught asking. Well, I wouldn't know whom to ask, so it's really lucky that we don't need to, that we have you to help us seek out your old master . . ."

And so on and on, a steady reiteration of why they were here and how well he was doing, talking the dogtooth through his doubts and hesitations. Jendre could feel those: long pauses, occasional abrupt reversals. Baris might have known these streets all his life, but he was losing them now.

Still, he had brought them—well, somewhere. The pinch-box stood four-square on the level; it was almost unsettling to feel so firmly grounded, after hours of sway to the rhythms of her bearers. She was glad to have had a calmer passage through the streets here after the toppling vertigo of the bridge, but it still felt like coming to shore at the end of a river trip, a dizzying shift in the world's balance.

Still, she had time to grow used again to a floor that didn't rock. Time to listen to the dogtooths' grunting and blowing, as though even their strength had been taxed close to its limit; time to listen to the dwarf's silence—another sudden alteration, from one world to another—and then the noises he made, sliding down from the box's roof. He must have landed awkwardly, unless all landings were awkward on those painful legs. He swallowed a cry and she heard the effort in it, then his stumping around, walking off the pain as he relearned the stillness of ground.

The stillness of stone, in this instance, she could hear that too: not wood he was stamping on, not gravel, not mud. She was patient for his sake, but that was effort of her own. She ached to be out of here: to see something, anything, even that cursed bridge or a band of soldiers coming. Well, no. Not that, but she would settle for the remitting darkness of a cloudy night in the rain. She'd like to feel rain on her skin, and stone beneath her feet; she'd like to feel anything, so long as it wasn't these six rough-made boxy walls. And she'd like to hear sounds directly, not filtered through narrow spy holes; and she'd like to breathe air that came to her on the wind; and—

And patience was said to be its own reward, presumably because it brought few others, but here was something more: the grunt of Djago at full stretch, the scratch of a key in a lock, the slow fall of the box-front to give her everything she wanted.

Stone, rain, wind, storm; call it freedom, and have done. There was no true freedom in the world, but she'd settle for an approximation. Tonight, she'd settle for this. She'd crawl out into it, indeed, and never mind her dignity. Her legs were too cramped to stand. She hadn't realised it in the box, but movement brought pain in every joint and a shock of pins and needles to her hands and feet. Like Djago, she wanted to be stamping, but she couldn't manage it yet.

It was still night, true night here, unsickened by the bridgelight; she cast a wide look skyward, and could see only a glow beyond a run of roofs to say where the river was, and where the bridge. Maras was a city that climbed, and you could always look down to the river. Sund was flat, and she hadn't really thought about it before, but its own houses blocked out its proper view. The river had formed both cities and the long history between them, in many ways it was the history between them, and it was all but invisible to the Sundain half of its people.

Issel—or no, more likely Rhoan; Issel didn't talk much, except to say what he wanted—Rhoan might have said that to the Sundain, the river was in their hearts, while the Marasi simply rode it like a horse. That the Marasi tried to own it, and therefore needed to overlook it, while the Sundain belonged to it and therefore were never out of its sight or reach. That—

Teo would have said that she was standing in the street with a dwarf and two dogtooths. In the rain, in the night, in a strange city where she might be surprised either by a Marasi patrol or a Sundain loyalist, and either one would be bad beyond measure.

She hadn't expected to find herself in the street; she'd thought a house, its yard, its shelter. But of course it was night, and no house was easy of access in the dark.

Her bearers had set the pinch-box down by a narrow gate in a high wall. Stone paving beneath her bare feet, wet and cool and welcome; this was a high-status district, despite the lack of lights and traffic. She said, "Master Djago, where has Baris brought us?"

"He finds it difficult to say, my lady; but I believe this house should be where Master Tel Ferin is to be found. If his information is reliable."

"Well then, shall we try the door?"

"It is perhaps a little early to be making social calls . . ."

"Perhaps it is, but I would sooner not stand in the rain till sun-up or discovery, whichever might come first. It's wise not to have gone barrelling in at the front door, perhaps, but I think we can be judicious at the side here. If the gate's not locked?"

"As a matter of fact it is, my lady—but I do tend to agree with you, so . . ."

He made a definitive gesture. Baris was seemingly too shy to force the gate of a man he knew and feared, but the other dogtooth had no such inhibitions. One brawny hand on the latch, one lean of the shoulder and there was a *crack*! too loud in the quiet night, and the gate was swinging open.

Beyond was darkness, deeper even than out here: wet dripping darkness, a luxurious overhang of trees. Jendre shuddered, but hiding was good, even if you couldn't call it shelter. If their collective nerve faltered before they reached the house proper, at least they could hole up in the garden and be safe.

She waited, but no one seemed inclined to lead; so she did, stepping forth boldly, setting an example, saying "Baris, will you and your friend bring the, the litter," she still couldn't say "pinch-box" with any comfort, any more than she could ride in one with comfort, "inside the wall, in case anyone should chance on it and want to ask questions? Thank you."

And then she walked through the gate, trying not to flinch as she brushed a low-hanging branch and unleashed a small flood of water down the back of her neck. Even that was welcome. Or so she told herself, firmly. After the dry dull nothing of the box, all her senses needed exercise.

All her senses were getting exercise, here in this garden. Her eyes strained to weave shape from shadow, from the barest grey outlines in the blackness. Her ears found insects and night-birds, the creak of new branches under their burden of leaves and rain, the hissing whisper of air as it worked on those same branches. All the smells of rampant overgrowth, rot and wet earth filled her nose while her mouth tasted the promise of overripe fruit that the same air, the same rain was bringing her, while her skin shivered and exulted under the constant impact of water.

There was a path of sorts, though it was more like a hole in the darkness, simply a way to walk that didn't involve walking into trees. She went that way, squeezed between one tree and another, walking it seemed against a wall of water as she dislodged more and more from the undergrowth, the overgrowth all around her. And walking became more and more difficult, as though she were walking into a web of water, but it still took her a while to realise that she was making no headway, that like a fly caught in a web she was moving and moving and getting nowhere at all, caught by a sticky proliferation, an entanglement of water, a trap that she had walked clean into . . .

She had seen water-magic already today, far worse than this. She had seen and felt and been entangled in the magic that saved her life, then seen Issel slaughter soldiers sent to track him down. Even so, this simple snare was a terror to her. Seized in the dark, in ways she couldn't comprehend, with all her struggles only tying her up tighter, she lost all the grip she had on being grown and strong and confident. She could invade an enemy city, an occupied city, pretty much by herself; she could seek out a rebel traitor in order to betray her own people, with barely a second thought; she had been dead and fetched back by an awesome magic, and it was hard to be afraid of anything after that; but she was afraid of this. She wept with it, that crawling fear like a chill in the bones. She would have screamed with it, but that a sticky strand of this not-water had wrapped itself across her mouth as she fought, and she could barely breathe. Not air enough to scream with, and she was too gagged to talk.

She knew that the others were caught too. She couldn't see—this deep-in-the-shadow darkness, and all the water in her eyes that she lacked a hand free to dash away—but she could hear grunts and gasps and scuffling struggles behind her, even above the noises she herself was making.

After a minute, she heard the dwarf's rough voice speaking, slow and steady. Lucky: his mouth must still be free. He was talking to the dogtooths behind him—or ostensibly he was—but she thought the words were aimed as much at her.

"Don't panic, this is not meant to harm us, only to hold us. Don't struggle: that will only bind you up tighter. Stand still, stand quiet, and don't be afraid . . ."

She could manage two of those instructions, she thought, though even so much was hard. Her fear, she could do nothing about. His voice might calm her body, but nothing could calm her mind, where it struck out wildly into fantasies of captivity and horror.

Time passed, and nothing got better. Her legs trembled, and even that little movement excited the strands that gripped her, tightening their hold; the muscles cramped in response, and she cried from the pain of it, or else from sheer exhaustion.

And the rain fell, and all that water only strengthened her bonds the more, and she wondered if even her tears were contributing to them; and time hung as static as they were, seized in the moment, and she wondered if they would be left simply to die here, abandoned to the trap. It might not take long, if these cruel strands kept tightening despite all she could do to stand still. Like riverweed they could pull her down; like riverweed they could drown her . . .

HOW long it was they stood there, she couldn't tell. How long it was since sun-up, she hadn't noticed; it was a late sudden realisation, that there were shadows in the gloom now, which meant that something had changed in the world beyond, time was not dead entirely. She couldn't lift her head, to look for light between the leaves; her back was pulled into a half-bow, and it was all she could do to hold a precarious balance. Soon now, soon she would be pulled crashing over, and be wrapped again in new strands, be cocooned entirely and unable to breathe at all, and it would only be a question of whether she suffocated before she was strangled or her bones were crushed.

But there was light and light was something; it was better to die in the light. She only wished that it didn't feel so pointless, that they might have accomplished something, passed the message on, left someone else to look for Armina.

Sidië, I'm sorry . . .

But perhaps there might still be time or opportunity, because here came people brushing wetly through the trees, and she might not be left here to die after all.

She couldn't see, but she heard how light their voices were as they talked together, even the gravelly bass was just chicken-skin with no meat, and she heard the oh-so-casual bravado in what they said—

"Well, see here, looks like we've caught ourselves some fishes in the net."

"What shall we do, throw the little one back and gut the rest for supper?"

"Nah, let's gut 'em all. Small ones are sweeter."

—and they gave themselves away with every word. They were young, barely more than children; and they were nervous, never done this before, anxious to do it right. And afraid, perhaps, despite their potent snare. Which meant they wouldn't be confident, they'd be careful; which meant small chance of getting away, even if they were only a pair of youngsters and she had three grown men at her back . . .

Well, one half-grown man and two dogtooths. Experience and strength, but not married, not likely to work well together; and she knew herself to be useless, buckled in body and crushed in spirit.

They came to her first, because she was first on the path or because she was weakest, or both; and just the touch of their hands dissolved all her bonds in a moment, and she would have fallen headlong a moment later if their hands hadn't been there to catch her. Whether they meant to hold her up or hold her captive, she couldn't guess; it was her arms they held, which achieved both at once. She was grateful for the one and cared nothing about the other, except that she would have liked one hand free to wipe at her wet and filthy face before she hauled her back straight and met them eye to eye and said,

"Please, we came here looking for, looking for Master Tel Ferin . . ."

That startled them out of their adopted swagger, either the name or her Marasi accent, or perhaps the two together. The small one almost let her go, before she did the other thing and gripped more tightly. The bigger one—who might perhaps have been Jendre's own age, though she doubted it—said, "Did you? And how did you know to look here?"

Which was an admission, but she didn't point that out; just jerked her head backwards and said, "We had a guide."

They looked, past the dwarf to the straining figures beyond; and one gasped and the other said, "Baris . . . ?" and then she knew for sure, they had found what they were seeking.

Not safety, she didn't feel safe, even after the children let her go; just one step further on this mazing journey where she had no sight of the road and no real faith in her arrival, only a blind hope and a pressing need.

And a sodden robe, cold and clammy hair, a desperate shudder in her that was nothing to do with either, and a hard interview to come. She tried to stand straight and walk proudly when the boy beckoned, while the girl ran ahead; she couldn't do it. She felt dizzy, her back hurt, her legs wouldn't hold her. She flung an arm out, almost at random, for something to catch hold on; it was caught instead, and held firmly until she had her balance back.

When she looked to see who had her, it was Djago. Of course it was, though he was reaching uncomfortably high to give her that support, though he must have been suffering badly himself after so long standing in the snare of the water-web.

She said, "Master Djago, thank you. I'll be fine now."

"I don't think so, my lady."

"No?" She bit her lip, suddenly close to tears again. "Well, perhaps not—but there's no need for you to hurt yourself in helping me. No, I mean it. Let go your hold and walk beside me, and I'll just rest my hand on your shoulder—such a handy size you are, for a girl who needs a friend—and that should be enough, only the touch of you, I shouldn't need to lean . . ."

Having said which, of course, she didn't dare to lean, but his simple presence at her side gave her what she needed: a point of balance, a source of comfort, a promise of resilience. Her back still hurt, but she could straighten it regardless; her legs still wanted to give way, but would not do it now. Even her dizzy head could settle, once she had that little gesture of support. She could swallow against the last residue of tears, blink against a sudden flare of sunlight reflected off a puddle in the leaf-mould, set her face to the house and her thoughts to the future.

———————

THE house was a surprise, if only because it was so unsurprising to her. She'd seen nothing of Sund, but she'd always assumed it to be as different from Maras in style and structure as it was in history, in attitude, in war.

This house might have been a previous home of her own, reflected. The wall, the garden, the trees: although Marasi gardens were better tended, their trees pruned and marshalled into attractive order, all of this was intimately familiar. The building too, once they came out of the trees to see it in first light. Marasi houses were taller and less broad, perhaps because they had less space to stretch in, because their hills were steep and crowded; even so, the brickwork and the windows were achingly alike, the angles of the roof, the portico, all spoke of somewhere else. She had been happy in that house; this image of it raised a momentary, unexpected lump in her throat. Was adult life all loss? It seemed so; she had lost sister, family, contentment, all in short order, once they had moved higher up the hill. And had lost more since, including her life and liberty; now she was losing her city entirely, giving it away . . .

The boy led with many backward glances, not quite trusting them to follow unchivvied. For that reason if no other, she did her best to keep pace, even to press at his heels.

Out from the trees and through a less wild garden, though it was still unkempt; round to the back of the house, where all her own houses had harboured their more interesting people, places, secrets, pets; in through a scullery, down a corridor with stores and workrooms opening off, into a kitchen, all of it wonderfully normal except that in Maras there would have been servants and slaves everywhere to tend a house this large. Here there were meant to be, surely, no one would build or buy such a house without the expectation of a staff to run it; but she could spot only the occasional child, tending the kitchen fire or fetching water from a cistern, all of it make-work, all of them come from curiosity to see the strangers. If this house had staff, it was sparse or elsewhere.

One or two of the children greeted Baris by name. Jendre wasn't sure if he recognised them or not; if he did, he showed no signs of it.

In the kitchen, a man was waiting for them: tall and self-possessed, undisturbed by the early hour—despite his long loose hair and his sleeping-robe, he wore both with an elegance born of wealth and training—or the manner of their finding. He leaned against a table, dabbling his fingers in a bowl where rose-petals floated. Jendre was reminded of Rhoan in the Marasi streets, making magic with a palmful of water. This was a threat, perhaps, or a precaution. More than that, this was the man responsible for the water-trap that had caught them in the trees. That was a guess, but a fair one. And that being so, then—

"Master Tel Ferin?"

He bowed. "And you are—?"

"We are wet through," Djago said dryly, the only thing about him that was dry. "And we are your guests, I hope, although it has felt remarkably as though we were your prisoners, and we would appreciate the chance to find ourselves dry and warm."

Surprisingly—well, it surprised Jendre—Tel Ferin smiled, although there was some little strain to it. "This is not my house, despite appearances. These are my people, though"—this motley collection of children gathering round—"and one of them will bring you towels, no doubt"—a small boy, galloping off when his larger fellows poked him—"while you draw near to the fire. Such as it is. We are very short of fuel this side the river, or I would ask you to the bathhouse."

Oh, was there a bathhouse? She would so dearly love a bath, a morning, a full day in the baths. She hadn't felt clean for weeks.

But here was a chance, and she took it, and never mind the risks: "Do you need fuel? Issel, I think, could heat a bath without. And chase all the water out of these our clothes with a touch, I fancy . . ."

"Ahhh." It was a sigh of envy, of desire, of possession lost: all of that, and more that she could not read. Now she was sure, this was the man they had been sent to find. "Have you come from Issel?"

"In a way." Directly, indeed—but that was one way to come, and she didn't want to give him too much, too soon.

"Well. You must tell me where, and how, and why—but not immediately. Let my people bring you dry clothing of their own, if you will, because I am not Issel, and it is wiser for me to spend my strength in the gardens, as you have learned; and when you are dry and warm—inside and out, yes, someone will make porridge—then we will talk further. If I am lucky, someone will bring me tea in the meantime. That was Issel's task for a while, and I am ill served since he left us . . ."

He left himself, with that whimsical plaint still hanging in the air. One of the children followed him shortly afterwards, with a steaming pot in hand.

————

TOWELS and clothes and porridge, all as promised, though the dwarf struggled between clothes that fitted his length and clothes that fitted his breadth, because none would do both. All of it was good, but the food was best; she could have cried again when the little girl who fetched it asked if she would like more, or perhaps some honey to sweeten it?

Instead—instead of eating, instead of crying—she said, "No, but sit and talk to me, sweets. Do you know Issel?"

A solemn nod, and a hesitant smile: she knew him, she liked him, but she wasn't sure she should. Well, Jendre could understand that.

"Was he one of you? And Rhoan too?" *My people*, Tel Ferin called them: more than servants, though they filled that role. Adopted children, perhaps, was he a philanthropist? But Issel was a water-mage, and so was Rhoan, and so was Tel Ferin, so . . .

When the child nodded again, she had another question hot and ready, "Do you all get to be like Issel?"

If it was so, she couldn't believe that Maras had survived this long—which was why she didn't believe that it was so, and was not at all surprised by the girl's sudden giggle, and the shake of her head.

"Issel was very bad," she confided.

"I'm sure he was—but very good at what you do, yes? The water-magic?"

A pause, as though she had been trained never to reveal this to a stranger;

and then a jerk, a nod of the head, and she was scooting off before Jendre had the chance to ask anything further.

———————

DRY and warm and fed, they had Tel Ferin back. In bound hair and what she took for formal dress, or its rootless survivor here, where all formal structures had been ripped out, he sat them most informally around a table in the kitchen—Djago perched high on cushions, the dogtooths squatting awkwardly on a bench and still looming, uncomfortable and ill at ease—and said, "Well, now, what will you tell me of my reckless pupil?"

"Your pardon, master: this is a school?"

It wasn't like Djago to be so slow. Jendre didn't believe for a minute in his guileless discovery. He must have some end in view; she kept quiet.

"It is, of course. That is my claim on these children's service, that they learn from me the proper uses of their gifts. It is my claim on Issel, and perhaps why he has sent you to me—but before I say more, I should not have said so much to the Marasi except that you have clearly met Issel, and you have met my own precautions in the garden, so I am giving little away here. Still, it is time that you gave something to me." His fingers were back in that bowl of rose-water, an implicit threat. "Your names would be a beginning, I think. A young woman, travelling in company with an elderly dwarf—this is unusual, even for your city. The chosen means of travel—a box, my children tell me, slung like a litter on poles: I take it they mean a black bier, such as I have never seen this side of the river—that is more unusual still. And that you should come to me, a proven water-mage and so condemned; that you should be fetched here by my own servant, whom I lost that same night I lost my own house, and Issel too; all of this has its story, I am sure, but I cannot see it in these pieces."

No, she was sure not. She was surprised to be trusted as far as they had been already; that would be Issel's name or Baris' company, or the two wielded together, but it was still a surprise. Another part of the same story, she thought, and wanted to hear him tell it. Instead, "I have run away," she said, "twice now, from sultans' palaces. My name is Jendre, and I was married to one, outraged by another, abused by a third. My friend is called Djago, and he served my husband's father, back so far."

"I was a fool," Djago said softly, "but death has robbed me of my follies. All but one."

"Well. That is a story that I would very much like to hear, given that it concerns our masters and their ways. It could be useful, if you will bear with my questions; we've never had the opportunity before, to talk to someone from the heart of the empire."

She was sure not; but, "Forgive me, Tel Ferin, the harem is barely the heart of anywhere."

"Oh, come: it is where your sultans are bred, trained, kept until needed. Anyone wishing to understand Maras must first understand the harem."

That was insightful, unless it was meant to be flattering, to make her feel herself and her kind more important than they were. She said, "You make His Magnificence sound like an animal, pedigree stock."

"Oh, and is he not?"

Mehmet and his uncle, surely; they had acted like animals newly released from the cage, wildly indulgent. Her Man of Men, though, he had been magnificent in every sense; she was resentful on his behalf, but then didn't have the time to defend him, because Tel Ferin waved his own question away with a long hand. "No matter. All of that is a tale of Maras, and we are in Sund, and so I imagine is Issel. You have run a long way from your beginnings, my lady Jendre . . ."

"I have, but so has Issel. I met him in Maras"—in the river actually, though she did not feel inclined to say so—"with his friends, Baris here and the others."

"In *Maras*? Did you so? Baris, what were you—? No, never mind. Forgive me, my lady, but I think this is a story I need to hear. In detail."

SHE told it him, in what detail she chose, confident that neither the dwarf nor the dogtooths would gainsay her. Her tale left Issel as she had last seen him on the beach, Rhoan—another of Tel Ferin's lost children, another startlement to him—in a Marasi courtyard, both of them working to achieve this, herself here and speaking to him; and so, inevitably,

"Jendre," he said, losing her honorific with his discretion, "I can admire all the intricacies of your journey, and particularly the courage of it, braving guards at every step and venturing over that cursed bridge—but you have still not explained the purpose. Why are you here, and why have you been sent to me?"

"Because"—as blunt as he was, at last, now that she was allowed to be—"we hope that you can send us on to Armina."

"To *Armina*?" Of all this morning's shocks, that seemed to be the greatest.

"Please."

"Whyever—?"

"Because we need her. We think we do. Issel says so. Without her, he can't get into the magicians' pavilion, wake the sleepers, break the bridge," *all these things that I want for my sister, you want for your city, don't deny me now . . .*

"I don't understand. Why does he need Armina?"

"Oh, I don't understand it either. He says she is of their kind, the magicians' people. He says she has bells in her hair. I can say, the women who tend the sleeping children, they do have bells. I don't know why that matters."

"No. No more do I. But Issel has stood there, and I have not." Jendre had stood there too; that didn't seem to matter now. "And Armina was, let us say instrumental in leading Issel to me; she has always been a part of his life, as for a long time she has been a part of mine. That was always interesting; more so now, if she has a connection with the dream-masters."

"Well then, will you tell us how to find her? I think we should be swift, to take her back." She didn't trust Issel, she meant, not to get into some greater trouble in the meantime. Rhoan might think she could control him, but Rhoan might be wrong; what Jendre had seen of Issel, he was straying out of all control, his own included.

"I'm afraid that won't be possible."

"Oh, why not?"

"I don't believe she would come with you willingly; I don't believe she would help, if you took her by force; I don't believe you have any hope of reaching her, either to ask or to abduct."

Suddenly she was tired beyond measure, tired almost beyond bearing; she did not need this. She said, "I'm sorry, I don't understand."

"Jendre, we had a network here, a cobweb of people opposed to Marasi rule. Some few of us were mages, some were like these children here, gifted apprentices, learning to use their gift under my tutelage or others'. More were what you might call soldiers in the field, or spies. Issel I think was a rebel against all of us. Armina was one of the links between us, who knew many of our secrets. Places and names. She was . . . convenient, as a means to keep in touch.

"I thought we were careful, but we gave our trust too freely; perhaps it is always so with a people under occupation, perhaps there will always be voices willing to spill a secret for money or security or an easier life.

"We were betrayed. We lost many friends; I lost my home, and barely had time to save my school. Even now, the children are scattered, a handful here and a handful there."

"And you think it was Armina who betrayed you." Not a question.

"We are certain of it."

So was Issel, she understood now; and Gilder, and Rhoan. That was why no one trusted her. Even so, "They still need her, in Maras. Whatever damage she has done here, she can put that right . . ."

"No. There are no reparations for betrayal. And I see no reason why she would; and besides, as I said, you cannot get at her now. She went to the Marasi, and now she serves them, however she can. Whatever use she is to them. I only know where to find her, which is in their barracks. How will you reach her there?"

Chapter Five

THE knife was still in his belly, and the man still had a blood-slick grip of it, twisting and ripping.

That was all Issel saw, all he knew, all there was left to know in his narrowing world: hand and blade, the cold instruments of his dying.

AND then one thing more, the iron bar that came down from above, splintering the man's wrist as it knocked his hand away. The blade jerked viciously, so that he and Issel screamed both at once.

And then the iron bar again, pounding down, skewering, so that the man spasmed like a gaffed fish, impaled in a cruder echo of how he had impaled Issel. Issel fell aside, into the great shadow of the dogtooth that loomed over him as he worked the bar deep and deeper, trying to dig it all through chest and spine and into the stone beneath.

And then there was a voice, pitilessly swearing, and that was Gilder; and his hands, and they were angry and pitiless too as they reached for the knife-handle and Issel could only just manage to lift his own hand, his own voice against him.

"No." It was a thin whisper, thin as water against the run of blood that he could feel welling out around that blade, but it had weight enough—just—to stop a man.

"Issel, let me see. It has to come out."

"*No.*" A breath, and that was thinner yet, and hurt deeply; but pain was one thing he was used to. *Slide through it, don't try to ride it or you ride it to oblivion.* "It has to stay. To plug . . ."

Blood was running from that tear of a wound, the blade couldn't block it altogether—but take the blade away and run would turn to flood, and one more thing Issel knew about, it was the flow and drain of liquids. The flood, and the stem.

"Issel, we can't move you with that inside! Every jar, it'll just cut you afresh . . ."

"Don't—move—me."

"But—" Gilder swore again, briefly, fluently; and used his last and most potent persuader, the ultimate weapon: "Rhoan will be angry with you."

It was, Issel realised, almost certainly true. But it was not to be avoided now; in truth, if Gilder and the dogtooths chose to play catch with him all around the harbour, there was nothing he could do now to avoid it. The last of his vision was failing, and he had no choice except to turn his gaze inward and let the world all go.

———

REACHING down into the dark:

Water-sense is not sight; it does not need the light. It is not hearing, or touch, or smell, or taste. If it feels like any of those, that is only because the mind has no other ways to understand what it is doing, sensing, reaching for.

Here is the blade, tangled deep in a wet and messy clutch of sundered flesh, a sucking swirl of blood. Here are organs, the lightless cisterns and sewers of the body pierced and broken and blocked, leaking their importance.

Here is pain, the light he has always worked by.

Here is that tingle, less and more than innocent pain; here is the taint of the Shine, that could make him glitter and glow even on the inside, see him, now . . .

———

THERE was, at last, another voice: one fit to draw him up from the dark, from the depths, from the slow work of blood and tissue.

"Oh," she said, "Issel . . ." And then, "I don't, I don't believe it—you left the *knife* in . . . ?"

"He insisted," Gilder muttered, somewhere behind her. "He said it would plug the wound, I suppose he meant to stop some of the bleeding . . ."

"Well," she said, "he's not bleeding now, is he?"

He's nearly dead now, that must be what she meant; and *it can't do any harm, too late for that.*

He opened his eyes then, nicely in time to see her reach for the handle of the knife, and curl her fingers gingerly around it. She must mean to draw it out, as gently as she could; but just as she took a grip, she must have felt how it toppled at her touch, because she snatched at it despite all her intentions.

And found herself holding the handle and the tang, no more, where they had not snapped but fallen away from the blade, which was left embedded in his body. After her first shock, she gazed at what she held, at the smooth soft break between blade and handle, and she looked down at last to find his face, and see the best he could manage of a smile.

"Issel," she said, "what have you *done* . . . ?"

Smiling he could achieve, just, though he couldn't imagine quite what it would look like; a death's-head grimace might be flattering in comparison. Talking was too much. He only waved a hand, vaguely, at his exposed belly.

Where she could look, and see how the steel of the knife blade had melted and run—like blood, like water—to fill all the ripped wound of its entry, despite the janizar's twisting and tearing. See that, and she would know that he had softened all the edges of the steel so that it was no longer a blade but truly a plug, to seal his blood inside and his damage from the world.

She said, "Well, some of us would have stuffed rags into the wound to stop the bleeding, but never mind. You do what you have to do. What are you doing else?"

He still couldn't answer her, and this time he had nothing to show. Water-sense couldn't be shared. She should be able to touch the wetness of his lips and follow that water down, all the way through his body, to find where he was rebuilding walls by sheer will over his water, where he was forcing blood and other wet to flow as it ought, where he was trusting flesh to heal on its own.

She was water-skilled, she should have all of that and more; all she lacked was belief. He had no way to give it to her now. He gestured and shrugged, and both those movements cost him in pain and trouble; she said, "Don't do that, don't move. Don't answer me, I'm stupid. I'm just glad you're still alive. Astonished. You don't deserve to be. I'm not sure just how stupid you are, Issel, I can't measure that low, but . . ."

And yes, she was angry, and she told him so; and he thought there were tears on her cheeks even as she spat her fury, but he couldn't be sure because his vision was leaving him again; and then his consciousness was sucked down in pursuit.

THE next time he rose, it was only high enough to hear noises. Voices, and the crack and rumble of great stones being heaped together; the soft insidious whispers of the river. Unless that last was only in his head, a lyric to the bass thrum of the water in his bones.

He tried to stir, but his body was clay. He could feel nothing, move not at all. They had transplanted him, he thought, into some slap-dash mockery made of river mud. He had no eyes to open, no mouth or tongue to make a protest. Nothing to do, then, but turn and dive down deep again, to where that plugged hole was, that gape where they must have poured him in. He could force the plug out and rush into the light to follow it; or he could do the other thing, the clever thing. He could seal it up from the inside, from below, smoothing all this rough-ripped hole into unmarked clay and so preserve himself, hide from the hot sun until the rain came to dissolve this useless body and carry him away in floods and gutters to the river . . .

THE next time he rose, he had eyes and could open them, onto a welcome shadow-world. There was sun, or there would be no shadows; but there was a roof of sorts, between the light and him. As there was a floor of sorts, between him and the ground. Not much, of either.

He turned his head from side to side—movement! a little miracle in itself, to a man who had been clay—and saw that there was a carpet up on poles, to overhang him like a tent. He was lying on another. Otherwise, he was where he had been, out in the open, between the fallen wall and the warehouses and the waterside.

The wall was not so fallen now. He could see how men and—mostly—dogtooths were labouring to build it up again, with those same stones he had ripped out of it. There was nothing scientific about their work, not a mason among them or else no time to be heedful of his craft; they were simply struggling to pile as much stone as possible in the breach, as quickly as they could manage. They heaved and strained, gasped and cursed as they raised great weights between them, encouraged each other with cries, sometimes with threats, and still occasionally had to abandon a stone too heavy to lift.

Issel lay still and watched, until a voice said, "He's moved—oh, Ailse, why didn't you tell me he's awake?"

"Gilder said to let him lie quiet."

"Yes, of course, but—"

"He said you would disturb him."

"Oh. Did he?" A pause, then, "Oh, damn him, I suppose he's right. But Gilder only wants to use him. Maybe you'd better go and find Gilder, so that we can fight it out with Issel watching. Who knows, Issel might even join in . . ."

Issel didn't move, he didn't need to. Rhoan came round to kneel on the carpet beside him, where he could see. Briefly, she touched his face; her fingers were wet, but it was she who gasped at the contact. He had been in the river, and on some level his whole body had been burning ever since. On another level he could feel nothing now, nothing was strong enough after that.

She was too close to be clear, just a silhouette against the light. It didn't matter. Hers was a shadow he was content to rest in, so long as—

"What's happening?"

"You're getting better, I think. Incredibly fast, but that's just you. How do you feel?"

You tell me how I feel, you felt me. "Over there, I mean. At the wall."

"Oh, they're rebuilding it. If they can, if they have time."

"Why?"

"Because," another voice, out of his vision but no need to see, no need to stretch the water-sense: it was Gilder, coming fast, "there is an army in Maras, and it will come out of those gates and down that road any hour now, and we need to hold the wall until you are fit to save us. Did you think that chasing them away would be enough, that defeated once they would give up their harbour and everything it brings them?"

"No." He hadn't thought much at all, but none of his thoughts had been about occupation, holding the docks. "The men were going to take boats and flee, while we went back to the sewers, to wait for Armina . . . ?"

"We couldn't move you, Issel," Rhoan again, reaching to touch him again, "once you were hurt. We didn't dare."

He would be hurt a great deal more if the Marasi caught them. No matter. "Why are the dogtooths still here?" Not for love of him, he was sure of that. He had freed them, yes, but that wasn't enough to buy their lives back for a war with the Marasi.

"Because you were hurt too soon," Gilder said, meaning *you were stupid, you tried to keep us out of it, and so you were hurt when we could have defended you.* "The big ships in the harbour saw what you were doing, hauled anchor and sailed out into the river. Beyond harm's reach, they think; but they're still there, and any little boatful of dogtooths trying to flee would be seized or sunk. If we can hold out till nightfall, perhaps the men can slip away then, if they dare to try. But . . ."

But there was no true nightfall down here below the bridge. The Shine would show them up like coins on a cloth, to anyone who dared be looking—and there wouldn't be a vessel out there tonight without a watch. Gilder knew that too, and must have impressed it on the dogtooths. He had his little army, and it seemed he meant to keep it.

Issel had one way to defy him, if he could reach those ships out on the river. He hardly doubted it; with all that water to carry him, what could hold him back? He closed his eyes and reached—and could barely find them, the most fleeting and ineffectual of touches, like a fingertip's contact at full stretch, just enough to know that they were there. He couldn't get a grip on them at all.

That was his weakness, a measure of the damage that he'd taken. The river might have been a friend to him, and was not. It could have lifted him, carried him, lent him all he needed of its strength; instead it almost overswept his spirit, drowning it as drums or thunder will drown out a voice. It was too grand, too great; he couldn't hope to use it.

He drew back into his own body again and found it shaking, Rhoan scowling: "I don't know what you tried to do then, Issel, but stop it. You're hurt, you don't know how bad it was; you could have *died*, anyone but you would have died . . ."

Amazing to himself, he found a smile lurking and offered it to her. "I'm the one who does know just how bad it was. It's my belly." He knew every nicked vessel, every punctured length of gut. He knew them intimately, from the inside.

And that little plug of steel that he kept softening and reshaping as he rearranged his body's flows: it was almost a part of him now, adopted into his flesh.

"Well, just be still, then. Lie quiet and rest. Don't, don't try to *do* anything . . ."

"If he doesn't do something," Gilder said, "he can have all the rest he wants, because we'll all be dead. Do you honestly think a handful of dog-tooths armed with crowbars and stones can hold off a regiment of janizars? Even for one day?"

"Do you honestly think," she countered, "that Issel can do anything to help? With a hole in his gut that he has to keep the blade in, because otherwise even he can't stop it bleeding him to death? Look at him, he can't even stand . . ."

"Then you'd best make your peace with the river, because that's where we'll all be headed. Living or dead. Should they sew you in a sack, or would you rather they slit your throat first?"

"I'd rather you slit my throat first. But—"

But Issel was pushing himself up on one elbow and so higher, sitting up into a sudden dizziness that had him reaching for her blindly; that had her swatting at him vainly, trying to push him down again; that had Gilder doing what was useful, offering him swift and necessary support.

"Issel, no, what are you *doing*?"

Proving you wrong. Aloud, he said, "I need to see."

"You can't! Look at yourself . . ."

He smiled again and shook his head, gripped Gilder's arm and was hauled swiftly, efficiently, brutally to his feet.

He did manage not to scream, though the look on Rhoan's face said that she'd seen it anyway, that pain that coursed through him like a tidal rip. At least it chased the dizziness away; and pain was in his nature; they were bonded soul to soul.

Even so, he would have doubled over if Gilder hadn't hauled him erect; he would have shaken loose and slumped back onto the carpet again if this hadn't been so important. If Rhoan hadn't been so close, and watching.

He couldn't manage another smile—he could almost see his own face reflected in hers, in her pallor and wide, appalled eyes, and a smile on that face would be monstrous—but he did hold her eye and say, "Show me," and he did take her arm. Once he was sure of it, he even let go of Gilder's.

Stiff and silent, she matched her pace to his slow shuffle as they ducked out from under that improvised tent into the wet light, hot sunshine on puddles and wet stone.

First to the wall, to the breach. At least there was no longer a ramp of rubble that soldiers could scramble over. The repair was rough and probably unstable, but it might hold against infantry, if it could only be defended. The Marasi would bring archers, though, and crossbowmen; this little dogtooth army didn't even have shields to protect themselves.

He said as much to Gilder, in as few words as he could.

"Shields?"

Gilder answered with even fewer, just a jerk of his head to where a couple of men were nailing planks onto a frame. No time to make individual shields, but screens to duck behind, they would be better than nothing.

Issel nodded.

It was Rhoan who said, "Issel, can you—you know, stiffen the work here, make the stones hold together . . . ?"

I thought you wanted me to lie still and do nothing. He said, "Of course, when I have to." But that was a lie. At the moment, absolutely not. In lieu of honesty, he said, "You can help. Especially if the rain starts again."

"I can't hide the wall, Issel. They know it's here, and they know we're behind it."

"No, but you could blur their sight of us, confuse their aim, maybe give them false targets to shoot at."

Rhoan fell quiet and looked thoughtful. If he did nothing more, Issel thought he'd done something worthwhile.

He wanted to see more, but the long walk to the gate was beyond him. He declined to be carried; instead, he made his slow way along the base of the wall towards the nearest surviving watch-platform. All the way, he was aware how sparse the defences were, how far the wall stretched, how easily the Marasi would be able to swarm it. They should know that; these were their own risen slaves, and they must have a count of numbers. What they couldn't count was the magic that opposed them: how many mages, how strong they'd be.

Just the one, and I am weak to the point of leaning on a girl—but that the Marasi didn't know, and their doubts were a weapon to his hand, their ignorance his only safety.

A wide path ran inside the wall, all the way around the compound. It would make reinforcement easy, if they only had reinforcements; in his pomp, Issel could have created water-soldiers to give at least the impression of an army, perhaps even to fight like one. Now, like this—no. Everything he had was in his body and needed to stay there.

Everything he had in his body, all his strength and determination—and all his pain, and his habit of endurance—might not be enough to see him up to the watch-platform. He was daunted, just by first sight of the ladder. Rhoan might call his recovery a miracle, but it was a rough field repair that he'd made, nothing like a healing. He was holding his insides together by will and craft, because he could. There was no flesh-and-blood knitting together in there, and wouldn't be until he could lie down and let his body work. Till then—

Well, until then there was pain and damage and rigorous control. Now there was a ladder to climb. Which meant stretching and tugging, heaving dull and heavy flesh upward, using resources he couldn't spare but had to. Grip the rungs, step up. Reach for the next rung, feel the pain—like a new blade, stabbing and slicing—and not ignore it but let it wash through, surf through shingle, there and gone and only the wet of it remaining. Step up. Feel the pain.

———————

AND so on, up and up, how many rungs he wasn't counting, but every one was a cost.

He did reach the platform, by himself, unaided; and had a moment to stand and sweat and shudder, before Gilder, then Rhoan followed him up. Issel turned away; he was here to look, not to be looked at.

Behind him, he heard, "Issel, how are you—oh, never mind. If you felt bad, you wouldn't tell me, would you? Not till you fell off the edge."

"I won't let him fall," Gilder said.

"You might not be quick enough to stop him," with its underlying accusation, *you didn't stop him getting hurt*. But she changed the subject quickly: "Shouldn't there be someone up here, on watch?"

"I can't afford the man, I need everyone working. The gate needs to be reinforced, as well as the breach here. We'll know as soon as the Marasi bring their army out. Though you can stay up here yourself, if you'd like to volunteer?"

"No. I'll stay with Issel."

"As you wish."

Issel looked along the length of the wall, and saw how a team of dog-tooths was indeed working behind the gate, wedging it with great baulks of timber out of one of the warehouses. They might have been meant for ship-repair, or maybe for the city . . .

The city: he lifted his eyes to it, this first close view he'd had, and saw how it hung above him like the lammergeiers that hung above the river cliffs, wings spread wide, poised at height as though the wind they rode were solid. To the birds, no doubt it was; to Maras, the empire was the wind beneath its wings, sure and certain, safe to soar upon. The birds were carrion-eaters, feasting on the bones of others' kills; the city had grown fat on the conquests of dead sultans. Fat and complacent, he hoped: fit to lose the tribute it depended on.

Behind the walls it rose in staggered tiers, up and back, echoing in worked stone the rocky heights it was built on, encompassing whole hills within its walls. Those hills were crowned with green, the famous parks and palace gardens of Maras, that the wealthy in Sund tried to emulate within their little acres. Issel had seen one of the originals, and might have died there, if Rhoan hadn't rescued him; now he was outside the city, where he belonged, and he might have died here too. He might still die, if his wound turned sour before it healed properly; he might die before that, when Maras sent its soldiers down the hill . . .

They hadn't far to come. Here was the dock gate in its wall; there was the road, which the garrison had fled along; and there was the city's dock-side gate, close enough that he could see the guards arrayed along the wall surmounting it. Too far to waste a crossbow bolt, apparently, but they could certainly see him. If they looked behind them, he supposed they'd see their own soldiers massing.

It wasn't clear what the Marasi were waiting for; perhaps it simply took time to assemble a regiment. The docks' garrison had been swift enough, but that was its duty, to defend these walls. In Sund the janizars were swift again to answer any summons, but they had reason to be ready. Within the walls of their own all-powerful city, perhaps their masters kept only enough soldiers to maintain the city's peace—why keep more, where soldiers could be as much a threat as a guarantee?—and all of those might be needed now, to quiet a restless population. They might have to send outside the city for more troops.

It was Gilder's dream, he thought, that they might send to Sund, closest and easiest, a quick march across the bridge. The more men he drew back to Maras, the fewer he would have to drive from Sund.

Whatever the reason, this delay was a blessing. It gave Gilder time to organise and reinforce; it had given Issel time to get back on his feet, though there was little he could do now he was up. He could look, he could worry; not much else.

The city gate was wide, the road was short. It was all too easy to picture soldiers flooding down and washing over the walls, unstoppable. A rapid slaughter for these rebels and workers of forbidden magic, no mercy shown; himself unable to resist, helplessly trapped inside his weakened body and the whole day his fault, his responsibility. Without his heedless magic the dogtooths would have stayed within their cage, safely in their chains; he and his friends would all be safely hidden in the sewers, no one would be facing death this day . . .

He looked about, and saw a little keg of water in one corner of the platform. Water with a dipper, drinks for the watch.

Gilder followed the direction of his eyes, and said, "Yes."

Said, "*Yes*, Issel. Something you can do."

"Not up here," Issel said. "I wouldn't manage the ladder, after."

"No. And that is not enough water, in any case."

Rhoan was slow today, unless she was distracted. Only now did she catch on; only now—too late!—did she say, "No. Oh, no. Issel, you can't. You can *not*! Look at you, you're barely holding yourself together, you can't put yourself through . . ."

"Rhoan. We don't stand a chance else, none of us does. If I can't fight for you, at least I can give you something to fight with. If you help me."

"Not me," she said instantly, putting her hands behind her back like a child, absolute in refusal.

For a moment, he could just be exasperated with her stubbornness, simple ordinary emotions, as any boy and girl together might discover. Then he had to puncture her entirely. "Gilder, then. He can do this."

"Issel, I won't let you."

"You can't stop me."

She glared, defiant; then crumpled, turned away, muttered, "No. Of course you're right, I can't. But—"

"You wouldn't anyway," he went on relentlessly. "Even if you could. If you thought I would listen when you said no, you wouldn't say it. Because Gilder's right, and I'm right; this is our only chance. If I have to suffer for it—well, I've suffered before." He was suffering now, and he still had the climb down to face; and that was nothing, simple physical pain, nothing at all compared to the pain that was coming.

"And if it kills you this time? You haven't *died* before."

"It won't kill me, Rhoan. This'll be the third time; I'm getting used to it."

"You haven't done it before with a hole in your belly, where half your blood's run out. Issel, you nearly died once today already. I can't believe you're even thinking of doing this."

"Yes, you can," he said, weary suddenly, "because you know I have to. All these people will die if I don't. And you will die, and me too. I do this, and we have a chance. You know it. You're only making noise." And then, the killer, "How are your hands, do they still hurt you?"

"No," she said coldly, ferociously, snatching them away from each other, where they'd been rubbing together like a memory of old cold pain regained. "They're fine. And no doubt you will be too, eventually. Even without Armina."

They hurt each other, because they were good at that, it was something they could do. They glared—or no, she glared and he absorbed it, which only infuriated her more. And then she went down the ladder, and he spent some time on the platform there with Gilder, looking and pointing, talking about how to make war on an army when neither of them knew anything about making war, or armies.

GRIP. Step.

He went down the ladder slowly, slowly, like a child on the stairs: one rung at a time, both feet side by side and his hands rock-steady before he thought about the next. His whole body burned around the ice-blade in his belly. It wasn't there—except for the warm steel plug that was almost a part of him now, so very far from the blade it had been—and yet he felt it. He felt it twisting, thrusting deeper, every step.

And he hadn't started yet, on anything that mattered. Being knifed was nothing; every step of this was nothing, next to what came next.

Gilder brought him to a barrel.

Down on the quayside, there were barrels of good sweet spring-water, standing ready to be loaded; no wise captain would ask his men to drink river water here, below the bridge.

Issel clutched at a barrel's rim, strained almost beyond endurance by the walk this far, after the efforts of the ladder. That was just his body, wanting to fail, because it was afraid.

With one hand clenched on wooden staves and their iron bindings, he spread the other above the surface of the barrel's water. Briefly, he thought he saw it rise towards his palm, hungry for him.

It would have him, soon enough. His thoughts reached down his arm, like a pour of water over his fingers and into the depths of the barrel, where he tried to claim that barrelful and turn it as Tel Ferin used to, as Rhoan and Gilder could. That process of inforcing, where it would pass through darkness and light, turn black and then silver and then clear again and be more than it was before, more potent, more ready to be used.

He tried it, knowing that he would fail; knowing that he was too tainted and his powers too corrupt, he couldn't achieve the clean transformation that he worked for.

Instead, the water turned a shimmering grey, neither black nor silver, shadow given life, sickness made tangible; and that life drew it up out of the barrel, up his arm, engulfing.

Where it touched, it clung; where it clung, it burned. Issel had screamed the first time, as that acid jelly rose, as it seared. The second time he'd been prepared, he'd been strong; he would have screamed none the less if he'd only had the air to scream with.

This time, too weak to scream, he was sobbing even before the not-water touched his skin. He did have a moment of hope, that perhaps he could let this pain too wash through him, as he had been doing all day; he had been in the river, after all, since he last tried to turn water, and everything was different now . . .

That kind of hope is really despair, dressed up; it was a fancy, a wild dream battered against the door that gives onto the real world. Even as he snatched, it frayed.

Pain possessed him, as though every fibre and flow in his body were molten metal. The river was distant, away from him, no help; he was alone, and not strong enough, and the not-water was flowing up his arm and reaching for his shoulder, and once there it would spread all over, consume him entirely, and then he would be the pain and nothing more, lost Issel . . .

———————

EXCEPT that there were hands suddenly, coolly on his head, and a voice in his ear, and that was Rhoan; and she was saying, "Come on, Issel, it's just a little water. Just a barrelful, what's that? You've been in the river. And I've been telling you all summer, it's not in the water, it's in you. You can turn this around, you know you can. You've done it before, do it now. Because if you don't, I'm going to have to pull that stuff off you myself, with my own hands, and you know how much it hurt me last time, and this time it'll be worse, I can see that already . . ."

The last time she had needed a healing that only Armina could give her, a magic that Issel hadn't understood, then or since. No Armina here, not yet, and he couldn't make Rhoan wait; he couldn't let her be hurt, not like that, all knowing.

Which meant—

Well, this was what it meant. This standing straighter beneath her touch, which was what told him that he'd been bent almost double over the water-butt before, barely holding on. This opening his eyes, which had been closed before; he hadn't realised. This shudder, this breath of air, this determined glare at that cloying ooze that he had perverted from the water.

He glared, he reminded it—unless it was himself he was reminding—that he made it, he owned it, he could command it. Whatever life it had, that came at his gift and was still his possession. He would accept the pain that came with, that was his possession also, and he claimed it. He would not be mastered, though; he would not be possessed.

He turned that water with a sob, he forced it moment by moment to retreat, down his arm and back into the barrel. There was no damage, not a mark on his skin, but every creeping, clinging moment was an agony, the price he had to pay in lieu of Rhoan's.

When the last had slithered off his fingers, he had two hands to hold on with, and used them both. He still had Rhoan's hands too, firmly at his temples; he used those too, the only way he could hold his head up long enough to see the end of this.

The substance in the barrel writhed, and reached towards him where his hands were gripping the rim.

"Issel, step away."

That was Gilder. Issel shook his head; he didn't think he had stepping in his legs anymore, and he daren't let go the barrel to find out. Besides, the mass inside it was leaning in his direction, as though the barrel sat on a slope; if he did step away and it tried to follow, it might tilt the whole barrel over. And spill out, dribble between the planks of the quay and so into the harbour, into the river itself: and what then? At best it would be lost, and he would have all this to do again; at worst—

He tried to imagine the river turned grey and greasy, glittery, half-alive; and shuddered, and leaned his little weight against the barrel.

"Be quick . . ."

It was his own thought, but Rhoan spoke it.

Gilder stretched his hands above the barrel, much as Issel had; but what he did was clean and pure, unsullied, even here under the bridge. The barrel filled with shadow for a moment, then with a flare of light; and then it held water, nothing more. Nothing that Issel wanted to touch, but Gilder scooped out a palmful and worked it lightly with his fingers, till it was a ball of gel. Then he looked around, and pointed to a lighter where it floated empty, moored to the quay.

Pointed, aimed, threw.

That little globule of jellied water flew, and struck—and there was an explosion, an eruption, a sudden catastrophe of wood and water. And then no boat, only a carpet of shards and splinters and broken planking spread on the water, surging wildly in the wake of its destruction.

"That's it," Gilder said. "That's *it*! With this, just with this one barrel, we can chase the Marasi back to barracks. Rhoan, if you take the eastern wall and Issel takes the gate, I'll hold the breach to the west there; that's the weak point, that'll be where the attack comes first . . ."

"Not me," Rhoan said flatly. "I didn't come here to slaughter slaves and conscripts."

"Those same slaves and conscripts killed our friends, and they will kill us and all of these"—their dogtooth army—"if we don't."

"I don't care. I'm not a soldier. Issel neither, you mustn't make him do this. Look, with this much we could defend ourselves against those ships in the river there, we could put everyone into boats and get them away; that's why we came here, why we took the docks . . ."

"It's too late to run now. Listen." Indeed there were the sounds of trumpets and drums somewhere beyond the wall, a far-distant shout of men. "If we don't man that wall and defend it, they'll come straight over and catch us before we get the boats away. Too many of them, not enough of us who can use this. It'd be the same on the river; we can't sail a ship, and we'd never keep a flotilla of little boats together in those currents. We'd get separated, and we could only protect our own. That wall is our defence, it's all we've got.

"If you won't fight, it's your choice," he said, "but Issel must. Between the two of us and the dogtooths, perhaps we can drive the Marasi away. It's about terror, and this"—a swift touch to the chill staves of the barrel—"this is terrifying.

"If we drive them away, though," he went on, relentless, regardless of interruption, "they will come back; that's what armies do, they swallow a defeat and try again. They couldn't leave us here, in their docks, cutting off all their river-access. And we can't sneak away in the night; there are too many here to hole up in the sewers anymore, there's nowhere else to go on foot, and we can't manage the river. Yet.

"That'll change," he said, "as Issel grows stronger, as those ships find reasons to sail off. We can see these people safe—but not yet. We have to hold out first.

"And what would help us most of all," he said, "help our city and us and everyone, would be an uprising in Sund. Right now, to divide their forces and keep them off-balance, make the army doubt the Sultan and him his generals. Every soldier taken to Sund means one less here, for us to face; every soldier taken out of Sund makes the rebellion easier.

"With a barrel of this," he said, "you could take the bridgehead and hold it, stop them sending reinforcements. When the city sees that, the whole of Sund will rise against them; and then we've won, even before the bridge goes down.

"What I'm thinking, Rhoan," he said, over her dawning protests, "is that if you don't want to fight, you could take a boat across the river. Just one boat, with a crew to row it. Any of those ships bothered you, you could drive them off; you wouldn't even need to sink them, just scare them away, if you had the water to do it. Or, better, you could hide yourself and your whole boat, they'd never even see you.

"And what I'm thinking," he said, "there's another lighter there, see it? With all those barrels of water already loaded? It must have been due to provision one of the ships, but it can serve us just as well. Half a dozen men, Rhoan, and every one of those barrelfuls changed, all that water—you could provision a revolution, with that. Couldn't you?"

She said, "Those barrels aren't changed, it's only water."

"They can be changed. It doesn't take long, does it, Issel?"

"He can't—"

"He can. Can't you, Issel?"

"If I must." There couldn't be more pain, or worse pain; it could only go on longer. Which he could endure, so long as Rhoan was there to hold his head.

"Well, but what do I do in Sund? I don't even know how to find Tel Ferin anymore. Baris could, but he's gone. And Tel Ferin wouldn't fight anyway, you know that. Who else is there? Everyone we knew was taken . . ."

"Not everyone," Gilder said. "There are other groups. Other hidden mages, even."

"Yes, but I don't know how to find them."

"Make a noise. They'll find you."

"I wouldn't know to trust them." *Remember Armina.* "And I told you, I don't want to kill . . ."

Issel said, "I'll tell you where to go."

"Where, then?"

"Up onto the roofs. Find Joss. He'll remember you. And he'll know who you should go to. He sees a lot from up there, and hears the rest. You can trust him. Go to Joss."

"Will you come too? You should be away from here."

"I can't. Joss doesn't trust me—and I'm needed here, anyway. Gilder can't hold this place on his own, however much water he has."

"Issel . . ."

"I know," he said, against the desolation in her eyes. "It just has to be, that's all. It could still come out well. If it doesn't—well, at least we tried.

Let's get down to those barrels. You and I can do this, we don't need Gilder. It won't take long."

"Long enough."

"Yes. That. But then it's done. You should take someone for company, when you go tonight. Take Teo."

"Issel, I can't do that. Jendre left him here, deliberately—"

"For his safety. I know. How safe is this? Take him, Rhoan. He'll like the roofs. And he didn't like being left behind. At least one of us can have something that he wants."

Chapter Six

JENDRE sat like a beggar in a doorway, trying to understand quite how she came to be here.

She had been a wife, then a widow, yes; to an exceptional man, yes, but the thing itself was not exceptional.

She had tried to run away since he died, which was unusual but not bizarre. Besides which, she had failed.

Then the abominable had happened, twice, her husband's brother and her husband's son; and she had resisted at the last, and so been sent to death. Yes.

And rescued, yes, impossibly so; and that had apparently made all things possible, so that now she was a rebel against her own people, and had crossed the river to find other rebels, who would lead her to a mysterious woman of uncertain gifts and unreliable loyalties, who would or would not go back to Maras with her . . .

———

YES. And so she was sitting here, because the woman Armina was said to be in that building there; and she was watching the gate because she could think right now of nothing better or more useful to do, or else she was just waiting for the next extraordinary thing to happen.

Perhaps the extraordinary thing was the building itself. In Maras, it wouldn't have attracted a second glance, unless it was a wary one; there were barracks at every level of the city. Not so large as this, perhaps—the imperial court liked to be discreet about how strong a garrison they kept within the walls of their imperial capital, whereas here those same minds were determined to be imposing—but the design, the build of it was intimately familiar. She had grown up with these heavy blocks behind their high walls, the solid and secretive gates, the roofs arched and domed like any roof in Maras, incongruous atop a four-square military barracks.

In Sund, this vast barracks looked utterly out of place. That was deliberate, she was sure; as its placement was, in this sudden void between the wealth of the merchant quarter and the cramped housing that reached down to the river. Here had been council chambers, the administrative heart of the city; her people had razed it immediately after the invasion and based their own harsh governance here with this highly visible symbol, the roofline of Maras behind an unbreachable wall.

What might almost be more extraordinary, what was certainly just as unexpected, was when a child came to sit peacefully beside Jendre in her doorway.

It was a boy, dirty of face and dressed in beggarly rags, and she was sure—well, fairly sure—that she had seen him in among Tel Ferin's pack of servants, pupils, apprentices, call them what you will. All of whom had been flatly forbidden this adventure.

"Hullo," she said warily, unfamiliar with the breed. Little girls she knew about, but boys were meat of a different matter. When they got bigger, then she knew them; at this size, barely at all.

He grinned at her, gap-toothed. "You want to get in there?"—with a jerk of his chin towards the gate, the wall, the building beyond.

"Yes, I do. I suppose I do." She'd rather wait for Armina to come out—but only if that were promised, and imminent.

"Come on, then."

"What? Wait—you mean, you know a way inside?"

"Easy. With you. Not the little hairy man."

"His name's Djago. It's all right, he won't hurt you—"

"I know that. I wouldn't let him. I've got water. But he can't come, they wouldn't let him in."

"But they will you?"

"Yes. And you, if I've got you. Coming?"

She didn't really understand, she didn't really want to—but yes, she supposed she was. This did appear to be her, on her feet and following that little skinny scrap of a thing.

Not to the barracks, first: a puzzlement, until he went to a cistern that stood in an alley, and took a bucket that might or might not have been his, and filled it there.

Hefting that—and leaning off against the weight of it, to the point where she almost thought she should offer to carry it for him, except that she had seen these people at work with water, and she wasn't going anywhere near it—he led her towards the barracks wall, but not to the main gate. Away down the side, rather, where Djago was watching.

Actively begging, indeed, a practice that looked good in a dwarf; and he was utterly convincing, begging from the Sundain, the servants who came and went through the side-gate. That was right, because for sure Marasi soldiers would not waste their coin on him.

When she was close enough, when they were private together, he said, "My lady?"

"This lad says he has a way in, but not for you."

"My lady, you should not—"

But the boy was forging ahead, disregarding the gate and the dwarf both. Something in his gait said, *if you want to come, come now*, even if his urgency lay only in the weight of the water that he was struggling with, that he was too proud to put down.

"Stay here," she muttered to Djago. "We'll look like a procession else. I don't know how, but he says we can get inside. If it's true, I think I have to go."

Djago might have protested; she wasn't sure. At least he didn't try to stop her. There were guards atop the wall, overlooking the gate. They might just have looked like two beggars quarrelling over a good pitch—but let the guards hear her accent, or let them once wonder why a Marasi-trained eunuch dwarf was begging in Sund . . .

Djago could find that thought and follow it to its natural end, as easily as she could. He let them pass, unhindered. The boy led her on to the far end of the alley and so out into a stretch of dead marsh country, the very limit of the city. Here the compound's wall was dark with age, great weathered blocks of stone, sharp contrast to the clean new build elsewhere. This must be a survival of the original city wall, perhaps the only stretch not demolished after the invasion; how practical, to take Sund's own failed defences and make them part of Maras' great statement, *here we stand: believe us*.

Except that the wall had not stood, entirely. Ahead of them were builders working from a scaffold that embraced a deep breach. Fallen stones had been stacked for re-use; frames and winches stood about, to raise another course of blocks when the masons were ready. At the moment they were busy with chisels and mortar, levelling and fixing the latest course. Jendre couldn't tell if they were Marasi or local workmen—or janizars, even: the empire's soldiers needed more skills than soldiering, and very likely could build their own barracks if they were called to do so—but those were certainly janizars overseeing the work, from the surviving parapets on either side of the breach.

"What happened here?" she murmured, still following the boy, although it felt like madness.

His shrug almost slopped water from the bucket he strained to carry. "We don't know. The wall came down, and soldiers died. We think it was a water-mage, but we don't know who . . ."

Jendre could guess. She thought probably the boy, the whole school had guessed already. They wouldn't talk about it with her. She had gathered already how uncomfortable Tel Ferin was with any active resistance; they wouldn't trust her not to be a conduit back to him. Even this boy, who was leading her into the kind of situation that would make Tel Ferin very uncomfortable indeed: even he would be discreet.

She wondered if Tel Ferin knew where he was. For sure the schoolmaster didn't know what he was about. And would be furious if he found out, furious with her, and rightly so; but it was too late now to turn back, with eyes on them from above and voices calling down.

That was only soldiers being what they always were, raucous and suggestive. Their victims could ignore it, perhaps—except that this wisp of a boy did no such thing. He tilted his head back, shaded his eyes against the sun and began to—

Well, it took her a minute to understand, between their borderlands accents and his argot, but he was dickering with them. Over her price.

She felt herself flush livid with embarrassment, with rage; and had to stifle it all, because any other choice would only lead to exposure. As it was, they could see her clenched fists and stiff silence, they could read her very real shame and fury and they were welcome to it, any proud girl might feel so, under such a barrage of abuse . . .

The boy laughed at last and waved their offers away with a grand gesture, as though he were far too important to waste time with them, or else she was far more valuable than they could afford. Happily, the troopers above took it in good part, and only chased them with a few choice descriptions that made her blush again.

She hissed at the boy, surprised not to see real steam spurt from between her teeth; she raged at him in whispers, but he simply shrugged it off. No doubt that exchange was normal currency in Sund. And not in Sund alone; not every girl in Maras lived the protected life that Jendre had, behind a harem wall. She wondered sometimes what had happened to those girls she'd run so free with, as they grew. Likely one of the answers was this, that their bodies were traded outside barrack walls.

Coming to the work-site, passing through the rubble and mess that such sites always generate, she saw kegs of water among the rest. No one would want to drink the marsh-water, but if these men had their own supply, then what excuse for the boy's bucket . . . ?

He was known here, though, he was welcomed with calls and gestures; and every man who called him took a dipper of water and drank it, and smiled, nodded, passed the boy on. At the scaffold, they lifted him up from height to height, carefully, with his bucket.

When he jerked his head, she scrambled after, hauling herself indelicately from pole to plank to avoid the inevitable offers to hand her up behind the boy. She didn't mind the dirt on their hands, it was the dirt in their eyes that troubled her; better to show herself well able to climb a simple framework, and let them enjoy what they saw of her legs, for whatever thrill that could give them.

The topmost level of the scaffolding was still only halfway up the wall, the breach only half-repaired. Up here, Jendre could see what had been hidden from below: that the scaffold was mirrored inside the wall, where another team of masons was at work.

So when he was done with the masons here, the boy could hop quickly over the highest course of stonework; he could offer a drink of water to the men on the further side; he could look back and summon her, with another jerk of the head.

Inside there were ladders, which made the descent easier. She was more puzzled than before, why these men would want the boy's water, when the compound must have its own wells; more puzzled yet when they came down to ground level, and the foreman beckoned them over. He slipped a small copper coin into the boy's mouth—paying, apparently, for what they must already have in plenty—and then he nodded at Jendre and said, "What's she for?"

"She's my sister."

"I'm sure she is," with a snort that denied it entirely, "but why's she tagging along?"

"Raff in the commissary said his officer would pay well, sir, for a nice clean girl . . ."

". . . And if he's wrong, well, there are plenty of officers else. Eh? All right, boy." He ran his eyes slowly up and down Jendre's body, bringing another of those fiery flushes. "You trot her in, say I passed you; and any money, on your way out a bite of it is mine. Yes?"

"Yes, sir, of course. You don't need to say, I know my duty."

"You know how to protect your little businesses, you mean."

"Sir, that is my duty. Not only for me, for my sister too . . ."

The foreman snorted and cuffed at him; the boy ducked and ran off, laughing.

"Go on, then, girl, get after him. You won't find others here so generous if they catch you wandering around on your own. And I don't suppose his fancy officer would be so interested, after a few of the sergeants have been at you."

She could curse this trick of sudden blushing, if it didn't seem so useful. She backed it up with an awkward curtsey, one of those little serving-girl bobs that she'd never had occasion to master, and scuttled off after the boy.

He was dawdling, giving her the chance to catch up without quite seeming to wait. At the back here, the solitary brutal silhouette of the barrack block was broken up by stables, training yards, archery butts. Round a corner, into shadow, unobserved: she grabbed his skinny elbow and said, "If you're my brother, hadn't I better know your name?"

"They call me Little-Bit here. Don't suppose you would, though."

"No. I don't suppose I would."

"Ion, then. If anyone asks."

"Ion. Good. Ion, why do they pay you to bring them water? They must have plenty of their own."

He snorted. " 'Course they do, but mine is sweeter, see?"

"No, I don't see. Why is yours sweeter?"

"They think I draw it from some special well, my secret. They tried to screw it out of me once, but I just cried and wouldn't tell. Then I didn't go back for a week. Now they're nice to me."

"Doesn't tell me how you do it. Or why."

"How is easy, stupid"—with a shifty little glance to see what the name would earn him. Just a scowl; he grinned, and went on, "I'm Tel Ferin's 'prentice, aren't I? I can't do the big stuff like Issel, not yet, or the clever stuff like Rhoan, but I can make water taste sweet. Or sour." A glance left and right, and he scuttled over to a cistern, spat in it, came back looking some-how sheepish and cocky both at once. "It's bad to spit, but my water turns theirs foul."

"So, what, they'll pay you more for yours? Ion, is that worth it? Is that what this is all about?"

A shrug, and a shake of the head: yes, it was worth it, but no, there was more to it. "It's good to make them unhappy, it's good to take their money. But it's good to be coming in here, too. I can talk to people, listen to them, learn what's happening . . ."

Of course that was all good, but—he was, what, eight years old? Nine, perhaps? Too young to be playing spy, when he knew too much that the Marasi should never learn. "Does your master know you do this?"

"Tel Ferin? No, he'd never—"

"No. And he'd be right. You can go on selling water to the workmen, Ion, that's a smart idea, but no more coming over the wall to foul their own, d'you hear me? And no more asking clever questions. Learn what they tell you, and be satisfied with that. Now go on back. I can find my own way from here on in."

"You can not. How, then? You don't even know how to find the com-missary."

"I don't want to find the commissary, I want to find this woman Armina."

Ion's face twitched at the name, but he had known that already. "I could ask Raff for you. He knows everything."

"I'm sure he does, but I'm not sure he'd tell you. He'd certainly want to know why you were asking. He's not your friend, Ion, he's an enemy soldier; he'll trade with you if you're useful, but he'll betray you without a second thought. Don't trust him with any secrets. And—Ion, I know you don't really have a sister, but did he really ask you to find a girl for his officer?"

"Yes, of course."

"Then I definitely don't want you introducing me. You go off now, and I'll find someone else to ask, someone who doesn't want to buy me."

His disappointment was not all for the money, or she thought not. She hoped not. Though she was sure he would have sold her, without a second thought.

She said, "Go on now, go," and—rather to her surprise—he did.

And left her alone, at the heart of what really ought to be most safe for her, a general's daughter in a Marasi barracks; except that one way and another this had become a double danger, because of both who she was and why she was here.

She skirted the stables, the smithies and workshops, all this clutter of a busy army life; she knew it intimately well, and how to avoid attention within it. Look busy, be purposeful, have something in your hands: it only took a minute to scoop up a basket of rushes from an outhouse door, and head towards the main block of the barracks.

She wasn't the only girl in view, nor the only girl wearing what she thought rags, what was presumably just cheap clothing for serving girls in Sund. She might have been the cleanest, but that was a small thought, a mean thought, and she ought to be ashamed.

With the basket under her arm, she stepped out of watery sunlight and into the shade of a passageway, and for a moment she felt marginally safer. Until a man stepped out of a cubicle there and said, "Well now, pretty, and who are you, then?"

She gaped at him and stammered meaninglessly, all unprepared.

He was patient, waiting her out; then, "Come on, lass. What's your name, and what do you want? You're not Brinie, who went out for rushes to dip and has got herself all tangled up with some lad there and will undoubtedly find herself beaten when she remembers to come back in. Without her rushes, even. So who are you?"

Flushed and flustered, she had only impossible varieties of truth or else a plausible lie to fall back on, and *thank you, Ion*: she said, "Oh, please, I was, I was told to ask for Raff, in the commissary? He, he promised us money from his officer, if I was pleasing; but I thought, if I just walked in as I am, everyone would know, so . . ."

"So you tried to look like a regular serving girl. *I* knew. I am Ballin, and I know everything in here, everyone who comes and goes. I'll know you again, girl, once you've given me your name."

She was too distraught to lie; she said, "Jendre, please," and only re-alised afterwards how safe a name it was now. There had been another, an infamous Jendre, but she was dead.

"Well, Jendre, next time don't steal another girl's duty, you'll only get her in trouble." He took the basket from her, quite kindly. "Now you hop along and find Raff's little officer, and be good to him, and I'm sure there will be a next time. Only don't do that with your voice, trying to put on a Marasi accent to please us; it's cute, but it's not convincing, and it won't be what he wants."

Actually she'd been trying to hide her Marasi accent by imitating the voices that she'd heard all day. She blushed one more time, only because she'd been secretly rather pleased with her effort, she'd thought she was sounding like a native. He laughed, and slapped her soundly in a place and manner that would have cost him his hand at least, his hand at best when she was her father's daughter and not an executed traitor to the realm; and she scurried off like a reprimanded servant or worse, a harlot come to sell herself.

Down the passage and then turning at random, left and right, and so un-heedingly into an empty corridor, wondering who she could safely ask and how she could ask it, what business any girl might have with this mysteri-ous Armina; and as she passed an open door there was a faint rustle of bells at her back, and a hand caught her wrist and dragged her roughly inside, and slammed the door behind her. And there in the half-light through a tiny window was a large woman with tangled plaits of hair, where bells chimed every time she moved her head, where mirrors caught the inadequate light and made more of it; and this was Armina already, confirming all the little that Jendre knew about her and doing more, doing this:

saying, "I'm sorry, little one, but I've no time to be gentle,"

and blowing dust in her face, a red and heavy dust that was caught by her gasping so that she breathed it in, and coughed on it as it burned the back of her throat, and then had to breathe again and so breathed more of it, and more, and . . .

Chapter Seven

IT was the Sultan who had made them wait.

ISSEL had seen the lighter away, broad-bottomed boat carrying barrels of one potent water over a riverful of another, carrying the boy Teo and a crew of dogtooths, carrying Rhoan.

He watched them row away from the dock, he saw the sail set, he saw it catch the wind; he all but felt the kick of the hull beneath their feet.

He was aware, then, when one of the big ships turned in pursuit. Only the one: they had gathered into a little fleet now, and they talked together with drums and trumpets. *One*, they said, *will be enough, for that rag-and-splinter boat.*

When Issel tried to intercede, to catch that ship in the water, he couldn't do it. He felt as though he was straining to grip something that was far, far out of his reach.

In the meantime, Rhoan had all the power she might need, to drive off or destroy that vessel and any others that threatened. She lacked the desire, as much as she owned the strength; Gilder ached to kill Marasi, and Issel had found this place where he could stand, where it didn't seem to matter much who died, but Rhoan was caught on hooks of guilt and sorrow. Still, she had other lives than her own to defend, and he thought he could trust her with them. He'd had more than one reason for suggesting that Teo go with her.

He followed their progress with eyes and water-sense, and it seemed as though they moved unbearably slowly across that broad, broad river, and yet they were all too quickly far too far away from him. Both of those at once. He hated to let her go, but she was far better gone; she went into danger none the less, and he could neither protect her nor go with her.

A shadow loomed beside him; a voice said, "Please, will you come?"

It was one of their men, halfway to being dogtooth, bulky past reason and his face beginning to distort. That must be worst, knowing what was to come and still having the intelligence to understand it, a way to measure loss. Issel glanced at him, felt that pang of pity, of dread, and preferred to look away—but when he turned back to the river, he couldn't find Rhoan.

A moment of panic, *that ship has sunk her already*—then his mind caught up with his eyes, and he reached instead with his water-sense.

And found her, of course, exactly where she ought to be. The ship that hunted her was lost, though, quartering the water, spotters up top and at every rail. If she could hide from so many eyes that were searching deliberately for her, it spoke loudly for the strength of the water she was using, and for her own increasing potency also; it said that he didn't need to worry.

Still, it was hard to turn back to the dogtooth.

The man was pointing to the breach: a walk from the jetty but not far, close enough that Issel could nod and step forward without needing an arm to lean on. There was still pain, of course, sharp and living, but he wasn't constantly struggling to hold the ragged pieces of himself together, deep in the wet dark there. Now that he had made all the walls that he needed to stand between one flow and another, to keep his blood from his gut, to block the holes and the leaks and seepages, he could maintain them with barely a fraction of his concentration.

He couldn't do that and walk and deal with the pain and follow Rhoan with his water-sense, all at once. He learned as much by trying. He stumbled dizzily, wrenching his belly and so doubling up around the pain of it, and so needed the dogtooth's arm after all to make the last of the distance to the wall.

He found Gilder organising the defences. Which meant another climb, up to the parapet: no platform now, but the wall itself was wide enough for a man to stand on. A man and a small keg, Issel noted, as he dragged himself sweating to the height.

"Issel, can you hold the breach here, are you fit for it? Even with the water, I can't cover both the gate and this."

In his own person, in his own strength, Issel thought he could have held both. Now—in his own person, in his own strength—he thought he could hold neither. But he too would have the water; and if he used that . . .

He never had done, yet. Not his own tainted water, remade by someone wiser. He touched it reluctantly and felt a greasy sting, sharp enough to make his fingers jerk away.

He reached back, cupped a palmful and stiffened it, rolled it between his fingers and cocked his arm, wanting to hurl—and was warned by a vicious twinge in his belly, and changed his mind; tossed the ball of water underarm, over the wall and a little distance off, towards a dune cloaked in straggly whin.

He kept it in his mind as it flew, as it fell, riding the little thing with his water-sense, that fine thread of connection; and when it struck, then he released all the force there was pent-up within it.

The dune erupted. Even here, high, they had to duck a sudden stinging rain of sand and gravel. When Issel could look again, he saw a pit.

"Yes," he said. "I can hold the breach."

"Good, good. Wait, though . . ."

Gilder whistled down the ladder and a dogtooth came up, that same man who had fetched Issel and helped him here.

"Issel, you make another ball of water, and keep a hold on it . . . Good. Now you—what's your name?"

"Malo."

"Malo, take this—don't be afraid of it, it's just a jelly, see, no harm—and hurl it as far as you can. See that wooden hut, down by the shore there? Think you can reach that?"

"Yes."

"You do that, then. Stay with him, Issel . . ."

The man Malo threw the water-ball, hard and high. That little slip of Issel's mind that had made it stayed with it all the way, and triggered it in its fall.

There had been a shed; a soft, explosive sound sent birds screaming into the air, among a lethal shower of splinters. When they settled again, there was no longer a shed or anything that looked like one, anything to remember that there had been a shed.

"Good," Gilder said. "Now you can keep the breach. Will this much water be enough?"

"Oh, yes," Issel said. "Plenty."

The janizars would run, long before he reached the bottom of the keg. He had no doubts about that. However well trained they were in battle, and however harshly disciplined in barracks, they were soldiers yet. There wasn't an army made or trained that would stand, he thought, against a few hurls of this water.

Rhoan would forgive him; there would be more terror than death, and a great deal of running away. He thought he could scare them back behind their own walls, then keep them there.

Gilder would never forgive him, if he had the chance to kill and passed it up. He thought he could live without Gilder's forgiveness.

For the moment, he could live without standing up. There was no question of going back down the ladder, but the wall was wide and solid, here at some little distance from the breach.

He sat with his legs overhanging the drop, and turned his eyes to the city.

The drums and trumpets had been sounding for a while now. There was an army issuing forth, officers on horseback and their many men on foot. No call for cavalry here, on this restricted ground with a walled compound to besiege; the officers only rode to give them stature and authority.

There were men enough to overwhelm the breach, the gate, and all the wall as well. Even now, though, they weren't marching down towards the docks. They were forming up, rather, on either side of the road: janizars and their officers too, all in neat display. And the trumpets sounded a long, loud peal, and more men came out on horseback, very grand men in bright and glittering costume. Issel had been starved of spectacle for too long, and besides, his belly hurt and he wanted out of his body. It wasn't raining now, but there were clouds building below the sun, there was moisture in the air; he rode his water-sense all that way, which was not sight nor hearing nor anything like them, but could stand in for both.

The men wore beards and jewels to express their great importance, both in increasing quantities, so that Issel struggled to remember that the new

Sultan was a beardless boy, and the grandest of these men must be an underling; and then there was one more brass-splitting trumpet call, and a great shadow looming in the gateway.

That was not a horse, nor any creature that Issel had yet seen. If he'd been close in body, he would have flinched away; perhaps he did, even sitting where he was on the wall. Even before the massive thing lifted—what, its nose? did ever nose look so like a snake?—and spread its ears like vast sails on either side of its appalling head and blasted its own dreadful response to those trumpets as it rocked forward into the light.

It was a grey thing, carved surely from rock that had been given life somehow. He'd always understood that the Marasi had no magic of their own, that even the bridge-magicians were bought or brought in from some far-distant country of their conquering. Perhaps that was wrong, or perhaps they had bought or fetched home some other magic too. For sure, this was no normal creature of the earth.

None of the soldiers was running, which impressed him; not even the horses were bolting, which impressed him more. One or two had their ears back, but nothing worse. They were used to it, then, troopers and beasts both; and it had that same barracks discipline, because it paraded down the road between them all and never broke to left or right.

There was a man on its back, he saw that, perched behind the ears and guiding it with a hooked and pointed goad. He took a while to notice that, only because it took a while to see beyond the ears. But behind that rider there was more, there was a belly-strap that held a box on its back, like a giant litter in gold and silk; and there was someone in that box, a young man, no, a boy, standing and waving, exhorting his janizars to come to the slaughter, come kill his enemies, the evil water-mage, the rebels and the traitors, come and joy . . .

That must truly be the Sultan, demanding his place in the line, leading his troops to the war. Except that the monster he rode was hauled abruptly to a halt, the Sultan descended by a ladder, and a horse was brought for him instead. He was no rider; it was skittish beneath him, despite men at its bridle. But the Sultan waved his sword and gave the order, and his army marched ahead.

He stayed to watch, up by the city gate, like a boy who has set his toys to play together.

THE men followed the horses, and the horses followed the monster; and if Issel thought that he could terrify the soldiers into defeat, for sure the Sultan thought the same about his monster. It swayed down the hill, and even half-adrift from his body as he was, Issel could feel the fear this side of the wall.

He came back to himself, to see how dogtooths were swarming down the ladders, away from the posts Gilder had allotted them. No matter: they could only be targets up above, for arrows or crossbow bolts. As was he, of course; but even as he thought it, there was grunting and blowing at his back, and here came Malo up the ladder with a cumbersome wooden screen on a strap across his shoulder.

"We can hold this," the man gasped, "to be a shield; then you can spy where to throw, and I can throw the water, and . . ."

And if he was that closely involved in sorcery, clearly no conjured monster was going to frighten him off the wall or away from Issel.

At first, it seemed likely that the battle would come nowhere near them anyway. The army followed the monster, the monster followed the road, and the road would bring it straight to the dock gate and to Gilder, who had his own keg of Issel's water.

But that goad went to work; the monster squealed and wheeled, off the road and over the rough scrub and directly towards Issel. Perhaps half the soldiers followed; the others stayed on the road.

The breach was a weak point, obviously. Any breach in a man's courage was another, where fear could force its way in. Perhaps they thought that even a water-mage would run from a monster like this, and then it could simply push its way in through the ill-patched hole in the wall, and the soldiers could flood after. Or else it was that no one lived now to remember what poor, weak, defeated Sund could do in her pomp, and so the generals simply didn't believe what their fleeing men had told them about the water-magic.

They would learn. Issel was hurt, beyond the ability to use his proper strength; but he and Gilder both had their water-kegs, and that would be enough.

Issel also still had Malo at his side, with his shield and his strong arm. The man was frightened, twice frightened—by the monster, and by the sheer size of the army behind it—but he stood his place on the wall. Issel was frightened too, though only by the wild power of the beast. Did they think they had that tamed? Whatever it was?

It had iron cuffs around its legs, he could see that now; and a harness bound its head, a harness with a great iron disk set between its eyes. Small mad eyes, no comfort there. The iron was dull and pitted, not for the glamour of display; which meant it was for work, today for warfare. Like the beak of a battering-ram, he thought: he could see just how that head would drop and thud into wood or stone, no difference, if it had all the monster's terrible weight behind it. He thought it could probably rip living trees out of the earth.

Left alone, it could doubtless rip through the breach here or the dock gate, both; and what did any army of man have to trouble it with? If arrows could pierce its hide, all they could do was sting. No hope of reaching any vital part of the creature. Fire, burning pitch might drive it off; a spear might get through to find its innards, if any man were fool enough to come close enough to spear it . . .

There must be pitch in the docks somewhere, but no time to fetch and fire it, nor to hunt up spears. Or fools.

Nor any need. The soldiers would be in crossbow range by now, and Malo had his great shield ready, but no one was stopping to shoot; they must believe in their monster quite as much as Issel did.

He would teach them also to believe in his water-magic.

He had water in his hands already, dipped from the keg. If it scalded Malo as it did him, the man showed no signs of it as Issel dropped it into his big palm.

"Throw it in front of the, the creature, I don't know what that is . . . ."

"They call it elephant," Malo said. And, "This will not hurt it."

"I hope not. I only want to scare it, send it back . . ." Send it back in panic, through the troops; that should scare them, as much as any magic would. More. To have a creature of that size, that monstrous shape, rampage through their ranks, out of all control or mastery . . . He thought the army would run. And then he needn't kill any of them, and Rhoan would be pleased with him.

Malo shrugged, and flung the ball of water. Issel found that he could direct it in flight, just a little; water-sense was not touch, but still he could nudge it, to make it fall just so. That was the first hint of his wider powers coming back to him. The strength of it was in the water, not in him, but he was glad to feel it none the less.

The ball struck earth, and it was like a thunderbolt cast down before the monster's feet. A great cloud of stone and soil and dust blew up, like a sharp and stinging rain; Issel was glad to have that wooden screen to duck behind. It would be worse, far worse below, under a hail of falling rock.

He heard the sounds of it, the cries and curses of men, and over all the screaming distress of the elephant. When the blast-wind of it subsided, he peered over the shield, expecting to see the great grey rump of the monster trampling men like corn as it fled—

———

—AND instead saw its head, its dreadful nose and ears, the whole of it come charging onward through the dust. The nose was curled up high, the ears were flapping, the head was tossing to and fro and it was squealing in fear, but on it came, and . . .

No. Not fear. It was pain, that made it squall so. The man on its back was working his goad, driving the heavy iron spike of it into the elephant's side, using the hook to haul its head forward and no matter the damage that did to its torn ears. Issel could see the blood in streamers, he didn't need his water-sense to find it.

And the creature came on, and there would need to be more blood, and he was sorry for it.

"Can you hit the man who rides it?" he asked Malo, handing him another slippery ball of water.

Malo nodded, and flung; the ball flew, and caught the man on his naked chest.

It must have bitten deep; the man burst apart, spatteringly. He had no time to cry out, as his mount was doing; little time even to feel the impact, let alone the pain. Issel could hope so, at least.

He wanted to see the elephant, unguided, turn away from the wall. He could drive it, perhaps, with another ball of water hurled ahead.

But the animal was still screaming, and still coming on; and now he could see why. The men behind, with long spears jabbing and thrusting . . .

Maddened with pain or else too well trained, too imbued with obedience to pain, the elephant went where it was driven, head down and hurtling towards the wall.

Issel was raging, but out of choices, out of time; he scooped out another ball of water and passed it to Malo without a word, without need of words.

That ball struck the elephant on the shoulder and broke the hide, broke the muscles, broke all the bones beneath. It was a cruel strike, but still not fatal: the animal fell on the shattered joint, shrieking and coiling its great rope of a nose, and yet desperately trying to rise again, caught in an ecstasy of terror.

Issel was close to weeping as he took another handful from the water, aimed and threw it himself.

Hard and true, straight at the monster's forehead.

It struck with a deep thud and two distinct cracks, as first the iron plate and then that massive head-bone broke.

The elephant subsided, all of a piece.

The men who'd been driving it forward were not slow to run now, they were only too late. Issel sent handfuls of water hurtling after them, and no matter if he hurt himself in the doing. Those men were caught in a storm of lethal rain, on a ground that erupted around them. Where the water struck, it smashed through bone and flesh, it killed; or else it struck the ground and raised a fury of splintered rock that tore the men apart.

Guilt and rage drove Issel until the surviving men were far out of his reach and still running; until he had a spear's-worth of pain himself buried in his belly, he could feel it at last; until sweat or tears had streaked his face and he wasn't sure which, but it didn't matter because he deserved both.

And more, worse, he deserved worse. He deserved this racking pain in his gut, and the hatred that twisted deeper. He had to spend a minute just standing, turning inward, repairing walls and channels inside himself; the pain was not so easily lulled, nor the churning emotions when he looked out and down at the wreckage, so many bodies, all his own sorry work. Rhoan wouldn't be pleased after all. He despised himself, so how would she feel?

And yet he had no regret, he didn't draw back from what he'd done. They had driven him to it, those stupid, vicious dead men, as surely as they had driven the elephant to its destruction. It was that ruthless, relentless cruelty that he detested, that stirred him up to these paroxysms of disgust; he had it in himself, and that disgusted him, but he had learned it from the Marasi. Whenever his Sundain nature—well, Rhoan's—tried to stay him, they did something more to provoke it. And so died, and he pitied them not at all. Their city had made them what they were, and it had made him too, and very likely he and they deserved each other.

———

WHEN he could stir against the pain, when he could see again, he looked along the curve of the wall and saw the gate still standing. That was good.

Then he saw Gilder on a watch-platform crouched behind a screen and lobbing balls of water over, virtually unaimed. That was not so good, but he understood it when a bolt, another bolt struck the screen and splintered a corner of it, twisted it in the grip of the dogtooth who held it, so that Issel could see for a moment how it was spined with shafts.

Even before the elephant fell, that second force of soldiers must have attacked the gate, and Gilder alone hadn't been enough to drive them back. He was holding them off—he and his dogtooths, those who hadn't fled, who were out on the wall throwing down rocks and fending off scaling-ladders, ducking arrows. Issel saw one duck not fast enough and fall instead, a shaft through his throat.

He'd have liked it to rain. At least the leaden sky was keeping the air wet: wet enough for his water-sense to reach those swarming soldiers and pick between them, find where the archers and crossbowmen were.

Malo carried the water-keg at his back, fussing just a little about the risk of arrows. Issel told him not to worry; all the bowmen currently had their attention on the beleaguered Gilder. That wouldn't last, but it meant he could walk the wall until he came to the first fretful dogtooth, heaving stones over the parapet to discourage a scaling-party beneath. Issel paused there, took water from the keg and hurled it down.

The wall shook.

"Too close," Malo said.

Yes—but the survivors were retreating from this stretch. Running, indeed. That was worth a little tremor, in a wall that didn't need to last until tomorrow. No one this side of it could last until tomorrow.

The archers had noticed him now. Issel felt the arrows as they were nocked, before they were shot; water-sense was not any of the other senses, and could work in tandem with them all, an extra level of awareness, alert to other things.

"Lie down," he snapped. "Quickly, both."

He would have pushed them off the wall, if they'd been slow; dogtooth bodies could survive the drop, sooner than they'd survive arrows.

Both men dropped, though, as though he had poison in his voice. Perhaps they only had fear in their hearts; perhaps it was fear of him. To Issel it felt like an age since he had been in the river, since he had been something to be afraid of.

Now he was only the man who had the weapon, this water. There was a watch-platform a little further along the wall, with a screen for shelter, but he had no time to get there; all he had was this handful of water, that he could toss up into the air in a crude imitation of what Rhoan did with her mists of discretion. Crude was good, for this; he wasn't after subtlety, misdirection, the deflection of a casual glance.

He tossed up that scatter of water and held it there, and rejoiced that he could do that much; and all the droplets reached and ran to link together into a kind of watery chain-mail, and what arrows struck it shattered or sprang off to leave him safe.

And he followed their paths back with hurled balls of water, which no man should have been able to throw anywhere near as far as an arrow could fly, but he lent that water the wings of his desire, and it flew; and where it fell there was a chaos of blood and broken bone, and no more arrows came.

———————

THERE were other archers, of course, and crossbowmen too, and when he found them he used them in the same way. Ball by ball, death by death, he and Malo drove the besiegers away from the gate, away from the docks altogether.

When he thought to look, beyond the army's rout to the city wall behind it, he saw the Sultan ride back through the gate, long before his running men could reach it.

And he felt that gate with his water-sense, and gripped it; and found that yes, he could take a grip even at this distance, he had more of his strength back than he'd thought. Unless it was just temper.

It made him scream, here in the docks, but no one in the city would be hearing that; and he gripped those brazen gates and tore them hinge from hinge, and flung them down in the wake of the retreating Sultan, in the face of his retreating army.

Chapter Eight

ENDRE, if she will.

It was a choice.

There was Jendre, the solidity of her, the strength of her, the limits; or there was this, here was this: the tenuous soar of it, the frailty, the reach.

She danced, she thought, in time to come.

The past was a fixity, irredeemable rock. Now was the beach, remade daily, shaped by wind and tide, fleeting. The future was the sea, vast and indeterminate, where she could stretch and wallow as she chose.

If she will. It was a choice always, a choice out of time.

There was dizziness there, that was more than the sick dizziness of a fevered body; there was confusion there, that was deeper than the confusion of a clouded mind. They existed as currents in the great swirl, as features, events, matter; they were an aspect of the music, unless they were another step in the dance. How could she tell? Where they came, she was drawn into them: shaken, lost, bewildered.

And then stranded, abandoned, left behind—but never fallen out of the music, never missed a step of the dance. How could she? It engulfed her, it possessed her. She was indistinguishable: a candle's flame in a furnace, unextinguished.

She was in the dance and of the dance, it expressed her and she it; and there was another with her every step—a guide, a guard, a mentor, an enthusiast—unless that was only another aspect of the dance, a constant beat of music, a singular thread of current in the swell and surge that drained her and uplifted her and was never still nor ever would let her be, so long as she remained within the dance.

It was a choice.

———————

JENDRE, as she would.

It was a choice, and she made it.

Not for a lifetime, though it felt like a petty death to leave the dance. There was a long, slow falling away from the music, losing the beat and the movement. There was a ruthless tenderness to her abstraction, like all a plant's roots being teased from the soil they gripped, unless it was the soil that gripped them; she was removed, gently and carefully and entirely, from all that was beautiful and sinuous and seductive, everchanging, everlasting.

She could go back. That was a choice. It was a promise.

She had a companion, taking shape from the music, finding solidity out of the relentless shifts of the dance, showing her the way of it with a kind of patient urgency. She had made the choice, and now was the time; time was, now.

———————

JENDRE, as she was:

shaking, dry of eye and dry of mouth, itchy with a sweat that had dried on her skin; staring wildly around her but that hurt her eyes and there was nothing to see, only the dimness of a closet that was strange to her and a face that was curiously not.

She closed her eyes, then, and even the woman's breathing, her smell, that unquantifiable sense of her body sharing the same small space, even that was familiar if not quite comfortable. This was someone she trusted and some-one she thought she could trust, though that trust might lead them both into danger. *A reckless plunge into deep, deep water*—this was that same guard, guide, mentor who had been with her in the dance. Somewhere about her was the rhythm they had danced to: beating, unheeding, unconcerned.

She was the gateway, the dive into the sea.

Jendre worked her mouth, her lips, her tongue; she worked air in her scorched throat; she said, "Armina."

"Yes." And then, "Open your eyes, child."

She did that, and the woman pressed a cup into her hands.

"Drink this."

She did that too, expecting some strange tea or a drug-brew that would act on her mind where it spun giddily from such a firm, tight core; she was astonished how balanced and secure she felt, just sitting here with a stranger in a place she did not know and had no right to be.

She drank, and it was only water, sweet and clean. But then, this was Sund—she remembered that, she remembered everything, though it was all the far side of a great event and didn't seem to matter anymore—and water was a drug to them, a tool and a wonder.

But then, this woman was not from Sund, and neither was her magic. Maybe this was only a drink after all.

She drained the cup, and its water was lost in the desert that was her body.

Armina chuckled—how could she do that, how could she make such a soft, wet sound when she had been to that same place as Jendre, and should be just as dry?—and refilled the cup, saying, "Slow now, drink it slowly. You have been a far way with me today, and you need to learn the ways of flesh again."

Was it still today? They had fallen entirely out of time's strict clock, she thought, and this might be yesterday, tomorrow, some day not yet counted in the calendar.

She sipped water, and said, "Where, where did you take me?"

"You know that."

"Yes." It was the wrong question, but it was hard to find the right one. Not *how?*—the answer to that could only be *magic*, which was no answer at all. There did need to be questions, though, and answers; she had come here blindly seeking a woman she didn't know, and in the finding she'd been offered something so utterly unlooked-for there were barely the words for it, and she didn't understand . . .

"Why?" she asked then. "Why did you do that?"

"Because it lay in me to do it, and it lay on me to do it, and it lies in you and on you to learn it. I have waited for you."

Clearly, she had been waiting ready in this closet, which meant that she knew Jendre was coming, and that would be her magic at work again; and that was equally clearly not at all what she meant.

"I don't understand."

"No. Understanding will come; I will bring you to it. As you were brought to me. It lies in your path, little one. I could show you that in a mirror, but we have taken too much time already, and you should not go back too soon."

She thought they had taken all the time there was, and danced in it; and yes, she ached to dance again; and no, she did not want to go back. Not yet. Her bones were still trembling from the first time, her blood carried the echo of the beat.

"What now, then?" She had come here with a purpose, but she seemed to have lost that entirely, or left it behind. Or else Armina had stolen it from her. The other woman had the initiative now; she had Jendre right in her hands there. Or tangled in her hair, perhaps, along with the little bells and the flashing mirrors and all the other bright adornments. Was she an adornment? She didn't feel very bright: shaky and sick, rather, and thirsty again, and only wanting to be told what to do.

"Now we wait. This is a good place to be."

The barracks, did she mean? Or Sund? She couldn't mean the closet . . .

But the building shook suddenly, and far off, through many walls, she thought she could hear someone screaming.

"What was that?" Not an earthquake, it was over too quickly—though here it came again, an abrupt and shocking shudder in this good strong Marasi building that should be fit to stand against anything.

Still not an earthquake, it wasn't the ground that shook the barracks; the ground was the only still thing, except Armina, who sat rock-solid in her patient certainty. This felt more as though the building were being struck, as it were by a giant hammer; but what could—?

Issel could, but Issel was on the far side of the river. Wasn't he . . . ?

Armina reached out an arm, and closed a hand around Jendre's wrist. Such a big hand, it made her own seem tiny; it made her feel delicate and frail, childlike. Her mother did this to her, and her father's slave Clerys could do it, and her husband had done it for one short night and a lifetime's regretful memories. No one else, since she ceased actually to be a child.

The woman drew her down to sit, and she had no resistance in her, only more questions and a greater need for answers.

"What's happening? Please?"

"What has to happen. What I have seen to happen, what I have helped, perhaps. I saw that I would help. It is why I took you on a see-sail."

That was a surprisingly good way to describe it—Jendre had been taken onto the river for treats all through her life, and yes, it was a journey just to see, to enjoy the breadth and grandeur of the world in glimpses—though she still thought it had been a dance. Perhaps Armina didn't dance, or took no pleasure from it.

"That isn't an answer." Though it was, of sorts, to questions that she hadn't thought to ask.

"Perhaps." The room shook again, and a drift of dust came down from the ceiling. Armina tutted, and said, "Pass a cloth, yes. From the shelf there, you can reach."

Not a cleaning-cloth she meant, but a great sheet of purple velvet that must be meant to clothe a table in the commander's quarters; Jendre had seen such in her father's house, but only recently, since he was promoted. Armina shook it out and spread it like a cape, over her head and Jendre's both.

Jendre glanced at her doubtfully. "That won't protect us much."

"Enough. It will keep the dust out." And she shook her head, the bells jingled, and Jendre pictured what a labour it must be, to wash a cloak of dust out of that assemblage.

Besides, she didn't understand much, but it was clear that Armina could read future events, in the swirling patterns of the dance. Truly so, not like the street fortune-tellers Jendre used to shriek her laughter at. They wouldn't be sitting here in this particular closet, if the ceiling was due to fall in on top of them.

That was so strange, to feel herself safe in a building under threat, surely under attack. Her mind told her to trust, while her body screamed to run. Others were running, she could hear them in the corridor: shrieking women, men with heavy feet and heavy voices. There were cracks in the plasterwork now, as another thud slammed through the brick and stone. More than dust was coming down, she could feel little impacts on the sheltering tablecloth.

"Armina, are you sure?"

"Of course."

Of course. If this was strange, just to sit here and persuade herself to an act of trust, then that must be so much stranger: to see, to know the future, to be this confident of what would come.

It was possible, of course, to be confident but also wrong. Something struck Jendre's head, sharp enough to sting even through the coverlet.

"Ow!" She reached up to rub the spot, very aware of Armina's shaking beside her. Silent laughter, she thought. Well, she did have to ask. "Are you ever wrong?"

"Yes, of course. It is all possibilities. That is why I must work, to make happen what should. What use to see it, if you could not change?"

She was right; it would not only be useless, it would be terrible to have that utter certainty and no influence. Knowledge without power. But, "Who is to choose, how you change matters? To make what should, happen? Who says what should?"

"I do. Because I can. Oh, I could go to your Sultan and tell him what I see and how to change it, I could go to anyone—but why would they trust me? How could they? I might lie, any day or every day, to achieve what I wanted. Better just to have my secrets, work for what I think is best. Your Sultan would kill me. So would most men, I think."

She was right, of course. Whoever sat the throne, he would come sooner or later to disbelieve her, to sense conspiracy. And yes, that would be death and not dismissal: how if she went to an enemy and worked her predictive magic for him instead? Saw what he should do to win the throne, and told him true?

No one in Sund would kill her, perhaps, because no one here had power worth the losing. She might choose not to go to Maras; it might be a wise choice. And Jendre certainly had no way to compel her.

Jendre said, "I have no magic."

"No."

"But you said, I can learn to see as you do."

"The magic is in the powder; the skill will be in you. Skill I can teach you. I have seen it."

"Why would you want to? And don't say because you've seen it. It's a choice, you've made it. Why?"

"For you, and for your people."

Her own people were dead or disfigured, lost or left behind. Some had no futures; some she would prefer not to see. How dreadful, to know what would come to someone you loved. Or to see it and avert it, to spend your time working the world, changing futures for their benefit or your own: that seemed almost as dreadful. To know what lay behind every door, and be the one who locked one door and opened another, walked past or led the way . . .

That was what Armina did, though, she confessed it; and it was what she wanted for Jendre. What Jendre wanted was not clear.

She said, "For the Marasi?"

"Of course. They are your people."

They were. And they had sentenced her to death, and seen the sentence executed. But no, that was the Sultan; the city could not be blamed. Her Man of Men, he had been the city in all its splendour, but this boy who sat the throne now, he was not and never would be. One aspect of the city, perhaps—venal and corrupt, that face of Maras that lurked in shadows and fed on cruelty and terror—but not the whole. It was him and his kind that she would rebel against, if she was a rebel. A traitor she certainly was, but that was only because of the bridge—which had been her husband's work, and his darkest moment, but he couldn't be blamed for that. He was his city and all its faces, Maras in all its moods.

She had tried to destroy the bridge and would still do so; she might join any rebellion against the Sultan's rule if she thought it stood a chance. Either way, she was no one her city would ever listen to.

"The Sultan has already tried to kill me once," she said. Armina had said it herself, this skill would be death in the court; and Jendre had one death sentence already carried out and two more owing, even without it.

"Even so. The next one will not."

No, because she meant to go nowhere near the court again. But, if Armina was saying otherwise . . . "And, what, he'll listen to me, will he?"

"He will."

She snorted, but only because she wanted to disbelieve. She couldn't actually achieve that, it was all pretending; she was glad when the building shook again, a shelf broke from its fittings and plates fell and smashed across the closet floor, and she could say, "You haven't said who it is doing this, or how. It can't be Issel, I left him in Maras . . ."

"It is not Issel. Although it is his strength that they are using. You will know them, some of them, when you see."

She knew no one in Sund, except Djago and the dogtooths, who could not do this or anything like it; she had met no Sundain except Tel Ferin and his school, some of whom might like it but their master would forbid it, and besides, she didn't believe that any of them had this kind of power. *Issel's strength*, Armina said, but that made no sense to Jendre. She had seen that boy do strange things and dreadful things—she had seen him glowing and she had seen him kill, merciless and masterless; worse, she had seen him under the river, been there with him, lived because he could live for both of them, it seemed—but she had no notion that he could pass his skills along. Armina could teach hers, perhaps, but Issel's powers were clearly in himself, wild and unconfined.

Something was breaking this barracks down, the stones of it and the discipline too. There was some very unsoldierly shrieking out there, and more fear and hurt than she could bear to listen to. She said, "Please, can't we go out? Perhaps we could help the injured . . ."

"No, child. There is death out there, and this is not your time to meet it. Nor mine."

Of course Armina had seen all of this; but what, had she seen all the way to Jendre's death? Or to her own?

That was one question, at least, not to be asked. Hard enough to think that anyone might carry that knowledge, that it existed indeed as knowledge to be carried; worse by far, to imagine carrying it herself. Stick to what was recent, then, and local. Armina had seen the two of them sit out this attack, here in this linen closet; very well, they would do that thing. Ridiculously shrouded against the dust, talking in circles—this happens, because I have seen it happen; I will make this happen, because it happens, because I have seen it happen—and digging deeper and deeper into murk and bewilderment for Jendre . . .

"Can't we go back to the dance again?" That had left her sick and shaken, but this was almost worse. No, this was worse; at least the dance was exultant. There was nothing here but dust and despair, thinly couched as shelter.

"Dance, do you call it? Well, and that will do. But no, we may not. You haven't the strength, and I am tired now. We will sit, and wait, and the world will play its battles out around us."

SO they did that, amid all the rumble and crash of a building being torn down about them. The screaming stopped before the other noises, which was a relief of sorts.

When there was nothing more to hear except an occasional creak-and-slither, as of one more beam giving way under its burden of displaced stone, Armina cast off the shrouding cloth and came groaningly to her feet.

"Now we go and see," she said.

I thought you had seen already, I thought that was the point. But Jendre held her tongue and only followed.

The near end of the corridor, the heart of the building was still standing, and so presumably the floors above; Armina had chosen their refuge well. The far end, though—well, that was gone. Open to the sky, its walls ripped and chewed away, its passage choked with rubble.

Rubble and bodies too, and not all of them were dead. There were men groaning there, and moving fitfully. Jendre looked at Armina, who looked impassively back.

"That water you had for me, in there—is there more?"

"There can be, if the scullery has not been eaten."

"Fetch it, please. As much as you can carry." She had lost all her curiosity suddenly, about who was out there and how they had been doing this, and why. She had work to do. She didn't suppose she would be very good at it, but—yes, what Armina had said earlier. These were her people. They might be soldiers from the far fringes of the empire, brought in as slaves and trained to be ruthless, ruthlessly trained; they were her people still, and she had been—however briefly—wife to their master and commander.

ONCE more, she had entirely lost track of time, and had no idea where in the day she was. She was kneeling above a boy who seemed barely older than she was, listening to him sob.

He had good cause for sobbing, and had forgotten entirely to be brave. So had she; she was sobbing with him, as she mopped his face and let him suck water from the rag she used, as she watched the blood run from where his hip was crushed and ruined by a fallen stone.

There was nothing she could do but show him a kindness that he was barely able to notice, and wait with him until the end. He wasn't the first whom she had watched into a death today, but he was the one who had touched her deepest. They barely had a language in common; those few words that he reacted to were words he must have learned in barracks, strict and military words, "water" and "listen" and "be strong." He couldn't manage that, but at least he understood her, if that was any comfort to either of them. His own babbling was a painful mystery to her, soft and liquid and distressed.

She sat and watched with him, and waited; and was disturbed not by Armina, who was doing similar work elsewhere in the building. She was disturbed by someone entirely other, who came padding over the rubble; who cried out gladly when he saw her, and called her name; and then corrected himself with a half-choked, half-hysterical giggle, and said, "Lady, my lady, are you well?"

"Teo? *Teo . . . ?*"

THEN there were more tears, and more hugging than the boy actually wanted in the middle of a battlefield. She rubbed her wet cheeks against the sand-rough sandy stubble on his head, where he had lost his cap; and then she hit him, and said, "Why are you *here*? What are you doing? I left you safe in Maras . . ."

And if he could be here, then perhaps Issel was too, which might explain what had been happening to the barracks—but no, Armina had said it wasn't Issel. Though it was his strength they were using, she had said that too, and Jendre still didn't understand it.

She did turn back to her young janizar, but he had died while her attention was distracted. She could feel sorry for that, and guilty, without being responsible; but those were indulgencies for later. For now, towing Teo firmly by the wrist—one part of her life recovered and not to be left behind, not to be let go again—she went scrambling awkwardly over the shifting mounds between her and the air, past other men's bodies, unclear whether they were all dead but not stopping now. She was still Marasi and would remember so, but again that could be later. For now, here was the Sundain revolution, and she was a part of that too; and out in the light she found Djago, sitting on a horse trough, side by side with a girl.

Coming closer, she saw that the girl was Rhoan. Who had also been left in Maras, and Jendre was surprised again that she would leave Issel, whatever the imperative. Or the provocation.

"See, Djago, I said that I would find her . . ."

"You did say so, and you prove true to your word. Enough words now, imp. Sit and be quiet"—down on the ground, where the dwarf's feet could rest on Teo's shoulders—"and don't wriggle. My lady, I am *very* pleased to see you."

"And I you, Master Djago." Though he had certainly had the greater cause to be anxious. He had seen her go by in the alley, he would have known that she'd gone inside the barracks; he must have worried exceedingly even before this attack began. In the meantime, she hadn't given him a thought. Nor anyone else. She'd had no particular cause to, but—

"Rhoan, Teo—what are you doing here? And how did this, this"—with a wave of her hand to encompass the chaos, the wreckage of what had been a mighty building and a mighty symbol, all brought low so swiftly—"how did it happen?"

"How all wars happen," Rhoan said wearily. "Someone found a weapon, and nobody managed to say no to using it. Even I couldn't say no."

"You did this?"

"Oh—no. Not actually. But yes, I am responsible."

"I don't understand." She was tired of saying that, tired of feeling it, extremely tired of having it be true. Once she'd had a grip on the world, she knew the way things worked, even where she had no influence; that was all gone now, and she missed it.

"No. I'm sorry, I was being obscure." A quick and guilty smile that didn't touch what lay underneath, layers of worry and shock and distress and a whole other level of guilt. "Issel can turn water into a weapon that anyone with a touch of the water-magic may use. He needs our help to do it, but he's the key. So he made a lot of this water, a lot, and I helped; and then I brought it across the river in a boat . . ."

"We didn't have any boats," Jendre said, when Rhoan seemed to have stopped talking for the moment. "That's why I, why *we* had to come over the bridge."

"I know. But things change. We couldn't leave all those prisoners running loose, to be rounded up again. So we, uh, we took the docks; and then Issel was hurt, and he and Gilder started turning the water, because we would need that, and it was Gilder who said I could bring a boatload over here and find the rebels and maybe we could do something which would help everybody, and . . ."

A flap of her hand told the rest of the story: how she had done all of that, and behold the result—death and mayhem, on an awesome scale.

"Teo came with me," she added, "and he wanted to find you, of course. And Master Djago too, both of you. The boys on the roofs took us to Tel Ferin, who said that you'd both come to the barracks here to keep watch for Armina. We found Djago, who told us you'd gone inside, and he was worried about you. I would have waited then, but . . ." A shrug said that it wasn't her decision, that others had been determined to act now, that one girl's welfare couldn't be the criterion for revolution.

Jendre had no argument with that. Besides, she was well, and always would have been; Armina would have made sure of that. She was more worried about another of the woman's protégés. "How badly is Issel hurt?" She hadn't known that he could be. Nor that Rhoan could leave him, if he were.

"I don't know. It might have been deadly, for anyone else. For Issel— well, I know the pain is terrible, because he admitted that it hurt. But he thinks pain is his due, he thinks he deserves it. I think he seeks it out. I don't think the hurt will kill him, and Gilder won't let him kill himself. He'll use him and use him, and never quite use him up. I, I didn't want to watch that, so I was glad to have the excuse to come away."

Less glad now, perhaps. Poor Rhoan had come as far as Jendre, and was still looking for an end to her journey. So were they all, though Jendre thought that perhaps she'd found a star to guide her, if no map yet.

She said, "So Sund is in revolt"—and even Tel Ferin had come out, striding through the ruin here towards them—"and we don't know whether the Sultan will send more janizars to crush it, or call the survivors back to defend Maras. If Maras needs defending. What's happening across the river? Does anybody know?"

"No, not yet—but the docks are on fire. See?"

She looked, and saw the great thick greasy pillar of smoke rising from beyond the river, somewhere out of sight. She still wasn't used to these low horizons, the lack of a distant view. But she watched the smoke in its rise, watched it tangle with the smoky span of the bridge, and said, "How soon can we get across?"

Chapter Nine

SSEL knew nothing about how to fight a war, or take a city.

Happily—if it could have made him happy—the war wasn't his to fight. He was only the weapon and the purpose, the deep, driving intent. There was no more thought of slipping away in boats, or hiding down in the sewers. At some point during the siege of the docks, all Issel's hopes and intentions had been utterly changed. It was when he saw how they treated the elephant, more or less, or perhaps it was that little time later when he caught a glimpse of how they treated their own men much the same, sergeants with whips driving squads forward against Issel's lethal hail of water. There had been nothing he could do but go on killing, until he worked out how to carry the water a little way further through the air, and so kill the sergeants. It was fuel to his anger, how those whips drove him as much as they did the janizars. He felt helpless and resentful, and didn't know how he could explain this to Rhoan.

It would be harder yet to explain what followed, but no doubt he'd find a way. In the meantime—well, he was the weapon. It was Gilder who planned the war and its strategies.

Was it a war at all, where you really only had one weapon and you weren't really fighting for your city or your people or any cause at all, only because you hated what you fought? Issel wasn't sure. It was easier to call it a war and to speak about Sund as though Sund had sent them, Sund supported them, Sund waited to learn of their success . . .

The rest of their little army didn't care. Some few of the dogtooths—largely those who were barely touched by the Shine, who showed little or nothing of its effects—had chosen to slip away along the shore, take their chances while Maras was distracted; that was another reason to wage war, to distract the city, keep its gates closed and its attention on him while little people scuttled off. Most of the freed prisoners, though, had stayed to fight. What they were fighting for was even less clear, perhaps even less clean. They were angry, that was all: betrayed by their own city and angry enough to kill.

Which they did, cheerfully, under Gilder's guidance. They weren't really troops, though, something closer to bodyguards and scouts. Issel was the weapon; sometimes, he thought he was the war.

Issel had his powers back.

———

NOT as before, not yet. He was still hurt, there was no miracle of healing in his magic; he still had that steel plug in his belly, he still had to maintain his inner makeshift mendings, it was still a constant drain on his strength, and the pain of it was a drain again.

But he had found a point of balance, an equilibrium, and he could work from that. He could reach out beyond his body and find that water responded; he could feed from it and so draw strength, and so draw more from the water.

He could feel the pools and fountains, the lakes at the city's crown, high in those palace gardens; he could sense the whole network of sewers and cisterns that fed them, that underlay the city. What he could sense, he could stir. Not quite as before, perhaps, when he was whole and in his terrible pomp; he couldn't drown all the city, all at once. But he could take what he needed, fetch water or find it; he could twist wet iron till it broke, buckle steel, clench the rain like a fist around a man's chest until he screamed, until he stopped screaming.

He was a weapon, and they couldn't stand against him. Gilder told him, when and where to strike; he only needed to see how. There always was a way.

"Why" was a whole different question, which no one seemed to be asking anymore.

Issel felt very distant from it all, too far to see clearly, too far to care; and at the same time very close indeed, too close to have any perspective at all. He could see nothing except the immediate, the men who wanted to kill him and the swiftest way to strike back.

Wounded already, he was very far from immortal. If they could come at him, they could kill him. That was what the dogtooth army was for, how Gilder deployed it: to be a shield-wall of flesh and steel and leather all around Issel.

———————

THEY rested through the night because Gilder insisted, and because Issel couldn't stand any longer. They left the docks burning at their backs and came to the city gate in the morning, his little army and his general and himself. It was the gate that he'd ripped down, that the Marasi had left lying in the road. They hadn't abandoned the gateway, though: enforced it rather, building a wall of stone overnight to seal it entirely. Between that hasty new wall and the arch of the old above, nervous heads watched them, crossbows pointed. Some few crossbows shot, but Issel was well protected; there were shields behind shields, and he was a small figure walking among giants.

Behind their walls, the Marasi might have felt as safe as he did. This raggle-taggle bunch of risen prisoners, how could it threaten a city, any city, let alone their own and golden walls? So few of the rebels, with a regiment of janizars to face . . .

But these fine soldiers, these janizars were looking at the bodies of their comrades, left to lie and rot between the city and the docks. They could likely see the elephant, its great corpse already starting to swell in the heat. For sure they could see what had been mighty gates of wood and brass twisted into ruin and flung down in an act of sheer sorcery, in a gesture of utmost contempt.

And now here came the sorcerer and his little, little army, walking up the road in the dim dawnlight, in the breeze off the Insea; and small wonder if those soldiers were afraid, if they loosed their bolts too early, if they prayed.

They must have felt confident, they must have felt unsure: both at once, and Issel understood that. Distantly. It didn't matter. He had the river at his back and a blade in his belt, another in his belly; he was here.

They had built themselves a wall across the road, and thought themselves secure. But there was a well in the gatehouse, just to one side of the arch there. Issel could have drawn all that water up and out, like a great glass-green slug rising from the depths; he could have oozed it all along their new-built wall, and they could have done nothing but stare, nothing but shriek, nothing but run; he could have reared his water-slug up and swung it like a hammer, smashed their wall to nothing in a minute.

Or else dispersed it like a mist and enveloped them, seized them, squeezed them to a pulp inside their armour. He could have done that. He really was very distant.

What he did, he didn't trouble with any of that. He just gripped the water where it was, there in the well, that deep shaft that undermined the gatehouse and the wall; he gripped it and spent a while feeling it, friending it, finding where the seepage was, in and out.

Then he seized it and shook it, as a terrier shakes a rat. He boiled it with a thought, a fling of his mind, and sent the steam of it exploding through all the cracks and crevices of the wall's foundation. Wherever that steam went, his own destructive temper followed. Water splintered stone; water erupted, gouting like volcanoes, dissolving soil and cement and throwing stone from stone with all the force it owned. From foundation to capstone, the wall split and fell apart, and the soldiers were left gaping. For a moment or two, those few moments before their legs understood what their minds were telling them, what their eyes were seeing.

Then they ran. Some were too slow and went down beneath a hard, hard rain, but it didn't matter; Issel was very far away.

Even clambering through the breach and coming down into the streets of Maras-city, he carried that distance with him. Even walking barefoot past a body crushed beneath a fallen stone, feeling something wetly warm in the grit beneath his feet and looking down to see the blood still trickling, still finding dust to soak it up—even then, he was a long way from feeling anything. If his anger had burned out overnight, it had left a scorched waste behind: no room for pity, remorse, responsibility. Issel was a weapon now, in hands other than his own.

———

GILDER was the general; he said, "We can't face down the whole Marasi army. No matter how strong you are, Issel. Or how strong they think you are. Any kind of pitched battle, they can just stand off and shower us with arrows, and they'll kill us all eventually. Or run at us and take the losses, we can't kill them all. You can't, I mean, and you're all we've got.

"You, and the fear of you, Issel," he said, "that's our weapon. We know they can be broken, squad by squad. They're trained to fight, but in the end it's fear that drives them; they're not fighting for anything that's theirs. Except their lives. Make them more scared of us in front than they are of their sergeants behind, and they'll run. We've seen.

"So we move fast," he said, "and hit hard. Keep the city scared. We can't conquer Maras, we can't occupy a whole city or anywhere near it; so what we do, we go for the head. Cut off the head, and pray the body dies. I know you wanted to break the bridge, Issel, but we've tried, and you can't do that. You can't get past their magic. This is next best, to break the power of the throne. Then with any luck they'll start fighting among themselves; vultures always squabble over a corpse, and Sund will have no value to them then. Besides, we have a mage to fight for us again. We can drive them out, bridge or no bridge. Once they're broken."

Issel felt very distant from Sund, and those purposes that had fetched them across the river. If they went back, perhaps he could recover the boy he used to be, left long behind. Perhaps he would find what mattered, waiting for him in his own city.

But he had crossed the river, and been in the river; he thought there was no going back.

Here, he was only a weapon. He didn't have a voice.

Rhoan would have noticed that, perhaps. She would have spoken for him. It didn't matter.

———

FOLLOWING Gilder's orders, Gilder's plan, they ran uphill from the gate. Issel couldn't see, shielded as he was by the bulk of armoured men all around him, but his water-sense flowed all around. He knew there were archers on a roof there; there was water too, it had rained overnight and the gutters were blocked. The archers found themselves cloaked in a sudden mist that blinded them even before it burned their eyes like acid. Issel barely broke step.

There was an open square ahead of them, packed with men: a reserve force, held back to reinforce the gate if needed. They hadn't heard yet that the wall was down, though they might have heard its falling. They were waiting for orders; they had waited too long.

A central drain channelled all the rainwater from the square to a cistern below a well-head. Issel could feel that, possess it, use it. Water was the weapon, perhaps, and he was only the trigger. Rhoan would tut and pull a face, he knew, but she carried too much of the school with her. She had Tel Ferin's teaching in her bones, and everything that man did or said was about exerting power over water, mastering it, keeping it strictly on a leash.

Issel unleashed it, as a falconer unhoods a hawk and lets it fly. It's the hawk that matters.

Issel unleashed it, and the well-head flew apart. Half the paving of the square was lifted up and swept into a storm, a whirling wind of water, like a dust-devil poised upon its point except that it had cobbles for dust, and as it tore them up, it flung them out like shot from a sling.

Where it passed over a body, it tore that apart and flung the shattered bones, while its core of water grew a reddish stain.

No soldier would stand against such a thing, forbidden magic, terrifying and lethal and right there among them. The janizars ran screaming.

Did Issel leash the water then, or did he let it go? It was a question, and he still wasn't sure of the answer.

Gilder said, "On, up. Panic spreads like fire; the more fires we touch to life, the faster it will overwhelm the city."

There were wide roads that led slowly up the hills of the city, with many turnings; there were steep and narrow alleys, sometimes flights of steps that ran directly. They took the alleys, the steps where they could find them.

They were already within the city's first defence, the ring-wall where the Sultan and his generals would naturally keep most of their forces. It would take time and organisation for the regiments to regroup, and—Gilder planned, Issel hoped—they might never catch up. It took time even for messengers to run from one quarter to another, longer for their messages to matter. This was a foot race, with Issel and his companions trying to outrun their own news . . .

————

IT was a race with obstacles, where they must fight their way through; it was a race with traps, where they must lose a man, two men, more. Even Issel could not protect everyone; even he could not find out every danger, on the run. These alleys had blind corners, sudden byways, hidden doors. Bolts or blades came unexpectedly; whether they were chance encounters or deliberate ambushes, there were bodies left behind at every rise, fewer men keeping company.

Distant as he was, Issel felt those losses. He called out to Gilder, "I would be swifter on my own."

It was a lie, he had a blade in his belly and could barely keep pace. Gilder didn't even need to say it, only, "What, then, will you leave these to fight their way out again, unprotected? They do better in your shadow, Issel, we all do. It's what we chose."

They came around a corner on one of those climbing stairs, and there were half a dozen janizars coming down, and he hadn't known. He'd been too turned inward to his own distress. And they were hand to hand with his men before he could do anything, before he could think what to do; and a dozen of the dogtooths lay dead before he got a grip on himself, before he could get a grip on the water in the janizars' bodies, in their blood.

Then he had them, and they died abruptly as the blood shattered in their veins, in their hearts, in their brains; but Issel dropped to sit there on the stairs, with his head in his shaking hands.

Gilder said, "What is it, what's wrong? We have to keep going."

"I can't," and that was as much as he could manage for a while; then, "I *hurt*, Gilder."

"We all hurt." Indeed Gilder was bleeding, from wounds that Issel hadn't been aware of; and that hurt too, that was another sign of his failure.

"No, but those men *died* because I was hurting, because I couldn't see." When that drew no response, he sent his water-sense on and out, and found that one officer at least had heard that they were coming: there was a platoon of archers across the road where this stair debouched, a rain of arrows ready, and he had no strength to meet it. There was water enough to hand, there was a stone cistern beside the road; but when he reached for that, he couldn't grip it. "I can't do this anymore, I need to rest. If we go up to the head of these stairs, we'll all die."

He told about the archers. Gilder said, "I have your water here, I can—"

"Perhaps; but how often can you do that and not take an arrow yourself? And what's the point? You can drag me along, but I can't do anything now. I'm not sure I can stand up." When he felt for it with his fingers, that steel plug in his belly was body-heat, no more, but what he felt in his gut was red-hot, like a brand. It was a conscious effort now, just to hold everything together—and he was suddenly unsure how long he could stay conscious.

"We can't stop now."

"We have to." He had stopped. Hadn't Gilder noticed?

Gilder the general, revising his strategy: "Very well. Ailse—"

"I will carry Issel," she said at his side. He hadn't even noticed she was there.

"No. Anyone can do that. I need you to find somewhere we can take him. A way into the sewers."

Issel could have told him that, his water-sense could find it. Not necessary; she said, "Yes. There is a well-house, back down these stairs."

"One of you men carry Issel, then—gently!—while Ailse shows you the way. I want a dozen with me; the rest follow her. Ailse, come back for us."

"What are you going to do?"

"See to those archers," he said grimly. "Anyone finds their bodies, they'll assume we've gone on up into the city. For a while. They already know we use the sewers; we shan't be safe for long, but we can buy you time, Issel. Just not a lot."

It was a good idea, better than Gilder knew. Issel had overspent himself drastically, and simple rest wouldn't restore him. It wasn't sleep that threatened, but something darker; in that darkness, he would lose any hold over the inner mending he'd achieved, and all today's work—running, yet!—had undone even the tentative start of real healing. He had something in mind, and the sewers were the place for it. If these bought him time, he thought he could pay them back.

Or die, he thought he could do that too.

Or both.

HE felt himself lifted; he smelled the strong, musky odour of unwashed man—*unwashed dogtooth*, he might have said before, but it was all one—beneath fresh linen and oiled leather. They had dressed themselves at the docks, from a bale in one of the warehouses, then from the bodies of dead janizars: for decency, and for protection. Human instincts, even in the slowest of them or the most degraded. He found that comforting—but then, without those instincts, they wouldn't be here at all. His was no conscript army, these were volunteers.

It was hardly an army at all, only a band of desperate men with one desperate talent to fling at a city and all its people. They needn't do this, they never had needed this; even now, once in the sewers, they could follow the water down and get away. Maybe find a boat and go to Sund, those who were willing; and so fight another kind of battle, cleaner and more honourable . . .

Could they? He could think it, he might even say it; he should certainly add it to his long list of sorrows and regrets, all the mistakes he'd made and the dead he'd left to mark them. He didn't really think it could happen. Not for himself, at least.

He'd have liked a little distance now, just when he felt so close. All he had to hold to was right here, his own internal damage and the little world around him: the smell of the dogtooth and the feel of his clothing, the strength in his arms, the jolt that burned Issel like fire at every step.

They were all steps down, which made it worse.

And then there was a doorway and Ailse was there, in a tiled room full of shadows; and there was a dark pit in the floor and more steps winding down to water.

"It will be dark down there," Ailse said, "and we have no lamps. Keep one hand on the wall, and stay close . . ."

She led the way. Issel's bearer followed close, rubbing his shoulder along the wall for lack of a free hand, positively leaning into it. Round and down, a wide, descending curve with the drop always at the heart of it; and every step jarred him deeply, but still brought him closer to the water.

When they reached it, the steps just went on down and so did Ailse. So did the dogtooth following her; Issel knew, even being carried in the dark. He could feel it through the dogtooth's touch on him, a tingle passed from skin to skin; no matter if the dogtooth felt it not at all, Issel could feel it for both of them.

He didn't need eyes or light down here; perhaps he ought to be leading. Their path was clear: some few steps into the water, there was an arch in the well's wall, a tunnel. Pure dark in there, no glimmer of daylight, but his water-sense described it in detail. Low and narrow, a simple channel with no footway, they'd have to wade. It would bring them soon enough to a wider chamber, and the water wasn't deep. Wet legs, wet dress, banged heads and bruised elbows: there was no other harm to be taken here.

Except for Issel, who could always find harm in water, but had never let that keep him away.

He cramped himself up as tightly as he could in the dogtooth's arms, and still collected barked knees and a scraped scalp as they squeezed through in Ailse's wake. She was feeling her way with her fingers, calling back to be careful. Once they came through into the chamber, as soon as there was headroom above and space to the sides, she said, they should move to the left, stepping up onto a pathway; two more steps straight ahead and they'd be in deep water, a broad cistern.

Issel knew this already. He was away and ahead of her, trying for distance again. And not really succeeding; his sense would run with all this water, on and on, but his sense of self stayed firmly rooted in his body, anchored by his pain.

His pain and more, his dread: his simple uncomplicated fear of what came next, what he had to do.

He only had Ailse to talk to, and her only for this little time before she went back to fetch Gilder. These dogtooths wouldn't do what he asked; they had a general, they only looked to Gilder now. Issel was a weapon, and not to be cast away.

Gilder would tell them so. Ailse, perhaps, he might reach.

He said, "Ailse. Listen to me."

His voice echoed strangely in the tunnel, a skinny wisp of sound. Voice enough: she heard it, and half-turned her head though her eyes were useless anyway, it was her hands that guided her.

He said, "At the end, you step right, and so do we. Send the men left. I need to talk to you."

Her voice came: "I meant to do that, to watch them onto the path and then leave them here. I have to go back."

"I know. But first, we talk."

She grunted, which he chose to understand as consent.

———

OUT of the tunnel, into a wide and echoing space with much, so much more water ahead of them. This cistern fed half a dozen wells, through similar channels; it was fed and refreshed itself by a constant flow from above, one node in the tangled web of sewers that kept the whole city watered.

The footpath ran all the way around, with breaks narrow enough to hop over where the channels came in. Ailse stepped up and to the right, and Issel's dogtooth followed; she ushered the rest the other way, "Keep moving along, make space for the next man. I know it's dark, but just feel your way, hands and feet, don't fall in. Where there's a break in the path, just step across, it'll be a stretch but you can make it . . ."

They weren't happy, groping and fumbling in the utter dark. Issel felt their fears and reached into the water, just a touch, he could manage that; perhaps he could even afford it.

The faintest glow arose from the cistern, enough to cast a shadow-light, to show them where to step and where to jump. He did it slowly, not to frighten them further; brave in battle, in here they were utterly reduced. Darkness and rock and water could do that to a man, he'd noticed it before. What was elemental took everything else away.

When the last of that slow chain had found his way onto the path, Ailse went to step down into the channel again, to make her way back for Gilder and his squad. Issel said, "No, wait. First you have to let me go."

"What?"

"Into the water, here. I need it."

"Issel, what are you saying?"

"You know what I'm saying. You've seen." Just talking was hard; arguing, persuading, being plausible would be impossible. "I went into the river, to save Jendre."

"Yes. That was your water-magic." She sounded really slow, suddenly.

"That's right, Ailse. That's right. And so will this be, no different." Except that this time he might not come back. It was odd to have been so sure of the river, and to be so doubtful now about a little pool, but—

"But you are hurt now."

That was right, he was hurt; and now he had to lie outright, he had to say, "That's right, Ailse, and the water will heal me. That's the magic." He was fairly sure that was a lie. He had never found any healing in his water-magic; Rhoan asserted that nothing in it led to any good. It was Armina's magic, her rusts and reflections and games with time that had healed Rhoan when she needed it.

"I don't like to . . ."

"Ailse, you must. I need it now. See . . ."

And he pulled up his shirt, and sent a little more of his little waning strength into the water to raise the light, to have the wet air shine around them so that she could see; and that meant he could actually see himself, and that was not so good.

There was the nub, the glint that had been the blade of the knife, that was now a steel walnut embedded in his flesh; but his flesh was swollen and dark all around it, and there were streaks that radiated out like patterns of pain. He was used to that, except that it was a sour pain now, bitter and enduring, not clean and sharp as it had been before. More, though, there was a feeling that all his inner walls were breaking down, if not breached already. There should have been distinct flows, where now there was a muddy lake. Precious veils had been ruptured, that once kept each from each.

In the end—which was here, now—there was the water. He needed that, to make something of this ending; he wanted it, if only to make nothing of himself. He hurt, and he was tired of hurting. That could be enough.

Ailse said, "Issel, that looks bad."

"Yes. The water will help." He didn't think that was a lie at all. To help was not necessarily to heal. He might die; he almost hoped he would die; but he would do it in a way that gave it value, all the value it could own. "You have to let me go."

"Gilder is only a little way away . . ."

"Or dead, or engaged in a battle that could take him an hour to fight, or it could take a day. Ailse, I don't have an hour."

And ultimately, all he needed to do was turn his head and look down into the water, and have it flare back at him, all that dim glimmer gathered locally into a sudden calling clamour, fabulously bright. She was scared then, of him or of the water, both; which he might have felt guilty about if the dogtooth who held him hadn't been stooping at her signal to let him slip out and down, down into the deeps of the cistern.

THE light welcomed him, gathered about him, burning, burning.

For a moment, he almost forgot that this was water. So bright, so fierce, it might as easily have been fire.

His water-sense leaped out and away—like flame over oil, he might have said—and it took a terrible effort to rein it in. He needed control, above all. This was a last chance for everyone he cared about; it wouldn't be he who paid the penalty if he failed.

First, then, he slipped out of his clothes, to have no shadow between him and the water. Everything hurt—every movement of water over his skin flayed him again; every movement of his own twisted and tore at his gut—but at least he wasn't choking, drowning, kicking for breath. He hadn't needed to think about that; the body remembered. And the magic was in the water, even here, deep in the heart of Maras. Sund was not so special after all.

Naked, he laid hands to his belly and found that plug of steel where it was buried in his flesh. Found it soft and pliable, almost molten already—like steel in fire, in a furnace—just from being there where the water touched him.

Found it, gripped it, eased it out.

It should have been followed by his own juices flowing, blood and other matter; nothing in there had healed enough to form a seal behind the plug. There was a pressure against his skin, though, potent and forbidding. This water wouldn't be tainted. He felt it like a searing hand pressed against his wound, and then a finger of it slowly, insidiously slipping its way inside.

He had seen wounds cauterised with hot iron—yes, and heard the screams. He threw his head back and tried to scream, but his throat was full of water.

So was his belly now, and he could feel it biting, blazing its way into his bowels, into his blood and bile, every wet cell of his body. Not like hot iron, which burned and sealed and passed on; not even like hot wires, probing and twisting and winding their way through all the fibres of his flesh; this was a liquid fire, that melted and mixed and flowed on, consuming as it came.

This was what he had hoped for, what he had gambled on: this acid burn, this pain, this dissolution.

———————

HE even thought he might survive it. Something, at least, might step up out of the water and call itself Issel. Whether it would be him was anybody's guess. There were a few people, perhaps, who would care enough to find out.

Or he might die here, swiftly and unconfusingly, overborne by pain and shock and weakness, too long trying. He had been sure that the poisons in his gut would die, if once he let the water at them; there might be no healing in the water-magic, but there was death, plenty of death. After that, it was only guesswork. He was too tired to cling to the slippery thing that was hope, and he found it hard to care. Death would be welcome, as this cleansing fiery bath was welcome.

For the moment, though, the swift and unconfusing pain of it was too much. He couldn't bear it, he couldn't fight it, he couldn't even scream against it—so he left it, he slipped outside his body and abandoned it.

This was what else he had hoped for, why he needed to be immersed in the water. Water-sense was not a horse or a boat to bear him away, not even a rope to haul himself along, but it was a light in darkness, a pathfinder and perhaps a path. If he could send a thread of his awareness out through the slightest wisp of water, then perhaps he could do the other thing, send almost all of him out there into this great turbulent network and keep just a thread attached, to link him to his body.

If that thread snapped—well, that might be the thing they called death, and he didn't know then what would happen to his spirit, his sense of self. He might haunt Maras for a while, but in the end he thought he would flow down and out and into the river. And then most likely be diluted, scattered, washed away . . .

Water-sense was that part of him that faced outward, that found the world or as much of it as he could reach. Issel was that part that faced inward, that found himself. That was his anchor, not the dense clay body, the suffering broken thing that had been given over to the water. He might need that too, but later.

For now, this was where he lived and who he was: this certainty, this bubble of awareness, *Issel, I am Issel*. He had turned himself inside out, and was here—not looking, not listening, not touching, but sensing this world of water none the less.

He found his body resting breathless and abandoned at the cistern's base. It might have looked dead entirely if it weren't glowing so. Not fiercely, but enough to light the water. He thought there was a pulse to the glow, which matched a pulse that still beat somewhere in himself.

That body was still hurting. He let it alone, and turned elsewhere.

There were men who lined the wall above and around the cistern. He knew about them; he was a little distant already, but he could remember. Down a channel—that one, there—were noises, people in the water, wading. He slid down to investigate, and here was a woman ushering men in from the well-pool. Ailse, Gilder: he remembered.

They were hurried, heedless and blundering in the dark. There were not so many men as there had been, and some were bleeding. All of them were afraid.

Issel was in the water, and he was of the water. There was no pain; he had left all that in the body. It was the work of a moment, a flicker of desire to raise a skein from the water, to seal the tunnel's mouth behind them.

There were steps echoing in the well, booted men coming down. His water-sense enfolded them in that wet air: they had weapons, armour.

The first of them splashed into the water, ducked into the tunnel, met the skein.

Screamed, but only briefly.

That fine web of water wrapped itself about him and contracted, crushing flesh and bone and metal all together. Behind it, another skein was forming.

This water had a memory, with Issel to inhabit it; it could learn. He didn't need to stand guard here. That skein would renew itself, every time it needed to; time and time again, perhaps, if the janizars were slow to learn.

Another scream, two screams overlapping: Issel was already elsewhere. He bypassed Gilder and his surviving men, and spread like ripples through still water.

Where he found living bodies, he interrogated them by the many ways he could: their size, their arms, their body-heat and more. Voices, breathing. Manner.

Water-sense is not sight or hearing, touch, but it can serve for all of these. In a time too small to measure, he knew those people better than their lovers did: which were dogtooth, which were runaways, which were soldiers.

The soldiers died, too swiftly to understand that they were in danger. Some were certainly deserters, hiding out; he could tell as much from what they did, the way they were holed up in backwaters. But he couldn't talk to them, he was disinclined to listen and less inclined to trust. He knew his people, by where they were gathered; for anyone else, arms and armour just meant death.

Back at the cistern where his body was, Gilder and Ailse were still talking.

About him, necessarily: and staring down into the water, at his stillness, at the light he shed.

He ought perhaps to draw back into his body, to confer with them; it would at least prove that he could. That he was not dead yet. They would be glad to learn it, and so would he.

But pain still waited there, a killing pain, the thing that he had fled. He was afraid even to be near it; he dared not slip inside. Let them be anxious, then; let them go unreassured. It could make no difference in the end. This was the end, he thought, the swelling wave, the shadow rolling in ahead of the catastrophe.

For himself, it had happened already: recently, with that blade in his gut; or a little while ago, perhaps, the boat across the river; or Baris snaring him for the school; or Armina guiding him there, guiding all his life; or his long slow exposure to the Shine, or . . .

That was his own, too late to save, but he still had time for this. For Maras, he would be the catastrophe.

————————

THIS web of water underlay the whole city, from wall to wall. It reached further, indeed, it fed from countless streams and springs and minor rivers, and in the end it all fed into the great river of the world. He could go as far as he could imagine, if he could stretch himself so thin. For now, though, he had all the city above him, and all water was the same water. Every great house had its own well, dipping into the common source; every house had its drains, its cisterns, its gutters for the rain.

It was raining again now, and all the city was his to interrogate, his to possess.

It was very full of people, and few of those were janizars. Those that were, they were on the streets, on the walls, manning the gates. They had closed the gates. Certain streets were crowded with the common folk; certain gates—those furthest from the docks, which were still burning, even in the rain—were besieged, but unrelenting.

If Issel wanted this city, he wanted it empty.

Every gate had its gatehouse, and every gatehouse had its well. They must have thought that a precaution, a wise defence.

They hadn't built these walls against a water-mage, because they had no cause to. Even at the height of their powers the Sundain stayed in Sund, and worked the river to keep the Marasi in Maras. Then the Marasi overleaped the river, and came to Sund. Now came the response, now there were Sundain in Maras, and the city would learn: it had hoarded altogether too much water.

The people had picked the right gates to clamour at. Those furthest from the docks were furthest from the water, from any water, and their roads led swiftly away over wide flatlands.

With pikes and staves, occasionally with violence, the janizars kept the people from pressing too close to the gates. That was good for Issel. The soldiers on the gate he didn't care about, particularly. If they were swift of thought and swift of body, they might be safe. By day's end, he hoped to teach whole regiments to run.

PICK a gate, any gate.

Reach into the rain and find the strength of it. Accept it, absorb it, possess it.

Hammer down that gate. From the inside, from the city side, so that it falls outward, so that the people can see a broad and empty road ahead of them. The soldiers doing pike duty will have their backs to it, but they'll hear, they'll know its fall; they'll look over their shoulders, that at least. They'll see the damage come from nowhere, from the rain; they'll see the road, perhaps they'll hear its beckoning; for sure they'll hear the crowd's desire, and know how thin a line they make and how little reason they have to hold it.

Now remember where you are and what you are: you are all the water in the city, and you do not need the rain.

With all that weight and sonority behind you, you don't need to seize the water in the well; you are the water in the well. You know how strong you are, and how sorry these walls that men have built above you, their dry stones with their dry, dry mortar.

You can bubble up out of your darkness, and if there's a man in the well-room he'll have a shock, he'll have wet legs, he may yell and scurry up the stairs. It doesn't matter.

You can spread out across the floor and lean against the thick dense stone of the turret walls, feel their age and their fragility, their desperate vertical balance, how they only stand because that's all they know to do.

You can teach them how to fall.

You can lean, you can push. With all the force of all the water at your back, you can break the mortar, crack the stones themselves, topple that balance and bring the whole gatehouse crashing down.

Men will run. And leap from those high and tumbling walls, and hurt themselves, and die, but mostly they will run. Some will run through the gate.

And once they have, once the first janizars have done that, then nothing will hold back the people anymore. They will run with the soldiers, or they will run over them. The only certainty is that they will run, out of Maras and away.

PICK a gate, and carry on.

MARAS had a dozen gates because its first great sultan had decreed it so when he raised its majestic wall, because there was a verse in the scriptures that spoke of a jewel with twelve facets, and another of the six angels that surround the throne of God, their twelve lidded eyes always on watch.

Issel broke them all that day, but only to open the ways to the world, to let the people run.

THEN he set about encouraging them to do so.

THOSE who had been massed at the gates and thronging the streets round about, they needed no encouragement. They were already spilling out into the country like dammed-up water from a breach, from many breaches; but after the first spurt there was only a trickle, and Issel wanted a flood.

All through the city, then, there were signs and portents. News flew, about the gates and their destruction, and how their guards had fled; soon there were rumours to spice the news.

A bronze statue cast in the shape of the great Sultan Abeyet, he of the wall and the twelve gates—a statue that offended religious teaching and should have been struck down, except that recent sultans had been careless in observance and this was a gift from a newly conquered province and so it was set up in a public square with its feet in water to show how the Abeyids now bestrode the river of the world, from Maras to Sund, as their magnificent forebear never had done—that same statue stepped down from its pool and bestrode the streets, roaring and shaking its wet beard, waving its mighty sword.

From every fountain in the city, the water gushed too high, too hard; and it flickered with an eerie light, and steamed, and lashed out unpredictably like the blade of a whip although there was no wind to drive it, and it burned whatever it touched.

Soldiers had the worst of it; was it not ever thus?

Where the troops marched, the rain turned to hail, except that this was a hail of splinters, glass-sharp and steel-hard, that stung them into running. Where they ran, they left a trail of blood behind them, which the rain refused to wash away. All the gutters were filled and overflowing, and all the streets ran red.

Where the barracks were, rain broke in at the doors and all the windows; it smashed through shutters and through iron-banded wood, through any grim defences that the men could lash together. Where it struck, that water broke bones as easily as skin, as easily as it tore leather or timber or metal. Where it pooled inside the walls, it shivered like a living thing, and crept together into masses that stirred and rolled and oozed deeper into the building. No man would go near it then. Few would watch or follow, even, so few saw how it slipped down into basement rooms and sculleries, to join with more water that was bubbling up from underfloor or out of well-shafts, the enemy within.

The next they knew above was a sudden shaking in the floor, then the irruption of a water-man from below, a great figure in the form of a man, too big, too terrible. It might be a child's drawing of a man, or else a man shaped only by shadows, where there was no detail on the wet sheen of the skin—no fingers and no joints, no face or hair—and nothing fixed beneath, no bones, nothing to harm.

It couldn't be attacked or parried or prevented, only fled. It swung its arms and broke things, whether they were weapons or furniture or heads; it walked through barricades as casually as it walked through walls.

Rooms collapsed in its wake. Soldiers ran through the barracks, and then from the barracks. And so out into the rain, the hailing rain, the savage slashing scarring rain that drove them through the streets and allowed them no shelter until they ran for the gates and so joined the steady stream of refugees leaving Maras.

Outside the walls, no weather bothered them, and no one chased. The jewel that was Maras had a flaw, a storm in its eye, but nothing leaked.

THOSE were the rumours, some of them, in the chaos and madness that beset the city that day. There were more; they all had water at their heart and terror in their voices, many left bodies broken or dead, and their blood mixed with the water. Mostly those bodies were soldiers', in the telling; mostly what the rumours said was *Run! Run from Maras, Maras is doomed! Run if you are military, run if you are not . . . !*

Truth was harder to assess than rumours were to hear, but there were bodies on the streets, and most of them were janizar. There was blood pooled here, there, almost anywhere, despite the endless rain; mostly the men who sat hunched and bleeding by the roadside were soldiers too hurt to walk, abandoned by their comrades.

Whatever people saw and whatever they understood by it, they hurried through the city by back-ways where they could, to avoid the barracks and the soldiers and the blood, the worst of the rain. They came to a gate and fled through it, as quickly as they might; and their only constant virtue was that wherever they went and whomever they met there, friends or strangers, they shared their own urgent message.

Run! Run from Maras, Maras is doomed . . . !

BY nightfall, Issel judged, the city was as empty as it would be. Not as empty as he would like it; it was vast, and even like this, with his water-sense dispersed along a thousand channels and stretching through uncounted drops of rain, he was not omniscient. There must be barracks he had not found, among these many, many buildings with the same such roofs; there must be more soldiers otherwhere, on patrol or off duty, mixed among the people or simply keeping low. He couldn't hope to find or scare them all. For sure there were thousands, maybe tens of thousands of ordinary Marasi also still within the walls. Some would have been too slow or too scared or too stupid to leave before this; and now it wasn't only the bridge and the dockside that were alive with an eldritch shine. Lights and colours ran like water in the streets, flowed down the gutters and bubbled out of the drains.

Some of that was wilful on his part, some had simply happened. As his own body shone in touch with too much water, now that he was invested in the water, so did all the water that he touched. It had been his choice to carry that light further, to spill it out from the sewers and cast it up into the rain; he'd pour it into the river if he could, if he dared, to make it seem from afar that Maras was bleeding light.

There were people left, he was sure, who would be running now if they weren't afraid of those lights. They should have run ere this; he was short on sympathy, and painfully aware of those who had not been let run, servants and slaves and prisoners, the women locked into their harems. He'd done what he could through the day, breaking gates wherever he found them barred, but he couldn't be everywhere. There were still people in the city tonight not by their own choice. That being true—and there being nothing more he could do about it—he would give short shrift to those who'd lacked only the courage to run.

He would give short shrift to them all, now. Aristocrats and servants, officers and men, free and slave: bold or terrified or stubborn, they were out of choices. So was he.

Not even he could destroy a city, not entirely, but he didn't think he'd need to. He'd done enough, almost enough already; all it needed now was one last push.

Something monstrous, unforgiveable, imperative . . .

THERE were hills and hills, within the ambit of the city walls. Each had its own springs, its own ponds, its own drains to feed the underground waterways; each had its own wells and fountains to draw on them. Each had its own cisterns to store and maintain the supply, its own pipes and channels to deliver it.

The higher the hill, the more grand the architecture, even down below. Issel had seen one magnificent garden in the flesh, where he had made his attempt against the magicians' pavilion; he had explored other grounds in the rain today. Those were the gardens and parks, the palaces that held the most water, that fed the most, that demanded the most in return. Their cisterns were elaborated caverns, where even the many pillars that supported the roof were tiled in gorgeous colours, to match the tiling on the walls. Those roofs themselves were extraordinary, the living rock carved to resemble or to echo the roofs of the buildings overhead, an inverted image of domes and semi-domes and arches.

The highest hill of all, the greatest palace with the most sculpted grounds, cupping its own great lake within its arms of green expanse—that was the Sultan's own. The New Palace, Teo had called it. Not where the magicians were, but there was no touching that, not now. Jendre having committed herself to cross the bridge, she would be ill served to come home and find her sister dead at his hand, in its destruction.

Besides, he had sent Rhoan after her with a boatful of water, to drive the Marasi out of Sund. That was being done; there was a steady stream of refugees coming over the bridge. Soldiers, mostly. If he took away their opportunity to run, they'd be stranded in Sund, cornered and desperate . . .

There was nothing he could do, but spare the bridge for now. His water-sense would not span it, there seemed to be no sense of water in it or anywhere about it.

Besides, the Sultanate was his target now, necessarily. What else?

TIME was slippery coin, but Issel spent some of it exploring that hill intimately, from the inside out: feeling his way not along the cut channels that he knew already but into and through all the natural ways that water found to make its course through rock. He found the little runnels and the cracks that dripped, and insinuated himself into those narrow squeezes; he followed them up into the weight of wet earth above, and understood it.

While he was there, while he had a grip on so much stony soil and the sprawl of the palace there below the peak, it would have been an easy thing, almost the thought of a moment to bring a deluge down onto the complex. He could bury it. But that would bury hundreds, thousands of little lives—his storms of today had barely reached this high: he'd broken a couple of gates in passing, but not enough, or else they had been too soon guarded again, or else few had had the nerve to flee—and by the time all the bodies had been dug out, there would be a palace again, empty but fit for use.

He wanted more than that. Not a symbol, a statement: *no more.*

Back into the hillside, then, down into the sewers. All this water and all of it his, unless it was all of it him; and more above, a whole lake of it that he had stretched his knowledge into, that was a source for so many little threads of water, all its leaks and overflows, its rivulets that oozed and spat and sang down through the rock to join him.

He held them all in his mind's hand—

—his water-sense, but it was so much more now, more even than an extension of his thought or will, it was himself, he thought, his own self, as much as that inward-thinking creature that called itself Issel—

—so many pools and runs and dribbles of water, like so many fingers to his hand, the grip he had; he held the palace, the gardens, the hill itself cupped within that hand; and gently, gently he began to tug and twist.

———————

NOTHING happened.

Of course nothing happened. One mind, one will couldn't shift a hill.

Not all at once.

What he could do, he could pick at the seams of it, break a little stitching here, a little there . . .

———————

THERE were many pillars that supported the glorious roof of the cistern underlying the palace, pillars like trees with their feet in water and their branches transmuting into the ribs and veins of the intricate vaulting overhead, and all of it gorgeously tiled. Even by his own weird light and with no eyes he could sense the beauty and the wonder of it. It was a forest, such as he had heard stories of but never seen; that it was a forest of stone and glaze, the work of men, only added to the glamour.

And he cast it down. One at a time to begin with, he broke those graceful pillars. In their falling, some of them smashed others; and then he made the water rage around their roots, that whole forest of trees, and he brought them all crashing down in a catastrophe of churning.

All those tiny watercourses, the paths they took through rock: he stiffened his fingers, those trails of water-in-rock, and worked them back and forth, and squeezed, and pulled, and—

———————

THERE was a scattering, a flindering, little chips of rock breaking off and trying to fall and wedging themselves where the flow of water would carry them away when he allowed the water to flow again; and some of them broke apart and were crushed between the mother-rock and him, his water, the hard slick thing that he had made of it; and there were more cracks that opened as he worked the rock, and there was more water that he could seize, or else he could melt himself a little—just a fingerlet from a finger, a twig from a branch—and infiltrate the dry cracks and so penetrate deeper into the mother-rock, and it was like being the roots and rootlets of trees over centuries, delving and stretching and eating rock, making it splinter, making it crack . . .

———————

UP through the darkness, making light, bearing light; and with every tiny shift in earth, every whispered crack in rock he had more water, because there was all that lake up there yielding it to him, and at some point the lake itself must have started to whisper its own light, as his little glow oozed through.

He hoped so, at least. He hoped it blazed like a beacon; he hoped that would drive the fearful out into the streets. And if that didn't do it, then this would, perhaps: that one mind, one will could make a whole hill tremble after all, when it had done work enough within that hill, when it had broken enough stitches to split those seams, when it had a cityful of water like a hammer at its back to drive its purpose home.

Issel heaved, and yes, he felt the shiver. Heaved again, and there were splashes in the cistern, a patter of debris falling into all the sewers round about.

Heaved again, and they must be feeling this up in the palace above, a shaking in the walls and in the ground beneath them; there must be hangings slipped, cracks in the plasterwork, vessels broken where they fell.

People must be running now, crying out, *earthquake*!

Even the guards must be letting people out of the palace, be they servant or slave, concubine or eunuch; no one would enforce a harem in an earthquake. Surely.

———————

ISSEL heaved again and felt a slippage, something major, like a great weight falling through his fingers.

The roof in the vast and beautiful cistern-chamber fell almost in a single slab, though it broke into several pieces on its way down, before it struck the water.

Issel felt the impact of it in himself, and needed a moment to remember that this was not his body that it struck; and then another moment to remember that he had a body, that his link to it was frail, a memory of a thought, no more; and that if that link were not snapped by a tidal rush of water, then the bones of his body would be; and that there were half a hundred other people in the cavern there where his body waited him, and they had bones too, and no idea that this surge was on its way, and nothing they could do there to prevent it—

———————

—WHICH left him time enough, just barely, to work with the water in between, to build a wall, to block one channel entirely so that the worst of the wave broke there and was turned back on itself, and spent all its energy against itself—

———————

—AND in the meantime he had felt the weight, the pure mass of what was coming, as a seam ripped apart in the hill there and all that lake of water began to drain down into the cistern-chamber, and he built more hasty walls to seal off this section of the network entirely, then turned back to where the hill was trembling of its own accord now, and he caught all that water as it fell and redirected the force of it with barely an effort and no doubt at all now, because one mind, one will and a lakeful of spilled water was plenty enough to overturn a hill, plenty and to spare . . .

Chapter Ten

HEY came to the bridgehead slowly, warily, no fighting-party. They had been promised, there was no one left to fight.

The docks at Maras had burned all night, a bright far glow across the water. Sometime in the darkness, something else had happened: something unseen and impossible to understand, that made Jendre fearful for her city and her sister. There was a deep slow rumble that resonated in the bones more than the ears. She thought the house and all the ground beneath had shaken slightly, for all the time it lasted. She was sitting on a pallet far from sleep, and the flame of her lamp had certainly trembled.

Teo had been out in the night somewhere with the children of the house, running wild: chivvying janizars across the bridge, she suspected, but was careful not to ask. He came back, though, soon after the event, and said that all the river had turned choppy and run strangely for a while. There were flights of birds, he said, and bird-cries that you never heard at night. It should have been an earthquake, but it was all wrong: in Sund, not a tile had slipped from a roof. Not an earthquake, then. But something.

The bridge was still there, so not that. She knew it already, before Teo said so; she had looked out of the window and seen the Shine refulgent over the lower town. Seen it with relief, for the first time in her life. If Sidië's dream survived, then so—hopefully—did Sidië.

Nothing to do then but pull Teo onto the bed with her, dirty as he was, blow the lamp out and try at least to rest, if not to sleep, for the hour or two that remained of the night. Dawn would bring its own counsel. It always did.

———————

WHAT dawn brought, in fact, was this: a slow walk down through Sund, with curious companions.

Tel Ferin led them, or thought he did, but only by virtue of being taller. He had half a dozen of his fellows with him, rivals for that leadership. Jendre had known the type all her life, born to wealth and trained to ambition; the Sultan's court had been infested with them. And dependent on them, she supposed. Her father had given her a military contempt for men whose place was a gift of birth, who need not work to rise, but she could recognise their value.

Their lives must have been very different in Sund, but types breed true all over: these were men who had had the money to survive the occupation, and the patience to endure it. Some must have the water-magic, as Tel Ferin did; perhaps they were all secret mages. That wasn't important now. They weren't coming to wreak mystical damage on Maras. That had been done already. They called themselves the Council of Sund, reconstituted; she supposed they had as much right as any, to speak for their city.

Then there were the children—Tel Ferin's apprentices, who had the magic and Issel's water and really did want to wreak damage, if they could only find a target—who were acting as scouts and outrunners, alongside Joss and his roofworld gang. Teo had run with them half the night; he'd be with them still if she hadn't added her veto to his torn loyalties. She understood that rush to a sudden freedom, the urge to kick and kick until something broke; she only didn't want it to be his head. Besides, she had Tel Ferin's assurance that all the children would be left this side of the river. That was enough—just—to keep Teo tight at her side, despite the lure of the roof-run.

Well, tight between her and Djago. One way and another, she and the dwarf had tethered him, and that was good enough. For now.

There was Rhoan, walking by herself, unhappy at everything: at being here, at what she had brought with her, at how it had been used. She flinched away from every sight of bodies: too many of them, half-buried still under rubble or sprawled in corners. Jendre had no idea what would be done with all the bodies. That would be for negotiation, she supposed, for the Council to determine. If the Marasi cared to negotiate over the bodies of their conscript slaves. It had best be decided quickly, whatever the result; these were hot, wet days.

There were the dogtooths, Baris and his friend who had carried Jendre across the bridge—an act of courage that she appreciated more every time she considered it, every time she remembered—and those who had fetched Rhoan over in the boat. They kept close company, the sharper careful of the slow. She couldn't imagine what kind of life they might be going back to. Neither could they.

The men and their troop of children, Joss and his, Rhoan, Baris, all of Sund; the dwarf, herself, her body-servant boy and the other dogtooths, all Marasi. The Sundain were invaders but not an army; they were leaving behind what strength they had; she and her compatriots were going home, except that none of them had a home to go to now. There was a dreadful cloud overhanging Maras, a shadow in the sky that was not smoke from the smouldering docks.

The Sundain, the Marasi—and one more. Armina walked ahead of Jendre: utterly confident, utterly alone. Rhoan and Tel Ferin wouldn't go near her, the kids actively spat at her feet. She walked by herself, in the silence she had earned herself, which was not of course silence at all because her own hair sang at her with every step. The solitude appeared not to bother her, nor the spitting, nor the muttered names and curses; she seemed entirely content with where she was, where she was going and who with, what she had done to achieve it. If she listened to anything, she gave the impression of listening to her hair.

Jendre supposed that the two of them could walk and talk together; but the woman was still half a stranger and all a mystery, and she wasn't feeling charitable. She missed her dead and her lost, and wanted only her precious close. That meant Teo and perhaps Djago, and she had both of them alongside. The dwarf was labouring to keep up, but he wouldn't let the boy carry him: "I want to see this day for myself," he said. "Which means from my own height above the ground, at my own speed and through the crystal of my own pain. If I hold you back, go on without me. I will follow; I am slow, but reliable in the end."

"I'm not leaving him," Teo said flatly to Jendre.

She nodded. "Quite right. We will none of us leave him. I am not in any dreadful hurry to see Maras." Which was a lie of sorts, but an easy one to maintain. After the night just gone, with all the forebodings of this morning, she could find all manner of reasons to drag her feet.

One of the best was the most immediate, and nothing to do with Maras or what she would meet there, how she could come back into a city that had seen her killed.

It was the simple question: how to cross the river?

There had been boats, there might still be a boat, if the fleeing Marasi had left anything riverworthy in the harbour. One of the scouts, a girl sporting bloodstains like trophies on her tunic and a genuine trophy, a Marasi sergeant's whip in her belt, had run down to see, but not come back. She might be in trouble, she might be using that whip and wishing for more water; she might be negotiating with some late or luckless captain. Tel Ferin had sent another scout chasing after her, but in the meantime he wasn't waiting. After twenty years of subservience and silence, he was blisteringly impatient today; he was leading them straight to the fountain square, which Jendre understood to mean straight to the bridge.

She had crossed it once, in a box, when she couldn't see anything but the stray sick light that broke in through the air-holes; that was bad enough. She didn't want to cross it again. Particularly she didn't want Baris and his friend to have to cross it again. So by all means let them dawdle, let Tel Ferin and his Council friends go over on their own; she and those who followed her could make their own way, find a fisherman on the strand . . .

But several of the dogtooths behind them were bearing burdens, little barrels on shoulder-straps, Issel's magic water; and Tel Ferin would not cross the bridge without them, and the other dogtooths hurried to stay with them—all one pack, indivisible—and everyone was swept up and swept along in that urgency, and somehow nobody got left behind at all, though Djago sweated and grunted with the effort and Jendre could have wept at the inevitability of what was coming, what she least wanted herself or her people to face.

They came to the square, and yes, there was the bridgehead, swooping impossibly down from the sky it stained; and no, there was no running messenger to bring a last-minute miracle, news of a boat waiting at the riverside, sails aquiver for the wind.

Heavy-hearted, heavy-footed, defeated before the event, Jendre kept her place in the parade and tried to distract her mind by trying to understand this place, a fountain square where no fountain played, a splendid open space at the heart of a living city but everything here was dead: dead tree-stumps, choked marble channels where surely water must have run. Bodies.

Many bodies. They must have been the bridgehead guards, too brave or too foolish to flee by way of what they guarded. Someone had dragged them into neat piles and then left them there, like awful warnings; and it struck her suddenly that it might be early but the streets of Sund were extraordinarily empty. It was as if the whole city was lying low under the weight of the night just gone, crouched like a beggar in the temple, waiting to see if there would be penance or punishment or bounty.

Jendre might have told them, only that there was no one to tell. Just the one man, rather, slumped against a great bowl of stone, a basin with a jutting fountainhead that threw no water. There was water in plenty in the bowl, and the man who sprawled there could have used some, so dirty he was.

The scouts had perhaps taken him for a body, so still he was; well, they were young, and there had been a great many bodies on this walk. Small wonder if they didn't want to poke.

He wasn't dead, though, and he proved it, lurching massively to his feet after Tel Ferin and his cohorts had already passed by. So had the scouts, almost all of the children; they were up to the bridgehead by now, or else fanned out across this wide square. There was only the one girl on hand to intercept him. She'd been talking to Rhoan and was not really ready for this, but she went anyway, all uncertain who he was or what he wanted. She ran right up to him in her urgency, and he brushed her aside, and she fell; and it seemed as though Jendre had suddenly become stupid, because obvious details could only drop into her awareness one at a time, and appallingly slowly:

—*that girl's not getting up*, because that hand he'd used to brush her aside, that was the hand he held a knife in;

—*he's a Marasi*, or at least he had fought for the Marasi, because that dress he wore—what little of it there was not torn away, sodden as it was with more than water, darkly stained—was janizar;

—*he's heading straight for Armina.*

————————

WHO knew, and was standing her ground, waiting for him. And Tel Ferin and his companions were barely aware that anything was happening, only just starting to look around; and with Armina having been walking so proudly determined on her own, and Djago being so slow, there was too much space opened up. Jendre had no hope of getting there in time. And Rhoan had fallen back to talk to Baris, and dogtooths were strong but not fast, and—

AND nobody was going to reach Armina before the janizar, and nobody had time to intervene any other way—except that Armina had something in her hand, in her fingers, a flash of brass as it might be, and she held it to her mouth and blew, and there was a cloud of red in the air between them, the finest of powders; and the man blundered into it before it could disperse, and seemed to be amazed, trapped in a single breath into some world of his own wandering.

Armina stood still, but he couldn't reach her. Jendre was coming, surprisingly ahead of Teo and with a knife in her hand, delighted that she had it; and it wasn't so far after all to get there, just this hectic plunge, and—

AND it wasn't needed after all, because the janizar suddenly buckled at the knees and fell, in an awkward collapse from which he made no try to save himself; and she thought that Armina's powder must have stifled him entirely, except that her momentum carried her on, too close, and she could see how one side of his head was staved in where he lay, and there was a pebble on the ground beside him, and she could hear a whoop from across the square.

Closer she could hear voices, anxiety, shouts; but she gasped a breath and they were almost music, she staggered to a halt and she was almost dancing, she stared wide-eyed at Armina—calm, solid, eternal—and she could almost see the sea.

She took another breath, and was almost lost entirely.

Where she stood, this firmity, this stony square was smoky suddenly and indistinct. The people who surrounded her were blurred, as though in constant movement, although they seemed to be moving very slowly. Over yonder, a boy stood on a roof, but she could see more than boy and roof, although nothing was clear. She thought she could see what he had done, hurling that stone from his sling to slay the perturbed janizar; and now he was calling down to the company, and she seemed already to have heard every word that he said, as though this was only a memory:

"Rhoan! Rhoan, the roofs of Sund are open to you, if you come back. And to Issel, too. Tell him . . ."

He was telling true; Jendre could see it. Not only the truth in him, but the truth as it might happen, Rhoan and Issel on the roof-run, somewhere in the dance. Or she could see the absence of them, the emptiness of Sund, another step; everything was fluid, it all changed and could be changed.

Even Armina could shift or be shifted, though she was far more certain than the people around her. Nothing was truly fixed, there was no hope of saying *these are here and this is now*. The only two clear points that shared this place with her were the body at her feet and the bridge yonder; that was because they danced with her, or else they were elements within her dance. And the body was already starting to blur, and then that would only leave the bridge.

But she heard Armina saying this, just as she heard Armina saying nothing, and saying other things, but this was closest or said most often, or most likely to be said, or there were more voices, more Arminas saying this than anything else, an instant echo across a thousand worlds, a theme in the music and a step in the dance:

"To cross the bridge in comfort, you need just a little of what that man had. All but Jendre, who has had too much already. You, boy, take your knife from her; she will cut herself."

She felt Teo's fingers, she felt the blade of the knife, both and neither, each in the other order. She heard Teo's voice, and others' voices too; most nearly or most often, she heard him say, "She has cut herself."

"Yes. I said. Now, each of you, see this rust in my palm here? Breathe out onto it, and breathe in. That's all. See, I do it first . . ."

And she did, and was less fluid to Jendre's eyes, slipping partway into the dance with her; and then there was Teo too, pushing forward to be next and regretting it, perhaps, gazing in a kind of dizzy anxiety until he found her, found her hand and clung to it and never mind the blood; and Djago followed with a kind of frowning interest, to take possession of Teo's other hand, and so there were the three of them together.

Not long after there were more, all, and they were walking to the bridge like a stately music while Jendre danced among them, before and behind and around, while Teo never let go of her hand and Armina always knew just where she was, although the sea was washing over her head while the rest of them were barely paddling.

Somewhere, some part of her clung to a different kind of understanding: that they were all of them floating just a little but she was spindizzy and falling, always falling in her head; that she was incoherent to them, and wouldn't be able to walk at all without Teo's help; that this magic and the bridge-magic were close kin, so that this would help them cross it without the terrors and the sickness.

That Armina had not exactly known that this would all happen this way, but that she had waded in these waters already and knew the suck of tides, the surge of events; she had been ready when they came.

That this was what she wanted for Jendre too, or else it was what she had foreseen.

———————

JENDRE set foot on the bridge, and it felt real to her, like something solid cast into a dream. She was suddenly not dancing, there was nothing liquid about her, and the music ebbed. Shadows swirled to either side of the span, and there was a summoning to their patterns that she felt an urge to respond to, only that the bridge had a prior claim, it kept her grounded.

For this time, as they walked the length of it, she knew herself exactly as she was, a girl in company crossing a river by means of this curiously physical bridge. At the same time, she knew more, she knew who she would be: a girl stepping off the bridge to meet a force of men, to speak with them, to lead them here and there within the city. She could see it with such certainty she could almost put a name to the men who were waiting. Whether it would happen because she saw it so, or whether she saw it so because it would happen, that didn't matter. She saw it, she understood it, she was ready for it.

Which being so, she needed to be first across the bridge. She slipped her hand free of Teo's, and left him with the dwarf; and walked forward, and felt Armina close as her shadow as she came past Tel Ferin and his Council.

He might have said something to her, which might have been a question, or a protest, or an assertion; there was nothing solid in it, though, and nothing to delay her.

So she led the way down onto the Marasi bank, and they stepped off the bridge below the Fishgate; and now there was nothing quite solid anywhere about her, except what lay behind.

She was dropping out of the dance, though, or at least not slipping back into it with the same engrossing fervour. There was a dryness in her throat, which was at least a reminder that she had a throat, a body with its needs for air and water; so much remembered already, it seemed a small step further to remembering that a body needed balance also, that a fading music offered no support . . .

THAT was a step into a stumble, and Armina's hand was there, right there to save her; and the ground she would have fallen on felt remarkably solid suddenly beneath her feet, and that disturbing strangeness at her back must be the bridge, as the world inverted once again.

She said, "Is it like that for you, all the, all the time?"

"No," Armina said. "Not all the time, and not like that. You will learn."

Which might have been a promise or a foresight, both; Armina, she guessed, did not distinguish.

The men who waited were a squad of janizars, but older than the norm: veterans, scarred and grizzled, fit to stand against whatever magic, whatever terror came their way. Even water-mages, out of Sund; even when the smoke of the docks was in their eyes, and there was something else, a grittiness in the air that lay like a drift across the river and was still masking the early sun.

Their officer was younger and familiar, a man she knew. A man Salem had respected but not liked, but they'd been rivals, and young men were like that. She stepped forward now, with Armina quiet and steadfast at her side.

"Hedin."

He was pale, fixed, staring. She wondered whether a smile might help, but decided not.

Instead, she gave him time; and in time he worked his mouth loose enough to say, "My lady," just as his legs took him a step backwards, and he obviously hated that.

She said, "Thank you for not having your men shoot. We don't need more harm to come here." There were bodies round about, but she couldn't see how they'd died, except badly. What she meant, what she feared was more harm coming to her city, here where the docks were burning on the one hand and there was something wrong with the skyline above, and Tel Ferin and two of his compatriots had bowls of Issel-water in their hands.

Hedin was the wazir's son, with all the position that gave him in the city and its government, even in this new dispensation. He came from a long line of survivors, and in himself he lacked neither courage nor intelligence. He said, "That's why I was sent, in case anyone came over the bridge. Not to defend it; we have no defence. I was to invite you to a parley. But—not *you*, my lady. I have, I have seen you killed . . ."

Now she could smile, and did, at an impossibility so well expressed. She almost felt she should apologise. She said, "I was saved by a water-mage," although she knew that the legend would always say that she died and magic brought her back. Sometimes, she could believe that of herself; sometimes— in the dance, under the influence of Armina's rust, as she still was, at least a little, now—she could believe there was no difference.

She said, "We will come to your parley," because she knew it, she had seen it. "We have somewhere else to go first, though, if you will accompany us, if you please," which was not quite an invitation, because a dozen dog-tooths had come off the bridge behind them now with Rhoan, and if the unlooked-for ghost of an executed woman couldn't enforce her own de-mand, then all the forces at her back most surely could.

Hedin recognised that and bowed his acquiescence, which was submis-sion in all but pride.

Jendre left it to the men to sort out just how they would march together, and in what order. She forged ahead, knowing where she wanted to go, be-cause she had seen it. Armina stayed at her shoulder, and if Jendre was right in her suspicion—if that was an amused satisfaction in the other woman as she followed her urgent, fierce apprentice through this first test—then at least Armina had the grace to keep it to herself, and Jendre had the wit to ignore it.

The gate was broken, the wreckage pushed roughly to one side; and not only the gate but the tower beside, and a whole section of the wall. Jendre had no time to stop and wonder at it; she was impelled onward, up into the city.

She found Hedin suddenly at her shoulder, and had to admire him all over again. He said, "If you told me where we are going, my lady, I could send my men on to be sure the way is secure. That is no longer true throughout Maras. I asked the gentlemen behind you"—that would be Tel Ferin and his friends—"but they had no answers for me."

"No, I am sure." They had not seen; what were their water-gifts, compared to what she had? But, "I can't give you an answer either, Hedin. If these alleys have names, I never knew them."

"A direction, then? A description?" He wanted *why* as well as *where*, that was inevitable; he had his crippled city at his heart's door, knocking. And no reason to trust Jendre, or to believe that she had its welfare anywhere remotely in mind.

"On the third level, a well-house off one of the rising stairs."

"There are many."

"Yes. This is in the eastern quarter." But that was clear already, just from the way her feet were tending.

"If you cannot describe it to me, how will you know the one you want?" Another step towards asking the crucial question, why it was so urgent she should go there, what this portended for the day or for Maras. He was being cautious, discreet, diplomatic, but there was an insistence underlying his manner; whatever it cost him, he did mean to learn.

I saw it, in a vision. Could she say so? Visions and foretellings were encompassed within the church's teaching, not anathema. Not necessarily anathema. She temporised: "It was—shown to me."

"For what purpose?" And then, "I dislike to question you, my lady, but this is unexpected, and not within my orders . . ."

". . . And you are dealing with it very well. Hedin, I don't ask you to trust me, but try to believe this, that I intend no more harm to Maras. I did not intend so much; I went to Sund in an effort to avert it, and was forestalled. I am as distressed as you are, despite all that Maras has done to me; I am still a daughter of this city. This byway I'm leading you along, it's important, it's urgent—and it is not another blow to you or yours. I swear that."

"And yet you have been wrong before," he said softly, "and so the city suffers."

"Yes." Nothing there she could deny, or argue with.

He held her eye for a moment, then nodded, as he had to. "I have no choice, do I?"

"No." She had seen it. Perhaps she might change things she saw, if they were far ahead and tentative. Armina could do it, certainly. This young man, blindly change a thing so close and so imperative? Not a chance.

"Very well, then. But I am serious, that the streets are not safe; tell me what you can. And be as swift as you may. There are important people waiting," *and the fate of our city hangs upon your meeting them.*

HIS men spread out ahead of them. She might have placed more confidence in the scouts they'd left the far side of the river, but even those sharp children had let a danger slip them by. She relied on her own inner vision—she had seen it, and so it would happen—and rather more on Armina's presence at her side. She didn't, she couldn't entirely trust her own foresight; how should she know that what she saw was true, or even likely? She'd found so many ways to deceive herself before, and this was a golden opportunity.

Armina, on the other hand, she thought she could depend on. The big woman was saying nothing, but she did radiate a kind of satisfaction. The young apprentice was apparently doing well.

If she slipped, the young apprentice was fairly confident that she would be hauled back into line, even if it must be line astern.

She wondered what it was like to be so confident, so informed: to see every day before you lived it. To see the choices, weeks and months and years ahead, and to order your life accordingly. And so to make choices for others, uncountable others, with uncountable consequences; and to carry the responsibility of all of that, the good and the bad together, and still to carry on . . .

Well, she was getting a taste of it now, against the promise of a lifetime to come.

She didn't like the taste; she thought—she hoped!—she would never acquire a taste for it; she was as unhappy as Hedin, and just as much choiceless. For now. She felt like a tool of her own vision, a slave to what she'd seen: *you will go here*, it said, *and do this*, and she did, because she'd seen, because it said.

Perhaps it was Armina she was slave to: the other woman's vision, not her own. She could live with this for a time, but not for long.

FOR now, she followed the vision and its urgency. She followed the streets and tried not to look at, not to see the damage. Superficially, Maras could be a mirror for Sund this morning: ruins and silence, bodies, emptiness. Those few faces she caught sight of were haunted, terrified, lurking in shadow.

But Sund was a city that had long dreamed of freedom, and would find it now. If the river were a mirror, there was light only on one side of it. And there was something more here she hadn't seen yet, not only fallen gates and broken barracks; there was something dreadful, high on the hill.

She might have thought to look from the bridge, with the true sight; she'd have to learn to use it, if once she could learn to trust it.

They came to a stair that led upward, and her vision-memory coincided with her childhood memories, and with some darker understanding of what she'd seen. It wasn't all recognition, more a deeper kind of knowing, but up here, and turn *here*, and—

Yes. This was the district well-house, the one she'd seen; she knew it, although there might be a hundred such throughout the city, or there might be more.

She hesitated at the open doorway. Armina looked at her, and she said, "Do we need to be careful? If they're wary in there, if they're keeping watch . . ."

"They are not the danger," Armina said briskly. "Issel is. We will need Rhoan."

That was good, that the girl should be needed; Jendre knew for herself, there was nothing worse than helpless anxiety.

They came into a square and simple room, whose only purpose was the great well-pit in its floor. There was a stair winding down into shadow, and here Armina flung an arm out to hold Jendre where she was, until Rhoan came forward.

They went down together, with a light that Rhoan drew from a bowl of water. Where the steps met the well-surface, they kept on going, down to a dark archway that stood half underwater.

Not entirely dark: Jendre could see some glimmer of light in its distance, and she thought perhaps an echo of that glimmer in the water all the way from there to here. There was something achingly familiar about that light, and the ache was in her heart, in her breathlessness, in her fear.

She didn't need Armina's hand locked firmly about her arm, to hold her still.

"Rhoan," the woman said, "now is for you. There is a snare set here, which your water-skills can find. Be careful."

"I don't—oh. Wait." Rhoan dipped her hand into her bowl and lifted a palmful of water, keeping a wary distance from the archway. It was hard to see her do anything more than that, as though her gaze cast all the spell there was; but now there was no water left in her palm and a gauze of water-drops across the archway, hung like a bead curtain against the dark. Unless it was the light it hung upon, like hooks: certainly it seemed to catch that light and glimmer with it, brighter and stranger than Rhoan's own water-light.

Armina grunted her approval. Rhoan said, "How do I—?"

"That is for you. What do I know of your water? I know it is lethal to touch that, because your Issel is behind it. If you want to reach him, find a way."

So many messages in that, too much knowledge. Hard to be sure in this coruscation of lights, but Jendre thought the other girl was blushing.

She drew Armina up a few steps and out of the water, to murmur, "I didn't see this."

"I know it. I saw you, blundering in there and dying badly. I saw Rhoan do the same, because you told her Issel was within. I saw one of Hedin's men, the same, because you said you had to be down there and he would not let you go without a scout. You are young, unpractised, you don't see enough. I see too much," which was perhaps one answer, how it felt to carry so much responsibility for other people's lives.

"Have you seen Rhoan get past—that"—whatever it was, the snare that Issel set—"without hurting herself?"

"Of course. She is very able."

"And have you seen her fail?"

"Hush. There was no need. See . . ."

She saw. The glimmer-curtain was gone, and Rhoan was peering a little anxiously down the tunnel it no longer veiled.

"Oh, well done!" Jendre splashed down quickly to join the other girl, not to leave her standing there alone. "Is it safe now?"

"I think . . ." For a moment, that seemed to be the whole thought; then, "I think Issel must have felt me do that."

Is Issel safe? was the question that came next to mind, that Jendre swallowed out of courtesy, out of pity; but she had seen some of the harm that boy could do, and she didn't like the dark stretch of this tunnel nor the water that lapped within it, nor the glimmer that came trickling down it from whatever waited within. The question came up again, hard and urgent like a bubble in the throat, and this time it wouldn't be swallowed.

"Is Issel safe?"

What it meant, of course, was *are we safe with Issel*? She had seen, but now she doubted herself extremely; and when Rhoan said, "I don't know," Jendre doubted everything, including whether she had understood the question.

But Armina stood behind them, wafting them onward with her great arms swinging. That was enough. Jendre took a breath for courage, ducked her head beneath the lintel of the arch and plunged into the dark.

The near-dark; there was Rhoan's light behind, that glow ahead.

Slowly, steadily, the glow resolved. There was a chamber at the tunnel's end, a wide one. She forged through the water towards it and saw a figure stepping down, a shadow lapped at by the light.

"Who's there?" His voice was tight, his pose threatening; he held something in his hand, and she didn't need to guess what that was.

"Jendre," she said quickly. "I've brought Rhoan, and Armina." *And Tel Ferin is outside with others like himself, and all the dogtooths you sent over with Rhoan, and there's a whole squad of nervous janizars and an impatient Marasi officer too, but you don't need to hear about those yet . . .*

"How did you—?"

"Armina." Briskly, to save more complicated truths. "She sees these things."

"I know she does." Gilder didn't want to relax his guard, step out of their way, set his water aside. If he knew that they had brought janizars to the well-house—well, it was lucky that he had none of Armina's gifts.

They came on, and he did reluctantly give way, backing up onto a path that circled the deep pool of the chamber. That path was full of men: dogtooths, most of them. Those Issel had freed, she supposed, those who had survived. Gilder's little army.

Behind her, Rhoan said, "Where's Issel?"

"There." A jerk of his head, towards the water. Here was the light-source; Jendre peered down, and *he is the light-source*. There was a figure lying on the bottom, and he glowed.

She had seen that before, but he hadn't been still at the time, he'd been rescuing her. Now he lay like a dead thing, and the only reasons she had for believing otherwise were that he was still glowing, which she didn't think he would if he were dead, and that she had seen this. Which was why they were here.

She said, "He's been too long. Rhoan, can you swim?"

"Nervously. I am Sundain; we respect water, we don't wallow in it." She was only talking, barely listening to herself, while her eyes were fixed on that shining boy in the depths.

"I swim," and that was a woman pushing through the dogtooths, the only woman among them. She had been with Issel and his friends; her name was, was Ailse. Yes. "Should he be fetched?"

"Yes. He must be; he'll never come back by himself. Between us, we can manage . . ."

"I can manage."

And she was gone, in one swift plunge. Jendre regretted that, a little; a chill bath would have cleared her head, and she thought she might need to be sharp. But then she'd have been sodden, with no opportunity to dry or change her dress. She was already wet from the hips down, but a walk in the sun would help, at least, with that; once wet, her hair needed half a day to dry.

Ailse was a shadow, occluding Issel's light. She was a rising shadow, that fetched the light alongside.

They broke the surface, and she laid him on the path as the dogtooths backed away. He did look fearful, with the water running off like liquid light, puddling around him where he shone. There was a cut below his navel, which glittered still with unshed water. One of his hands was closed into a fist; as she looked, the fingers opened and something rattled onto the path. A nugget of metal, she thought it was, that had melted in his grasp and reshaped itself to the folds of his clenched hand.

Armina stooped for that, then reached inside her dress and drew out a package wrapped in greasecloth. She added that little nugget to it, and laid it down by Issel's hand.

Jendre said, "Rhoan, this is for you too. He has gone too far; you have to fetch him back into himself."

"How?"

"I don't know. Armina neither; this is your magic, as the veil of water was. We found his body, but you must seek his spirit in the water and call him home. These things may help"—the package that Armina had brought from Sund.

"Oh, his little things, yes, those are his life . . ."

That was what she had seen; and this too, that she and the older woman turned now and left the girl as she bent over the boy, left them all—no, all except Gilder. He came after, as they waded back into the channel. He said, "Where are you going?"

She could lie, but he'd never believe her. He had done his fighting, that was clear, and it hadn't been enough. Whatever had emptied the city, it must have been Issel who had done it. Issel in the water, while Gilder and his little army stood off the janizars, that at best. Until Issel hung his veil over the well-mouth, and then they had nothing to do.

Gilder wanted more, and she could give it to him. He knew that. Very well, then. She hadn't meant to tell him, but suddenly it was needful; she said, "To the palace, I think. To talk to the Sultan, I think. There was a deputation to meet us at the bridge. An escort. There is a party of us and a party of them, but we are quite peaceable together. If you can be peaceable, you may come too." He had earned that, she thought; and he knew what had happened here in the city while she was gone. Besides, she doubted she could shrug him off now. He was coming, by his choice; she might as well make an invitation of it.

After a moment, he said, "If I can walk with—that woman"—meaning Armina, clearly—"and not kill her, I can walk with the Marasi, and talk with them too."

"Good, then. Come along." She didn't think Rhoan or anyone would miss him.

They climbed the well and went out to where the men were waiting. Jendre said nothing of what they had done in there, only, "This is Gilder, and he will be coming with us," as though he had been the sole point of this diversion. "Shall we go?"

And then she made watchfully sure that all Hedin's men followed along, that none was sent inside to discover whatever she might not have said.

———

AS they rose higher in the city, so did her bewilderment rise and so did her understanding, the two together. The air was thick and gritty in her throat;

they walked through a layer of mud and stone that seemed to have blanketed the entire city. In the lower town she'd thought it was strewn rubble from wrecked buildings, but up here it was so clearly more than that, portent of some inconceivable ruin. She read the signs and understood their potency, but at the same time it was too vast and mysterious, she was stunned by it before she knew its name.

Then they turned onto the first of the great boulevards, from where the whole of the upper city was clear at last to be seen, on its several hills—and it wasn't, because there was a hole in the world.

All the way up, she had thought they'd be taken to the New Palace, the heart of the city's governance, where the Sultan lived and met his generals, where he planned his conquests, where he ruled his empire. At least, when he had been her husband, all of that was true. Now the Sultan was a boy and his Sultanate in other hands than his, but she had still expected to go to the New Palace.

The palace wasn't there anymore.

Neither was its hill.

———————

INSTEAD there was . . . a great brokenness, a sudden waste. A chaos of rubble and mud where there had been park and palace, high walls and strength and beauty, the story of the empire writ in stone.

Fallen stone, now. Its walls overturned, all its strength and beauty ploughed heedlessly under.

After a time, Jendre understood that she was standing stock still in the centre of the boulevard, and that Hedin was at her side. Her hands were drawn to her face, her teeth clamped hard around one finger.

After a time, she took her hands away; she said, "The people?"

Even with the harem emptied once and not yet filled again, there must have been hundreds, many hundreds living in the palace complex.

"Some got out," Hedin said. "Maybe most; we did have warning. The buildings shook, and we thought it was an earthquake. We didn't know that even the Sundain witches could do this. There are still many dead under there. No one has tried to count."

No. Nor ever would, she thought. They were dead and buried already, and the survivors fled beyond counting. No wonder the city felt so empty; she was astonished that anyone had stayed at all.

And no wonder there had been this deputation waiting at the bridge. Not all the legions of Maras in its empire, all its armies, every janizar it owned could fight an enemy who would do this.

She thought of Issel in his water, and wasn't sure if she wanted Rhoan to recall him after all. If she had seen this first, she might have left him there till he was lost from his body altogether.

"The Sultan?"

"We brought him out in safety."

No doubt they did. "Where are we to meet him, then?"

"I was to take . . . whoever came"—*not you*—"to the old palace."

Of course. It seemed fitting, one more time. Wherever and however she tried to run, she always came back to the Palace of Tears. It might be a brave, a defiant gesture, having seen one hilltop throne eaten by the ground it stood upon, to retreat to another; but that was Marasi thinking all through, the habit of height and isolation, the Sultan sat above his people . . .

"So let us go," she said, and set off without a glance behind, making an entourage of all her companions, where no doubt some at least had thought themselves principals.

IT was a longer walk, if a slower climb; she had walked this way before. She could have whiled away the distance in memories, but those were traps. She could have whiled it away in awe and wonder, gazing about her to see how her city was broken, but that was a lamentation and another trap.

She could have talked to someone, anyone, she could have company at a gesture. It would have been wise, perhaps, to talk to Tel Ferin, to discover his strategy and intentions; or to ask Djago's advice, he who had known the imperial city and its rulers far longer and perhaps more closely than anyone here. Or to listen to Hedin about conditions in the city and the night just gone, who had fled and who remained, with whom she had to treat. Or simply to let Teo talk to her for a while, to take whatever comfort he could offer.

But the boy and the dwarf were together, some way back; Djago couldn't keep up, and she didn't want to dawdle. And actually she wasn't interested in Tel Ferin's plans, whatever they were, they didn't touch on her concerns at all; and she couldn't talk to Hedin any more without asking about specific people, were they fled or dead or here, which would give away her concerns entirely . . .

And she was aware, even as she ran that list through her mind, that it was all a string of excuses; but she clung to it none the less, because it gave her what she truly wanted, the opportunity to walk through her devastated city alone, with her eyes on her feet in the mud as it dried in the sunshine. She didn't have to listen, she didn't have to speak. Or to look, or to think. She could wrap her misery around her like a cloak, and call it solitude . . .

———————

THROUGH the city and up the hill, then, making believe that she was on her own and no part of this foreboding party, until she was stalled by her first sight of the palace gate. The first time through, it had been the limit of her life, the last gate she ever would pass through. Now the way was open, and the gate was shattered beams dragged roughly to the roadside.

There were stones too, from the fallen arch above. Those too had been levered out of the path, but instead there was a stronger bar to her passage, a squad of men with weapons drawn.

She paused, until Hedin had come up to her; and might have let him by, let him lead and followed with the others, except that this palace had briefly been her home and she was still Marasi and she would not tie herself too closely to these Sundain, nor separate herself too far from her own people.

Besides, she wanted to see their faces when she walked in. Whatever they expected, most certainly it was not her. The Sultan might scream witchery—which it was, of course—and demand her death, but she was tolerably certain that would not be granted him. If the truce of parley didn't protect her, then that same cry that condemned her probably would. The Marasi must have had their fill of witchcraft, this last night. They had tried to kill her once already, and clearly failed; she didn't think that they would try again. Not with Issel's work an ever-fresh vision behind their eyes, a monstrous stain on the empty city. They'd be afraid to touch her. Probably.

These guards didn't know her. They saluted Hedin and stepped aside; she kept neat pace beside him, as though he were her escort and those salutes intended for her.

The barren court behind the gate, that was familiarity itself; but they turned right instead of left, through this narrow door instead of that, and she was abruptly in another world. She only knew the women's quarters, here as elsewhere, in lost palaces and houses left behind. Now she could learn how the men lived, or one breed of men at least: how the sultans of Maras used to live before they built their bright new palace on the highest of their city's hills.

Disappointingly, it seemed—until she remembered that for their pleasures, for their comforts they mostly came through to the harem. Hedin led her and her entourage down corridors with open doors to either side, and these rooms, at least, were smaller and more austere than she was used to: rooms to conduct business in. Rooms to govern from, she supposed, picturing them as they were meant to be, busy with clerks and officials, the hub of an empire that stretched from sunrise to sunset.

With the New Palace gone, perhaps these rooms would be that busy again—though if they were, it would be first to save an empire, not to govern it. That mighty grip was loosened, and the news would be spreading fast, with every refugee who rode or sailed or ran from Maras. Many of those were the same clerks and officials who would be needed here. Many would come back, of course; first they had to stop running, then they had to stop being afraid, then they had to realise they were hungry. Some would find new ways to feed themselves, but many would not, especially in a countryside overrun by hungry men. There would be panic, desperation, no law; communities would find leaders, erect walls, guard their fields and drive strangers away. Maras would not stand empty long. Those who had fled would come creeping back. Some would take anything they could steal; some would take any work they were offered. Something would rise again, but not the city that she knew.

For now, all these rooms stood empty still, abandoned, as they had been for generations. Hedin led past them all, to wider doors at a corridor's end. Waiting soldiers drew them open; he walked through, and Jendre followed.

Now here was a room. It was room enough to hold all the men it held, and to take Hedin and her and the men who followed her, and still to leave space for a great table and a screen and divans along the walls, and still not to feel crowded.

These men who waited here—though not for her, they had no notion of her—were the true court, the men who held the empire in their hands. She didn't think they had done well by it, but she wasn't here to criticise. Only to observe.

And of course to be observed, she could hardly help that. Given the choice, she'd have preferred a clean dress, but none of them was staring at her wet and grubby robe. Only at her face.

At least they remembered her, then. As she did them: half these men she had known all her life. Many of them she had seen at her first trial, before her second Sultan, when Salem was condemned.

Here was the pasha Obros, at the forefront, his scars standing out starkly where his skin had paled at the sight of her. Even more than her father, he was the man who had shaped and misshaped her life. He had chosen her to wed her husband, her first Sultan. He had fathered Salem, and let that young man escort her about the city on her wedding days. He had allowed her husband's brother, her second Sultan, to sit the throne too long, and so he had seen Salem condemned, and still not risen till it was too late; and then he had installed Mehmet, her third Sultan, and let that boy play with her as he would.

And so she had been condemned in her turn, and the pasha had once again done nothing, while she was sewn into a sack and thrown into the river. All the city had seen it.

And now he and these were seeing her risen from the river, rather wet; small wonder they were staring. Behind the pasha was the wazir, Hedin's father. And then all the generals in the city, all the men of power and wealth, all those who had a child given over to the magicians, trained to dream the bridge.

Necessarily, that list included her father. He was there.

He was the first to move, or at least the first to come towards her. Among the others, there was a general shuffling away. They were men of war and long service, brave men, hard men; magic lay largely outside their experience, and what they knew—the bridge, largely, that their children dreamed—they did not like. This, now, this frightened them.

She frightened them.

Even her father: he approached slowly, with one hand on his blade.

"Jendre . . . ?"

"Yes." There might be many ways to have this meeting, in public or in private; there might be many moods, and in future years she might come to regret not having arranged it differently, or felt differently about it. But she was here, and he was here, and—oh, she was angry. Suddenly and entirely, she was furious with him.

"How is this possible?"

"This is *possible*," she said, spitting it, "because you and your wise friends there made a Sultan out of a greedy, vicious little boy, and then you gave him all the playthings that he wanted. You gave him *me*, Father. And then you let him kill me. How else could I be risen from the dead, except he killed me?"

He had no answer for her, only a voiceless shrug, because everything she said was true. Truth could be like that, building a case that was indefensible, constructing a crime that had never been committed. He might have had some responsibility for the original decision, but it would have been made just the same without him; and that once done, Mehmet declared Sultan, he had had no voice and no choice in whatever came afterwards.

Her anger might be unreasoning, but it was still hot; it made her stupid, as it always did. When his eyes flickered to the side, to the pierced screen that shaded one corner of the room, she thought he was only being awkward, embarrassed, unable to meet her glare.

Perhaps it wasn't even his own behaviour that embarrassed him. Perhaps he was humiliated to be scalded like this by his daughter, in front of his colleagues and seniors.

Or else it was fear again, he wouldn't look her in the eye because her eyes had looked on death and worse. She had come here in the company of mages, her city's enemies; she was witched, touched by witchcraft, and a traitor too. That could be his thought.

Never mind that he had come to her, never mind the churning feelings in her belly and the stunned question in his voice. He could wait. She snapped, "Oh, get back to your cronies." And, astonishingly, he went.

She had already turned her back, to make her position and her loyalties clear. In her head they were anything but, this was still her anger moving her; and she was still stupid, she was startled to see how few of her companions had come into the room behind her.

Tel Ferin and his cohorts had somehow managed to separate the others and leave them behind, unless it was Gilder who had done that. She knew it wasn't Hedin, he'd been with her and had sent no orders back to his men; but they hadn't followed this far, nor any of the dogtooths, and neither had Teo and Djago. Perhaps they'd all been taken off to be fed. She could hope so.

Armina was here. She seemed to be a fixture now. She stood at Jendre's elbow, in her shadow, and nobody challenged her right to be there. The Marasi were challenging nothing, Jendre realised, asserting nothing. They must be stunned by what had happened to them, with what speed. Two days ago they had ruled their world, and now they were here to surrender what remained of it.

They would need to surrender the Sultan, that was unavoidable. No surprise, though, that he was not with them; that boy would be no advantage in a negotiation.

Or was he, perhaps, here after all? When she had spoken of him, her father's eyes had flickered to the screen there, and perhaps that wasn't anything to do with shame . . .

Tel Ferin said, "We speak for Sund," which Jendre thought was presumptuous, but inevitable; she wished she could have brought Rhoan here to dispute it with him.

"And we for Maras," the pasha said; and in the long round of names that followed, Jendre felt her arm gripped, and allowed herself to be gently tugged backwards, then sat down, with Armina plumping heavily beside her.

"They will do man-talk now," the woman said, "for too long, before they decide to do what is obvious, what I could have told them in a moment. If I gave you a breath of rust now, I could guide you to see it, then you would be ready; and it would save sitting through their endless talking, if you and I were away."

She was tempted, but, "No. No, thank you. I want to listen, and I'd better keep alert."

"As you wish. You will learn that there is more than one way to know what happens, and what matters. But you are right, you have not learned it yet."

Did she know, then, that Jendre would turn her down? And if so, why did she offer?

"Armina, did you really manipulate things to make all this happen, or did you only see it coming?"

"Both of those are true." And she sounded very comfortable with them. "It happened as I knew it would, because I made it so."

"Why, then? What's your interest in Maras, or in Sund?"

"You will need someone to be with you, after this," Armina said. If that was any kind of an answer, Jendre couldn't see it.

The men had settled on the long divans, facing each other across the width of the room. Armina and Jendre were on neither side, at right angles to both, sitting apart at one end. That seemed entirely fitting. Jendre's father and others on the Marasi side kept casting sidelong glances at her, but she ignored them. Loftily, she thought.

Armina was right, the talking took too long. Neither side seemed keen or urgent to come to the meat of the matter. She was glad, though, just to sit and listen, to gather the mood of the meeting, the moods of the individual men. Which on the Marasi side were more frightened than furious, and which the other way around; which on the Sundain side were more greedy than aggrieved. Harem life hones a girl's sensibilities to a lethal edge; when she was alert she could shave nuances of meaning from the simplest words.

Just now she wasn't alert, she was better than that: her mind running ahead of the men's slow speech, knowing what they would say before their thick tongues and heavy jaws could shape the words. It was like listening to a conclave of dogtooths, she was so sharp, so fast today . . .

Ah. Sharp enough to look at herself, to understand herself: Armina didn't need to give her that promised breath of rust, because she still had traces of the dose she'd taken earlier. Her mind wasn't racing to conclusions; rather she was getting unconscious glimpses of the way ahead, the road these men were fixed on.

It seemed to come in waves, like ripples on a pool, and it was a shifting, uncertain effect, far short of the dance she had known and pined for. For a while she could ride the leading edge of the men's conversation and hear their words before they spoke them; then she would have a sudden insight, a revelation on some matter that had not even been discussed; then she would be rooted in her own body and her own time and have no grasp at all on anything outside it. For a while. Never very long, never long enough to feel stable or confident in herself or her judgement.

She knew, though, what lay behind that screen. She knew it with such an absolute conviction that she couldn't understand Tel Ferin's denseness as he said, "There is the matter of your Sultan . . ."

"No, there isn't," she said tiredly, the first time she'd spoken in a long, long hour.

Tel Ferin startled around. "I beg your pardon? We must address this, Jendre, it is a matter of the utmost gravity. He cannot—"

"He is not," she snapped. "Don't you *see*? The pasha has addressed this already."

And when he continued to shake his head at her, bewildered and a little outraged, she was too impatient to let the pasha explain himself, or Tel Ferin fumble to his own understanding.

She hauled herself to her feet and stalked across to the far corner, couldn't be bothered to fold the screen aside, simply pushed it over.

Now they could all see clearly what she had seen in broken shadow and in implication, the slumped body in its heavy robes. To dispel whatever doubts, whatever questions they might have, she stooped and lifted, carried the dead weight of it to the great table in the centre of the room and threw it down.

And lifted the head by the hair and showed it to them, one eye and poker-scar and the livid weal around the throat where a bowstring had dug deep.

"That is Mehmet," she said, "who was lately Sultan of Maras. You may take my word for it. I made two of these marks myself, and the third will have been the pasha. Or one of his eunuchs, if he was feeling traditional. I think we should leave Mehmet here, so that you none of you forget that you are arguing over his bones, like the lammergeiers on the river."

And then she was abruptly herself again, with no foresight, only a sickness in her stomach that she thought was not due to the rust. She fumbled her way back to her seat through the dead silence that was followed by the inevitable clamour of voices, and was already sinking down into it before she noticed that Armina was gone.

Her turn to startle, she'd thought the woman was permanently attached. But Armina had only gone to the doorway, where she was speaking to a guard outside. She came back after a minute and sat down again, and squeezed Jendre's hand between her two. There was strength in that, and dependability, and very little comfort; she was not a comfortable companion.

Soon a parade came in, men with trays: the palace might have no servants, but janizars were adaptable to any duty. These were the High Guard, the elite troops, and they served drinks and titbits as though trained to it. Jendre gulped water gratefully, almost desperately, and thought for a while that this was the only reason Armina had gone to the door. She'd had no sight of that at all, nor anything that came from it; and oh, she did have so much to learn . . .

To her astonishment, once they were past the refreshments and the private murmurings, the men seemed to have accepted her edict, that the body should remain between them as a token of what they were about. It led inevitably to the question of how Maras should be governed now; and she was twice astonished when it was the Sundain delegation who proposed that there be a new sultan decreed. She'd thought they would seize this dual opportunity—himself dead, and his palace eaten by the ground it stood upon—to impose a whole new rule, a council of themselves, perhaps, to oversee their new dominion, with Marasi representatives to advise how best to keep the people quelled.

It seemed they had no interest in governing Maras, only in keeping it peaceable. Or so they said. They did, of course, want a voice in who should sit the throne. It would be another puppet, then, but this time puppet to an alien dictation. Her anger had burned itself all out already, or else she would have been angry. As it was, she was only despairing. Her beloved city had been ruined first by internal conspiracy, murder and bad governance; then it had been torn apart by Issel in his chilly rage; now it was to be crushed in spirit, kept quiescent under a toy Sultan. There were still more of her husband's sons surviving, kept in store . . .

Indeed, they were discussing one already, how best he could win the hearts of a distressed people. It was Armina who rose suddenly to her feet and said, "No."

Again, consternation and astonishment, and Tel Ferin saying, "You have no voice here. Keep silence, or leave us . . ."

"No," she said again, and went on, "You talk of this boy, and think that you can make him what you will. You are wrong. Tel Ferin, he knows that my sight is true; you of Maras, you should know it also, for you use my own people and a twist of my own magic to keep your pretty bridge in being. All your dreaming children believe it must be there, and so it is.

"Believe this, then, when I tell it you: that none of that dead man's boys would give you what you seek. This one did not"—a gesture at the body—"and another will be worse.

"What you need," she said, "is not a child. You need a man: one who will understand, and sacrifice for his own city's sake. One who has a name already in the city, whom the people know and will follow. One who can re-build Maras and not seek to rebuild her power across the water. Set that whole line aside, put an end to your Abeyids and look elsewhere."

There was discontent, dissent among the Sundain; Tel Ferin found a way to crystallise it. "A new man will want to establish a new line, his heirs to rule after him; and then he will be ambitious to give them something better than he had, a city free of oversight, he will begin to pine for empire again . . ."

"Then choose a man without heirs," Armina said flatly. "A man who can establish no line. You have one such before you, and I have sent for him. Sund can talk to such a man; and then, on his death, there is no heir, and Sund can debate with Maras to select another sultan. Of that same kind, if you will, but that is far ahead. Too far, even for my sight. This much, I have seen."

Which was like saying, *this much, you will do*—but half of the men there did not know that yet, and they fell to a great deal of arguing while Armina only waited, and Jendre was so slow and dizzy she really didn't understand at all, until Salem was brought into the room.

———————

POOR Salem, unwarned, quite unprepared: he seemed dizzy himself as his father seized his shoulder and talked to him in a hard, fast undertone. And that was before he had looked around and seen who else was gathered here, besides the Marasi he had known all his life and the Sundain who were mostly strange to him.

Before he had looked at the central table, and seen his Sultan's body; before he had looked to the room's end and seen women, seen Armina, seen Jendre.

Seen Jendre.

Seen her, taken an instant step towards her; and faltered, swayed, seemed close to fainting. And remembered who he was, where he was, who was watching him; and so caught himself, straightened, walked directly to her.

Dropped to his knees before her, and took her hands; and asked no questions, asserted no impossibilities, said only, "I never believed you dead. I couldn't, how could I? They took me from you, but I kept you here"—and he pressed her hands to his heart—"and so long as that still beat, you lived for me."

I have always lived for you, she could have said, to match his folly with her own. It wasn't true, of course, but nor was his; of course he had believed her dead, he had known it absolutely. He could be an idiot, but he wasn't stupid, nor inclined to deceive himself. She tugged her hands free and stroked his head, where he was growing his hair again. He still had a fevered, haunted look; she said, "You've not been well."

"No. Better now."

"Perhaps. You will be better yet. You need to be. They want you to be Sultan."

"So my father tells me. It's—too much. That, and this. You."

"Both of us," she said. "Back from the dead."

"Perhaps. I think they want a dead man on the throne. They want a client sultan, picked to do their bidding and never to act for himself or his city. I do not want to be that man."

"That may be what they want, Salem. It does not have to be what you are. Once you are Sultan . . ."

"If I went against their wishes, they would visit Maras with their witchery again."

"Not like this," she said confidently. "They won't have," *Issel*, "the ability. But it would need a subtle man, to work for the good of Maras and not provoke the Sundain. You can be subtle, if you try. If you listen to others. I know you don't like him, but listen to Hedin. It's the young men will see us come through this, our fathers are too fixed in the old ways . . ."

"Young men and their women too, I think." He stood then, and turned to find the pasha; and quite without warning her, said, "I will take the throne, Father, if you wish it—if I am let marry Jendre."

THE consternation died at last, though the doubts remained. Salem was adamant; Armina was smug, which was what allowed Jendre to believe it.

She drifted then, and nothing to do with residual rust in her blood. Her eyes were on Salem, and her mind was empty.

What brought her back to herself, to the room, was the sound of his voice. He'd been listening, saying nothing, while the men debated; he must have been dazed himself, dazed beyond measure. But he was engaged now, contributing, arguing; and if he could recover so quickly from such a shock, such a sequence of shocks, then she owed it to them both to do the same.

So she listened, while they discussed the janizars. They couldn't be dismissed and sent home, it would be like unleashing ravening wolves on the countryside, the destruction of all order; but Maras couldn't be left with such a powerful standing army—Sund would not allow it.

"They must be a Sundain army, then," Tel Ferin said. "They must look to us for their allegiance. Maras bought them; Sund can claim them. They will be garrisoned here, of course, in Maras. Their uniform has an evil reputation across the river, and the Sundain will not tolerate them."

"They will stay as an occupying force, you mean." That was Jendre's father, speaking as though he had rinsed his mouth out with bitterness. "Of mercenaries."

Tel Ferin shrugged. "If you will."

"And who will pay these mercenaries?"

"Maras will. Some part of the reparations, after twenty years of bearing down on Sund."

"Very well"—and this was Salem—"but they must have Marasi officers."

That raised a chorus of denial, of utter rejection; he sat it out, then repeated himself.

"They *must*. They are wolves, we have said it; and while they were ours, it was only our leadership and our discipline that held them in check. Who is there in Sund who can captain such men? Where are your generals? You have none. You never had a military; you don't know how to train it or how to contain it. If the janizars stay in Maras, they do so under the Marasi. Who will report to the Sundain, of course. They are your men; so are we all."

"And what," one sharp voice from the Sundain side, "will you use them against your own people when they riot?"

"Of course." Salem shrugged. "We always have done. Why do you think there are so many barracks in Maras?"

For now, though, there were precious few people, and rioting would be the last thing on their minds. For that matter, there were precious few janizars, but they could be recovered; and their first duties, Jendre suspected, would lie in rebuilding the city. Both cities, perhaps, once Sund understood what a work-force they were. Maras would pay, both sides of the river, but that was a price worthwhile.

The dogtooths would be co-opted, conscripted most likely, into that same work-force. They'd labour much as they had before, she supposed, only without the chains. If they wanted to run, then let them; but while they worked, they'd be paid, and where did they have to run to . . . ?

———————

THOSE thoughts, other thoughts led to one inexorable conclusion. It was one of the Sundain delegation who broached it indirectly, with a sour, "You Marasi have claimed for twenty years that we were one city, Maras-Sund. Now in defeat you might still say the same, it seems to me. Time was, when we had a river between us and nothing to do with each other. That was better."

"It seems to me inevitable," Tel Ferin said, "that for a time we must both go forward together. Sund must stay watchful, which means we must keep a presence this side of the river; Maras will need our guidance, and, yes, our governance for this while. There will be no Sundain empire, but a Sundain mandate, yes. Which we will enforce when we need to."

If they could. Well, to some extent of course they could—but she really didn't think they'd have Issel. What they would have, what they couldn't do without . . .

"No one has yet mentioned the bridge," Tel Ferin observed.

"There was no need," Salem said hastily. "Of course we will bring down the bridge; it has been the symbol of our oppression for too long. Not only for the Sundain, it has oppressed our people too. All of us. We will send the magicians back to their own country, and—"

"No."

No. Well, at least he had tried; but they weren't stupid, these Sundain. Nor were they inclined to be kind.

"We have no ships," they said, "and your docks are ablaze. They will need entirely rebuilding, as will ours. How could we keep any measure of control in the meantime, without the bridge? For the moment, at least, it must remain. Perhaps we could move the magicians and their, ah, their dreamers across to Sund . . ."

"Perhaps you could give them your own children," a Marasi voice spat, "instead of ours."

Perhaps they should, not as hostages but as a reminder of the price of power. They would not; Jendre knew that without seeing. Just as she knew what Salem would say.

"Where the children are to be found, how chosen, we can discuss that at another time. The bridge exists; if it must survive, so be it. But this, at least: my wife"—and he paused for a moment at the taste of that on his tongue, something so new, and said it again—"my *wife* has a sister Sidië in that pavilion, and she must be released."

Oh, Sidië. It had all been for this. Everything Jendre had done, every theft and every betrayal had been for this, to have her sister free; and she rose to her feet now and said no.

Said, "No. We all, we *all* have family in that pavilion. Children, brothers, cousins. Sisters. What shall we do, replace them with the children of the poor, the crippled, the slave? Will it not matter then? *No.* So long as any children sleep and sicken in that foul place, let them be our own. Sidië stays, and so do all the rest."

One more betrayal, then: last and greatest, worst. The words were ground glass in her mouth, in her throat, she thought she ought to choke on them; the idea was a poison, bitter and brutal.

It was also a trap, and they couldn't see it. They saw the tears she would not shed; they saw—she supposed—her honesty, her commitment to a workable peace, at whatever price she had to pay. They didn't see how she laid her sister down as a token, to buy time.

Just until, Sidië. I promise. Just until . . .

Salem was right, the Sundain had no generals and no generalship; they had magic, but no understanding of war. Or of empire, of how to govern. For a while, Maras must bow its head, but time would come. She and Salem between them, they could do this thing: they could soothe Maras and be amenable to Sund, a kind of bridge themselves; and they could wait. Eventually Sundain vigilance would lapse, Marasi determination would rise. Jendre would know more about the magicians, and their workings, and the bridge. And then, one day, there would be no bridge; and after that—well, let come what would. She did not think it would be an army of occupation.

Whether Sidië could wait long enough to see the day, that was another question, impossible to answer. She and all those children were the sear on Jendre's soul, the living brand: one more use she made of them, to keep her fierce and focused.

Oh, Sidië . . .

———————

LATER, yawning and struggling to hide it, it occurred to her to wonder just where and how she should pass the night. The harem here was empty, and its gates thrown down; every alternative she could think of was improper. At the least.

When the meeting finally broke up, though, Salem seemed quite ready to scandalise propriety, claiming her hand and her company. In his bed, he intended, clearly.

"Salem, we can't! We are not married yet! However much you like saying 'wife,' it isn't true."

"It can be. There's a parcel of priests holed up in our house, fled when the temple roof came down. They can marry us."

Oh, it was tempting; but, "Tomorrow. Tomorrow at noon, in the temple ruins, where the people can see." If he meant to be true Sultan, it must all be done properly. Maras would never accept him else. First in a line of eunuch princes: how strange it was, but she could see it work. No Sultan had ever truly been able to trust his brothers, his wives, their children; perhaps this was best for all, city and throne together. It would still lead to its own cruelties. Men would castrate their favourite sons to have them eligible, and there would be rivalry, conspiracy, purchase and betrayal. That was Maras.

"What of tonight, then? We could still be private together . . ."

"Tonight, Salem," with a hand against his chest, for the touch of him and for the push that she needed, to fend him off, "I will sleep with your mother."

"What?"

"And her sister-wives, and all your father's women. You have a harem in your house, and I don't suppose the pasha's wives have all run away."

"No, of course not, but . . ."

"But they will make me welcome, then, and comfortable." With luck, they might even feed her; oh, but she was hungry. "And I will see you in the morning, early, when you pay a dutiful breakfast call upon your mother . . ."

———————

IN the meantime she sent for Teo, but it seemed no one could find him. She had Armina's attendance, then, and Salem's promise, and that would have to be enough.

Chapter Eleven

OWN in the Shine was Issel, leaving.

The docks were still burning, a lower light to rival the bridge, but there were boats out on the river. The trading ships had shown the wisdom of long years at sea, shown their sterns to Maras and Sund both, fled away; they'd be back, but not till both banks of the river were quieter. What lay out there now were the freebooters, the privateers, lacklords in their piracy: vultures, come to pick over the bones of Maras. There would be rich pickings if they could once get a foothold in the city. They were holding off for now, but soon—later tonight, or tomorrow night—the boldest of them would venture ashore to try for whatever could be looted.

Issel picked the soundest of the smaller vessels, and had the river bring it to him.

There was rising consternation aboard; they could hear it quite clearly, cries and curses rolling across the water. The boat came inexorably in to the beach, where Issel and his friends stood waiting. Some of the crew would have liked to make a fight of it, but he sent balls of weird light rising like fire from the river, flowing up the boat's rigging, stinging anyone it touched. There was a succession of desperate splashes, and by the time the boat came to shore, it was deserted.

One by one, Issel's friends hauled themselves or helped each other up the side. Teo couldn't climb and carry Djago, so that fell to one of the dog-tooths. Baris and Ailse were there, and they had brought half a dozen others, more or less of their kind.

Rhoan had to help Issel, who was desperately uncertain in his body, certain only in his pain. The water had purged infection from his wound, as a hot iron would, but he still glimmered in there, where water was keeping it open. Healing would be a long, slow process, and for now it was a constant hurt. His little things didn't help, the greasecloth package held close against his belly, beneath his shirt. There was one more piece in their number now, more awkward than any, but he would not let them go.

Other things were better. Rhoan was better. Leaving was right, for her. She looked at him on the deck of this little new world of theirs, while the crew grew accustomed to oars and sails, the non-Isseline ways of motion; she said, "Which way, then? Upstream, or down?"

The Insea, or the ocean? Wide, wide waters with their endless coastline, known lands shading into lands of legend; or waters beyond measure, lands beyond legend, beyond the reach of history or help?

He felt the river's surge beneath the hull, and smiled.

"You choose," he said.